Death

Deathangel

Charles Meyer

Boaz Publishing Company
Albany, California

ISBN 0-9651879-7-7

For information about permission to reproduce selections from this book
write to:
Permissions
Boaz Publishing Company
PO Box 6582
Albany, Ca 94706

Library of Congress Cataloging-in-Publication Data

Meyer, Charles, 1947-
    Deathangel / Charles Meyer.
        p. cm.
ISBN 0-9651879-7-7 (alk. paper)
    1. Episcopal Church--Clergy--Fiction. 2. Terrorism--Fiction. I. Death
Angel. II. Title.
PS3563.E8726 D43 1999
813'.54--dc21
                                                                99-052237

For prisoners of evil,
and their liberators.

Deathangel

Prologue

It was a weird call at a weird hour, but Father Joseph McCaslin was used to both in this parish. St. Jude's Episcopal was not the rich church on the hill; it was the poor church by the river. The Hudson River. More specifically it was the church by the prison. Sing Sing Prison.

McCaslin picked up his rumpled black clergy shirt from the bathroom floor and gave it the sniff test. Who cared? His jacket would cover it anyway. He looked in the mirror to button the hard white collar around his neck and decided against shaving. What was the point? It was dark in the sanctuary and the penitent would be behind a screen. He threw water on his face and took a drag of green mouthwash from the bottle. No sense punishing the sinner with dragon breath.

Half asleep, he pulled on the rest of his clothes and went downstairs to the kitchen. The call was probably from an ex-con who got out at midnight. Who else would wake him up at one in the morning with a request to meet immediately in the confessional?

What the hell, he thought, slugging down a cup of muddy coffee from what his housekeeper called the Eternal Sludge Pot. He kept the urn on twenty-four hours for such occasions, and for the multitude of cons and homeless who rang the bell wanting handouts. Maybe the guy who called wanted to make a clean start from the get-go. Maybe the rap groups at the prison were bearing some of that proverbial fruit. Or maybe the man wanted to mug him, as others had done. He zipped his black coat and headed into the cold September air toward the small Victorian church. These days he kept Mace in the confessional.

The red front doors to the church were always open, regardless of vandals, exactly for times like this. McCaslin believed the church should be a sanctuary where God's people are always welcome, their needs met, regardless of the hour. Though he did wonder why the man couldn't have waited until after breakfast—and more sleep—to make his confession. Either it was vitally important or he didn't want to be seen by anyone, or both. McCaslin walked in and saw the small blue light was on, indicating that the man was already in the booth. There was no car parked in front, so he could have walked the two blocks from Sing Sing.

A chill ran down the priest's back. He stopped. What the hell was he walking into? Why did this penitent insist on meeting him in the booth, first, not in the church as everyone else did? Was it the nature of the sin? Or was it something else? He had done this dozens of times in his years at St. Jude's—heard every scam, fallen for every sob story—so what was different now? He shook his head and continued up the aisle.

He pried open the door to his side of the confessional and saw, with some comfort, that the Mace was in its proper spot, ready. He settled into the well-worn cushioned seat, took down the purple stole from the nail in the door, and aimed the small canister of disabling chemical at the screen.

"I am Father McCaslin."

"I know this."

American, McCaslin thought, but with some European influence. Ten years of confessions made him adept at spotting accents, like a blind man who detects the slightest nuance in language. Americans would say "I know," not "I know this."

"How long since your last confession?"

The man paused, breathed deeply. Was he calculating the time or getting ready to do something?

"Fifty years."

Oh, great. This was going to be a long one. McCaslin would need coffee, not Mace. Still, it was curious. "Why now?" he asked.

"Do you mean why after all this time or at this hour?"

McCaslin frowned. Most people just answered or got on with it. It was unusual to be engaged in this way. "Both."

"I came because I had to, Father. I am at a turning point in my career, and I cannot proceed further without getting some things off my chest."

"And the hour has to do with not being seen, or known?"

"Right."

It must be someone high profile, but right now McCaslin didn't care if it was the mayor of New York or Mickey Mouse. He just wanted to stay awake through the confession and get back to bed. At least it was clear there would be no mugging tonight. Just to be sure, he kept hold of the Mace. "Let's begin, then."

"There is one more thing, Father." The voice seemed to deepen with seriousness. "As I understand the sacraments of your church, you need not comprehend entirely my sins or my circumstances. You need only witness my confession to grant absolution. Is that not true?"

The quicker the better. "True."

"Very well, then. This will be a short confession, but it will not be in your language."

"I'm sure God understands whatever it is you're saying," McCaslin said, starting the ritual. "The Lord be in your heart and upon your lips that you may truly and humbly confess your sins."

The man prattled nonstop in a language that could have been Polish or German. McCaslin strained to make sense of words or phrases, but his college Spanish was no help. He listened carefully, despite his weariness, increasingly aware of the strangeness of the situation and beginning to feel uneasy again. How could the man switch languages so quickly, from perfect English to perfectly accented something-or-other?

After a long pause, the priest asked, "Is there anything else you would like to say?"

"No. Nothing."

McCaslin pronounced the blessing. "From these things and all others left unsaid, I absolve you and send you forth into the world cleansed by the power of the Holy Spirit. Now there is rejoicing in heaven; for you were lost, and are found; you were dead, and are now alive."

A short laugh came from behind the screen. "That's true in more ways than you'll ever know, Father."

McCaslin shook his head. The man did not sound particularly penitent or sorrowful. He wondered what would happen if he withheld the final words but decided not to find out.

"Go in peace and sin no more."

"Thank you, Father McCaslin." The man sighed. "But we both know I will sin again."

McCaslin caught the glint of the booth light on metal, heard a loud snap, and panicked at the thought of a gun. The now malicious voice whispered, "Like Jesus, you've served your purpose here. Now I will guarantee your place in paradise."

Trapped and terrified, McCaslin pushed himself back against the confessional, bracing for the shot. He imagined his bloody body being found the next day, a casualty of his own stupidity. As he hopelessly lifted the Mace to the screen, he heard the church door bang open and two teenage voices shout into the sanctuary.

"Hey, God? Anybody home?" the first voice said.

"Nope? Great!" the other replied. "Then I guess we can take what we want."

The sudden distraction his only chance, McCaslin bolted from the booth and ducked down the aisle toward the two boys, yelling at them to get down and run. Startled by his appearance, the pair turned and raced for the church entrance. McCaslin followed them to the door, where he risked glancing over his shoulder and saw the outline of a figure rushing toward the shadowy exit to the side street. Outside, the boys vanished, and the priest heard a car around the corner squeal away into the darkness. Taking deep breaths to calm his pounding heart, he clutched the Mace in his pocket and hurried home to the rectory.

Shaking in fear even when he reached the safety of his kitchen, McCaslin jotted down some notes. It was not coffee that would keep him awake the rest of the night.

It was knowing he had encountered evil.

Chapter 1

It was a perfect September night, and that worried him. When things were perfect, something always happened. It was the only thing you could count on.

Matt Beck sat on a flat boulder jutting out over Long Island Sound. The incoming tide lapped beneath him, splashing small spurts of foam into the light wind that was always present at Umbrella Point. He pulled his legs to his chest and watched the ascending yellow moon metamorphose into a white silver dollar.

"Everything changes," he said, turning to the dark-haired woman beside him. He held his wine glass up to the moon and then to her. "Except us, of course." He smiled and sipped the Chenin Blanc. "We're the same as we were when we met."

"Right," Anne Demming said, with enough added drawl to remind him of her Texas roots. "And bullshit don't draw flies, neither." She laughed and handed him another piece of bread. "No, Matt. You and I have changed a lot in ten years, but I'll tell you one person that hasn't—Tod Engel."

Matt lowered his glass and looked out over the sound. "So you said in your interview." He tried not to be annoyed that she had brought the man into their celebration tonight. *CityMag* had just published her ten-year update on the serial killer who had launched her career. Beck had questioned doing the article from the start, but Jackson Twitchel, Anne's editor and mentor at the magazine, stuck to his bright idea that people might like to know what had happened to the man responsible for the brutal, random murders of eight people over a three-month period in Westchester County.

The Deathangel murders. Matt breathed in the cool breeze from the sound, trying to push away the images. The police had dubbed them that after finding a hand-carved wooden angel at the scene of each killing.

"Hey." He felt Anne's hand on his. "Come back," she said. "Sorry to raise old ghosts. I know you were reluctant about this whole thing and, just for the record, I appreciate your help in actually pulling it off."

"The bishop's help, actually," Beck said, shifting his attention back to her. Bishop John Langert and he went back a long way, to Matt's seminary years. He was not just an old friend but one of only a handful of people who had maintained Engel's innocence all this time. "He was glad to pull strings to get you in, especially since it bothered the hell out of everyone else."

Both the county commissioner and the warden at the prison where Engel was doing his life sentence had called Twitchel to urge him not to pursue the story. But, with his usual Texan arrogance, Twitch had ignored all pleas, including Matt's, and ordered Anne to run with it. The result, he had to admit, was a stunning collage of photographs and copy, though perhaps not stunning enough for a Pulitzer nomination like the one Anne had received for her photojournalism coverage of the original Deathangel murders.

"The piece came out exceptionally well." He clicked her glass again. "You're one hell of a lady, lady."

"Thank you. And thank Twitch for this good Texas wine." She lifted the bottle from the clay bucket and poured them each another glass.

"It's the least he could do for dredging all this up again."

"You know it's the same one—"

"It's a Fall Creek Chenin Blanc. The same one I gave to you to make up for my great first impression the night we met." The scene was still vivid, one of two indelible images he would never forget. Beck had been chaplain at Westchester County's Grasslands Hospital for less than a year. Responding to what he thought would be a routine call to the ER, he walked into havoc. The room was a blue and white sea of police and doctors. Bobbing uncertainly in their midst was a large, disheveled man bleeding from cuts and gashes on his face and arms. Beck, in his black shirt and white collar, remembered forcing his way through the waves of humanity to the man before he even knew who it was.

A state trooper had tried to push Beck away as a flash went off, capturing the offensive movement–Cop Shoves Priest Assisting Battered Suspect. Temporarily blinded, Beck's squinting eyes opened to see the photographer's face as her camera was knocked to the floor.

"I forget," he said. "Did they press charges on you for decking the cop who broke your camera?" He always wondered how her thin 5'9" frame packed that much punch. She was amazingly strong from the rigorous exercise routine she began in college. Even today, between her biking and tai chi, Matt often had a hard time keeping up with her. At thirty-four, she was one year younger than him, loved to eat and lord her high metabolism over his constant struggle to diet, and hid her muscular frame under loose-fitting slacks and tops like the green and white silk ones she now wore.

"No charges were filed by either party," Anne answered, slicing a piece of Jarlsberg. "They figured a nose for a camera was fair."

"Not to mention biblical."

"And the cop didn't want it said in open court that a lady broke his nose for him."

"Don't mess with Texans."

"You did," she replied coyly, "and see what happened?"

He grinned at her. What happened was a roller-coaster ride. At first meeting, he'd been pissed at the reporter for invading the privacy of his emergency room, not to mention the rights of the poor man who had obviously been beaten nearly senseless by the cops. And she was pissed that he was pissed because he was intruding on her First Amendment rights to wrap up a story she had been following from the beginning and it wasn't his damned personal emergency room anyway–darlin'.

But there was something about the way they connected over this criminal that became the basis for his getting to know her. She wanted truth as much as he wanted justice. Besides which, she was gorgeous, and that was part of the problem, because he had not wanted to be attracted to her.

Beck also remembered how hard it was to minister to Tod Engel in that ER once he figured out he was helping the man the police believed to be Deathangel. He had to bury his feelings, to objectify the man and the situation, to see him as someone in need, hurting, being brutalized by the very protectors of the peace. If he had not, he knew he could have let his feelings run wild right there and killed the man himself, for Kate.

"So, ten-year anniversary today, Matt. Think that bottle will hold us another ten?"

He reached over and kissed Anne. "I'm hoping it'll hold us another twenty," he said, though he wondered if that was true. They had been together this long time, tolerant of each other's unfinished business with former loves, and he had recently begun thinking maybe he could move seriously into Anne's life and let her fully into his, beyond where he was with Kate, his first wife. As a chaplain, he had a reputation for being an expert on grief, so he knew the pattern of change. That was why he was so blown away by his reaction to the rehashing of the Deathangel story, the churning memories that it brought of Kate's murder. She was Tod Engel's fourth brutalized victim. It struck at a deep level that he thought, perhaps foolishly, he had resolved. As he watched Anne in the moonlight, he hoped that twenty years from now they would not be saying the same things they were tonight, as Engel still did.

The thought reminded him of something, and he glanced over Anne's shoulder. "Not to wax too nostalgic, but the first killings were right over there, weren't they?" He pulled himself upright. "Is that why we're here?"

Anne looked and shook her head. "We're here because this is the midpoint between the hospital and the magazine in case you got paged." Her round eyes grew rounder. "Though now that you mention it and we're here all alone in the dark of night with nobody else around—yes, this was the site of the first murder." She hugged her legs. "Thank you very much."

Matt handed Anne her glass. "Wine cures goosebumps." He pulled her toward him. "It was merely a ploy to get you closer."

"Well, it worked." She squinted at him and looked around suspiciously. "Now I'll probably find a bloody hook on my car door handle."

He laughed at her feigned squeamishness. She was one woman he knew didn't need his protection. Before coming to New York, she had skulked the slimy halls of the Texas State Capitol in Austin, the body-filled bayous of Houston, and the neofascist training grounds of the Panhandle Militia while Beck worked his way through General Theological Seminary, juggling school, a part-time job, and a full-time marriage.

"It's funny, or actually it's not." Anne took a sip of the crisp white wine. "Nobody's bothered to check on Deathangel since the trial. They sent him to Weston State Prison for the criminally insane, where he may have been languishing in a hole or watching color TV in a La-Z-Boy all this time. It's like they locked him up and threw away the key. Forgot about him."

"Understandable," Beck said, "considering."

Anne twisted around to face him. He knew she had something to say, something she hadn't quite gotten to, maybe something that would bother him. That was why she kept circling back to Engel all evening—not because of the article, but because of this something else.

"Look, Matt, I know this is difficult, but—"

"But there's nothing we can't talk about, remember? That's the deal we agreed on a long time ago." He picked up his glass and hoped the wine would insulate him from whatever pain was coming. "Go ahead, I'm listening." Sort of.

"Well, it's just that Engel—he seemed exactly as he was at the trial ten years ago. He looks the same, almost as if he hasn't aged. He's saying the identical nonsense phrases he kept spouting in the courtroom. I know that, for you, he has to be guilty, but I have to tell you, seeing him again, hearing him again, it made me question his guilt, whether he could have really pulled it all off."

Matt sipped the wine and looked at her. "You know I love you, right?"

She kissed him. "I assume that's why we put up with each other's idiosyncrasies."

"It's why I put up with yours. I have none." He set the glass down again and held her. "Yes, I believe Engel is guilty of all the murders. Not just because I have to, but because he was convicted and sentenced by twelve people who examined the evidence and decided it was so. Maybe Engel likes it that way, living in the past. Maybe he has to do that for some reason known only to the weird internal workings of his psyche."

Anne snuggled closer. "Maybe, for him, not changing is better. Which is another thing." She stared up at him. "I felt kind of bad disturbing him once I got in there."

"Yeah, I always say 'Let sleeping serial killers lie.' "

Anne graced him with a grin. "That seems to be what everyone wanted, everyone but Twitch. I hope he's right."

"Given Engel's benign response to your questions, this is one piece that won't upset anybody." Beck held out his glass. "A half and that's it. I'm on call tonight and it would be good if I were sober."

"A pity, really," Anne said, moving her face close to his so he could smell her rich perfume. "I thought we might continue this little celebration at your place."

Funny that they still called it that, he thought. It was true, he had paid for it with his family trust money. So it was his house, technically. But Anne's touch ran through it like a seamless thread. Just as his influence could be seen in her Brooklyn Heights condominium.

"Why don't you go on and I'll meet you if the hospital's quiet?" he said, knowing better. There had not been a quiet night at Grasslands in his ten-year career. Something was always happening at night at the county trauma and transplant center. "I can slip home and leave the beeper on."

Anne embraced him. "I'll make it worth your while."

A sudden gust of wind carried the sound of a gunshot across the harbor. Beck flattened himself over her as their glasses tumbled into the rising foam.

"Nice timing," she said, kissing him. "But it was just the metal masts on the boats in the marina."

"Sorry." He felt embarrassed at the heavy beating of his heart, the sudden band of sweat on his face, the dizziness that was about more than the wine. The sound had triggered the shock of finding Kate, and he had to force it down deep to prevent its intrusion into the present where it did not belong. He pushed Anne's hair back from her face and returned the kiss.

"This place, and talking about Engel, I guess I spooked myself."

"Listen." She held his angular face in her long fingers. "I saw Tod Engel only a week ago and he's safely locked away in the bottommost cell of Weston Prison all by his very own self." She untangled herself and began picking up their things.

Beck replied, somewhat to himself, "After all this time together, he's the last thing we should be frightened about."

Their footsteps crunched on the gravel path leading to their cars. "Got really dark all of a sudden," Anne said.

Beck glanced at the dark clouds covering the moon. "Looks like we're leaving just before the storm."

They reached his car and she turned to hold him. "Be nice and cozy up on your mountain in the rain tonight, Matt."

He hugged her back. "Barring DOAs and Code Blues, I'll be there." He kissed her deeply. "Nice celebration tonight."

"It's a start."

He unlocked his car as she walked ahead to hers. From the darkness he heard her voice.

"Hey, Matt? Could you come get this hook off my door?"

Father Joseph McCaslin poured a cup of coffee from the Eternal Sludge Pot and glanced at his reflection in the mirror by the sink. His brown eyes were sunken, and gray strands streaked his temples. He looked a gaunt decade older than his late thirties.

He had found no sleep that first night following the incident. And even last night he had tossed and turned, hearing every noise in the creaky rectory, certain it was the man after him. At two o'clock he rose and headed for the kitchen, knowing he'd have to caffeine his way through two communion services, an adult bible class and a finance meeting. He kept replaying the scene of his near death the night before last.

What the hell was that about? It couldn't have been a theft. There was nothing to steal. Even the teenage vandals who saved him would have had trouble finding anything of value in the chapel to fence. He shuddered. Actually, he felt more like he had been violated, raped; the man got what he wanted and was done. He had used McCaslin for absolution and would have disposed of him if the Lord had not sent those two angels in the form of hoodlums to interrupt the murder.

He sat down at the kitchen table and propped his black-socked feet on a chair. He cut a piece of chocolate cake, solemnly placing it on the plate in front of him. Old Mrs. Harmon, his housekeeper, had brought it "only for yourself, Father." Longtime bachelor that he was, McCaslin gratefully accepted her culinary lavishings.

He had to do something to relax, to eject the incident from his mind. Pouring a small amount of half-and-half into his coffee, McCaslin glanced at the headlines of the *Sunday Times*, which he had picked up late Saturday. Same old, same old, he thought. He ate a bite of cake and washed its sticky sweetness down with hot coffee. He skimmed the pages of small print, looking for something of interest, then threw it aside.

Damn it all, he thought. He had faced things like this before at St. Jude's. Gangs. Ex-cons. Sadistic guards. Robbers and vandals. He had been mugged at gunpoint once, and knives were not that unusual. He had to view this as one more incident in the long list of professional hazards in his line of work. Still, this was the first time he'd heard the snap of the bullet into the chamber not six inches from his head. He would notify the police later if he still couldn't get it out of his mind. Maybe he needed to call someone else, too, someone he could safely tell what had happened, to help him decide how upset to be.

McCaslin drank his coffee and absently picked up a magazine Mrs. Harmon had left on the table. As he scanned the contents page, the lead article grabbed his attention.

"Deathangel Maintains Innocence after Ten Years."

It was written by Anne Demming, his friend Beck's "significant other"—he thought that was the term they used—and her photos were incredible. She had the ability to capture on film the emotion of the victims' family members, and her then-and-now shots of Engel were especially telling. They looked identical. McCaslin remembered when he'd heard about the Deathangel murders. He'd just returned from a year in an English parish. They'd already locked Engel away by then.

He read the opening paragraph:

> In a bare, solitary cell in New York's Weston Prison for the Criminally Insane, convicted mass murderer Tod Engel gave his first public interview.
>
> In many ways, it is as though ten years have not passed for this overweight, 43-year-old man. Engel smiled throughout the interview much as he had at the entire trial, as if he enjoyed the publicity but was not sure why he was getting it.

McCaslin's cup was empty. He put down the magazine and forced himself to the counter for a refill. He sat back down, propped up his feet, and looked at the photograph accompanying the interview—the appearance of a madman gone wild in allegedly civilized Westchester County, New York.

He skimmed the rest of the article. There had been no common tie between Engel's choice of victims, no recognizable theme beyond the small wooden angels Engel apparently carved himself and left by the bodies, nothing except what was in the crazed mind of the man called Deathangel. So crazed, in fact, that Engel had waited at the crime scenes until the bodies were discovered. Reprints of police photos showed Engel standing amid the crowds gathered around the gruesome deaths, and it was those pictures that had helped to convict him at the trial.

One particular item in the photo collage caught McCaslin's eye—a picture of one of the victims. Kate Beck. He couldn't imagine what his friend had gone through. Then, as the events of the other night came back to him with a shudder, he realized he could imagine it after all.

He turned to the photo of Engel in the courtroom. The man looked pitiful, like the men who showed up at the front door of St. Jude's. How could this street person have concocted such horror?

> What kind of confession can one accept from a man who, ten years later, has the same vacant stare, makes the same inappropriate gestures and blurts out the same unrelated, insane phrases as Tod Engel?
>
> As I interviewed him today, it was as though the convicted killer was still chanting to himself, repeating esoteric words to ward off evil, fend off police and courts and prison and leave him alone, smiling and alone.

McCaslin's cup froze in midair as he read Engel's mantra like words, phrases the killer had reportedly said over and over again as he rocked back and forth at the trial, and that he still said today.

> "Concentrate longer. Concentrate longer."
> "Toad sticker. Toad sticker. Matthew's son's a toad sticker."
> "Grabbin' wieners. Grabbin' wieners. Death comes to grabbin' wieners."

Gasping for breath, McCaslin read them again. He could not move. His heart raced and the cup trembled in his shaking hand. He spilled coffee over the cake and on the tablecloth.

"No," he said. "This can't be." He set the cup and magazine and tried to block the logical progression of thoughts that chilled his body.

He had heard those words before. Not ten years ago, but last night. In the confessional.

And not from Tod Engel. From the man with the gun.

What if this pathetic person in the photos was not the killer?

Then Deathangel was someone else.

Someone whose voice he knew. Someone who knew him.

McCaslin stared at the widening brown stain on the white cotton tablecloth. It was as though he had opened a vein from a corpse.

Beck watched as the slim, bearded man drew back the plunger on the syringe. The nurse injected just enough air through the rubber top and into the small vial of milky liquid to change the pressure, then pulled back the plunger again with his thumb and forefinger, sucking the drug into the plastic barrel. Matt knew it contained more than enough cc's to quell the thrashing, enough to stop the pain and end the suffering. Holding the syringe vertically, with the needle straight up, the man shot a stream of liquid into the air and glanced at Beck.

Matt gently moved the family aside and nodded at the nurse. He checked the wristband of the elderly woman. She grimaced as she labored to drag air in and out of her lungs. Wiping the rubber surface first with an alcohol patch, the man forced the syringe into the plastic tube that ran between the IVAC pump and the Heparin lock in her wrist.

A moment later her breathing eased, as Matt knew it would. He watched the nurse speak calmly to the family before departing.

"You'll find she'll be much more relaxed now."

"Thank you," the weeping daughter said. Beck gathered her and her two adult siblings back around the bed. His ease of manner in the face of death inspired confidence, assurance that he knew the path they were traveling and they could trust his lead. His job was to make death normal, to still the panic so people could part, and depart, in relative peace. He walked through it with them, like a guide showing the finer points of dying: the grimace here, the change in breathing there, the need for ice chips on the tongue, a cold cloth on the head, perhaps some favorite music playing in the background, the importance of talking to and touching their comatose loved one, who could hear but not respond. The death rattle in the lungs that, like snoring, sounded unpleasant but was not painful, the final sip of air he knew was not far away. He handed out tissues from a small box near the flowers on the windowsill.

The white-haired woman breathed more and more softly.

"Would—would you—say a prayer, Father Beck?" the eldest son asked, without looking up.

"Of course." But the priest's words were eclipsed by the whine of the pager on his waist. He cursed himself for forgetting to switch it to vibrate; he hit the hold button and finished the brief prayer of thanksgiving for the life of the woman dying in front of them.

"Excuse me a moment," he said, pulling away from the bed and moving to the phone on the nearby table. He hit two digits to take the incoming call and spoke softly.

"Matt Beck here."

"My God—" The voice on the other end sounded frightened. "I thought I'd never find you."

Matt glanced at the clock on the wall. Three in the morning. He hoped McCaslin hadn't called the mountain and woken Anne.

"I got the recorder at your house, so I figured Anne wasn't there and you must be at the hospital."

Beck shook his head. Nearly everyone in the Episcopal Diocese of New York, including McCaslin, knew of his long relationship with Anne Demming, knew it had started only a few months after Kate was murdered and had continued without the alleged benefit of marriage. When some of the clergy had complained to the bishop about this "immoral" relationship, Langert had shown immeasurable understanding, even support, defending Matt at the Diocesan Council with the equivalent of "cast the first stone." Beck was certain it had helped that Langert knew him well and was, in fact, his mentor. It also had helped, as the bishop told him later, that Langert had enough dirt on the priests accusing Beck to defrock them if they persisted.

"I'm with a patient, Father," Beck whispered, caught between wanting to hear what had so upset McCaslin and desperately needing to get off the phone.

"I'm sorry, Matt. This is urgent. I'll hang up now, but you must call me back when you finish, regardless of the hour." Matt paused. He wondered what the crisis could be. He had known McCaslin since seminary, leaned on him for support in the years after Kate's death. They talked regularly, had a beer together every couple of months, were close enough for Beck to be his medical contact in case of emergency. Joe was not easily flapped, but now he sounded terrorized.

"Please. It is a matter of life and—"

"Yes," Beck said, observing the breaths in front of him become nonexistent. "I'll do that. Good bye." He hung up the phone. First deaths first.

As he knew they would, the lines of worry and age gradually dropped from the woman's face. Her jaw clenched for one brief moment. She squinted as her tongue pressed hard against the inside of her teeth. Then she stopped. The daughter and two sons leaning over the bed looked up at him.

"There may be one or two more spasms," he said calmly, taking her blue, bruised hand in his. As a hospital chaplain, he had witnessed this event hundreds of times, understood its possibilities, from defecation to exsanguination, witnessed its predictabilities and uncertainties. This family was lucky. Their mother's death would be a clean and quiet one.

The woman's face tensed as her diaphragm reflexively dragged itself down in one last futile attempt to suck air into stiffened lungs. Bodies were tough machines. They did their damnedest to stay alive, or functioning anyway. Although this woman hadn't really been "alive" for some time.

He hit the call light and the bearded nurse appeared, stethoscope in hand. The man placed the official object of power, like a scepter, on the old woman's chest. He listened and nodded at the priest.

"Yes," Beck said to the three looking at him. "She has died." He hated the word "expired." Parking meters expired. People died. He put his arm around the weeping daughter. The two brothers on the other side of the bed clung to each other and stifled their tears, as men are supposed to do.

Death was so hard in our culture, he thought. Even when long expected, its finality came as a surprise, a shock, an unanticipated event for those left behind. Beck seldom felt sad for the patients anymore. After years of tending to dying people and their families, it had become clear to him that, more often than not, the patients were far better off. They usually handled their deaths more easily than the families and actually suffered less. Of course there were other times of tragedy or trauma when the patient suffered miserably and the survivors would bear pain for years to come. Pain like his own.

He went to the brothers and wrapped his arms around them. It was, as Matt knew, enough to push them over the edge. They wept openly as their sister came to join them. Interesting that we cry, Beck thought, remembering his own tears over Kate, and for his father only a few months before that. It was true, as someone said, that we cry not because crying helps, but because nothing helps.

Beck could, after all this time, usually observe the tender scene before him without getting caught up in it. Death was a normal bodily function like birthing babies, digestion, bowel movements, sex; a normal bodily function that medicine so often ignored or prolonged with machinery and chemicals. But the delay could last only so long, and then, as had happened tonight—as had happened with Kate—everything would be withdrawn and the patient would be made more comfortable with a bolus of morphine.

Kate. In every death there was a fleeting moment of her. Her face. Her voice. Her memory. Her murder at the brutal hands of Deathangel.

Like a split screen, one part of Matt comforted the grieving family while the other replayed the past. He had just graduated from General and become chaplain at Grasslands. Kate taught English at Larchmont High in Westchester, as she had while supporting them through seminary. They decided to celebrate his first paycheck by ordering take-out Chinese and renting a movie. As they walked from their small apartment to the corner shopping center, he had not wanted to separate, even for a few minutes. Deathangel had struck twice, and everyone in the county was nervous and alert. Kate joked about Matt's paranoia. They were only two stores apart, she said. What could happen? Only everything. How long could it take? Forever.

"Father Beck, what do we do with these?" The woman's voice abruptly halted the images, sucking him back to the hospital room. She held up a large pack of blue plastic pads.

"Those are the undersheet pads. You can take them with you or leave them and get them credited. Actually, they make really good crib sheets if you have any babies in the family."

Matt vaguely heard them say something about a new grandchild as he tried to brush his hand nonchalantly over his wet eyes. He took a deep breath and focused. It was late, or early, depending on how you looked at it, and perhaps he had seen one death too many this week. He didn't usually tear up like this, run his own personal movies that intruded into his work. In fact, given how many deaths he stoically attended at the hospital, he'd wondered lately if he was growing hardened. He thought of himself as simply being realistic. Death was part of life. The next chapter. Hopefully quiet. As he prayed his own would be when the time came; as he had tried to make Kate's.

Why, then, this breakthrough of his own grief tonight? Maybe it had to do with his celebration with Anne, with the article and the memories it had aroused. Hell, maybe it was just the wine. Not enough of it.

Beck helped pack the patient's belongings, get the family coffee, and call the funeral home. When they were ready, he wound up the scene with a prayer and a short walk with the siblings to their car. As he returned alone to the sliding-glass door to the hospital, he gave a nod to Betty, the night switchboard operator. "That's another wrap."

She shook her head. "Nobody takes 'em out like you do."

"You make me sound like a hit man," Beck said.

"You are a hit, man, in my book." The plump, older woman grinned.

"Thanks, Betty." He yawned, peering up at the clock. Four-thirty. "I have to say I like it better when they have the good sense to die on the day shift."

He took the elevator up six floors to his office. Flipping on the light, he checked the wall calendar and read its command: "7 a.m.—Inservice Docs—Medical Ethics." There would be no time to go home, see Anne, and clean up. He would have to catch a couple hours here on his couch, shower in the doctors' lounge, grab coffee and breakfast in the cafeteria around six, and try to be coherent when he lectured to the new internal medicine docs on why and how to let people die.

He sighed and stripped off his shirt. Anne would understand. She always did. Just as he understood when her assignments interrupted their time together. He would wait until six-thirty to call so she could sleep through the night before heading back to New York. He laid his pants over a chair and pulled a quilt from his office closet, wrapping it around him as he lay down on the overstuffed couch. He thought of Anne's warm body sprawled over his side of the bed. He winced. This was not exactly how he had hoped to spend the night.

He switched off the lamp and closed his eyes, trying to slow the visions whirring through his mind like a roulette wheel. When the whirring ceased, the black ball fell in one slot and stayed there, staring at him until the wheel stopped.

On call.

Call.

Phone call.

"Shit," he said, as his eyes popped open. "McCaslin." Should he phone or not? He reached up, turned on the lamp, and sat up. There was no way he could not call.

He rearranged the quilt, cocoon-like, and grabbed the phone from his desk. As he dialed, he noticed the small green light blinking. A Voice-Mail message, probably a pre-op call for a Catholic priest. Catholics always waited until just before surgery to remember they might die without Last

Something-or-Others. He would check the message when he finished with McCaslin. Life and death, he thought. This shouldn't take long.

The phone rang once.

"Matt?" the anxious voice shouted.

"God, Joseph. Calm down!" Beck leaned his head back against the couch and shut off the lamp. "What's the matter?"

"I'm sorry to bother you this late, but I've been up all night, hearing noises, checking outside. I knew you'd think I was nuts for this, but I had to talk to someone who'll pay attention."

Just as you've done for me in the middle of the night, Beck thought. "Go ahead."

"I'm even sorrier for what I have to tell you, 'cause I know what this means to you."

Beck frowned in the dark. What the hell was he talking about? "Joe, what—"

"Matt, unless I'm going crazy, I heard something in the confessional the other night that leads me to believe Tod Engel is not the Deathangel killer."

The black before Beck's eyes changed to red, then his anger faded to bewilderment. What could McCaslin mean?

"Joe." Beck tried to speak calmly. "I understand you're upset about something, but that issue was dropped long ago. Now I really have to get some sleep. Call me tomorrow. Good night." He started to hang up.

"Matt, wait a minute! I swear somebody's been watching my house. There's been a strange car parked down the street all night. Once or twice I'm sure I heard someone in the yard. This man—he wants to kill me."

"Did you call the cops?"

"Right. In this neighborhood? With Sing Sing next door, the cops only come if there's actual blood flowing."

"Okay, let's talk reality a minute," Beck said, closing his eyes and taking a deep breath, speaking as much to himself as to McCaslin. "Tod Engel was caught red-handed with the murder weapon in his grimy little apartment, which, by the way, contained filings in the carpet from the wood carvings he'd strewn over the corpses."

"I know that, but—"

"Hear me out a second," Beck said. "Then there was the little detail of his full confession, not under duress, but right in front of the TV cameras on the six o'clock news."

"Matt, listen—"

"And his name, Joseph. The man's name, for crying out loud." Matt felt his patience slipping. "Tod Engel in German means 'Death Angel.' "

"Yes, you told me that before." McCaslin paused. "And yet—and yet I'm sure the man they arrested is innocent."

"And you're sure this isn't just one more pathetic person miraculously surfacing after all these years seeking notoriety or publicity or some damn thing? Anne just came out with an update story on the case. That could have given your sinner ideas."

"I saw her article. But there's more to it than that. There was his tone of voice. You didn't hear it." Beck did hear the panicked pleading now. "I—I can't say anymore on the phone. Just let me come by and see you tomorrow." McCaslin paused. "Today, I mean. Later today."

"Jees ... Joseph, what do you think I can do about it?"

"You can listen to the whole story and then decide how insane it is." McCaslin drew a ragged breath. "And if I'm right, you can possibly help me get an innocent man out of jail."

Beck realized he could argue for another half-hour or concede and hang up. He felt worn, but he owed McCaslin. A lot.

"My house at one this afternoon."

"I'll be there. With a bottle of Bushmill's Black."

"Right. I'll need it. See you then." Beck hung up the phone and snuggled back down into the quilt, trying to pretend he was home in his own bed. But the images played before his eyes. Headlines sensationalizing each new Deathangel victim, news photographs of the remains, he and Anne arguing about Twitch wanting her to do a story on the families. It had been a mistake to dredge all this shit up again.

He touched a button on his watch. The digits glowed softly in the miniature light, reminding him of the damned voice-mail message blinking the same green. He reached for the phone again and punched in his code. The mechanical voice announced, "You have one message." The high pitched, three-syllable "one" sounded like the person was strangling.

"Just get on with it," he said. "Give me the room number and I'll send a Catholic priest up there." He hated voice mail. The term, like others jerry-rigged to accommodate technology, made no sense. Why didn't they just call it a damned answering machine—which it was?

"Hey, Matt. Me." Anne's voice came over the line and Beck's eyes opened. "It's about four. Twitch called at eleven to tell me the magazine's received a lot of flack on the Deathangel piece. Mainly relatives resenting the pictures running again. He wants me to come in early and do some follow-up. I tossed around waiting for you to get here and then I woke up nervous about my stuff at home. So I'm heading there now. See you after work. You're not on call, so dinner's on you at the mountain. Adios."

Fine. He could do that. Grab some sleep. Listen to McCaslin at one, run to the store, throw something together. He closed his eyes once more and began to drop through drowsiness into sleep.

Somewhere along the way he saw himself carrying the bag of Chinese takeout and not finding Kate in the video store. Sirens blared in the distance. The clerk assured him no one in the store had seen her. Frantic, worried because their neighborhood was an area of high-rise apartments, gang tags, and drug deals, he searched each store in the shopping center, asking about her, finding nothing, his heart pounding, imagining the worst.

Then he found it.

The sirens came closer. The EMS vehicle raced behind the shopping center, back where they brought the delivery trucks and kept the dumpsters. Matt dropped the food and ran to the alley. By the time he reached them, Kate was getting CPR, IVs already started, chest paddles shocking her heart, thumping her back to life. She lay in a pool of dark liquid, her blood. It had soaked her clothes and her soft, blonde hair. A police car pulled up, its lights adding to the blue-white glow shimmering across her body from the ambulance.

Matt crouched beside her and saw the small wooden angel on the ground, soaking up her crimson life. He reached out to touch it, but stopped. Kate's eyelids fluttered.

He rode in the ambulance, the EMS techs working to keep her vitals up, to close the hole the bullet had made in her heart. He knew it was impossible and yet he urged them to keep trying. They had only been married two years, their whole future ahead of them—kids, careers, school recitals. This was too fast, too damned unfair. This only happened to old people, not to people young and in love and just starting out!

But in the ER they could barely keep Kate's vitals going, and Matt found the courage to tell them to stop, to turn off the ventilator, pull out the tube from her windpipe, discontinue the IVs. And finally, to leave her alone with him.

In the silence of that white room Matt held her hand, told her he loved her, and watched her take her final, tiny sips of air, then stop for eternity. He bent to kiss her one last time—and realized it was Anne's face that stared back at him.

Suddenly the pager screeched his name. "Chaplain Beck, call ER. STAT." He bolted awake to the sound of sirens.

Chapter 2

The large man in the starched uniform adjusted the dials on the dashboard. "That enough air for you, Bishop?"

"Fine back here, Earl," the Right Reverend John Langert said. The black stretch limo sped up the narrow Taconic Parkway, taking the curves and hills with little effort.

Befitting his rank, Langert sat in the backseat, sipping Chivas Regal and going over some papers. Earl was good at taking care of him, of anticipating his needs before he asked, like the little thing of turning up the air.

"Don't know what I'd do without you," Langert said, raising his glass to the rearview mirror so the driver could see the toast.

"You got lotsa people'd take care of you, Bishop," the gravely voice responded. "Just like now."

Langert sighed. It was true. He was surrounded by the privileges of his office, by people wanting to treat the bishop of the Episcopal Diocese of New York with due respect, due deference, and sometimes, he supposed, due fear.

He removed his half-glasses and looked up from the work on his lap. "We've come a long way, haven't we?" He stared out the window at the changing colors of the maples and sycamores. He liked to believe it was the push of the Spirit and not just his adept handling of power and church politics that had placed him in the back of a chauffeured limousine.

"Long way from a damned do-gooder."

Langert smiled. Damned do-gooder. That's what they had called him in his early years, an epithet he wore with honor. His social action bent had landed him in failing mission parishes at first; the bishops preceding him had far more conservative leanings. But their attempts to bury him in obscure, poverty-stricken churches were rewarded with highly successful outreach programs, fund-raising and rebuilding projects, and growth that catapulted Langert into the diocesan and national spotlight. As the diocese changed, and as he made the players change it further, Langert's style became more accepted, even sought after.

"Excuse me, Bishop," Earl said. "But do you want to stop for a sandwich or something before we get there? Once we hit the Weston exit, the pickings are a little thin."

"That won't be necessary, unless you want to grab something to eat while you wait for me at the prison." Langert had eaten a big breakfast and had a dinner meeting planned. As part of his rigorous schedule, he rarely ate more than two meals a day, a strategy that had always paid off. Everything he touched seemed to turn to silver, and, if he stayed long enough, to gold. But success was bought only with much hard work, stress and excessive hours, and a slavish devotion that bordered, some said, on the idolatrous. Perhaps they were right, he thought, watching the blur of evergreens pass by. There had been no time for a wife or family. The few lovers he'd had were, quite frankly, not as passionate or exciting as his work, which turned out to be much more demanding and harder to break away from.

"How long till we arrive?" he asked, sounding to himself like an anxious kid who had to pee.

"Ten minutes max. Why? You need something?"

"Just thinking about the reception committee when I arrive. Warden Williams wasn't too happy about my visit."

"He never is."

"That's why I'm coming now, while he's in Albany defending his budget. One less bureaucrat to tolerate."

Langert saw Earl smile in the mirror and smiled back. He knew neither of them was afraid of a fight. Earl had had a few in his day, and he had the scars and holes to prove it. Langert's own scars came from the political and emotional battles he had gladly undertaken. For this, he knew his critics thought him egotistical, narcissistic, and unreasonably demanding of his clergy and lay staff. His supporters found him compassionate to a fault, understanding, and committed to the growth and expansion of the church into every area of the community—political, social, educational, and religious. He was, as were all powerful people, both hated and loved, often by the same people. He only hoped he could tell them apart.

He offered Earl a cigarette, but the driver refused. "Unlike you, Bishop, I'm gonna quit those damned things." The silver-haired prelate smiled, sipped the Chivas, and went back to reading under the tiny, powerful light in the backseat. Though it was only midmorning, the tinted glass of the limo windows made it seem dark and dusky inside. The smoke from Langert's unfiltered cigarettes swirled in the rays from the bulb over his shoulder. It was the only obvious sin he allowed himself, and he swore he was cutting back.

"I'll take a bit more air back here, if you please."

"Yes, sir. Oh, and Bishop," the driver said, "we're coming up on the

Weston exit in about a half a mile."

"Thank you, Earl." Langert turned off the light and propped up his long legs on the plush seat. Of course the limo was ostentatious and unbecoming of his social commitment, but it went with the office, one of those conveniences he had grown to live with and even like. Besides, it gave him extra time to read diocesan reports, brought him to his destination rested, and provided work for his driver, who might otherwise be locked up in the same prison they were visiting. And it intimidated the hell out of public officials who operated on a "mine's bigger than yours" mentality.

"Weston State Prison entrance next, Bishop."

Langert stashed his drink and rearranged the wet bar. He combed his hair, took a swig of mouthwash, and spit it into the small basin. It would not do to have the diocesan prelate breathing alcohol onto a prisoner—or worse, onto the warden's surrogate who would meet him.

"Positive you don't want one?" He lit another cigarette and sucked in its warm, smoky flavor. "These are from France. Really strong."

"Get thee behind me," Earl said, leaning his hand over the partition. "Hand me one of those babies."

Langert knew Earl wouldn't quit any more than he would. The tobacco was bad for him, but the comfort was worth the risk. Besides, he came from a long line of smokers—and drinkers for that matter—and he believed things like disease and time of death were genetically programmed. He had stacked the deck in his favor with a relatively healthy diet and a rigorous daily exercise program of weights, Nordic Track and treadmill. His physician told him he had the heart and musculature of a man of fifty. Still, he deferred to genes. His body would break down on genetic cue when his DNA, like limes on a one-armed bandit, lined up all at once to start the process. Exercise would prolong his well-being and strength as long as his genetic makeup allowed the rest of him to exist.

He finished the cigarette as the limo slowed near the gated area of the fortress-like facility. Although the sign they passed didn't say it, Weston State Prison was home to most of New York's criminally insane. Security was several notches above maximum, and the guards were trained more in restraint than correction. Langert knew he was one of only a handful of visitors who had the haunting experience of driving up the long, winding road. Not many families or friends came. Most had rejected or disowned the inhabitants at the time of their trials, and those who did venture near were frequently ignored, if even recognized. They seldom returned to face such futility.

The mammoth steel gates swung open, and Langert thought of the welcome statement over Dante's Gates of Hell: "Abandon hope, all ye who enter here." That was certainly true for the man he had come to see—Tod Engel, the man they called Deathangel.

Leaving Earl outside to chat with the guards, Langert endured the usual formalities of signing in, walking through the two metal detectors, greeting one of the deputy wardens—the one he knew had drawn the black bean and had to escort him into the bowels of the institution.

"This way, Bishop." The tall, red-haired man inserted a key in the steel lock and pushed open the first gate.

The dark, dank hallways reminded Langert of the basements of his early churches. That many of the prison's inhabitants had come from environments that looked exactly like this was no coincidence.

"You know, of course, that Dostoyevsky said you could tell the freedom of a nation by looking inside its prisons—not that his country had room to talk, mind you," Langert said.

"Yeah, and not a guilty man among 'em," the officer replied, glancing around, obviously wary of his surroundings.

What Langert saw here, as he had seen in the other correctional facilities he visited in his official rounds, was poverty. "If Tod Engel had had money for a decent lawyer, or if I had been able to get him one, the man would be in a private sanitarium with quite a different view."

After the public defender assigned to Engel died six months after the trial, Engel had been exiled to Weston. It was the only prison in the system that could guarantee his safety and security.

"Well, I guess you failed then, didn't you Bishop?" The guard unlocked two more doors and ushered Langert through.

Paint peeled from the drab green walls. The slimy dampness that slicked the walls and floors hung in the air, sank deep into one's clothing, wet and cold next to the skin. Even on this bright September day, the sun's rays could not penetrate the barred windows, which were caked with dust. The few shafts of light that made it through were swallowed by the ubiquitous damp.

They approached the visiting room, the best of the sorry, seldom-used lot. Langert could tell it had been recently scrubbed. The smells of disinfectant and insecticide assaulted his lungs when the steel door opened. To counter it, he lit a cigarette.

"Your buddy'll be brought right out," the deputy warden said flatly. He stood at the door until the prisoner was escorted in by another guard.

"Have a wonderful chat. Officer Barden here will sit in with you."

At first glance, Langert thought Tod Engel had not changed much since the last visit. His thick black hair had begun to turn gray these last years, to thin out on top, like a tonsured monk. The wrist shackles bowed his large frame almost piously. He walked more slowly than last time, slower than necessary for a man in leg irons, like a man who has nowhere to go, nothing to move toward.

Langert stood as the guard sat Engel down at the square wooden table, obviously made in the prison shop. Engel, his head bowed not in reverence but in a catatonic stare, did not acknowledge his visitor in any way. Langert sat down across from the man, reached into a shirt pocket, and extended the open pack of cigarettes to him.

No response. He offered his own lighted cigarette.

Nothing.

"Take the shackles off, please," Langert said, keeping his eyes on Engel.

"I'm sorry, Reverend, but I can't."

"It's Bishop, my son." He paused long enough for the title to have its intended effect. This was a time to use the power. "And I believe Warden Williams has given me that option." He glanced up at the guard. "Would you care to check?"

Langert's gaze told the heavy-set guard he did not want to confer with his superior. Nobody questioned an order from Williams, much less countered one. The guard uncuffed Engel. Langert knew the man hoped the prisoner would severely injure him before the guards could break them up. Maybe he would even pray for it. The guard, who looked ready to strike a stunning blow at any second, cautiously lifted the leg shackles from Engel's bruised ankles. In the age of chemical restraints, they still used these medieval tools for show.

What kind of life must this be for Engel? Did he know? Did he care? Langert asked himself the same questions each time he visited Engel, each time he saw the man's despair. Maybe this was merely his own projection of what it would be like for him in this situation, not an accurate reflection of the dulled, lethargic mind of Deathangel.

Engel still did not stir when the guard moved behind the prisoner and stood, leaning slightly against the wall.

"That will be all, Officer," Langert said. "Thank you very much for your assistance. I would like to be alone with Mr. Engel now." No matter how dangerous the prisoner was, or how dangerous the guard thought he was, the man was entitled to a private visit with his priest. Perhaps that would motivate Engel to stir from his catatonic state, to smoke a cigarette and demonstrate how lucid he really was, maybe even to speak. It was a risk, but not the first one Langert had taken with Engel. Somewhere down deep the man knew it, understood that Langert had stuck his collared neck out further than most thought he should for the convicted killer. More than was politically correct then or now, more than made sense to anyone but him.

"There will be no problem," Langert said, with his inimitable tone of authority. "Don't worry. I take full responsibility."

The guard thought a moment. "You got it, Rever— Bishop." He suppressed a smile as he walked away.

The heavy steel door clanged shut, sealing Langert and Engel inside the small, pungent room. If something did happen, Langert was sure the three closest guard posts would be alerted to come to his assistance, but not too quickly.

He lit a fresh cigarette from the tip of his current one and crushed the glowing embers of the spent stub on the antiseptic floor. He leaned back in the hard wooden chair, sucked the smoke deep into his lungs, and stared at the man across from him. He blew the smoke above Engel's head.

The prisoner gave no acknowledgement of his visitor's presence.

"It has been too long since I last came to see you, Tod," Langert began. "I apologize for that. I am ... very busy ... with ... things." His voice faded and he looked away for a moment. "Anyway, my life is too busy, and that is not why I have come to see you."

Engel seemed to blink more frequently. He took a deep breath of the smoke-filled air. Langert wondered what was going on in that strange brain, wondered if the smoke reminded him of the past, the world outside. Did he think of barrooms or clubs? Of women who smoked with him, or after having him?

"I read the interview by the Demming woman, and it reminded me that I hadn't been here in a while." The Bishop flicked ashes on the floor. "So, here I am." He smiled and relaxed a little. "And you as talkative as ever." He sighed, pushed his chair back, and crossed his legs. "I hope you are feeling well, Tod. And that you're getting some exercise. Do they ever take you out in the sun? You look quite pale, more so than when I was last here."

Indeed, the man looked like a specter or one of those albino animals that lives in caves and never sees daylight. What if you wanted to die before your DNA had programmed it? Could you will it to happen? Was Deathangel doing it now? On his own or with help? The bishop made a mental note to remind Warden Williams of the New York "sunshine requirement," even for convicted murderers.

"When was it that I was last here?" Langert furrowed his brow and blew smoke at the ceiling. "I guess it was a little over five months ago." He looked at Engel. "I am sorry, Tod. I had meant to come here every three months to see you, check on your progress, find out if there was anything I or the church could do for you. If there was any hope."

Engel slowly raised his head. His hollow eyes stared at the Bishop through gray holes clouded in shadow. He showed no emotion and did not move his hairy hands.

"That's better. Thank you for looking at me. Would you like a cigarette now? I know they don't always let you have them because you've burned yourself in the past. But you won't do that with me, will you?"

Engel continued to stare.

"How about if I light it for you?" Langert lit a new cigarette and held it out. He leaned across the table and tried to stick it between the man's lips, but it would not stay.

"Too bad, Tod. I thought—" He crushed out the tip on the floor. "I thought maybe there was something you would like to say to me, a confession perhaps? You know I befriended you when no one else would. I was the only one who spoke out for your kinder nature back then, the only one who testified for you in the courtroom. I'm the only one who has believed that you aren't guilty all along."

Engel pulled his huge hands up from his lap, interlaced his fingers, and placed his braided fists on the table. He looked earnestly at the bishop, knitting his brow as if he were trying to figure out who this visitor was, what he wanted.

Langert avoided the fists on the table. "That's a start." He glanced at his gold Rolex. "We haven't much time together, so we must make the most of it. I've continued to visit you all these years, hoping for some sign, some word of encouragement from you to indicate your innocence." He leaned forward and stared into the dull, vacant eyes that searched his own. "A word, Tod. Anything. It couldn't have been you. We both know that."

Engel squinted as though his head suddenly hurt. It seemed to Langert that a painful memory had forced its way through the haze of drugged brain cells, through the pathology and into the cerebral cortex that, only partly damaged by years of abuse and malfunction, was still part of him.

And when that electrical impulse fired and hit home, Engel's face grimaced in a twist of rage.

The bishop watched Engel's neck become blotchy and was certain something had connected. "What is it? What's going through your mind? You can tell me. You can—"

Suddenly, Engel crashed his huge knees into the underside of the table.

Langert let the table fall over and kept his eyes on Engel, who raised his clasped hands above his head as if to strike him. It was Langert's turn to be motionless.

Engel stopped. He put his hands back into his lap. Feet slapped against damp concrete in the corridor. Before the guards could unlock the door and rush into the room, Engel had dissolved—into laughter.

Langert held up his hand to stop the men from grabbing the prisoner. With their hands on canisters of liquid Mace, the guards hovered nervously and watched Engel laugh and point at the Episcopal Bishop of New York until tears streamed down his reddening face. What in God's name was he thinking? It was the strongest reaction Langert had gotten out of him in years. Had the interview triggered some memory, some thought or emotion that an attorney might use in a new trial?

Whatever it was, he would have to arrange another follow-up visit very soon. Perhaps he should also arrange to have a talk with Anne Demming, the *CityMag* reporter, about her article.

The Bishop stood and raised his hand in blessing over Engel. The prisoner stopped laughing long enough to look up and spit in his direction, muttering a few words under his breath.

"What was that, Tod?" Langert asked, kneeling near Engel. "Did you say something?"

Engel reached out and pulled the prelate to him. The guards jumped, but again Langert raised his hand.

With his foaming mouth at the bishop's ear, Tod Engel screamed, "I am Deathangel!"

The officers could restrain themselves no longer. They swarmed in, wrenched the prisoner from Langert's neck. One man, clearly relishing his job, put shackles on Engel. The others cuffed and dragged him through the door before righting him on his feet for the long journey to his cell.

Langert walked with the smiling deputy warden to the front gate of the prison.

"Looks like you failed again, Bishop," the man said, locking the iron gate.

"I suppose that depends on your definition of failure," Langert said. As he climbed into the limo, he could hear the echo of Engel's insane laughter rolling through the corridors. But he had seen the man's eyes, and he knew the laughter was anything but insane.

Anne Demming rolled her eyes, listening to the angry voice on the phone. She tried to respond.

"I'm sorry. Really. What I meant was—" The person hung up with a slam. "Shit." Anne looked out her office window at the spire of Trinity Cathedral. "Double shit."

There was a knock at her door, and she swiveled to see Jackson Twitchel enter without waiting for her to wave him in. It was, after all, his magazine, his family's money that had bankrolled them in the beginning, that brought them both here from Texas, where they had already made the controversial *!SAXET!* magazine into such a screaming success. He could stand on her desk and piss onto Wall Street if he wanted. In fact, right now, she wished he would.

"Oh, no problem," she said, as sarcastically as she could. "Come right in."

The tall man had an unkempt mop of white hair slathered like whipped cream on top of his wrinkled waffle-cone of a face. He moved her phone and sat on the edge of her desk, frowning, his clothes hanging on him like an unmade bed.

"What's the matter, Missy? Don't like the latest assignment?"

She glared at him. He was the only man in the world who could call her "Missy" and live. Not even her daddy called her that. But Twitch had taught her to see Texas inside out, as though they were looking at it from behind a mirror, an idea that had given *!SAXET!* its title. From him she learned the minuscule details of investigative reporting and the subtle angles of photojournalism he wished he could have carried out. She loved him like a father and hated him like a brother.

"Oh, no, Twitch. I love the assignment." She frowned at him and raised her voice. "I love calling people ten years after their loved ones have died and asking them for follow-up information." She picked up the phone. "Excuse me for interrupting your life after all this time, but would you please exhume all your feelings about the murder of your family member so I can get an interesting emotional angle on the story for my retrospective? Would you mind if I cut your guts open one more time for the public?" She dropped the phone onto its cradle. "This sucks, Twitch. Big time."

He unwrapped a small sweet cigar and bit on it. "So—"

"So it was one thing to do the Deathangel piece. That was good journalism. But your idea of contacting family members to see where they are now?" She tossed her pencil on the desk. "I've dealt with militia that weren't this rabid about their privacy rights."

Twitchel crossed his arms and held the unlit cigar in front of his stained teeth. She knew he wouldn't smoke in front of her, although his own office reeked of the smell. After his last cardiac event, he'd given up cigarettes. Maybe his next one would swear him off these things.

"So, you turn anything up yet?"

"Only animosity, but thanks for the sympathy. Half the victims have no families to call in the first place, and those who do think we shouldn't have done the retrospective on Engel at all. They'd rather have him rot in Weston in anonymity."

"That's about like the calls my office has been getting. It's funny about articles like that, though." He moved from the desk to gaze out the window. "It was a really good piece of photojournalism, Missy." He glanced back at her and then to the street. "And those people down there bought more copies of this issue of *CityMag* than any other in the last three years. To top it off, we've received the most phone calls ever, castigating us for giving Engel more publicity and accusing us of reminding every other borderline psycho out there that they, too, can be famous."

Anne picked up a piece of paper from her desk and joined him at the window. "The family angle's bombing out, so here's my next line of interviews. What do you think?"

The crooked little cigar stuck out the side of Twitch's mouth as he smiled. "That's why you're the best, Missy. You think just like I do." He gave her the list. "Keep plugging, honey, and holler if you need backup." He left the office, the musty scent of his rumpled clothes and the sweet cigar wafting behind him.

"Anything for you, dear." Anne closed the door and returned to her desk. She hit the speed dial for Matt's pager, she was thankful Twitch hadn't suggested she interview him as a family member. Of course, if the others had worked out, she would have had to include him. As it was, she felt glad they hadn't. She punched in her number and hung up.

Matt had been a bit testy lately, since the Engel interview, anyway. She needed to corner him about what was on his mind. They had talked almost incessantly about Kate's death early on. They had to. When they met in the ER, Kate Beck had been killed just three months before. But such talk had tapered to almost nothing since the trial. Anne sipped at the flat root beer that sat on her desk—her comfort food. In some ways, she felt relieved that the Deathangel story had brought Kate into the open again. She was always in the background anyway, hovering, making Anne feel like the intruder, even though she and Matt were closer than ever.

She took the drink and walked to the window again, checking her watch. Matt must be in the middle of something or he'd have called back by now.

The sun glanced off the steeple like a beacon of truth at Broadway and Wall Street. God knows they needed one there. Her own truth was, she had to admit, that Kate wasn't lurking through any fault of Kate's. She was Matt Beck's emotional ace, the card he could play whenever he needed to trump his feelings of affection for Anne. She understood why he wouldn't commit to marriage again. She couldn't say she would either. She closed her eyes to the glinting sun and saw her own trump card, just as powerful as his. Peering beyond the church, out over the waters of the Battery, she wondered if it wasn't time for them to move on, to dredge up all the old issues and put them away. She shook her head. Easy for her to say about him. What about her? The American hostages? The failed rescue mission?

She jumped at the ringing of the phone.

"Hey," Beck said.

"Hey, yourself. You in the middle of something?"

"S.S.D.D."

Same Shit Different Day meant he didn't want to talk about it. It also usually meant he hadn't gotten much sleep. "Spent the night in the office?"

"Just a few moments of shut-eye. I'm heading to the mountain to catch up. How's your morning?"

"No luck with the victim's families, so I'm setting up interviews with the principals from the trial."

"Which ones?"

"Let's see," she said, examining the list. "How about James Rinski, Martin Ehrhart, Richard Williams, and your very own John Langert?"

"A cop, a politician, a prison warden, and a bishop. You've got your work cut out for you."

"If they'll talk to me."

"They'll talk to you. They're all in such high-profile positions now that they can't afford not talk to you." She heard his voice lower just a bit, an emotional sign for him. "Just, well, be careful, will you?"

"With the interviews?" She laughed. "What could possibly happen?"

"Don't say that," he snapped.

Clearly, something serious was bothering him. "You okay?"

"Kate said that."

Whoa. There was a showstopper. He never said things like that. "What's going on, Matt?"

"I know I'm just tired. And I know that this Deathangel story has me stirred up. But I had a sort of bad dream last night and, uh, the bottom line is, I don't want to lose you."

This was not the time to discuss this. Not on the phone. Not at this distance. Not sleepy and labile. "I don't want to lose you either, so stay awake at the wheel of that Spider till you make it home and get your butt between the sheets. We can talk tonight."

"Over a bottle of Texas wine."

"Right. And turn your pager off."

"I already have one interruption scheduled."

"Whatever it is, you can cancel it."

"No, not really. Joe McCaslin called."

Matt's friend at St. Jude's. "And?"

"Bottom line is he's pretty upset about something and I agreed to talk with him this afternoon. I'll tell you more about it tonight."

"With wine."

"With wine."

Anne smiled. "Right now, I'm more focused on your butt between the sheets. And a nice butt it is, too."

She could hear his smile through the phone. "Later, Miss Demming."

"Later, Father Beck."

She hung up the phone and shook her head. God. They sounded like an old married couple. Routines. Code phrases. Hi, honey, how was your day? Fine, dear. Three DOAs, two cancer deaths, an overdose in the ER, and one guy in his thirties diagnosed with ALS. How about you? Great! Dealt with irate family members of victims of a ten-year-old multiple murderer and upset readers who hated the story so much they sold out the print run of the magazine. Wow! Okay! Let's have dinner.

On second thought, maybe it was better if they stayed focused on the past.

Black letters on the rippled, opaque glass window were neatly framed by an old, smoke-embedded walnut door. He stared at their backward symmetrical march across the glass and wondered how some worker had stenciled them so neatly.

James I. Rinski
Police Commissioner
Westchester County, N.Y.

The descending order formed a pyramid, like his own shape behind the huge wooden desk. The once handsome, even dashing street patrolman whose photos filled the bookshelves had been replaced by an overweight bureaucrat unable to see his belt buckle or the increasing bags under his blurry eyes. What the hell, life was short. You had to grab all the T&A you could before it was over.

Rinski took a drag on the cigarette and crushed it out, drank his coffee, pushed back his chair, and tugged at his collar. He always felt uncomfortable, in the wrong position, out of sync with himself. He sensed the buttons bulging on the over-starched white shirt the cleaners had screwed up again. He was fat and hated it. In his head he looked like the muscled cop in the pictures, which had been taken ten years ago. His life was a mess. But that would straighten out soon, he thought, fingering the out-of-fashion paisley tie his ex-wife had bought him for his forty-fifth birthday last month. She had used the occasion to tell him she was getting remarried "to a man who could afford her tastes," as she had so disdainfully put it.

Fat chance.

At 12:05 P.M. he stared at the same glossy pages in *CityMag* for the sixth or seventh time. If he read it again maybe it would sound less provocative. Maybe the words and photos would magically go away. But the bold cover caption stared back at him: DEATHANGEL: TEN YEARS LATER.

Damned nosy reporters, he repeated in his head like a mantra. Damned nosy reporters. Why the hell can't they let sleeping dogs lie? He pulled a small pocket-knife from his vest. The pearl-handled knife had been a gift from his father upon his rapid advance from inspector to captain, a promotion resulting from his leading the bust of that maniac, Tod Engel—Deathangel. He neatly severed the magazine pages from their binding, tossed the rest of the issue into the trash, and fingered the edge of the razor-sharp blade as he read the byline. A thread of blood formed on his thumb as he fantasized about what he would like to do to Anne Demming.

Rinski remembered first crossing paths with her during the manhunt and the trial. At the time, he admired her dogged persistence, annoying to the police though it was. In those days, he had thought she might even be useful in unearthing clues the official investigators couldn't access legally. He found her attractive and at one point suggested they might like to get together and discuss the case over a drink. He found out later, through police sources, that she had dismissed him because she was schtupping that priest at the hospital, the grieving widower of one of Engel's victims, no less.

Over the years, her investigative reporting had led her to Rinski's office for the usual denials. He sidestepped and politicked his way out of things so the police could handle the county's problems their own way. Efficiently. Quietly. With no publicity. And now this shit. Let sleeping dogs lie, damn it. Ten years was a hell of a long time ago.

The phone startled him. He blotted the blood on his thumb with a greasy napkin and punched the intercom.

"Yeah, Charlotte," he murmured to his secretary. He used her name because he liked the sound of it. It fit her like a glove. Like he did. "What is it?"

"The county executive is on your line, Commissioner," she squeaked. Her voice was her least desirable asset. Charlotte Kinney was the otherwise unemployable daughter of a high-ranking county official. She had been offered to him five years ago as a way of settling a campaign debt, and he had taken her. All she could do was answer the phone and type, but that bottle-blonde head of hers didn't ask a lot of questions either.

And there were other things she did well, after hours.

"Yeah," Rinski mumbled. "Put him on. And get me a coffee." Maybe she'd help him cream it later. He grinned.

"Good morning, Commissioner," Martin Ehrhart said, softly. "Or, I guess, looking at the clock now, I should say 'afternoon.' "

"Long time no hear, Marty," Rinski said, swinging his feet onto his desk and leaning back in the brown, leather, high-backed chair. He had expected Ehrhart to call. The surprise was it was so late in the day. Maybe the old man slept in with a new honey. Fat chance now that he was high-profiling his way to the next senatorial election. That's what this was about. Power. That's what everything was about. And money. Even Charlotte.

"I know it's been a while, Jimmy," the older man said. "I'm remiss in my duties." He paused. "That's why I'm calling you now, to see if you might come over to my office for lunch today."

"Geez, Marty, that's some offer, there, you know?" Rinski surveyed the colorful pages spread over the desk. "So how did I know it was coming today?"

"Maybe you're psychic?"

"Maybe so, Marty. Maybe so." He folded the article and slipped it in the inside pocket of his jacket. "Or maybe we just read each other's minds, so to speak."

"Perhaps that is it, Jimmy. We do go back a long way."

The commissioner waited.

"So...how about it? Is your calendar clear?"

Ehrhart was talking as though the conversation was being taped, which meant it probably was. The man would keep his ass clean no matter who went down around him. But if it came to that, Rinski would make damned sure he didn't go down alone. There was too much at stake for all of them.

"What're you servin'?"

"Whatever you want. Like the old days."

"Yeah, the old days," Rinski said. "Whatever happened to them old days?"

"Perhaps they are back."

If they were, a lot of people were in deep shit. "Pastrami on rye, Marty. Some fries and a coffee regular." He reached for his jacket and started to drape it around him. "Just like the old days, huh?"

"See you in thirty minutes."

Rinski hung up the phone, then punched the intercom.

"Yes, Commissioner?" Charlotte squeaked.

"I got any messages out there?"

"Just one."

"Hold onto it. I'll call them later. Right now I'm goin' over to the Old Man's office across town. I may not be back this afternoon. You know how to reach me tonight, don't you, if anything comes up?"

"Certainly. About what time should I call?"

Rinski checked the watch straining at the pillow of his wrist. He wanted to work in a nap so he would have energy for her. With a little alcohol and a little coke, she was hell in bed, and he loved it. "Not before eight, Charlotte." The thought of it stirred him. "Make that seven."

Twenty minutes later, Police Commissioner James I. Rinski parked his official black Lincoln in his personal spot at the County Office Building. The neogothic structure reminded him of the temples he had visited in Rome many years ago with his wife, his now ex-wife, his soon-to-be-off-the-alimony-dole ex-wife. He smiled at the thought of more money for himself, though he made plenty with the county on and off the books.

Appropriate, he thought, as he climbed the stairs to the ornate entrance of the county temple. We deify our public officials and then wonder why they act like Roman gods with affairs, plots, and narcissistic scandals. He snickered at the words over the portal: "In God We Trust."

Fat chance.

"Mr. Ehrhart said to send you right in," the dark-haired secretary said when Rinski walked through the office door. The young woman wore no makeup and sported a tailored, long-sleeve suit; she smiled only slightly, barely looking at him.

Rinski eyed her from the back and opened the waxed mahogany door. Nice body, he thought. He wondered if Marty was—?

"Jimmy!" The man stood from behind his huge oak desk and came around to greet the police commissioner. "It is so good to see you!" He extended his hand to the unsmiling Rinski, who shoved the door shut.

"So are you schtupping her or what?" Rinski said. He was pissed at being summoned like a dog and then welcomed like an old friend after barely hearing from this asshole for years.

"What?" The old man smiled. "Jeez, Jimmy! Still the old kidder."

"Who's kidding, Marty? If you aren't, maybe you could arrange for me to meet her. Maybe as a little 'I'm sorry' present for not calling me till you need something nobody else but I can take care of for you."

Ehrhart spoke seriously. "You are exactly right, Jimmy. Exactly right." He put his fist to his chest. "Mea culpa. Forgive me."

"Whatever." Rinski would see about forgiveness later. He was suddenly taken with the opulence of the office. "Some space you got here. 'Course, I haven't seen you much since our metal desk and file cabinet days."

The last time they'd had a meeting was before the election, when Ehrhart had swept into office on a strong anticrime platform, with Rinski's help. Obviously, that kind of clout demanded better digs. The police commissioner walked around the high-ceilinged room, admiring the plush blue carpet. A white leather couch sat in front of the county executive's desk, where flying pigs and dragons floated across a new computer screen. Oak-paneled walls with antique glass cabinets gave the impression of intelligence and influence, like those photos people made with fake books in the background to pretend they were all Ph.D.'s, right down to the damned dog. Dog shit, Rinski thought. Just like this.

"What do you think?" Ehrhart said.

Rinski smiled. "Suits you to a T, Marty. Really, it does."

"Then sit down and feed your face and get in a better mood." Ehrhart pointed Rinski to a table beautifully set with white linen, china, and silver. "What'll it be? Coffee first, or your pastrami?"

Rinski looked at his boss. Ehrhart could still be mistaken for an airline pilot, a psychiatrist, or a surgeon. His black and silver hair waved reassuringly over his blockish head. The sagging wrinkles on his square-jawed face appeared inviting and friendly; voters no doubt thought they were the lines of experience and hard work and too much caring. His huge hands, once hard and dangerous, as Rinski remembered too well, were soft, like the leather of a well-worn baseball mitt. With that fatherly appearance and deep, resonant voice, the county executive of Westchester County, New York, seemed a cinch for the U. S. Senate in next year's election.

"Dessert," Rinski muttered.

"How's that again?"

"I said, dessert. I would like to have a piece of that chocolate cake with my coffee first. Then I'll try the pastrami on rye."

Ehrhart stared at him. "So that's how you came to look like this, Jimmy," he said. "Why, I remember when it seemed like you needed a meal."

"Yeah, Marty," Rinski said, sitting down at the table and dragging the piece of cake toward him. "I remember lots of things, too." He stuffed a huge bite into his mouth and talked while he chewed. "I think maybe ... that's ... what you called ... me about ... isn't it?"

Ehrhart sat down across from Rinski. He unfolded his napkin and placed it neatly on his lap. Taking the silver cover off his plate, he delicately pushed a fork into a small piece of broiled fish. Rinski wondered if the man wished the fork was going into him.

"You know, Jimmy," Ehrhart said, gazing at the china plate in a way that made Rinski slightly nervous, "sometimes you forget what you should remember, and you remember what you should forget."

Just to annoy Ehrhart's gentility, Rinski stuffed in another large bite of cake, then sipped his coffee to mush it up in his mouth. He continued to eat as he talked. "So is this place clean or what?" he sputtered. "I mean, can we talk here or is this polite conversation we're having for the taped memoirs of Senator Ehrhart?"

"It's safe here."

"How can you be sure?"

"I have it swept every morning."

"But it depends who does it."

"By people I trust, who know better than to miss anything."

"Okay. Okay," Rinski said, finishing the cake with another gulp of coffee. "So the place is sanitary as a toilet seat." He flipped the silver cover off his plate and bit into the pastrami sandwich. "Can we cut the shit and talk?"

"I think I remember a James Rinski who had somewhat better manners and was in less of a hurry. No, I take that back. You've always been in a hurry, haven't you?"

Rinski looked up from his food for the first time. "What's that crack supposed to mean?" He didn't like the tone and wasn't about to take any threats from this asshole.

"We both know what it means, Jimmy. And we both understand what we're doing here."

The Police Commissioner put down his sandwich and gulped the ice water sitting before him. "Yeah, we understand it. So what do we do about it, Marty?"

Ehrhart finished the remaining steamed vegetables and the last bite of fish. He pushed his plate back and pulled a dish of peeled apple slices toward him. "I was hoping you might have some suggestions about that yourself."

"My first suggestion is we do nothing." He bit into the pastrami again and took a slug of coffee. "That story is gonna be yesterday's garbage in a day or two, just like it's been every other time somebody got a hot lead and tried to reopen the case. Hell, even that Demming chick will be onto some other damned cause by the next issue. And even if her story does get people exercised about it again, there's absolutely no reason to think anyone might want the case reopened." He swallowed hard. "I mean, read the damned thing. The idiot thinks it's ten years ago. There's nothing new here."

"I think you may underestimate some of the people affected by this story."

Rinski threw the chunk of sandwich on his plate. "And I think you got this pastrami from a goy deli." He poked a fry into a mound of ketchup and sucked the red substance off before tossing the thin potato strip into his mouth. "I say we sit tight and see what happens. Who gets into what with who. If the chick pursues the story, tries to take it any deeper, we lean on her a little bit to slow her down or push her off it."

"She is pursuing the story," Ehrhart said. "She called me this morning for an interview, and she said she contacted you."

Rinski remembered the message Charlotte mentioned. He was glad he hadn't asked who it was. He would stall Demming as long as possible. What annoyed him was that Ehrhart knew about it.

The County Executive shifted his chair away from the table and crossed his legs. He poured himself a cup of coffee from the smaller pot with the Decaf label on the front. "The timing of that story on Engel is unfortunate," he said. "I received a call this morning from our overseas partners. They phoned to say they hoped it would not distract us from our goal."

Rinski stared stoically.

"I told them that, if anything, raising the case might increase our chances of election, especially when people remember how we took Deathangel down."

Rinski looked around the room. "Depends on who remembers what, doesn't it?"

Ehrhart ignored him. "They said they'd watch things carefully from their side of the pond."

Rinski stuffed down the rest of the fries and poured himself another cup of coffee—regular—with two lumps of sugar and an ounce of cream. "You can tell them to relax. We're watching it from here. Their investment is secure."

Ehrhart looked down his nose at Rinski. "Well, maybe some of us are."

"That crack meaning what?" Rinski glared back, narrowing his eyes.

"Meaning that you as police commissioner are unaware that Tod Engel received a rather lengthy visit at Weston State Prison this morning, a day after Demming's piece appeared in *CityMag*."

"What? I'm supposed to get a report any time that slimeball has visitors."

"You did. You just didn't know about it. I checked with your secretary—or whatever she is—after you left, and she said it was buried under other papers on your desk."

"What the hell's going on here?" Rinski said. He hated to be caught up short. What did Ehrhart know? What else was he hiding behind that placid demeanor?

"Perhaps your table manners are not the only things you've gotten sloppy about." The county executive dropped an apple slice on his plate. His voice lowered. "You are supposed to be monitoring Engel's visits, especially at this critical juncture in my career—our careers."

"And you're going to watch my every move from now on, are you Marty?" Rinski said, feeling his face turn red. "Is that like the old days too?"

The older man relaxed, and a thin smile touched his mouth. "No, it is not. It is certainly not. I don't like doing it, but if you don't do your job, I will do it for you."

As long as it benefits you, Rinski thought. "Okay, okay. So I screwed up once. Give me a break."

Ehrhart nodded. "Yes, this time I will. But you must realize that this is a delicate period for both of us." He looked at Rinski in the menacing way the police commissioner recalled from earlier days. "There will be no more screw-ups, Jimmy. The next one will be your last."

"I gotcha, Marty." Rinski sat up straight. He would play this game, pretend to be attentive. But if Ehrhart tried to mess with him, he would find the county police on his senatorial candidate's ass until they discovered something that made him a former candidate. "I'm on the case." He tossed the magazine article on the table. "This Demming chick, she owes me."

"Good. Then maybe you can deter her when she interviews you." The county executive drank his Evian.

Rinski asked, "Who was the visitor at Weston?"

"Bishop John Langert of the Episcopal Diocese of New York."

"Shit!" Rinski frowned. The guy could be a problem if he was still as feisty as he'd been at the trial. "I thought he'd given up visiting there. He hasn't come to Weston for months."

The County Executive leaned back in his chair. Rinski could see he was more and more displeased. "I'll have to slap a tail on him."

"Not yet, not yet. As you know, he has a rather extensive system of security around him, no doubt due to his support of unpopular liberal causes—Engel being one of them. If he suspects he's being surveiled, it may just increase his interest in the case, maybe convince him to try and open it again. For the time being, let's just see if he visits again soon. If he does, then we need to take some protective action." He paused and put his hand on his chin. "Prisons are dangerous places, you know. It is very likely that Engel might experience a serious accident or psychological downturn."

Rinski smiled and shook his head. "Great talk from our future senator from New York."

Ehrhart scowled. "I am not the only one at risk here, Jimmy, as you will recall."

The police commissioner grinned. "Yeah, but you have a lot further to fall than I do, my man."

The County Executive grinned back. "I wonder which of us would make the bigger crash?"

Rinski swallowed a final sip of coffee. Enough was enough. He pushed himself out of the chair. "I gotta get back to work."

"Back to work," Ehrhart said. "Yes, that would be a good idea."

Rinski chose to ignore the putz. "I'm putting a tail on the Demming chick and also on her hump. He's too close to this case. Who knows how he may be helping Demming? Maybe this was all his idea in the first place. Maybe he wants to reopen the case too. I want to keep an eye on both of them for now."

"I think it's premature, but I'll leave it up to you. You are the police commissioner, after all."

"That's still right, Marty." Rinski turned toward the door. "Anybody else you think might have read that piece and be messing in our business?"

Ehrhart shook his head. "Not yet," he said evenly, joining Rinski at the door. "That's why you must keep monitoring the case for inquiries of any kind. When you learn of them, let me know at once. I'll do the same." He put one hand on the doorknob and the other on Rinski's shoulder. "We've come too far to let up now. All of us. Zero screwups from here on. Perhaps nothing will come of this at all, and next year we'll be in Washington, myself in the Senate and you on my security team, grabbing all the ass you want."

Rinski removed the hand from his shoulder and, without speaking, left the office. The secretary glanced at him as he walked past her. Ehrhart wasn't schtupping her, he thought. He should be, but he wasn't.

He left the stone temple and got into his car. He wondered about the secretary, then shook his head as he forced his stomach behind the wheel of the Lincoln.

Fat chance.

Father Joseph McCaslin slipped off his alb and hung it in the sacristy. The noon Rite I Eucharist had run forty minutes instead of his usual succinct thirty, but it still left enough time for the prison guards and business people from town to get back to work from their lunch break. The Monday crowd had been larger than usual, given the remote location of St. Jude's, and he had enjoyed greeting new visitors at the door as they left.

Ten minutes after the service, the street was again deserted and ominously dark. Clouds gathered for a fall rain. McCaslin checked his watch. He would be late to Beck's house, especially with the wet roads, and he wanted to drive through the burger and shake place on the way. Maybe he'd better call, he thought, as he locked the silver chalice and vestments in their cabinets and tidied up the sacristy. No. That would just take more time and, worse than that, might wake Beck. Anyway, Matt would forget about his being late when they opened the bottle of Black Bush. He smiled. And if his friend got a bit more sleep, he might be in a better mood to convince McCaslin he was being foolish to worry so much, and to turn things over to the police, like he knew he should. It would be good to see him.

As he exited the sacristy, he noticed that the bright red front door was closed with the thick bar lock placed over it. He hadn't touched it.

The sound of footsteps near the front west pillar drew his eyes. He glimpsed part of a jacket behind the column. He flicked off the lights. Even at the noon hour, with the sooty stained-glass windows, the church was dark. If he were going to be a target, it would not be a well-illumined one.

The priest crouched at a pew and spoke. It was, after all, his job. "I am Father McCaslin," he said. "Is there some way I can help you? I can find you lodging for the night, or a meal, or possibly some work tomorrow."

His words stopped when he heard the click. Was it a gun clip or just a cigarette lighter flipping open?

He moved as quietly as he could across the pew to the far left side, using the pew in front of him as a shield. If he could get behind the figure, whose thin outline was now visible to his adjusting eyes, maybe he could surprise him.

And then what? What in God's name did he think he would do then? It didn't matter, really. What mattered was making sure the other person could not detect exactly where he was. He moved to the aisle, still crouching, and began working his way toward the left entrance—a recently installed fire door that would sound an alarm when he pushed the bar to leave.

It was then that he felt the cold steel blade on his neck.

"Do not move," a voice said. "We do not wish to hurt you."

The cadence again. European, but different. McCaslin realized that the first figure had been a decoy for the second, who had hidden in a closer pew. The click he'd heard had been the sound of a switchblade snapping into place. He felt incredibly stupid—and now angry.

"You can get up now, my man," the person behind him said. "A little at a time. And don't try nothin', please."

As the other figure moved toward him, McCaslin saw he was wearing a long coat of some kind, not an American cut at all. He was probably in his forties. Peripherally, McCaslin could see that the one with the knife was in his late teens or early twenties, in leather and metal, lots of both. Probably a skinhead. He hoped he could talk them out of whatever it was they were there to do.

"What do you want?" he said, as confidently as he could.

"Just be quiet," the accented voice in front said. "We were supposed to rough you up a little, just to let you know the one who sent us meant business. But there is really no need to do that, not if you shut up and cooperate."

Righteous indignation fueled the priest's response. "What the hell are you talking about?"

A knife grip smashed across McCaslin's face.

"I tole you to shut up!"

He took a deep breath and resolved to get out of this alive. The next step would come later. Survive first. He licked the split in his lip, tasting the sweet, hot liquid he knew was his blood.

"Better," the man in front of him said. "Much better. Now here it is, Father. We were sent to ask you, politely at first, if you told anybody about a recent confession you heard right over there in that box." He pointed to the confessional near the front door.

"Of course not," McCaslin said, buying time, thinking of a way to the street. He'd already considered the Mace in the confessional, but he remembered he had carried the container to his kitchen. He could attempt a short run to the side door, but he would have to get by the one without the knife. It was the only way out, and he had to do it now because they would not believe whatever he said. They could not afford to.

He stood straight, as if to stretch his back.

A hard right cross sent him sprawling backward over the pew. "Don't mess with us, man," the skinhead said, hauling him up from the floor. "We don't give a shit for priests or whorehouses like this building either."

McCaslin spit out blood and teeth so he wouldn't choke on them. He unintentionally splattered the black shirt of the younger man.

"Oh great, asshole. Now I got your blood on me." He backhanded the priest, knocking him into a pillar. "Hope to hell you don't have AIDS or nothin'." McCaslin saw him glance over his shoulder, looking for approval from the older man, who nodded. "You probably do. You're probably queer as shit, man. Maybe we should strip you down and see." He slashed McCaslin's shirt and shoved his fist to his abdomen. McCaslin doubled over in pain.

"Perhaps we should give the good cleric a moment to catch his breath before he tells us who he informed about the confession." The older man waved the punk away.

In his shock, McCaslin knew he had to move fast or he would never move at all. When the skinhead stepped back, he used his remaining strength to pull himself up and hurdle the two back pews, heading for the side aisle and the exit.

Within reach of the door he felt something strike his right shoulder. The pain forced him to his knees. He reached back to feel the handle of the embedded knife. The two men ran toward him. Fueled now by fear and pain, McCaslin yanked the blade from his own body, screaming in agony. As the skinhead leapt toward him, McCaslin rolled to the floor and thrust the knife into the youth's belly.

The older man was quickly on him, smashing his face into the stones of the aisle.

"Last chance to live, Father," the man yelled, unconcerned for his fallen cohort. "Who did you tell about your conversation in the confessional?"

Through a haze of red, McCaslin sputtered, "No—no one."

The man seemed about to ram the priest's head against the stones again, but the muted sacristy phone rang and he stopped. "Perhaps that is the no one?"

His head swimming and his eyes dim, McCaslin felt himself dragged back across the front transept to the sacristy door. The intruder fished the key from the priest's pocket, opened the door, and listened to the answering machine record the voice.

"Hey, Joe. Matt Beck. I'm at home, but I just woke up. If you get this message and want to hold off coming over for another hour, it would be fine with me. I'm looking forward to hearing, as Paul Harvey says, 'the rest of the story,' but even more to the bottle of Bush that goes with it. Take your time in this rain and drive safe."

"Is that him?" the man said to the bleeding priest beneath him. "What was his name? Matt Beck?"

McCaslin whispered, barely able to speak. "No. No. I spoke to no one. He called ... about a church ... matter." He wondered if the blackness beginning to surround him was the entry to death. What would it be like, the final minutes? All that mattered was to get Beck off the hook, if he could.

"Certainly." The man shook his head. McCaslin watched him close the sacristy door. He bent to help the priest to a walking position. Where was he taking him? Was it over now? Would he leave him alone? Alone to die here or what? He was now so weak, so unable to resist, that it didn't seem to matter.

"We just need to escort you out the back door to your car in the alley." He heard the man's voice as though from a deep canyon. "We cannot have you identify us now that my young friend has gone and let you kill him."

McCaslin opened his eyes to find himself slumped over the steering wheel of his car, which faced down the steep incline of the alley behind the church. The man was outside doing something under the hood. Blinking his eyes to clear them, the priest clenched his left hand on the brake release. A thick curtain of coma began to descend, dulling the excruciating pain. McCaslin used his last strength to force his right hand to grip the stick shift.

He saw the man begin to close the hood and, in one fast lurching movement, McCaslin twisted his body hard to the right, released the brake, and shifted into neutral.

The priest heard a shout, and felt two bumps as the car, its steering wheel locked in place, jumped forward and rolled over the body. But McCaslin had no energy to lift his leaden foot to the brake. He wanted sleep, rest. He would go wherever the vehicle took him, but he wanted the bumping to stop.

He sighed as the curtain dropped and closed his eyes to the images flashing past him. Somewhere in a dream he heard a car crash through a barricade, felt it drop suddenly and splash onto a pillow of cold, black water.

Chapter 3

Instead of the busy main highway, Matt decided to take the back roads and hook up with the Sawmill River Parkway. They were more fun in the drop-top Fiat.

He had come home, slept, and waited for Joe McCaslin to arrive and explain what he claimed he'd learned about Deathangel. At first he thought McCaslin had gotten the message he'd left and was coming later. But when two o'clock rolled around and the priest still had not arrived, Matt called and left more messages at the church and the rectory. As he entered the ramp to the Sawmill, he grew annoyed again about McCaslin's call. He wondered if Joe had simply thought better of the ridiculous idea and blown it off, or if he had come up with a logical explanation for whatever had happened.

But how much did Matt really want to know? He had come to terms, or thought he had, with Kate's death. He had resolved that her murder was the random and senseless act of a hopelessly retarded man. Now McCaslin said he was convinced it wasn't Engel. He'd frantically phoned in the middle of the night to beg Matt to hear him out. What was that all about? He could at least have called to say he changed his mind.

Beck downshifted, glanced in his rearview mirror at the car behind him, a blue Chevy, and turned onto the access road. Anne had checked in to say she'd be home later than she expected. He thought he'd go to the office for a couple hours, unnoticed. While the on-call chaplain covered the shift, Matt could get some records logged and be home with dinner fixed and a glass of wine in hand before Anne made it there. Maybe getting caught up at work would take his mind off McCaslin. Maybe he had left a message at the office.

Beck loved the crisp September weather. Just before dusk, the canopy of multicolored leaves over the parkway shimmered, liquid against a cloudless sky. The Spider convertible made it all the better, open to the view above as the cold air whipped against his reddening face. As he took the Valhalla exit at the blue "H" sign, he realized that with the open air came a vulnerability that closed-top cars did not risk—both from accident and intruders. There was a message in there somewhere. He ought to use it in a sermon. The more open and vulnerable, the greater the risk and the greater the joy. It seemed profound as hell right now, but he knew that was because he wasn't at any great risk of danger.

He glanced in the tiny mirror on the dash. The blue Chevy that had been behind him on the meandering two-lane road was still with him. Had it not been for McCaslin and his wild story, such a coincidence wouldn't bother him. But it seemed unusual for the other car to take the same— longer—route to the hospital.

Beck told himself to get a grip. He was sleep-deprived and overloaded with stress from work and home. He turned left and pressed harder on the gas pedal to see if the Chevy kept up with him.

It did.

Either they were going to the same place or the driver was totally stupid, he thought. He lost the other car as he slipped down a residential street in the opposite direction from Grasslands Hospital. Whoever was following him would certainly know where he worked. If he was heading in that direction, why didn't they go ahead and look for his car in the lot—unless they meant to catch him?

Matt scanned the neighborhood as he drove. No sign of the Chevy. He was being ridiculous. He found his way back to Route 9 and continued on back roads, his mind adrift with memories and questions. The early evening chill enveloped his body. He shivered, suddenly aware he had reached the 900-acre Grasslands Reservation. He passed the traditional white pillared pavilions of red brick, built early in the century to house the county hospital, poor house, and sanitarium. Now the place had been renovated—Beck called it "wordsmithed"— into the medical center, geriatric facility, and psychiatric unit. He pulled into the ground-level lot and parked in his space, shook his head, and tried to collect himself, distract his mind for a while with mundane work.

Beck turned his head to the sky and took a deep breath. Painful as it was, maybe he needed to remember the past to be absolved of what had happened so long ago. Maybe he had to expunge the memory by reliving it. Maybe he would talk again to Anne, in the darkest hour of the night when she could not see him; she would hold him as he held her when her own painful memories beckoned.

Like a screen going black, the pictures vanished, leaving Beck sweaty and exhausted. He waited another minute and searched the parking lot one last time for the Chevy. Stupid, he thought, and grabbed his canvass briefcase from the passenger seat. Waving to Betty at the entrance switchboard, he rode the elevator to his office.

Damned voice mail. He flipped on the light and punched his code on the speaker phone. Shouldn't even listen to it. Nothing that couldn't wait until tomorrow. Then again, it could be Joe, explaining it all. That would be good.

He felt both disappointed and relieved that the voice on the machine was Anne's. Still no word from McCaslin, but Anne would bring food for dinner. She sounded as tired as he had been. He listened to the message again just to hear her voice. It was the kind of familiar comfort he wanted right now. He looked at the couch and remembered the waking dream he'd had the night before. He shivered.

He stared at the stack of papers from his in box. He would work through the charting and reports, maybe catch up on a couple of "D&D" articles to get him up-to-date on the latest death and dying literature. That should give Anne time to finish up and drive to the mountain. Maybe they would have a good night together. Maybe he would talk, really talk.

First things first. He reached for an interoffice envelope at the top of the box. As he opened it, his pager screeched at his hip, startling him.

"You are jumpy tonight," he said to himself before he looked at the number. Ordinarily he would let the shift chaplain handle general pastoral care, but this call was to his personal pager.

He punched the phone digits for ICU.

"This is Chaplain Beck."

"Thank God you're here, Matt."

He recognized the voice of the gray-haired, veteran ICU charge nurse, Loraine Cooper. "I'm not really here, Lo," he said. "Just picking up something in my office. What's up?"

"We need you—you personally—down here right away."

Beck tensed at the tone of her voice. It had to be a doctor or hospital family member in bad shape. "What happened?" he said, feeling short of breath. "Who is it?"

"We just received a direct admit to the unit from ER. EMS dragged him out of a car that tried rafting down the Hudson." Her voice was as nonchalant as his would be in the same situation. They had both seen cases like this hundreds of times. They knew the outcome. "Looks like a GOMER to me. Multiorgan system failure. EMS intubated him so he's on a vent, but you and I both know how long that will last."

Not to the next shift, he thought. Still, why did they need him? The list of possibilities ran through his mind. "Name?" he said, not breathing.

"That's why I called you," Loraine said. "Wallet they fished out of his pocket says he's a priest."

Beck was out the door before he could hear her say the name McCaslin.

Warden Richard Williams pressed the buttons on the remote control and shook his head as he adjusted one of the four color monitors showing separate blocks of the prison. Playing on the fears of the neighboring wealthy suburbs, he had installed every modern surveillance method he could request, knowing that funds would be gladly appropriated by the state assembly. It seemed rich and powerful citizens didn't much like prisoners getting loose, especially not the crazies from Weston. His annual visit to Albany this week had been, as usual, successful. New laser equipment in next year's budget.

Williams went to the full kitchen in his office, poured a glass of milk, and carried it to his desk. Except for the thick steel bars over the windows, his spacious command center was more like an apartment built in the days when the remote location of the prison dictated that the warden live on-site. He hit a button to freeze a close-up shot in B Block of a guard handing an inmate a small bag of white powder, then punched another button to print the frame. He would do nothing now, but his options with both men had increased greatly. If the bag was indeed drugs, he could search the cell, throw the inmate in the Hole until further charges were filed, and fire the guard. He could also arrange to have the bag laced with strychnine so the inmate injected a hot shot and died. In either case, the guard was his now and would do whatever it took to keep that picture out of the hands of the police.

Williams smiled as he watched the monitors, confident in his ability to view almost any part of the prison at any time. There were still a few areas where the walls were too dense for signals to penetrate: the old infirmary, the deeper isolation cells, some of the original rooms and storage areas. As technology improved—some of it soon—he would figure out a way to relay audiovisual signals from those places as well. For now, there were cameras the inmates and guards knew about and those they didn't.

Knowledge was control. And control was everything. It was the basis of his career. He had moved up through the ranks from hack to sergeant to assistant superintendent and finally to warden over the dead or mangled bodies of his predecessors. He had gotten to know them, gained their trust, found out who they were screwing (whether women or the state) and made it his business—anonymously, of course—to expose them at just the right moment. One or two committed suicide, and a couple had disabling heart attacks; only one resigned graciously, having purchased the incriminating evidence at a price high enough to provide Williams with a seat on the Concorde for one of his regular trips to Europe.

He drank the milk and propped his feet on the desk. Now, at forty-eight, he could sit his well-toned body in his black leather chair and run his prison the way he wanted. It was entirely in his control—the guards, the prisoners, the visitors, and especially the vendors who mailed deposits to a private account in Quebec for the privilege of doing business with the institution.

The light from the monitors reflected off the bookcase and drew his attention to the photographs there: infant pictures of his siblings, one stern couple in dark clothes. No spouse. No children of his own. Despite an attractive face, sandy hair, and blue eyes, Williams had never married, or never married a woman anyway. His career was his mistress and he treated her to everything she wanted and needed to survive: time, money, and what passed for devotion.

His heart beat fast as he stared at the photos. He managed to block his past from consciousness most of the time, but when something triggered the memories, he became melancholy and depressed and sometimes strayed from the control he so desperately required. It was then that he rummaged through the clippings he usually kept hidden.

Distraction, he thought, as he went back to the kitchen and poured another glass of milk. Returning, he flicked on the sound to one monitor and listened to the guards' conversation with the prisoners; he flipped to another monitor, then muted them all and pressed a button on the console on his desk. Instantly, he heard the interaction of prisoners in the A Block day room.

Control. His parents had lost it. He had made a career out of regaining it.

Warden Williams stood and clicked off the monitors. He was about to put on his sport coat and go home when the phone rang. His secretary had left two hours before and he could tell by the ring that it was an outside call on his private line. He grabbed the phone.

"This is Williams."

"Good evening, Warden." The sonorous voice on the other end was both firm and solicitous. "I hope I did not catch you at a busy time."

"Not at all, Mr. Ehrhart. How are things down in the county executive's office?"

"Not nearly as neat and orderly as things at Weston, I'd wager," Martin

Ehrhart said. "You've gotten yourself quite a reputation for running a tight ship."

"Thank you, sir." Richard Williams closed his eyes and puckered his mouth. His muscular fingers tightened around the telephone receiver. This was not a social call. And it was not just to compliment his ability. Ehrhart wanted something and was taking his damned sweet time getting around to it.

"Do you have a minute to talk, Warden?"

"Yes, sir. I do." *Here comes the ploy. Watch it.* "What can I do for you?"

"Actually, I was hoping there was something I could do for you."

"Oh?" *This was a switch. Or maybe it was the bait. The switch would come later.* "What is that?"

"As you know, I'm a candidate for the U.S. Senate in the upcoming election."

"Yes. I do know that."

"So, as you might well imagine, I find I'm in need of someone to advise my campaign on the issues of prison reform and determinate sentencing. And, to make a long story short, I would like you to be that person, if you would consider it."

Williams paused. *Ehrhart wanted something big. But what?* "And... how... might this be beneficial to me, Mr. Ehrhart? Aside from the honor, of course."

"A good question. I like a man who looks out for his own best interests. I certainly do." Ehrhart had his script worked out, and Williams understood that he was reading his own lines well, one by one. "I can tell you that my campaign coffers are quite healthy. So I can assure you that you would be well paid for your consultation with my campaign managers and advisers."

"I see," Williams replied, apprehensive now that the stakes were climbing, hearing the setup in Ehrhart's voice, the windup before the pitch.

"And, of course, I'll need people who think the way I do to continue with me after the election. I understand there are some federal judgeships coming up in this jurisdiction, for which your background would be well suited, don't you think?"

What Williams thought was not anywhere close to that. He thought this man wanted to use him, to control him, and instinctively he hated it. "Once again, Mr. Ehrhart, I am quite honored that you would even consider me for such a position."

"There is, however, one thing of concern to me for which I particularly need your assistance."

Of course. Here it is. "And what is that one thing, Mr. Ehrhart?"

"I would like some information about one of your inmates." Information? Surely he desired more than that. This had to be just for openers. "Depending on what it is, I think that might be arranged," he said.

"Let me finish before you answer." The county executive's tone was harsher. "His name is Tod Engel."

Williams frowned. Engel had grown too popular. First, that damned reporter Anne Demming had pulled strings to finagle an interview, then Langert had barged in, and now this. "You mean Deathangel."

"Yes. That is what we called him nearly ten years ago. I was the prosecuting attorney from the D.A.'s office at the time, as you may recall."

"Yes, I do." And a vicious bastard you were then, too. Some things never change.

"It seems that the recent *CityMag* story has stirred interest in the case again. And I must say that I cannot imagine why you allowed such an interview to occur."

Williams started to sweat. He didn't like criticism, having his decisions questioned by this outsider who knew nothing about the delicate sense of balance needed to run this institution. "I didn't have much choice in the matter," he said. "Pressure from Albany, you know. And, of course, my adamant refusal would only have drawn more attention—and reporters— to the case." Something you should already know, you idiot. "We certainly couldn't afford that."

"I suppose you're right." Ehrhart pushed ahead. "But I should like to find out if there has been any other new interest by reporters or attorneys visiting Engel."

That was an easy question. Too easy. "No. None. As I already told your office, the only one who came out was Bishop Langert."

"Since you know him better than anyone, Warden, how did Deathangel react to the bishop's visit?"

What did he mean by that? Williams calmed himself to answer. "Engel was pretty upset. We had to chemically restrain him for several hours and keep him under constant surveillance."

"And now?"

"Now he has settled back to his old self. Making the same meaningless statements. You know, that stuff about 'toad stickers' and 'concentrate longer.' None of it makes any sense to anybody."

There was a long pause. Williams frowned. This wasn't all of it, and he wished like shit Ehrhart would get to the point. "Mr. Ehrhart?"

"Oh, sorry, I became sidetracked for a moment." The county executive cleared his throat. "And there have been no other visitors today?"

"None. But I don't quite see the importance—"

"The importance is that I'd hate to have any negative publicity at this critical time in our careers. Engel was certainly useful in bringing you this far in yours. We wouldn't want him to suddenly turn into a detriment to you. To us and our careers progressing the way they should."

This was still too easy. But if that's all he wanted, fine. "I'll be happy to keep you informed."

"I'm interested in a little something more than that."

Here it came. Williams closed his eyes again. His breathing became more labored. He heard the threat in Ehrhart's voice, felt the man's power billowing into his office like acrid smoke through the phone, taking over his space, clouding his vision. He could barely force the words through his constricted larynx. "And—what—might that—be—Mr. Ehrhart?"

"I think you should maintain an extra close watch on Mr. Engel for the next few days."

"How do you mean?" Williams squeezed his eyes shut as if to wall out the words. Control, he thought. He must retain control.

"I just feel that he ought to be under close surveillance. We wouldn't want anything to happen to him, you know."

The Warden felt overcome by the smoke, unable to see anything but the images of his past, of what had happened, of his parents.

"As I said," Ehrhart continued, "it would be terrible if Engel met with an accident or was seriously injured by another inmate, or became depressed and killed himself."

Williams stretched his head back and up, lifted his chin high to gasp for air. He sensed his control diminishing with each word from the man on the other end of the line.

"Are you still there?"

Williams coughed to clear his lungs and his mind. "Yes. I heard what you said." You said you want Engel dead, you pompous bastard. Well, it might not be a bad idea. It might remove the threat of damage to both of them.

"And your answer?"

"My answer?" Williams wondered which thing he was referring to.

"About accepting the consultant role to my campaign?"

What else could he say? It was an offer he couldn't refuse. Once Ehrhart was in the senate, he could pull strings to have the warden sent to Dannemora or Attica or some other godforsaken place in the cold. Or he could have him retired from the system entirely. He hated Ehrhart's pressure. The only way to maintain control was to assent and buy time. Besides, he could agree now and change his mind later.

"Yes," he choked. "Yes. I, uh, thank you for calling. Again, I am honored that you would include me in your plans."

"And you will remember to closely monitor Engel and inform me about his visitors and his progress on a regular basis."

His demise, you mean. "Yes. I will."

"Then I'll bid you good night, Warden. I look forward to your input to my successful campaign."

The line went dead. Richard Williams fell back in his chair. He gasped long, deep breaths, but none would halt the visions in his mind. He felt the smoke in his lungs, saw his childhood home in flames, himself racing to the door and being stopped by firemen in black, wet coats smothering him in their rubbery arms.

Immediately, even then, he understood what had happened. His parents, his crazy parents whom the children had protected all those years, had finally broken. All their insanity came pouring out that night as they systematically went through the house, killing each of the four children with a bullet to the head. Then, in some final act of contrition, they opened the gas outlets, doused the rooms with gasoline, and lit a match.

To this day he wondered why they had spared him, their eldest at fifteen. Why had they waited until he was out of the house for the night? Had they even known? Had they cared?

Tears streamed down the Warden's face. His panicked breathing began to subside. He had not had an episode like this for years. Usually the memories stayed in place. Usually he trapped the indelible scenes in his mind under lock and key, kept his own guilt and insanity, his own obscene fantasies out of public view—just like his prison.

But now he had been encroached upon, his power diminished, his control shaken. He must do what needed to be done to get it back, to take charge of his internal and external environment. He reached for the cassette behind him, removed it from the recorder, and labeled it with the date, the time, and a name. "Ehrhart." You never could tell when it would be useful in the future. To keep control.

He pushed himself up from the chair and haltingly made his way to the window. He hit the electronic button that opened it behind the bars and breathed in the musty air of late September. It cleared his mind, cleansed his office of the intrusive phone call, made his eyes sharp and his vision bright. It blew out the smoke and restored his balance.

The warden gripped the steel bars with both hands and gazed out over the complex. No, he would never be in that position again. He would not lose control as he had done on other occasions, occasions that shortened the distance between him and his charges at Weston more than he hoped anyone would ever know.

Matt Beck was ready to kick down the door by the time he reached the bright hallway to ICU. He had mistakenly taken the elevator instead of the stairs from his office four floors up to the second-floor intensive care unit. Why the hell did they make hospital elevators so slow? In a place where a few seconds made the difference between being present when someone was still breathing or missing their last moments, why did the damned elevators operate as though they were trying to force you to relax?

Smells of alcohol and feces reminded him that they didn't pay nurses enough, much less housekeepers. The odors also prepared him for what he would find in ICU. Beck slammed his fist against the metal wall plate, and the two doors swung open before him.

Loraine Cooper waited for him at the front nurse's station. "What I didn't have the chance to tell you before you so graciously hung up on me was that your buddy here took out two attackers on his way down to the Old Mill Stream."

"What?" Beck was stunned. He steadied himself against the desk.

"He put up a hell of a fight. The cops found a body, complete with tire treads, in St. Jude's sacristy. Apparently he dragged himself in from the alley. That was after they discovered the other guy skewered like a toad in the church aisle."

Strange, Beck thought. McCaslin had told him about being accosted at St. Jude's for money, even threatened. Probably because he had grown used to it and seldom got defensive or lost control, such encounters had always ended peacefully. This time, he must have been cornered for his life.

"Bodies are in the morgue. The M.E.'s going to do a post in the morning to try to identify them for the county police." The nurse led Beck to a glass-enclosed cubicle and showed him the numbers on the chart. "You can see this poor man won't last like this. The only question is how much we prolong him. And according to the plastic card in his wallet, my dear Chaplain Beck, that decision is now up to you."

Matt recalled the night, years ago, when he lectured to a clergy gathering at St. Jude's about advance directives and had everyone fill out the forms before they left the room. McCaslin joked that there was good news and bad news. The good news was that he'd named Beck his decision-maker, and that meant McCaslin trusted him to know what to do and do it. The bad news was that Beck was his decision-maker, and that meant he would not be in McCaslin's will.

Beck looked at the charge nurse. "Okay, Loraine. I've got a question." He had worked with Lo since his arrival at Grasslands. They had been through the insanity of aggressive ICU docs supporting the unrealistic hopes of anxious families, resulting in long, drawn-out, bad deaths. But what he was about to suggest was definitely pushing the limits, and he wasn't sure she'd go for it. "He's going to die, right? We know that."

"Yeah, and I know that look. We can't hasten this along with Vitamin M, if that's what you're asking."

Beck smiled at the ICU euphemism for morphine. They had often watched dying patients grimacing and suffering and called for more Vitamin M to ease the transition. There was no good reason for anyone to die in pain. But right now he wanted something else.

"No. As his designated surrogate decision-maker, I'm going to direct you to remove all that shit and do everything you can to make him comfortable. But before that, I'd like three minutes of as much lucidity as you can give me."

The charge nurse pursed her lips. "You want to find out what happened, right?"

Beck nodded, understanding that she would be venturing outside the bounds of allowable practice. "You can argue it's a comfort measure. It will give him great comfort to tell me everything he can about this before he dies."

"The attending wrote orders for comfort measures. You have the patient's power of attorney for health care, you direct his comfort measures, so this is a comfort measure. Sounds logical to me." She winked. "I've worked with you too long. I'm as sick as you are."

She left and returned shortly with two syringes.

"I can't promise you lucidity. I don't know how long his brain was waterlogged. If he was anoxic longer than five minutes, he may not be able to tell you squat. All I can do is shoot him full of a morphine antagonist and a heart stimulant and see what happens. While you're in there, I'll prepare a bolus of morphine to inject fast if he becomes delirious or overwhelmed by pain."

They walked into the cubicle, which was full of humming machinery. It was a familiar sight. Blue boxes read pulse and oxygen levels in crimson digits. Squiggles in various colors drifted monotonously across a TV screen, barely visible through the plastic jungle of dangling bags and tubing. Amid it all, dwarfed by technology, lay Joseph McCaslin.

Matt thought he looked insignificant by comparison, a gross distortion of humanity subservient to machines. The charge nurse administered the two syringes through the Heparin lock in McCaslin's forearm. She left the cubicle, but she would wait outside and do charting until Beck called for the morphine.

Matt let down the bedside guardrail and dragged up a chair. He reached over and clicked off the cardiac and pulse oximeter alarms—the drugs they'd given McCaslin would send them beyond their alarm limit.

"Joe," he spoke directly into the dying man's ear. "It's me. Matt." He touched McCaslin's hand and forehead lightly, not wanting to startle him or dislodge the delicately placed IV's. "I assume you can hear me somewhere in there. We're giving you something to try to open a window for you. I need you to come up to that window and do your best to tell me whatever you can about what happened."

McCaslin jerked in the bed as the drugs pushed back the cloud of nonresponsiveness, forced his heart to pump faster and his consciousness to surface from the depths of pain and injury.

"I know this is hard, Joe." Beck gently held his hand. "And I wont let the pain overwhelm you, but if there's anything, anything at all."

The man's eyes blinked several times, then opened wide. His mouth moved, pushing out whispered words behind the oxygen mask.

"Matt—"

"Yes, Joe, I'm right here." Beck removed the green straps of the mask from the priest's head and laid the plastic cup near his chin. "Who did this?" He saw the grimace of pain on McCaslin's face, felt it in his tight grasp, and wished it were gone. But he also wanted his friend to speak to him.

"Not sure." McCaslin pulled Beck's hand up to his chest. Matt could feel the heart thumping wildly.

"I have to know something," Beck said as McCaslin's eyelids started to close. "Listen to me! I have to know if this was related to your phone call last night. Was this a random mugging or was it about Deathangel?"

The priest opened his eyes and gazed at Beck. "Yes," he whispered, "Deathangel." He closed his eyes. "Come—"

Beck moved his face next to McCaslin's. Pictures of Kate flashed through his own mind. Kate on a ventilator, her battered body further invaded by tubes and machines; Kate as they were withdrawn; Kate peaceful at last. He had to shove the images aside, listen to the man dying inches away from him.

"My—house. File."

"Computer file or cabinet file at your house?" McCaslin was fading and the drugs were dissipating. In a minute he would surface into pain and suffering, devoid of the morphine, his pulse speeding up violently. Beck was pushing now, with only seconds left, but he needed more information. He spoke slowly. "Okay, then. Where?"

McCaslin kept his eyes shut and was silent so long Beck thought he had died. Matt called out to Loraine and nodded, then held up his hand to stop her as the weak voice barely whispered, "John three—" McCaslin fell silent again. It was the end. No more time for questions. McCaslin was telling Beck he wanted the comfort of scripture. "Yes, Joe. I understand." It was a common verse, plastered all over road signs and on placards at football games. "For God so loved the world, that he gave his only begotten Son, Jesus, that all who believe in Him might not perish, but have everlasting life."

Matt thought for a second. He had to try one more thing. As bad as he felt about it, he would want McCaslin to push him the same way if the tables were turned. Then he'd leave him in peace. As the window of lucidity began to close, Beck put his mouth next to his friend's ear. "Is there a password?"

He held tight as McCaslin jerked, writhing as though he needed to shed his skin, working his legs as if to crawl away. He barely breathed through clenched teeth. "Ab ... solve."

Was it a password or something McCaslin wanted? Just in case, Beck made the sign of the cross on the man's forehead, lips, and heart. "Deliver your servant, Joseph, O Sovereign Lord Christ, from all evil, and set him free from every bond; that he may rest with all your saints in the eternal habitations; where with the Father and the Holy Spirit you live and reign, one God, for ever and ever. Amen."

He motioned through the cubicle window and Loraine Cooper entered with the morphine syringe.

"Goodbye, Joseph," Beck said, tears filling his eyes. "May the angels greet you this day in paradise." And may one of them be Kate, he thought, leaning close to McCaslin's grimacing face. "God's got you. I've got your story. Neither one of us will let go."

Beck turned to the charge nurse. "Do you have enough to quell the thrashing?"

The nurse nodded and injected the morphine. "I already called and talked to his attending about your instructions as his proxy."

Matt glanced at her, noting her tone of voice. "Any problem?"

"No. Not really. You know the story. Horsey new doc wants heroics as long as he doesn't have to take them home and care for them or pay their bill, or deal with the people honoring their wishes."

He smiled at her. "Thanks for running interference."

"Somebody's got to teach those puppies to do it on the paper."

McCaslin had stopped moving. His breathing was quieter, the lines of agony fell from his face, and the tension in his muscles vanished. "Even in death, you taught someone a lesson about life, Joe," Matt said. He turned to Loraine. "This guy helped me through some difficult times."

"And now you're helping him through his." She handed Beck a damp washcloth to wipe McCaslin's sweating forehead. "What next?"

"Honor his wish. Withdraw everything except whatever he needs for comfort."

"I will if you'll chart that you directed me to do it as his proxy. He'll quit quickly without pressors on board."

When Beck returned to the bedside, McCaslin was already apneic, not breathing for long periods, but the morphine had calmed him. He looked peaceful at last, with no signs of discomfort. Matt touched his arm and thanked him for being there so many times for comfort and support, for his friendship. In a choked whisper, he said. "Hug Kate for me when you see her."

The monitor lines went flat.

Beck made the sign of the cross and tearfully pronounced the final blessing: "Depart, O Christian soul, out of this world; In the name of God the Father who created you; In the name of Jesus Christ who redeemed you; In the name of the Holy Spirit who sanctifies you. May your dwelling place be this day in the Paradise of God. May your soul, Joseph McCaslin, and the souls of all the departed, through the mercy of God, rest in peace. Amen."

When Loraine came around the bed, Beck reached for her and held on. He cried, sad at the loss, relieved that the pain had gone, and jealous, irrational though it was, that McCaslin would be with Kate and he would not, not yet. In a minute, he composed himself and thanked her.

Loraine turned off the monitors and noted the time of death. Beck picked up the small plastic sack of McCaslin's belongings. He would call the funeral home tonight and notify the diocesan office and McCaslin's relatives in the morning.

"Take it easy tonight, Matt. You look like hell." Loraine pecked his cheek.

"Thanks. I love you, too," he said as he left the unit.

Matt took the back stairwells and basement corridors out of the hospital to avoid seeing anyone—or anyone seeing him. He walked to his car, his emotions swirling. McCaslin's panicked call. McCaslin's death. Anne's elation over the Deathangel story and her frustration with her subsequent investigation. Anne's face on Kate's dying body in his dream.

The frigid September air shocked him. He climbed into the car and looked back at the bright lights of the hospital. McCaslin's dying words were that his murder was about Deathangel. What did that mean? And all the vivid memories of Kate, intermingled with his feelings for Anne? What he had believed were settled issues—Kate, Engel, Anne—were unfinished, uncertain.

Beck suddenly felt a sense of urgency. He had to hurry to McCaslin's house—and return home to Anne before something happened. To him. To her.

He jammed the car into reverse, backed out of the space, and raced off the grounds of the medical complex. Speeding through the night in the open sports car, he knew the chill he felt was not entirely due to the cold.

Chapter 4

Anne Demming turned from the Crosstown to the Henry Hudson Parkway and snapped off the radio. She'd had enough input for one day and wanted to drive to Matt's house in silence. Well, not total silence. Her brain was speeding faster than the car. What had started as an innocuous recap of Tod Engel now required interviews with people who had long buried the pain of this case. Maybe if she sorted through it all one last time she could put it to rest before she reached the mountain.

She grinned as she sipped the root beer she had picked up on her way out of the *CityMag* building. Why did root beer taste so comforting? Maybe she associated it with carefree days on the ranch. She remembered her horror the first time her daddy said he'd make her a black cow to drink, and how relieved she'd been to learn it was just ice cream and root beer.

Like the first time she heard Matt call his new place The Mountain, as though the forest-covered hill in Somers was the Wagnerian retreat of some superhero like Batman or Captain Midnight. She soon learned it was his retreat from the world of death and medicine. He could relax by the pool in summer and the fireplace in winter—both with views of the Muscoot and Croton Falls reservoirs. "The mountain" sounded remote and secluded, mimicking Beck's aloofness when they first met. She braked suddenly to avoid a pothole. Driving the Henry Hudson was like driving on the moon, except the moon had fewer craters.

A lot had preceded her first view of Beck in the Grasslands ER, and it was those events she needed to consider now. Given the heavy traffic, even at 7 P.M., she'd have plenty of time to do it.

Twitch had first put her on the story—the murders at Umbrella Point in Larchmont—on a hunch that they would not be the last. She had managed a particularly good photo of the crime scene but had not been allowed to take pictures of the wooden angel, for fear others might copycat the murders. If identical pieces were discovered, the police would know it was the same person.

They were found; it was the same person. Tod Engel killed eight people—five women and three men—and left a carved angel at the scene of each crime. Anne remembered interviews with police baffled by a murderer who struck and vanished almost at will, and talking to ordinary citizens who barred their bedroom doors at night, weapons handy. She had spoken with gun-store owners and sporting-goods clerks doing a booming business in weapons and locks. But Deathangel seemed undaunted by either. It was as though he walked through walls, killed, and disappeared. Ironically, the angels, the flaunted symbols of heaven-bound souls, ultimately tied Engel to the victims and assured his conviction.

Anne slowed the car and tossed her quarters in the basket at the Bronx tollbooth, where the Henry Hudson became the Sawmill River Parkway. Checking the rearview mirror, she waited for the gate to lift and hurried to beat the other toll lines converging into two narrow lanes.

She was finally allowed to photograph an angel when Engel was arrested. James Rinski, the investigator in charge of the case, had tried to elicit her help all along. Contrary to what he believed, she had not unearthed anything in her own digging. If she had, she would have turned it over to someone else, to avoid encouraging Rinski's obvious advances.

Anne shivered, recalling how slimy the man was back then. She made a face at the thought of interviewing him tomorrow. Ten years ago he had one thing on his mind. No, two things. The second one was Deathangel. But the sleazeball was persistent. Even though she had refused to deal with him, he gave her the exclusive on the bust. She sipped her root beer and smirked. "Probably thought I'd return the favor," she said.

She remembered it as if it were yesterday—accompanying the police as they barged into Engel's apartment and subdued the big man. She snapped the flash of the angel sitting on the table in plain sight and felt the same chill she did now at the realization that it was meant to go beside the body of another victim.

The parkway sign for Yonkers reminded her of the grimy apartment Engel had rented near the New Rochelle station. Rinski had been incredibly generous to her at the time, allowing her to take pictures simultaneously with the police photographer, including many photos of himself with various objects in the murderer's rooms. When they emerged from the apartment building, she was stunned by the horde of faces, the dozens of other media to whom the bust had been leaked—slightly later. The clamor for information from her and Rinski had propelled them into the national spotlight.

She asked Twitch to send Rinski a case of champagne as a thank-you. The lewd message on her answering machine made it clear that was not the kind of thanks he wanted. But the calculated publicity had not hurt his career either, she thought, changing lanes to pass a camper. He had used her media expertise to catapult himself to the place he'd been ever since—police commissioner for the County of Westchester. Their paths had crossed over the years, but never for long.

She changed lanes again. A blue Chevy darted around the camper and squeezed into her lane about two cars behind her. Some people had no idea how to drive.

Funny. She couldn't call up much about the defense attorney at Engel's trial. He'd been a public defender, very young and inexperienced. His name was Carpenter. Carl Carpenter. Everyone thought it ironic about the wooden angels and the name Carpenter.

Six months after the trial, she and Matt were supposed to meet for dinner in Larchmont. He called her from the hospital to announce he'd be late. A DOA was en route to the ER. When he finally arrived at the restaurant, he told her the DOA. was Carpenter. The man had gotten drunk, passed out, and puked, aspirating vomit into his lungs and choking to death. A neighbor dropping off a package found him.

That evening they'd speculated about his death. Carpenter had told her in a post-trial interview that he had failed an innocent Tod Engel. Matt thought he had fallen off the wagon, drunk himself into an early grave. Anne speculated that it was mob payback for a previously fumbled case on an organized crime figure.

Of course, it hadn't helped Carpenter that the chief attorney for the prosecution was Martin Ehrhart, whose reputation equaled "Flea" Bailey and Bill Kunstler. Now Ehrhart would likely be the next U.S. senator from New York. He was probably burning the midnight oil right over there in his White Plains office. Anne glanced at the lights on the horizon. Did he ever spare a thought for Engel, the man responsible for his rise to power?

Sweet Jesus. She shook her head. she could have won the case with what they had. Engel's smiling face had met the jeering, camera-flashing crowd outside his apartment with gratitude for what must have appeared to be his fans—and in some ways they were. He obliged their shouted questions by confessing in front of the rolling cameras in time for the eleven o'clock news. Anne remembered his exuberant words captioning her cover photo in *CityMag*: "I am Deathangel!" Add that to the angel, the wood shavings, and the carpentry tools in his apartment, right next to the 9MM, and his proverbial goose was cooked.

Anne adjusted the controls for a little heat in the car. Just remembering the murders and the look on Engel's face always made her double-check her door locks. She was glad his retarded delusions could no longer cause others pain. Though during her interview with him he seemed devoid of harm, as if whatever possessed him had slipped away, leaving his hollow shell locked up in prison. Maybe whatever that was still floated about, waiting to connect with someone or something, to give it life again. Maybe it was the same spirit that appeared time after time, as Jack the Ripper or the Boston Strangler, resurfacing to kill again. Back home in Texas, where Anne had mainly worried about drunken cowboys and scorpions, there had been the likes of Henry Lee Lucas in Houston and the still unsolved Yogurt Shop murders in Austin.

She checked her gas gauge and realized she was scaring herself. She turned the radio back on for distraction, then clicked it off. She'd left out one major detail in her review. The hair. The one time Engel left a note at a crime scene, the police lab found a hair sealed in the flap. Ehrhart made a major point of it in the trial, arguing that genetic analysis had proven it conclusively the same as Engel's. But the young public defender had him here, and he was able to malign the accuracy of this as yet unproved DNA testing. The hair was inadmissible as evidence. Ehrhart, she remembered, went red in the face over it and then turned it to his advantage, talking extensively in his summary about the fatal hair, reminding the jury with a wink that it was, of course, inadmissible and they should give it no weight whatsoever.

That was when John Langert, a mere parish priest then, had lost it. He stood up in the audience and yelled at Ehrhart, the judge, and the jury. It made for wonderful press and a great photograph. As did Engel's repetitive statement at sentencing: "I am Deathangel." Crowds booed him as he was escorted from the courtroom to travel to Weston State Prison. There he would sink into oblivion for a decade until she had resurrected him with her article.

Anne slowed to watch for state troopers along the section of the Sawmill they favored. A few other things had been resurrected, things that were clearly major issues for Matt. What else could have been going on with his call to her office today? Not wanting to lose her? He had never spoken like that before the other night at Umbrella Point, when Deathangel had reemerged. And he almost never mentioned Kate anymore, not after their early discussions.

Anne thought she handled Kate's hovering memory well most of the time, partly because of her own ghost. If pressed, she had to admit that a part of her still hurt from her fiancé's death in Iran. They put their engagement on hold when Robert told her he would have to be out of sight for a few weeks. She knew what that meant, and she knew he couldn't talk about it. His work with the Defense Intelligence Agency was secret, though his expertise as a marksman and strategist was not. Three weeks later she read the headlines in the Times: "Americans Killed in Failed Hostage Rescue Attempt." Robert's name was in the caption under a grainy photo. She greeted the body bag at the airport.

Was it the same thing that inhabited Engel, that lurked around eternally, that had also taken Robert's life? If so, maybe all you could do was to take a stand against it like Langert did at the trial. Like Robert did in Iran.

Suddenly too warm, Anne turned off the heat and rolled down the passenger window to get some air. She couldn't believe her eyes still clouded with tears all these years later. She supposed Matt was right; there were some losses we grieve all our lives. Robert was hers. That was another reason she and Matt were drawn to one another. Both knew what they wanted and didn't want. Both were unwilling to commit, but both needed someone to hold against the terrors of the night, the skulking thing that had wounded them so deeply. Someone who understood.

The cold night air chilled her as she closed the window and passed the Chappaqua exit. Those were exciting days, pursuing the Engel case, but, these were better. More settled, more secure. She drew in a deep breath as she took the ramp for I-684. The last stretch before home, and she was ready to be there. She was hungry, looking forward to a nice hot bath with or without Matt, and to the comfort of his king-size bed, where she could sprawl to her heart's content and still reach for him when she wanted.

The Deathangel material would still be there tomorrow: the phone calls, the stories, the interviews, the pictures. Right now she wanted to forget it. Her eyelids were heavy. She turned off at the Somers exit and took a left.

As she drove through the town center, she noticed that the same battered blue Chevy she had seen on the Sawmill was trailing slowly behind her. Someone else commuting to the city from here, she thought, and made the turn for the narrow, darker road that led to the mountain. Five minutes later she hooked a sharp right at the unmarked drive that wound up to the house. The Chevy sped past behind her.

To her surprise, Matt had not returned. Perhaps he'd left word on the answering machine. She pulled into the garage and electronically closed the door before she unlocked the car doors.

As she carried her bags inside, she made a mental note to ask Matt if he knew someone in town who drove a blue Chevrolet. She flicked on the light and stood perfectly still in the kitchen. She was suddenly aware that she was alone, not only with the feelings she'd dredged up about Robert, but with that force she sensed was once again prowling about.

She returned to the car and retrieved her LadyHawke, the chrome-plated .38 she had purchased years ago in Texas. The mountain retreat had indeed become a fortress.

Warden Richard Williams took a deep breath and picked up his phone. He had thought about it long enough, and it was clear. That pushy bastard Ehrhart had actually played right into his hands. Tod Engel had been a liability for longer than anyone knew, even before he became a guest of the Weston Hilton. With Deathangel taken care of, Williams would win twice: he would rid himself of a nagging loose end and have a little something on the next U.S. senator from New York—a favor that could be his ticket out of Weston, even out of the country.

He flipped on the television monitors and pressed an intercom button.

"Yes, Warden?" It was the guard in F Block.

"Have you been observing Tod Engel closely tonight, officer?"

"Not particularly, sir. No more than usual."

"That's what I thought. I've been listening to his cell and I'm concerned about his increasingly agitated condition, possibly related to that article and the unexpected visit from the bishop."

"But, Warden, I haven't seen any—"

"I want you to put him in solitary confinement, officer."

There was a moment of silence.

"You know how he hates being alone."

"What I know is that I am charged with keeping the man secure and out of danger, and that is exactly what I'm doing." He paused. "Do you disagree with that goal?"

"No, sir."

"Then follow the orders given you. Unless you would prefer working another shift, perhaps in another institution."

"I'll take care of it within the hour, sir." The guard's voice was taut and resigned.

Wrong answer. The warden shook his head. My schedule, not yours. "I want it done now. Do you understand?" Williams would remember this and mark the guard's file for no promotion, ever.

"Yes, sir. But we'll have to sedate him first. He'll figure out by the direction we're taking him where he's going."

"Then do so," Williams barked. "And notify me when it is accomplished."

"Yes, Warden, but what about belongings?"

"Engel may take whatever he wishes, but he is to be strip-searched before he goes in the isolation cell." Williams smiled. "And I want a close watch on him. I don't want anything to happen to him."

"But, sir, begging your pardon. If we let him have all his belongings, couldn't he take something dangerous into isolation, strip-searched or not?"

"Just follow my orders and contact me when you're finished. I want him isolated, but there's no need to be cruel. He may have his belongings." Williams was finished. "Clear?"

"Yes, sir," the officer lied. The warden heard it.

Richard Williams turned up the sound for the monitor trained on F Block. He was back in control again. He would manage this intrusion as he had managed others. He wouldn't allow Ehrhart or anyone else to tamper with his careful system. He would protect his psyche and his position at all costs, and he would get the job Ehrhart had promised him and maybe more, just as he had taken what he needed to get where he was today.

The Warden watched as the guards approached Engel's cell. He remembered his own days working the blocks, taking the orders, handling the prisoners. It was like viewing videotape of his past. His recent past, anyway.

As for the distant past, the fire and smoke in his head had been extinguished. He would do his best to see that they were never rekindled.

Beck turned into McCaslin's driveway, switched off the engine, and sat motionless, gripping the Spider's smooth, wood steering wheel. He cursed his cell phone, which had gone dead at the end of the message he left for Anne at his house. He wondered if the last bit had recorded—the part where he said he loved her. They said it more often to each other now, but he knew each was still holding back a part of themselves that would not let go, would not commit, would not be loved.

Until now it had worked. But McCaslin's death appeared to be linked to Deathangel. It was a turning point. He could back out of this driveway, return to the mountain with Anne, and let things work themselves out. They probably would. If there was something amiss about the Deathangel case, the police were obligated to follow the speculation to its logical end. It might take a long time and the results could be inconclusive, or the cops might affirm again that Engel was the murderer, but it would be out of their hands—and their psyches. Matt and Anne would be safe. Things would remain as they were.

He started the car and jammed the stick into reverse. He looked over his right shoulder toward the street and began to let out the clutch. His eye caught the yellow crime-scene tape flapping in the alley, separating the church from McCaslin's house. Then he stopped.

If he went into that house, there would be no turning back from the case, from his feelings, from dealing with Anne, from the memories of Kate's death—and from finding her killer. If he left the car, he risked everything.

Beck shut off the engine.

"Shit," he said, getting out of the Fiat.

He followed the stone path to the door. Lights were on in the living room and kitchen. Hopefully they were attached to a timer. His breathing tensed, and adrenaline heightened his senses to every sound or movement.

Matt used the key he had received with McCaslin's belongings. The creaking door made the silence even eerier. He stood still and looked around the living room. Something seemed wrong. He was about to take a step forward when a crash came from the kitchen.

Beck's heart nearly exploded. He moved toward the source of the sound slowly, rounding the corner. McCaslin's black and white cat was sitting in the sink, surrounded by broken dishes. Beck shook his head, regained his breath, and picked up the shorthair so it wouldn't get injured by the shards that surrounded it.

"Poor Reinhold," he said, stroking the animal which was named for the famous theologian. "I'm afraid we'll have to find another home for you, pal. Maybe Anne's Abby would like a learned housemate." Instead of purring, the cat nipped at him. "Bad idea, huh?" Beck wondered if the normally docile feline was skittish because it wanted food. As he poured dry food into the bowl in the hall, he realized another possibility. Maybe the cat had been frightened by something.

He tried to examine the room as his dad would have, coming up on an FBI crime scene. Then it clicked. For the first time, he saw it. And it sent a shudder down his spine.

Objects were barely out of kilter: a cupboard door slightly ajar, a vase on a table a bit off center, a paper on the floor, a lampshade slightly askew—things McCaslin's notoriously tidy housekeeper would never tolerate. The place had been searched but left to appear undisturbed.

Beck couldn't tell how long ago someone had been there. It must have been hours earlier, based on the time it would take to go through McCaslin's possessions and try to move them back. But why? If someone wanted to ransack the place, what difference did it make what it looked like afterward? Unless they hadn't wanted to draw further attention to McCaslin's murder. The priest's death would seem like a random mugging unless his house was later searched. Then it would look deliberate.

Beck went to the bedroom. The drawers of the dresser and desk were out of alignment—just enough to have been searched and hurriedly closed. This was not a routine burglary. Normal burglars chose items of value that were easily fenced. The gold crosses and Sony Watchman were still intact, though out of place on the desk. No. Whoever had been here was searching for the thing the dying man had whispered, the one connection that could pinpoint the time and day when Joseph McCaslin claimed he had heard the critical confession, the one that proved Tod Engel innocent.

They were after the file.

Though there was no way they could have known about it specifically, McCaslin's intruders might have assumed that he, like many clergy, kept the usual official records and, possibly, unofficial personal notes about marriages, baptisms, funerals, and even confessions, notes that might or might not be incriminating enough to reopen the case.

They had not been gone long. Beck put his hand on the computer terminal. Still warm. He switched the computer on and scrolled through the titles in the word processing program, scanning for a file name that might connect. McCaslin could have concealed the document under another, unrelated title, but Beck suddenly realized that the priest might not have stored it on the hard drive at all. In fact, he probably hadn't. If somebody stole the computer, they would eventually be able to break into the files.

It had to be on a floppy.

He turned off the computer and swiveled around in the chair. Where the hell would McCaslin have put it?

After a fruitless search of the bedroom, Matt returned to the living room. He sifted through the stack of books by the fireplace. He remembered sitting in this room with a glass of wine, swapping seminary stories with his friend. They had gone to different schools, but both institutions were in urban high-crime areas, Yale in New Haven and General in New

York. They had learned to keep their belongings intact by being illogical.

The logical place for the disk was in the bedroom or at an office desk, so the file had to be here in the living room, or maybe in the kitchen.

Beck smiled as he remembered McCaslin's answer to his question. He had not said "John 3:16," as Matt had surmised at the time in the emotion of his friend's dying moments. He had said "John 3."

Matt shook his head. The house was a two-and-a-half bath. He ignored the master and guest bathrooms—Johns 1 and 2— and headed for the smaller one adjacent to the kitchen.

John 3.

He searched through the cabinets under the sink and on the wall. Nothing. He paused a minute and stared at the only other object in the tiny bathroom. He should have taken McCaslin even more literally.

John 3.

Beck lifted the porcelain cover from the toilet tank as a loudly meowing Reinhold scurried underfoot. He gently nudged the cat out of the way and peered in.

There it was, in the most illogical place in the house, double-bagged in the plastic sealers divers used, anchored with a brick at the bottom of the tank. Great idea. And it saved water, too. He grinned and pulled out the dripping bag.

He caught a sudden movement in the mirror. Too late, he saw the black-jack and raised his arm to deflect the blow to his skull. As he collapsed to the floor, he made out a blurred form in a black ski mask. The blur grabbed the bag with one hand, wielding a knife in the other. Kate's image flashed before him, and his reeling senses told him this must be her killer. Through the ringing in his ears, he heard a venomous hissing voice.

"Thank you, Father Beck. I never would have found this if not for you." The person moved closer and bent over him. "You will never know the service you have done for us."

Beck's mind whirled, his body limp, his vision fading. He felt the sharp edge of the knife at his neck, the pressure building to make a deep incision over the jugular. Though there was a time when he would have welcomed death, it was past. Through the haze he pulled up ten years of indignant anger; fury roused him, fueled his strength to draw back his leg and smash it into the gut of the hooded killer. The man stumbled against the toilet. Matt felt as much as heard the knife clatter on the floor. Car doors slammed in the driveway outside, and voices sounded like they were fast approaching the house.

Beck barely saw the form jump up and, cursing, retrieve the knife and vanish out the kitchen door. The voices outside faded. His eyes closed to blackness. The house was silent, except for the rough licking of the cat's tongue on his face.

First it was the Morse Code he learned as a Boy Scout. Then it was the backbeat to a sixties song. Finally it became a familiar beeping. It brought him back to awareness, made him resurface from the black depths to the bright light above him. Beck shakily gathered himself into a sitting position and gradually focused his blinking eyes on his pager. His head pounded to the cadence of the beeps. Waves of nausea washed over him, wrenched so deep into the pit of his stomach that he thought he would throw up. He forced a few deep breaths and assessed the damage. He seemed able to move everything. There was blood on his hand when he touched the matted wet spot on his head, and a thin line of pain creased his neck. He rolled to his knees, leaned against the john, and looked at the number on the pager.

It was Anne. The good news seeping into his clearing consciousness was that she was there and safe. The bad news was he had to call her.

He struggled to his feet, walking unsteadily to the living room so he could look out the window at his car. The driveway of McCaslin's nearest neighbor ran alongside the rectory. Their house was scarcely twenty feet away. Neighbors arriving home must have sounded like someone coming toward McCaslin's house. Thank God.

He cautiously made his way back to the kitchen sink for a glass of water. It braced him as he picked up the phone on the counter.

The line rang once.

"Where the hell are you?" Her voice was more concerned than angry.

"What time is it?" Beck said, widening his eyes to look at his digital watch.

"Eleven thirty. What happened? I got your message about McCaslin and that you were going to his house. I'm so sorry, Matt. Are you okay?"

"I'm fine." He stalled, trying to sort out what to say. He should have waited until he felt more alert.

"Yeah. And my daddy's a sheep rancher. What's going on?"

"Long story short? Got sapped by the other visitor to McCaslin's house. And he took the information that McCaslin wanted me to find." Beck coughed and grimaced at the throbbing in his head.

"God, Matt! Do I need to call EMS for you?"

"I don't think so," he said, wiping the back of his head with a cold towel. "I'll be home in thirty minutes. Boil some water and pour me a glass of Black Bush."

"You sound like you're having a baby."

"My head feels like it." He started to laugh, then coughed. "Listen, be extra careful out there, will you?"

"I've got my LadyHawke. We'll be waiting."

"See you in half an hour." Matt hung up and wandered back to John 3. He replaced the tank lid and glanced around one more time, knowing the disk was gone but looking all the same. Silly habit, he thought. He turned off the bathroom light and went to lock the kitchen door.

Or maybe not.

Beck stopped and surveyed the kitchen. Memory of McCaslin's own silly habit emerged through the throbbing and nausea. Bearing a basic mistrust of computers, Joe had continued the silly habit he had practiced since his first sacramental act after ordination.

Keeping written notes. By hand.

In the last two years, when McCaslin finally succumbed to the ease of a computer, he still maintained his handwritten journal as a backup for when technology inevitably failed.

"Or when a masked killer steals your disk," Matt mumbled. His eye fell on a shelf of books above the sink. Cookbooks. He smiled. Illogical. Right. One by one, he opened them.

Diet For A Small Planet was not it. Neither was The Radical Vegetarian. He flipped through a few more with no luck.

He was about to check the books in the living room when he saw it sitting on the counter by the toaster: Helen Corbitt's Guide to Gourmet Cooking. The brown plastic cover was too large for the book. Inside, on page after lined page, was the unique scrawl of Joseph McCaslin.

Beck thumbed through the journal and read a few sentences, getting the flavor of its contents. His friend had violated the vows of confidentiality by writing down the exact content of some of the confessions, although no names were attached.

At the end of the book, McCaslin had meticulously copied down the words he heard in the confessional Saturday night. They were identical to the phrases Engel had repeated for ten years.

"Hold still!" Anne Demming grasped Beck's forehead and dabbed at his blood-stained scalp. "I've branded calves that were more cooperative."

Matt grimaced. "It feels like that's exactly what you're doing." He took a sip of Irish whiskey. His emotions were pitching like lava at the top of a frothing volcano. He felt sad over the death of McCaslin, angry at the murderers, humiliated by the attacker at the house, embarrassed at needing Anne to tend to him, and grateful she was here to do it.

She had been horrified when he came in the door an hour ago, carrying Reinhold. He sat as patiently as he could at the kitchen table while she put food on the deck for the cat and nursed his bloody wounds. He told her the details of McCaslin's death and the events at the house.

"It's awful about Joe," Anne said.

Her hands were soft and comforting on his whiskered face, and he felt absurdly grateful when she hugged him, kissed his neck. He felt the tug of loss again and pulled her close.

"I know what he meant to you, how good a friend he was."

Beck nodded toward the cookbook on the table. "Maybe still a good friend—for both of us."

She pointed to the chair. "First things first."

He sat still and let her finish. As she worked, she recounted her thoughts on the ride up from the city, checking the sequence of events of the Deathangel case with his memory as she stuck a gauze bandage on his head.

"Just remember, what goes around comes around," she said.

"I hope so," Beck muttered. "I know you'll quote me the 'vengeance is mine, says the Lord' line, but quite frankly I'd like to do this to them myself."

"Only in a Christian manner, of course," she said, kissing his forehead. "All done. You were lucky. That blow was meant to do more than knock you out."

Beck touched the cut on his throat. "Obviously." He picked up his drink and the journal and headed for the huge living room. Its wall of windows overlooked the surrounding forests, black except for the few twinkling lights of scattered houses. Anne poured herself a glass of white wine and settled beside him on the soft brown leather sofa. He kissed her and took her hand. "Thanks."

"Hey, blood's no problem for me." She grinned. "You should see what I can do to bulls."

Beck grimaced. "I'd rather not." He picked up the journal. "Ready?"

Anne nodded, and they struggled through the last few pages of

McCaslin's life. The writing was difficult to read, both because of the priest's cramped handwriting and because of the poignancy of his final thoughts. He had written it all down: the 1 A.M. request last Saturday night, the words in the confessional—"Grabbin' wieners, concentrate longer"; the gun, the heaven-sent church vandals, the article in *CityMag*, the fears of being watched, and the call to Matt.

They closed the book and sat for a moment in silence.

"A lot's at stake here," Matt finally said.

"Everything."

"Your article may have opened a wound that's been festering for ten years." He sipped the whiskey. "And covered is the right word, from the very beginning, if Joe's speculation is right."

Anne pointed at the diary. "You thinking what I'm thinking?"

"Depends," Beck replied, anger slipping into his voice. "If you're thinking we need to rip the scab off the wound, then yes."

"Only in a Christian manner, of course."

"Reexamine the evidence piece by piece. Of course."

"That also means dealing with the ghosts in the room—yours and mine."

Beck raised his glass. "I'll drink to that, and to them. Maybe they'll help us find out the truth."

She clicked her glass to his. "Here's to ghosts," she said. "And truth."

Whether we want to know it or not, Beck thought. "Right now the truth is my head hurts like hell. I need an aspirin and I think we ought to call it a day."

Anne gently touched the bandage. "I think we ought to call it boot camp." She put out her hand to help him up. "Let's go to bed."

"Best offer I've had yet." He curled his arm around her and they walked side by side to the bedroom. "You mind if I tag along with you tomorrow when you interview Rinski? There's a cop I know at the courthouse who I'd like to visit while you're there."

"No problem." Anne yawned. "The difficulty is getting up in six hours."

Later, as they lay close in bed, Anne said softly, "There was something I was planning to ask you, and in the excitement I forgot what it was. Something about a neighbor."

"I live on a mountain," Beck mumbled, half asleep. "Don't have any neighbors." He kissed her and rolled over. The part of him that was still awake felt the throbbing pain at his throat and shuddered at what would have happened if McCaslin hadn't had any either.

Chapter 5

James Rinski stared out the window at the woman and the priest as they entered the building five stories below. Her high heels accentuated her muscular legs, and he imagined where they went. Thank God short skirts were back in style. It damn near made this interview worthwhile.

He took off his glasses and sat at his desk, buttoning his shirt where his overflowing bulk sought daylight above his belt buckle. Fat chance he'd have with her. Fat chance he'd ever had with her, even after that once-in-a-lifetime break he gave her. Ungrateful bitch. Like all reporters. All they wanted was your blood. So you learn to bleed a little. Feed the leeches what they want and they're yours. That was how he had used them so effectively all these years. Just as before, Anne Demming would be no exception now.

He closed the manilla folder on his desk and tossed it into his out box. Then he put a magazine over it so the woman who would be sitting opposite him would not see her name on the front. It never hurt to run a check on your visitors, especially to update where they've been the last ten years. Although he'd occasionally encountered her snoopy ass on one case or another, there was always the chance a little dirt had crept into her folder, something he could use to turn the leech in his favor—or to get her to suck something else.

Unfortunately, the only comment consistently noted by his sources was "good instincts." He would see how good they were.

He sat back in the chair and propped his feet on the desk, holding his cup of coffee and a cigarette in one hand. He was a cautious man, and he enjoyed his reputation of paranoia. Hell, that was how he'd gotten this far by the age of forty-five. It kept people wary of him, just hoe he wanted them. Wary people weren't aggressive. Wary people made nervous, stupid mistakes that paranoid people took note of and used. But even paranoids had enemies. He smiled and sipped the coffee.

Enemies. It was difficult to tell anymore who was who. Ehrhart, for instance. His behavior yesterday was sure as hell threatening, but then Rinski himself had not exactly been cordial. They went back too far to be enemies now, each knowing what they did about the other. But they were a long way from being friends. Maybe there was a third category—opportunists who used you as long as you were in their best interest and dumped you mercilessly when your utility ended, when your deficit outweighed your benefit.

He pulled at the cigarette and exhaled. He had done that with people through the years, many of them foreigners who deserved it. He'd become a master of political manipulation, second only to Ehrhart himself. Sometimes better. The two of them together, at higher office, would accrue benefits, financial and personal, that he could only dream of now. Opportunist fit. Use 'em and lose 'em.

Hearing the front office door open, Rinski closed his eyes. He knew the scenario by heart. Charlotte the Barely Competent would announce the reporter's presence. He would pause for a minute or two, make the person wait to convey his generosity in taking time from his busy schedule for this important interview. The reporter would come in and sit in the chair opposite the desk, providing distance between them. About halfway through the interview, Rinski would light a cigarette, snuff it out if it proved offensive, and stroll around the desk to sit in the chair across from the reporter. If the interview became intrusive or in any way not to his liking, he would move back behind the desk and hit a foot button, which would alert Diddling Charlotte to interrupt him with urgent business. If things went well, he would terminate the interview after fifteen minutes. That was long enough. Anything you had to convey you could do in fifteen minutes. After that it risked getting out of control. He would never permit that.

It was always the same, and the press always went away with something he would hint was privileged information, or a convenient leak, or an inside scoop that they would not print but would flaunt with colleagues. If he was lucky and there was a little something in the manilla folder, sometimes they went away working for him.

He opened his eyes at the buzzing of the intercom.

"Commissioner Rinski?"

He mashed the miniscule button with his fleshy forefinger. "Yes, Charlotte?" He imagined her in his bed the night before and hoped it showed in his voice.

"There's a Miss Demming from *CityMag* here to see you."

"Please ask her to take a seat, and I'll be with her in a minute. I'm just finishing something. See if you can get her some coffee."

"Yes, sir."

Rinski picked up his glasses and went back to the window. He drew up the shade to let in more light. He hoped it would counteract the dull pall of answers he would give.

He tossed his cigarette into the coffee and plopped the paper cup in the trash on top of the latest copy of *CityMag*. Just as Ehrhart had feared, the piece had spawned renewed interest in the case. Demming was digging up bones better left buried. He agreed with Ehrhart that they must appear to have nothing to hide, especially at this stage of the political game. Maybe she'd drop the bones. Maybe the interview could even produce good press for them both.

Fat chance, he thought as he opened the office door.

"Welcome, Miss Demming," he said, looking her over on the way to her chair. "Sorry to keep you waiting. Unfortunately, some crooks demanded my attention before you did today."

"I understand," she said, shaking his hand. Her high heels put her just a few inches taller than him, and Rinski knew she had done it to intimidate him. Nice try, lady. Behind Demming's back, the police commissioner nodded at his secretary. As the door shut, he saw her set her watch for ten minutes. Good old Charlotte. He'd reward her big tonight.

"Please sit down, Miss Demming," Rinski said, pointing to one of the two leather chairs in front of the desk. He moved into the high-backed chair and leaned back. "Now, what can I do for you this morning?"

"For openers, you can come sit here across from me," she said, fumbling with a square metal object in her purse. "And you can grant me permission to tape the interview."

So much for the foot button. Rinski checked his angry response and smiled. Better view from there anyway. "Good idea," he said, strolling around to the front of the desk. "If I can have a copy of the recording."

She started the tape. "Done deal, Commissioner Rinski. I will send you a copy of this tape tomorrow, now that you have agreed to the audio-recording."

"Fine." He crossed one large leg over the other and pushed his back into the chair. He would have to regain the balance here, maneuver control into his hands but let her believe it was still in hers. "Mind if I smoke?"

The woman looked at him and smiled. "Yes, actually, I do. Cigarette smoke makes me gag."

The commissioner tucked the pack away. "No problem, Miss Demming," he said, getting up to walk across the room. "But I do have to satisfy my oral gratification with something." He poured a cup of coffee from a small pot on the table. "Can I get you a refill?"

"No, thanks," she said. "I'm fine."

He carefully positioned the cup on the desk beside him. "Now, I believe you wanted to discuss the Deathangel case?"

"Partly," she said. "I covered the case pretty thoroughly at the time, as I'm sure you remember." She crossed her long legs and held her pad of paper in her lap. "I never did have the chance to thank you personally for allowing me to follow you on the bust."

Rinski sipped the coffee. You sure as shit didn't, sweetie. The champagne was nice, but I wanted you in it. "No problem, again."

"So let me do that now. I appreciated it at the time and it doesn't seem to have harmed either one of our careers, would you say?"

"Yes, I would say that," he shook his head and removed his glasses. "The press has generally been kind to me." Especially when I set them up for it like I did you. "And you're right that it was largely through their exposure that my name hit the lights, just in time for promotions." Stall her with niceties, he thought. Keep her cordial and we'll never get to the interview.

"I know you're a busy man, Commissioner, so let me come right to the point." Demming glanced at her watch. "This is a follow-up investigation to my story in *CityMag* about Tod Engel. I'm trying to piece together some details that might have slipped by us ten years ago."

"Like what?" Like what color panties you're wearing? Rinski mused. Or not wearing. He smiled. "I thought the press scoured every part of that case back then. You all knew more about Engel by the time you were done than I did."

"That's exactly right, so I'm not as interested in him as I am in the others involved in the case, like yourself. How was it that you ended up directing the bust? I believe you were the chief of police in Mamaroneck then?"

"Yes, but I can assure you I'm a dull character. I was given the assignment by the acting police commissioner at the time, Wright Jackson, because I had serial killer experience from working homicide in the city before I came to the county. I worked closely with Martin Ehrhart putting the case together against Engel, so it was logical I would lead the bust." And a nice bust it is, he thought.

"So you still believe the evidence you gathered was conclusive?"

Rinski shifted in his chair, concerned at this new angle of conversation. "I'm not sure what you mean." What was she getting at? What did she have?

Demming uncrossed her legs and leaned forward. "Let's say, just for the sake of conjecture, that new evidence surfaced, casting a shadow of doubt, great doubt, actually, on the conviction of Tod Engel. Would you investigate that, or would you blow it off, thinking the jury made the right decision?"

The police commissioner bent forward slightly to match her stance and to glance down her open blouse. "You're really asking two questions, aren't you? To the first I have to answer that I would be bound by my oath of office to investigate, of course. But do I think anything—anything—would come to our attention at this late date, a decade after the deaths, that would change my belief that Engel committed them? No, Miss Demming. May I call you Anne?"

"Miss Demming will be fine." She leaned back. "Interesting that you term them 'deaths' rather than 'murders.' "

Shit. He had gotten too relaxed. She had counted on it, dressing like that, the short skirt with no pantyhose. He grasped the coffee cup in both hands to maintain his steady calm, hoping she would not make too much of the slip. "Death, murder. Murder, death. What's the difference in my line of work?" Then, before she could answer, he said, "No. Nothing would convince me otherwise. We investigated every kook conspiracy theory, ran down every lead, talked to every idiot who claimed to be in on it with him. Nope." Rinski finished the coffee and rose to pour another cup, turning his back to distract the conversation. "Engel whacked 'em all by himself." He turned to her and caught her adjusting her bra strap. He imagined his hands on her breasts. "Of course, if you have any information that might be useful, you would be withholding evidence if you didn't turn it over to us."

"I'll come back to that," Anne Demming replied. "But first let me ask you about motive. Refresh my memory on what exactly that was at the time."

She was good. Too good. He would work his way back to the foot button, but not until he found out what this new evidence was supposed to be. "I believe the majority opinion was that the man was simply crazy. You go around whackin' people with no connection whatsoever and spoutin' stupid phrases about it, people generally conclude you're nuts, right?" He held the coffee and remained standing. The view was better.

Anne smiled. "Now that's an oxymoron if there ever was one, isn't it?" She looked at him over her coffee cup. "Simply crazy. He was never declared insane, you know. I believe the prosecution denied that defense from the beginning. There was no doubt that he was mentally retarded and delusional. The question for the jury wasn't his mental status. It was his guilt or innocence, whether he did the crimes or not."

"Do you think otherwise?"

"I don't know yet, Commissioner."

Rinski heard the "yet" and didn't like it.

"It's just strange that Engel is still saying those phrases after all these years." She pulled a paper from her briefcase. "And nearly always in the same sequence. Listen: 'Concentrate longer.' 'Toad sticker. Matthew's son's a toad sticker.' 'Grabbin' wieners. Death comes to grabbin' wieners.' "

"Clearly sexual language. Most multiple killers are sex freaks," Rinski said, feeling a stir below his belt as he looked at her. "I believe the shrinks brought that out at the trial, that the murders were some kind of—what did they call it?"

Demming glanced at her notes. "A masturbatory act."

Rinski took a deep breath. Hearing the word from her mouth was the next best thing to being there. "Yeah, like the guy was masturbating by killing people." The word was having an effect on him. "Those phrases were somehow related to all that. The shrinks made it sound like he had to do those deaths and he had to get himself caught to stop himself." Rinski smiled and stuck his hand in his pocket. "Like maybe if he kept it up he'd go blind." He walked around the desk. It was time to terminate this interview. What the hell was Charlotte doing out there?

"Psychiatrists can make something out of almost anything, can't they, Commissioner? From the way you stand there with your hand in your pocket and coffee cup in your other hand to the way I sit with my legs crossed."

Rinski removed his hand and perched on the edge of the desk. He had already made something of the way her legs crossed. She was sharper than he remembered. He was aware of her watching him as she continued. Good instincts.

"They make everything seem merely an internal battle between the good and evil forces of the psyche," she said. "But wouldn't it be interesting if the phrases actually meant something else? Something that had less to do with Tod Engel and more to do with the particular people he chose to kill?"

Rinski drained his coffee cup. The stirring in him vanished. She was fishing but using the wrong bait. "That theory was chased down at the trial also, as I'm sure you recall. There was no obvious connection between the victims."

"None of them knew the others?"

Was Charlotte dead or what? Maybe she needed a watch that beeped so she'd stop doing her nails and do her damned job. "No." The police commissioner grinned. "They weren't even members of the same church."

Demming leaned over to retrieve another pen from her purse, frowning as though she had not considered that, then looked up at him. Rinski flushed, half at being caught staring at her breasts, half at his flippant remark which might have given her a lead. He tried to change the subject. "Well, what has the response to the article been so far?"

She ignored him. "Were the victims all the same religion, Commissioner?" He noted her formal tone. She was through schmoozing.

Rinski wrinkled his brow. "To tell you the truth, Miss Demming, I don't remember anyone ever asking that question."

"The church gets left out again," she said. "Even in the case of serial murder."

Good place for a new topic. He checked his watch. "I guess you have a personal interest in organized religion." He smiled. "Didn't I see you come into the building with a priest?" What did a looker like this see in a minister? Must be hell in bed. "Matt Beck, isn't it?"

"That's right."

Good, he thought, she seemed surprised. Now they were getting somewhere. "Of course, he would have a personal interest in this case, given his wife's death and all."

"His wife's murder."

"Whichever. And of course, you have had your own loss." He moved from the desk back to the chair opposite her. "Which was Robert Ludeman's, Miss Demming? Death? Or murder?"

He could see by her reaction that his question clearly stung. Excellent. He meant it to. Where the hell was Charlotte?

"I guess that depends whose side you're on, Commissioner."

Rinski loved it when her neck got red.

"You seem to have gone to great lengths to find information about us."

Rinski smiled, at ease now, on the offensive. "Not really. Personal profiles are easy to put together if you have the right sources." And he always had the right sources. "So, other than escorting you, what is Father Beck doing here?" He used the formal term purposely, to dig at their unwed relationship.

"He's visiting a former patient from the hospital who works in the police department."

She was good. Kept her answers factual. Bought time to recover. Rinski was about to ask a cutting question about the boyfriend when the intercom finally blurted out the raspy voice of his secretary.

"Commissioner?"

He moved behind the desk. "Yes, Charlotte?"

"Your eleven o'clock meeting is waiting on you."

"Thank you, Charlotte." Nice of you to wake up. "Tell them I'll be right over."

He turned to Demming. "As you heard, I really must call this to an end."

"Not just yet, Commissioner," she replied, remaining seated. "I need about ten more minutes of your time."

Wait a minute. The worm was turning again.

"While I'm here, I'd like to ask you about Mr. Ehrhart and his political plans this fall."

Rinski considered a moment. So what? It was not on the subject of Deathangel. He had made his points and stood his ground. Marty would like the press coverage. Besides, he hadn't seen nearly enough of her thighs.

He pushed the intercom button. "Tell them I'll be there in about fifteen minutes, Charlotte," he said, and sat back in the chair across from Demming. He picked up his coffee, his eyes drifting to her legs. "Now, about the county executive."

Waiting on a bench in the police anteroom, Matt Beck heard footsteps approaching and looked up at the paunchy, balding man with bushy black eyebrows. "Hey, Vincent!"

"That's Sergeant D'Angelo to you, Father!" the cop said loudly, reaching out his hand and pulling the priest from his seat.

"Hey, Vinnie," one of his colleagues yelled across the room. "You tryin' to look good for promotion or somethin'?"

"Naw," another answered. "He's tryin' to nab a fast track to heaven."

"Yeah," a third uniform echoed. "He's gonna need it, too."

"Okay, okay," the sergeant said. "Enough showin' off for the Father here." He motioned around the police reception and waiting room. "I want all youse to meet Father Matthew Beck, an old friend of mine from when I had my heart attack two years ago."

Matt smiled and nodded to the men, then turned back to his friend. Clearly, D'Angelo had learned nothing from the hospital experience. His black suspenders bulged down his blue shirt and over his belly, and the skin was taut over his rosy Italian cheeks. His wife did not exactly follow the cardiac cookbook diet. "Vinnie—"

"Don't say it, Father," D'Angelo said, ushering him toward a green steel door and nodding to the guard behind a thick glass window. "I might have another one right here and now. But if I do," he patted his gut, "I'll die happy and full of Marianna's pasta and good paisano wine." The door clicked and he motioned Beck through.

The first hurdle, Matt thought. Like getting into a computer maze. He hoped D'Angelo knew all the passwords. And how to beat the dragons.

"Where ya goin', Sarge?" A tall policeman held the heavy door open while they entered the hallway.

"I'm takin' Father Beck on a tour of my area, Russik." D'Angelo smiled and hit the cop on the arm. "He's never been in this kind of place before and I figure he needs to learn somethin' about sinnin' to keep preachin' those good sermons to sick folks." He stared the man in the eye. "That all right with you?"

"We aren't really supposed to have civilians back here, you know," the tall man said politely.

Could be over, Beck thought.

"Does he look like a civilian to you, Russik?"

The man smiled. "Yeah, I guess you're right. Long as you stay with him, I think we can trust him." He let the door slam shut behind them. "We could trust him better if you weren't with him."

Another one down, Beck said to himself as they disappeared down the long corridor and turned a corner, out of sight and earshot of anyone.

"Okay, Father," D'Angelo whispered. "What's this all about?"

"Like I mentioned on the phone, Vinnie, I have to get a look at that evidence without anyone knowing." He glanced nervously over his shoulder. "Did you find what I need?"

D'Angelo kept his voice lowered. "It took a while, but I rummaged around the property storage right after you called. Dust made me sneeze so I thought I'd be noticed, but I wasn't. It was pretty well stashed up under some other old cases, but I removed it and filed it under another name like you asked." He paused a moment, then put his hand on Matt's arm and said, "You sure you wanna do this, Father? Being as how you, you know, were intimately involved here? I mean, you know what's in there, right?"

Beck had thought about it, and though he felt reluctant, there was no other way. "I appreciate your concern, Vinnie, but a lot of water's gone over the dam since then." He patted the man's shoulder. "I can handle it if you can."

"Then we gotta hurry, Father," D'Angelo winked. "Follow me."

Beck stayed behind the squatty cop through corridors and stairs to the fifth floor, where they came to a wire cage filled with floor-to-ceiling steel shelving. D'Angelo unlocked the door and walked in first, leading Beck through a rat's maze of narrow aisles, each with rows of boxes marked with case names and trial numbers. Finally he stopped. On a bottom shelf, misfiled in the "M" section, sat a large cardboard box labeled with large black letters: DEATHANGEL.

"Take a walk around the next aisle, Vinnie," Beck said.

The sergeant shook his head. "It'll take you half a day to sort through that stuff, Father." He squeezed by Beck and bent over the carton. "I'll tell you what it is and we'll be out of here in nothin' flat."

Beck thought it was a bad idea. He didn't want to jeopardize this man's job or pension. His career-FBI father had always told him agents worked best alone, using cover to enter and exit. But there was no time to argue. "Just remember," he cautioned, "this never happened."

"Right, Father," D'Angelo replied. "Just like everything I confessed to you up in the hospital when I thought I was dyin'."

Matt reached into his pocket and pulled out a pair of latex gloves.

"Doing operations now, Father?"

"Right," Beck said. "I just want to make sure there's no connection between me and this evidence. The last priest who raised questions about this case went for a drive in the Hudson with the windows down." He slipped on the gloves and knelt beside the basket opposite D'Angelo.

It was time. Opening this box would reveal it all. Ten-year-old spirits would rush out and surround them like ghosts from Pandora's box. He felt queasy, a little dizzy.

He reached in and pulled some plastic bags from the box. "Don't you guys ever dust these things?"

"What for? We hardly ever have people lookin' through stuff this far after the event. Actually," the sergeant said, "I'm surprised it's still here. By now the old stuff is usually moved to the warehouse."

"Where it would be more accessible to people?"

"Yeah." D'Angelo looked around. "It's harder to get into this place, unless of course you're wearin' a clerical collar."

Beck brushed dust off a property envelope.

D'Angelo nodded toward it. "That, in your hand, is the letter Deathangel left after killing the old couple. He'd become pretty bold by then, and he left a note addressed to the main cop on the case."

"Rinski?"

"Yeah. Just a lowly chief of a three-man department then, but now he's commissioner." D'Angelo leaned against the cage. "I believe it was the hair in that envelope that eventually convicted Engel."

"Refresh my memory," Beck said. "How did that happen?" You never knew what new details might come out of old stories.

"The guy was M.R., but he wasn't stupid. He'd kept himself well hidden until he got ballsy and left that note. He probably scratched his head and a hair stuck in the glue on the envelope flap." D'Angelo leaned down. "Look there at that separate, smaller plastic bag."

Beck held it up. "See, there's the hair." D'Angelo said.

Beck studied it closely, then pulled a small magnifying glass from a leather pouch in his pocket and examined the plastic packet.

"Oh, great," D'Angelo said. "All the priests in the world, I gotta get the one who thinks he's Sherlock Holmes—with surgeon's gloves no less."

"You'd be surprised how often it comes in handy for things." Matt put down the packet and tucked the glass into his shirt pocket. "Do you know if you can tell whether a hair has naturally dropped off someone's head or whether it's been cut?"

"I would guess if it was cut it would be a clean break."

Matt looked at him. "Uh huh. It would. Just like the one in that envelope."

D'Angelo protested, "But forensics would have discovered that."

"Unless they were in a hurry to get the conviction." Or, he thought, unless they were directed not to find anything by the people running the case, by Rinski and Ehrhart. "What else?"

D'Angelo motioned to a long item. "That's the knife Engel used to carve the angels. The cuts in the wooden pieces matched the particular blade style. It's like the grooved rifling in a gun barrel—each one leaves a distinctive mark." He pointed to another bag. "And those are the wood shavings they found when they arrested him."

Matt held up a small envelope that appeared to be empty. "And in here?"

"Clothing fibers. They were taken from the house of the woman in Katonah, and I think there may be one or two from the other murders. They all matched the fibers of the clothing found in Engel's apartment."

"Tidy and convenient." Beck examined them with the magnifying glass, then folded it into its tiny leather case and put it away. "More nails in Engel's coffin."

Beck picked up a large bulky envelope before he realized what it was. He started to open it, then set it down.

"Those are—"

"I know." Matt took it up again and laid the contents of the package on the floor. Six small evidence bags, each containing a wooden angel. His heart beat fast and he felt flushed, his palms sweating inside the latex gloves as though he himself was in a bag, sealed shut. He forced himself to breathe.

Each angel was labeled with a victim's name, like a toe tag in the morgue. He read each one aloud, remembering who they were, a litany of death.

"Rita Haines and William Mills." The young couple at Umbrella Point in Larchmont.

"Connie Bartus." Katonah business woman.

"Latosha Simms." White Plains prostitute.

"Garnet and Arthur Reid." Elderly Port Chester couple.

"Josef Melin." New Rochelle. A dwarf.

He came to the last one and his head throbbed, nearly blinding him.

"Kate Beck," he whispered, his eyes filling with tears.

D'Angelo's hand on his shoulder reminded him to hurry.

"The discoloration?" Matt said, clearing his throat.

"The wood's pretty porous, so, well, what you see there is the blood that soaked into it. Engel had a habit of placing the angel close to his victims so their blood would stain it. At the trial, they figured it was part of some ritual, remember?"

Matt remembered. He looked at the angels individually. "Each one is different," he observed.

"Correct, Father. Nobody could determine whether the differences had something to do with the victims or not. One of the psychiatrists thought they did, but it didn't really matter. All the other evidence against him was so overwhelming that—"

"Did they check the carving marks on all the angels to see if they matched the knife? And the shavings—did the shavings all match these particular items?"

"Affirmative to both, Father. I remember because I was a court bailiff at the time. I escorted Engel to the courtroom every day and stood guard during the trial, waiting for him to go berserk in the courtroom, which he never did. So I heard the whole thing."

Matt put the angels back in their envelopes, holding onto the one with his wife's name for a moment longer. In his head he blessed it, and her, and wondered if they would ever know the truth. Then he returned it to the darkness. "Six angels. Eight victims."

"Right," echoed D'Angelo. "Six incidents, eight murders."

Beck lifted out a green telephone wrapped in plastic. "Did they ever find a connection between the victims?"

"Nope, never did. From what I recall of the trial, there wasn't any. They were just random, based on some crazy thing in Engel's mind. And I don't care what anybody says, he really is crazy, Father. He really is." The sergeant looked at his watch. "We need to be goin'."

"Right. Thanks." Matt replaced all the objects in the carton and stood to leave. "The phone. I don't remember it from the trial. Whose was it?"

D'Angelo shoved the box into the rack behind the others. "That came from Engel's apartment, too. Engel apparently was into electronic gadgetry and that fancy model appealed to him. It's also part of what convicted him."

"The buttons?"

"Yeah, one of the numbers programmed in was to the house of the old couple. Neighbors testified the old man and woman had received threatening phone calls the week or so before they were murdered."

"Convenient again." Every base had been covered. Either they had been dynamite investigators or the evidence was more than coincidental. "I mean, it's just interesting. Were any of the other victims' numbers programmed in?"

"None. But who knows, Father?" D'Angelo guided him back to the front door of the cage. "Your problem is you keep trying to make sense out of the retarded mind of a nut case."

"Maybe." And maybe not. Beck was about to ask another question when a powerful voice bellowed down the corridor.

"Sergeant D'Angelo! What the hell are you doing in there?"

"Oh shit," the sergeant whispered. "It's the Captain. Steiner's gonna have my ass."

Beck spoke loudly as he pushed past the chubby man. "Yes, Sergeant D'Angelo, I do have to be going now." He led the way down the aisle to the locked wire gate, pretending not to see the man waiting on the other side of the grill. "And thank you very much for the quick tour of this place. I'll give you a call next week about bringing in my Explorer Scout troop."

"Just what is this, D'Angelo?" the angry-looking man said, his face bisected by a thick black mustache.

"Well, Captain," the sergeant started.

"Are you his superior? Captain Steiner, is it?" Beck extended his hand. "I'm Father Matthew Beck, chaplain at Grasslands Hospital. And Sergeant D'Angelo has been kind enough to agree to let me bring some Explorer Scouts down for a tour of the property room and booking office. They're doing a unit on fingerprinting and crime detection, you see."

As Beck anticipated, the Captain saw the collar and calmed down. "I see. Well, all that is well and good, Father, but the sergeant should have at least made his superior officer aware that he was showing someone around a highly restricted area." He glared at the sergeant. "In the future, D'Angelo—"

"Yes, sir. I just figured, since he was a priest and all, and the scouts and all."

"Just do it right next time, all right?" The captain escorted them back to the steel door and into the waiting area.

"We'll look forward to having your scouts come visit us, Father Beck," the captain said. "Perhaps I will be asked to talk with them?"

"We would appreciate your time." Matt smiled, hoping the man was as gullible as he seemed. Somehow, he doubted it. D'Angelo would be suspect for a while.

"I'll leave you to the sergeant, then." The tall man nodded, turned, and left.

D'Angelo walked the priest into the outer corridor. "Sweet Jesus, that was close," he said. "What was all that with the scouts?"

"Only lie I could think of, spur of the moment."

"Well you'd better get some in here next week or my ass is grass."

"Okay, Vinnie," Matt said, patting him reassuringly on the back. "I'll dig 'em up somewhere. And thanks for the tour. It helped."

"I hope so, Father," D'Angelo shook his hand. "Sorry about the memories."

"Don't ever be sorry about memories, Vinnie. Sometimes they're all we've got."

D'Angelo whispered, "Well, Captain Steiner has a long memory. That little tour may be more costly than either of us can guess."

Beck glanced over his shoulder as he stepped into the elevator. "I hope you're wrong about that," he said. But from what he had seen in the property room, he doubted it.

"And your future, Commissioner?" Anne Demming flipped her notebook closed.

James Rinski's face remained passive. He had been calm and reasonable for the last ten minutes of political bullshit while he enjoyed wondering whether Demming wore low cut briefs or a thong. "Who can predict the future, Miss Demming?" He pushed himself out of the chair. "That is beyond my capability."

"Oh, come now. No further political ambitions?" She smiled. "Perfectly content to stay where you are until retirement?"

Rinski reached into his pocket and pulled out the pack of cigarettes. It was time to annoy her out of the room. "My only ambition is to continue to serve the people of Westchester County to the best of my ability."

"For as long as the county executive will have you, is that right?" She stood and smoothed her skirt.

"Correct." And that would be forever if all interviews ended as well as this one. He had definitely regained control at the finish and sidetracked her from the Deathangel case.

"What if he should choose to tap you for higher office?" she said, putting away the recorder and pad.

He loved it when she bent over. "I would, of course, consider it." He jabbed the cigarette between his lips. "But let me hasten to add that no such offer has been made. As I've told you, I'm quite content where I am now. I only hope the people of the county think I'm doing a good job—with your editorial help, of course." He escorted her toward the door, his hand slightly touching her waist.

Demming placed her hand on the doorknob, then turned back to face him as he dug out his lighter. "Good interview, Commissioner," she said, seriously.

"How do you mean, Miss Demming? Was I politically aloof enough to cover all my bases without offending anyone?"

"Yes, you were. And you said enough complimentary things about the county executive to justify your raise next year."

"But did you get the information you wanted?" He hoped not.

"Most of it." She put one hand on her hip. "But I would like to ask you something else, and it can be off the record."

"Shoot," Rinski said, starting to light the cigarette, then stopping. If the question got rough, he would light it and blow smoke up her nose.

"It has to do with those phrases Engel uses over and over."

"What about them? I thought we cleared that up earlier." She was calculating the effect of this, had been saving it until the end. What did she know?

She leaned against the door and stared at him. "As I said when I walked in, what if I had new evidence about the Deathangel case?"

Shit. On her way out the door. The bitch. He would have to remain calm, keep his own neck from splotching under his tight collar. "You would be obligated to tell me what it is," he said with restraint. And she wouldn't leave this damned room until he knew.

"I see," she responded with equal flatness in her voice.

Rinski stepped closer, invading her space, hoping to make her uncomfortable. "Do you have new evidence?"

"Possibly," she said, moving back. "You know, of course, about the murder of the priest in Ossining yesterday? Joseph McCaslin? Have you identified either of the bodies of the perpetrators?"

"Semantics again, Miss Demming. You call it premeditated murder, I call it a routine mugging. Potato, potahto, tomato, tomahto." She had better call the whole thing off. "As to the two muggers, the younger one had a lengthy rap sheet as a member of a hate gang, and the other was an illegal with no passport, I think." He tried to stay calm. Maybe he should light up now. No. He needed to learn more. Besides that, this close he could smell her. "Why do you ask?"

"Because McCaslin was nearly murdered two nights before the mugging—as you label it—for hearing the confession of someone using the same phrases as Engel."

Rinski snickered. "That's your big deal? Some obviously misunderstood words by a terrified preacher? I think I'd need more than that to reopen the case. Don't you, Miss Demming?" He flicked his lighter and Demming grabbed his wrist. He smiled, excited by her touch.

"But do you know what the phrases mean?"

She let go, but Rinski could not control his reddening face. "Of course not. Nobody does. Nobody but that moron Engel." He cocked his head and smirked. "But now you're going to tell me you know what they mean. Right?"

"When we do, you'll be the first to hear."

He was sure she noticed his sweating face. "You can—and will—do what you consider best." He struck the lighter again. "But I think this is all a waste of your very precious time. And it would, of course, dig up much ill feeling that has been comfortably buried for years."

"So you wouldn't do it?"

He touched the flame to the cigarette. "It makes no difference what I would do," he said, approaching her. "But take my advice." He stood close so she could smell the smoke on his breath. "Stay away from it." He put his hand on the doorknob. "It's always been my philosophy to let sleeping dogs—of all kinds—lie." He opened the door. "That way I'm less likely to get my ass chewed off by a pit bull."

"I'll keep those quaint words in mind, Commissioner, along with those of Tod Engel."

"You do that."

"Thank you again for the interview today." She shook his sweaty hand and he felt her soft flesh, wondered what it was like elsewhere. "And for the opportunity ten years ago." She released him. "I still have the originals of those photos."

"Any time," he replied, and he meant it. Any time at all. He waited until she had left the office, then glared at his secretary. "Can't you tell time, you idiot?"

"Hey, don't yell at me, Mister Commissioner," Charlotte said, putting on more lipstick. "You're the one who kept her another fifteen minutes. What'd she do to deserve that, huh? Show you her panties?"

"She wasn't wearing any," Rinski snapped and disappeared behind his closed door. He stood at the window looking over the city of White Plains. Smoke hung in the air cocoon-like, stirring only as he raised the cigarette to his face. His thoughts groped through an even darker haze, stirring only at the sound of the intercom on his desk.

"Commissioner?"

Reluctantly, he broke through the cocoon, returned to the chair behind the desk, and pressed Charlotte's button. "Yeah?"

"Captain Steiner called from downstairs while you were in your interview. It was about an unauthorized person in the property room. It sounded kind of urgent, but he said it was all right if you got back to him at your convenience."

"Right." And maybe his convenience would include someone else tonight. He frowned at the news, but he knew Steiner could handle it. Just like he would handle the disappearance of those two bodies in the morgue. The priest's muggers. Rinski would have to order it done today, before that nosy Demming bitch sniffed any closer.

"And Jimbo." The voice became sing-songy, little girl like. "I'm sorry about what I said."

"Okay." So they were still on for eight. "See you tonight." As he passed the window to retrieve his jacket, two figures walking from the courthouse caught his eye. He stopped and watched Matt Beck and Anne Demming get into an SUV. Grabbing a piece of scrap paper from the desk, Rinski jotted down the make and model and as much of the license number as his nearsighted eyes could see from that distance. He watched them drive away.

He breathed deeply, closed his eyes, and savored the heavy smell of his tobacco mixing with the delicate remains of Demming's scent. He wondered again if he should be more worried about the priest than the lay. Beck had the more emotional bond, would be less likely to drop the issue than a reporter who had new cases to investigate.

Rinski opened his eyes and mashed the intercom button. "Charlotte?"

"Yes, Commissioner?"

"Have Captain Steiner come to my office immediately."

Rinski picked up the phone. The automatic dialer beeped seven numbers.

A deep voice answered, "Yeah?"

"I want the tail report every three hours. Where they went. What they ate. When they took a shit. Page me." He hung up and inhaled more of the smoky, perfumed air. He would think of her tonight while he was doing Charlotte.

In another minute Rinski heard the captain's voice outside and, without waiting, he yelled into the intercom, "Send him in."

Al Steiner shut the office door behind him, looking worried.

Anne tossed him the keys to the Forerunner.

"You drive," she growled through tight lips. "I want to hit something too much." Matt knew growing up in Texas had taught her how to deal with drunk cowboys, bigoted rednecks, macho Tejanos, and frat rats. When they got out of hand, she walked away. If they wouldn't let her or laid a hand on her, she scooped up the nearest heavy object and nailed them. He wondered what Rinski had done that had stuck that kind of burr under her saddle.

"I need a shower. I've been slimed," she said, as Matt pulled out of the lot and headed for the Cross County Highway. "Ever been talking to somebody and you just know in that all-knowing place right behind your navel that there's definitely something wrong about this person? Well, there's definitely something wrong with Rinski. The man gives me the shivers. I don't remember him being that bad ten years ago."

"He's had time to get worse."

"With his position and power, not many people could deny him whatever he wanted." Anne shuddered. "But it was more than that. It wasn't so much what he did as what I think he's capable of doing."

Beck turned onto the access road for I-684 east.

Anne shook her head. "Could you take the back road instead of the expressway? I don't need the noise and speed right now. I need to calm down."

"This guy really got to you." He put his hand on hers and turned off the access road. "I can take Old Mamaroneck Road just as well. It's secluded and wooded and, above all, slow."

"Maybe I'm just goosey after what happened to McCaslin, but yeah, this guy got to me. I kept to my questions, and stayed as much in control and as assertive as I could be. I didn't relent when he clearly wanted me to leave, and I dropped a lug at the finish like I planned. And still I had the feeling that it rolled off him, that his mind was elsewhere, down my blouse and between my legs." She took a deep breath and looked at Beck. "You're going to think this is truly weird, but I felt more frightened around Rinski than I did sitting in Weston Prison with Tod Engel. I believe our police commissioner is capable of crimes that would make Engel look harmless." She sighed again. "That veiled threat at the end was the clincher."

"He threatened you?" Beck grinned at her. "And lived to tell the tale?"

She shook her head. "Not a direct threat, of course. But he strongly hinted that I drop any interest in opening the Deathangel case. 'Let sleeping dogs lie and you won't get your ass chewed off by a pit bull.' " She popped open the glove box and handled the LadyHawke. "That sucker even thinks of biting me and I'll use his nuts for target practice."

"So how will you write the interview?"

"I know how I'd like to write it." She replaced the gun and pretended to type on her lap. "The man whose bust of Tod Engel a decade ago catapulted him into his current fat and happy position is a slimy pervert psychologically capable of committing the crimes for which Engel was arrested. That would make lovely reading, don't you think?"

"Yeah, especially for Rinski's lawyers."

Anne smirked. "I'll be careful." She leaned over and kissed him. "Thanks for the scenic view. The leaves are lovely out here. I'm calming down."

"I noticed."

She stared out the window a minute, then said, "I wonder if Ehrhart and the bishop will have the same attitude about laying off the case."

"We may find out about Langert in a few minutes. I'm taking us to lunch at the Harbour Master in Rye. He often stops there on his way in or out of the city."

"Good on both counts. I'm starving." She twisted toward him. "How'd your chat with D'Angelo go?"

Beck told her about D'Angelo sneaking him into the evidence room, the hair that seemed cut, the clothing fibers, the phone with the old couple's number on it, and the angels.

"The angels?" Anne said. "Did you see all of them?"

Matt nodded. "Including the one with Kate's blood." Somehow it wasn't as hard telling Anne as he thought it would be. The lump in his throat was more controllable. He took her hand.

"I wondered how it would go," she said softly.

"I'm okay. Really." He did feel more peaceful for some reason. "When I picked it up, I don't know, I swear her ghost, whatever, her spirit, was there. It's like you said, helping us find the truth."

"And did you?"

"Maybe." Beck noticed a car coming up at a steady speed in the distance. He was taking his time and eventually would have to slow to let it pass. "Something wasn't right about those angels, and I'm not sure what it was. It was macabre seeing them all together, like a blood-stained heavenly chorus screeching out songs of death."

"It must've been awful."

"Not awful, just striking, distracting me from what I was supposed to be seeing, I think."

"Speaking of songs of death, that reminds me of something Rinski kept saying. He kept referring to the killings as deaths not murders. Like they were accidents or unfortunate casualties of war."

"Or hits?"

"My God! I hadn't considered that. If that's true, and Rinski or others were involved, it's no wonder no one wants the case reopened."

"Now wait a minute, Anne. It's a long jump from Engel not being Deathangel to Rinski somehow being involved in a conspiracy to frame him." Beck shook his head. "That was just an idle speculation. I don't really think it's true."

"Well somebody wanted Joe silenced, searched his house, and nearly killed you to get that journal. There's sure as hell something going on here, and it keeps pointing in the direction of Engel's conviction being very convenient, maybe covering the planned executions of eight people."

Matt accelerated around a curve so fast he nearly tipped the top-heavy SUV.

"What was that for?"

"To keep the blonde in the blue Chevy out of our exhaust pipe. She came out of nowhere. She's been tailgating us for two miles. I tried to let her pass, but she won't do it."

"A blue Chevrolet?" Anne's voice tensed as she looked behind them. "Matt, I saw that car yesterday. It followed me from the city up to your house last night."

"It trailed me to the hospital, too. But she seems to be tired of just following us. Here she comes again," he said, watching the speeding car approach him. He floored the accelerator, but the bulky SUV was top-heavy on the narrow curves.

"Gravel on the right! Watch it!" Anne yelled.

Beck cursed as he lost control on the soft gravel shoulder. The world spun as the SUV did a one-eighty. It skidded to a halt a hundred yards from the stopped blue Chevy.

Matt reached for Anne. "You okay?"

"I think so. You?"

Before he could answer, Beck saw the blonde climbing out of her car with a weapon. "Gun," was all he could say. "Listen to me. I'll distract her and if she shoots—shoot back, I guess."

Anne grabbed the LadyHawke from the glove box and Matt slipped out the driver's side door. The woman slowly approached the SUV and raised her pistol to fire at him. His heart in his throat, Beck heard a piercing siren, then caught sight of a police car speeding behind her. The blonde froze, then spun away and fired into the windshield of the oncoming police vehicle. The glass shattered, but the car kept coming; it knocked her down and rolled over her body.

Beck raced toward the woman. Two uniformed men with guns leapt from the car.

"Don't touch that!" one of them said.

Matt stopped in his tracks. The two showed their badges and lowered their weapons. Anne joined him and took his hand. One cop went over to the body and the other came up to them. It was the man Beck had met thirty minutes before outside the property room.

"White Plains police. You two okay?"

"We're not hurt, if that's what you mean," Matt said, his heart still pounding. "Captain Steiner, right?"

The cop nodded and glanced at the LadyHawke in Anne's hand.

"Mine," Anne said. "And I've got a permit for it."

"Where'd you come from so fast?" Matt said. He felt like he had been a spectator at a well-orchestrated production. One that ended in a horrible death. Whatever their explanation, he wasn't going to buy it.

"We were cruising the area on our way to lunch when my partner thought he heard tires squealing. Good thing he's so alert, huh?" A cacophony of sirens announced the arrival of EMS and more police. "What happened, anyway? Why was she tailing you?"

Anne stared at him. "Who said she was tailing us?"

The police captain bit his lip.

"Nobody. I just assumed, since she was advancing at gunpoint, that she might have been tailing you."

Over his shoulder, Matt watched EMS zip the body into a black bag. "Shouldn't we check the woman out?" he said. "See if we recognize her?"

"Nothing to see," Steiner said. "Her face is a tire track. But we'll let you know what happens when we run prints."

Beck wondered if his cynicism was due to Steiner's tone of voice or the incredible coincidence of the cop's presence on Old Mamaroneck Road.

"Can we go now?" Anne asked, glancing at Matt.

Steiner shook his head. "Not when there's been a death involved. We'll need you to follow us back to White Plains and help with the report."

"Not a problem, Captain Steiner," Beck said quickly to halt the words he knew were on Anne's tongue.

Killed. Murdered. Semantics.

When they were back in the Forerunner, she said them.

"No," the captain reported to his superior, "they were surprisingly cooperative. It was like they talked about it on the way over here and agreed to answer questions but not volunteer information. Short. Sweet. To the point. But I got the feeling if we pushed them, they'd have lawyered up."

James Rinski sat behind his desk and smoked a French cigarette. Strong taste. No filter. The way he liked his women. "As long as they recognized who was in charge."

Steiner nodded. "No problem there. They got it. By the time they left, they were exhausted."

"Excellent work, Al." Rinski gave the well-timed compliment like conferring a blessing. "I trust you'll tidy things up for us and take care of that other pressing matter I mentioned earlier?"

"Of course, sir," the captain said, standing to leave. "As always, no problem."

Rinski watched him close the door. He inhaled the thick smoke of the Gauloises. Something was wrong. He had never given orders to shoot. So either the blonde bitch had screwed up royally or she'd also been working for someone else. If it was who he suspected, it would take a while to deal with him and it would have to be done very carefully.

The commissioner stubbed out his cigarette butt and rested his head in his hands. In the meantime, it was good to have trained people he could count on, like Steiner, who would be sure to come up with a creative way to dispose of another body.

Chapter 6

Arthur Allen flicked cigar ashes into the tin can next to the picture of his father and noted his own reflection in the glass. His gaunt face stuck up from the discolored white clerical collar that hung on his frail frame and made him appear older than his thirty-five years. The heavy cigar smoke that coated the glass seemed to have impregnated the pores of his sallow skin, making the sweat on his wrinkled shirt more pungent. Even the yellow legal pad, on which he now tried to compose a sermon, seemed worn and faded.

The small, dimly lit office where he had spent the last ten years was like a cell, he thought, as he put the slimy cigar back between his yellowed teeth. It was safe here, secure, not like the outside world where you never knew who the real crazies were. Here you knew, here you could tell. It was obvious. They were the ones running the place.

Allen struck a match and relit the cigar, puffing clouds of smoke into the still air. It was an easy job, being chaplain of Weston State Prison for the criminally insane. Nobody expected much from him. He was given the bare minimum budget required to run a religious services program, and that was fine with him. He understood the inmates because he felt like one of them. Ever since his father died of pancreatic cancer, he had felt like one. Adding insult to injury, the disease had rapidly deflated the big man to nothing, just as his FBI career had deflated him once he realized the truth. Maybe some day Allen would come out of his funk into the world again. But if not, that was okay, too. He subscribed to the theory that he couldn't die until he completed his quota of cigars and whisky, and he wasn't half through with either.

He jumped at the ringing phone.

"Call for you, Chaplain," the prison operator said. "I'll put it through."

Allen waited, sucking nervously on the cigar.

"Hello?" the voice came over the phone. "Art?"

The chaplain exhaled thick brown smoke. "Who is this?"

"It's Matt Beck, you slimeball. How the hell are you?"

"Always nice to hear from you, Beck. Goodbye." He hung up the phone and returned to the sermon. Why the shit had Beck called? Whatever the reason, he didn't want to hear it. They had been friends long ago, good friends. He looked again at the picture of his father. Like brothers. Their fathers had worked together in the FBI, their families so close they practically lived at each other's houses. But it was different now.

Minutes later, the phone broke the silence again. Allen coughed, let the phone ring ten more times, and picked it up.

"Yeah?"

"Another call for you, Chaplain."

"Great." The priest swung his feet up on the desk.

"Don't hang up on me this time, Art. I've got some good news and some bad news."

"The bad news is that you called me. What's the good news?"

"Okay, whatever. Just stay on the line. The good news is that you may have the wrong man locked up in your prison, and you can help get him out."

Allen sighed. "Thanks for calling."

"Damn it Art, don't hang up on me!"

"Give me one reason why. The last time you called me, you wanted me to run some friggin' BCI check on a guy that dumped me in so much hot water they damn near transferred me to Buffalo. I don't need that kind of aggravation, with no return, if you know what I mean." He didn't have time for this bullshit. Just hearing Beck's voice reminded him of things he'd rather forget.

"If you mean I haven't been in touch with you since then, you're wrong. I called and wrote, but in your usual fashion you didn't respond. You've holed yourself up in that nuthouse prison for the last decade and cut yourself off from everybody who used to count as your friends, so don't give me this—"

"Shit." Allen slammed down the phone and rose to pour himself more cold coffee. "You'll call again," he said as he chewed on the frayed, wet cigar. He smiled when, five minutes later, the phone rang. "Same old Matt."

"Try not to get cut off this time, Chaplain Allen," the operator said politely as Beck's voice broke in.

"Damn it, Art, listen to me."

"Okay. You got me curious now. Let's hear it." Matt had probably heard some sob story from a dying patient who swore her husband-brother-father-uncle-son was innocent and being held unjustly at Weston. He'd fall for that shit in a minute, especially since Kate's death. "What's up with the inmate? Who is it?"

"Well, actually, it's Tod Engel."

Allen laughed. "Tod Engel? The Tod Engel? My main man Tod Engel?" This was even better than he figured. "Joke, right? You called me up to make me laugh one more time before I hang up on you again, right?"

"No! And before you do, we believe it's possible his conviction may have been manufactured, maybe by the police, to cover something bigger."

Allen laughed so hard he choked. He took a drink of coffee and tried to calm down. "Excuse me?" he said, restraining himself. "Has someone mysteriously swapped our brains in the last ten years? Is this the Matt Beck I grew up with who believed in America, apple pie, and liberty and justice for all?"

"Art—"

"The one whose father built his career on that shit?"

"Art, don't—"

"Or am I really talking to myself here? The one whose father came clean on his deathbed about running a setup with your father to send an innocent man to the chair just to protect what the Fucking Bunch of Idiots jokingly called national security? Don't give me this shit about unjust imprisonment, Matt. You don't know what it means." He was about to cut the line again, with the phone in midair, when he heard Beck shout.

"Damn it, just for once listen to me!"

On second thought, he wasn't done yet. "Listen to you? This isn't about you, Beck." Allen pushed back in his old wooden swivel chair. "I had this figured out the second you said Engel's name." He chewed on the cigar. "This is about your buddy Langert, isn't it?"

"No, it's—"

"I read Anne's piece in *CityMag*. So here's what happened. That article stirred the pot and now Langert thinks he can cruise right into the presiding bishop's chair on the back of Tod Engel, just like he used your wife's murder to get where he is now." He knew that would sting, but what the hell, Beck could hang up if he didn't like it. He didn't trust Langert. Shit, he hadn't trusted anyone in authority since Watergate. When he and Beck were in seminary he'd thought Langert was on their side, the side of the underdog, the poor, the needy. The three of them had been really tight back then, a team. But that changed, too.

"Stop it. You two haven't seen eye to eye since, well, since ten years ago."

"Eye to eye?" Allen's anger surged. "We've never seen dick to dick, and it has nothing to do with my dad's death. Langert's been a phony ever since that Deathangel bullshit. He manipulated that whole fiasco—including Kate, I'm sorry to say—to catapult himself into the limelight, and ever since then he's taken himself and this entire diocese down a pseudo-liberal path to destruction, or don't you see the financials his office sends out every year?"

"The financials I see are in order, audited, and show a black bottom line, contrary to the results of the other bishops we've both survived. Face it, you're still pissed at Langert for your father's funeral."

"Lack of funeral, you mean?"

Beck knew the story. He'd been there for it, only six months before he lost Kate to Engel's madness. After thirty years of devotion to the bullshit FBI, Art's dad is forced to retire after Matt's Dad, his partner, is killed in a fatal car accident. Five years later, Agent Allen develops cancer and dies, leaving Art and Matt sworn to silence and stunned about the wrongdoing their two fathers had conducted in the name of patriotism and justice. Then, against the wishes of his family, Langert chooses to conduct the elder Allen's funeral in the old tradition, with no eulogy, using only his first name in the prayers. Insult to injury. "I want to be the one to conduct Langert's funeral. Call me back when it's about the bishop's death."

"Actually, right now it's about Joe McCaslin's."

Sure thing. "No, it's not. Though I'm sure you assume otherwise, I do read the papers. McCaslin was killed resisting muggers."

"Wrong, you disillusioned bastard," Beck said, his voice sharp with pain. "Maybe we have had brain swaps. This time I'm the one seeing murder and conspiracy under every confessional, and you're the one clinging to motherhood and apple pie. You know your father would have jumped on this."

"And yours would have let it alone," Allen shot back. "Unless, of course, his superior told him it was a matter of national security." Beck was after something. Engel was just a foot in the door. Sometimes his distrust made sense. Like now, when Beck was fumbling for what to say. "Son of a bitch. Why do I even talk to you?"

Matt was silent for a moment. Then he said, "Because we used to be family."

Memories flashed across Allen's mind. Matt at the house. Matt at birthdays. Matt on vacations. Matt at school. His dad smiling and laughing with Matt's father. Shit. "Someday you won't be able to blackmail me into helping you by exhuming my father—or yours."

"I'm not exhuming them. I was hoping, have been hoping for years, to resurrect the relationship you and I once had."

Allen looked around his dingy office. He sighed and planted the cigar in the ash-filled glass tray. "A lot of whiskey has gone under the bridge since then."

"Yes, and a lot more will before we pack it in, I hope. I'd just like to drink some of it with you."

Allen started to blurt out a sarcastic remark, but checked himself and said, "What the hell. I've been getting stir crazy in here anyway."

"Good. Can you come to my house tomorrow afternoon, say around five?"

"Let me check my busy social calendar." He picked up the black book on his desk. "Let's see here. No executions scheduled. Nobody showing up for religious education class. Nobody in the prison hospital ward needing last rites or absolution. You lucked out. My schedule's free."

"Good."

But Allen knew Beck still had not dropped the bomb. "So what is it you really called to ask, now that our relationship is all patched up and friendly again?" he said, an edge still in his voice. Maybe this meeting wasn't such a great idea after all.

"I want to find out everything you know about Tod Engel."

That wasn't what Allen anticipated. "Deathangel? You better grab the information while you can. The guy got himself locked up in administrative solitary."

"Which is what?"

"That's when the warden wants to keep you extra safe."

"From whom?"

"Don't know. Seems Williams sent down an order to have him shut up right after Anne's article updated the world on Engel's status. Williams told the guards he was afraid the piece would fan the flames with other inmates, maybe even get these crazies in here in the mood to make a name for themselves by offing Deathangel." Allen sucked on the slimy cigar. "As if they cared. Funny thing is, it will have just the opposite effect."

"Meaning?"

"Meaning I've been with that man at least once a week since he's been here. Engel hates solitary confinement. It makes him more delusional than ever. The last time he was sent there, they had to redo the cell after he finished ripping it up—and himself in the process. Engel spent three weeks in the hospital from self-inflicted wounds. God only knows what he'll do now."

Matt spoke haltingly. "I probably shouldn't ask you this on the phone, but—"

"Why? You think the warden's listening?" Allen laughed. "Shit, Beck. You're more paranoid than I am. There are some boundaries even he wouldn't cross."

"Okay, if you think the line's clean. Bottom line. Do you believe Engel did those murders? Killed Kate?"

Allen took a deep breath. "Listen, Matt, I'm sorry I said that."

"Good start. But just tell me what you think."

Allen crossed his legs on top of his desk. "To tell you the absolute truth, I'm not sure."

"That puts you one step on the side of the bishop."

"He's just posturing for press coverage. Makes him look like the defender of the underdog. It's bullshit, like everything else he does. I'm not on his side. I just said I wasn't sure. I've spent a lot of time with Engel. More than anybody else in the last ten years. I guess if I were really pressed to form an opinion I'd have to say—probably."

"Based on what?" Beck said.

"Based on my years of prison experience, all of them here at the Weston Home for the Reality Impaired. Engel is certainly aware enough to have done it. But I'm not sure he'd remember it if he did. So, my clinical opinion is probably."

"Probably will do for openers."

"Is that all? I don't even have to see you tomorrow if that's all you want."

"One more thing."

Here it came. Took him long enough. And if it was what he assumed it was, Beck could shove it. "If this is about BCI records, you can take your invitation and your alleged friendship and your sloppy memories and stick them where the sun don't shine."

"I am going to ask you for them, and not because of your father, Art."

"Then because of what?" This should be interesting.

"Because back in seminary you used to care about justice, even the justice of a man like Engel, maybe especially of men like Engel."

Yeah, right, ancient days ago, maybe. "You want Engel's BCI sheet?"

"Hell, no," Beck answered. "That one's public knowledge. I'm after the sheets on Engel's victims."

Allen hesitated, surprised. "You think some of them had criminal records? Not Kate, of course, but maybe the others? There's an interesting twist. That's why they were killed?"

"No." Beck paused. "Just the opposite. I'm not expecting anything other than basic Bureau of Criminal Information background material like birthplace, age, family information, including Kate's."

"And what will that prove?" This didn't make sense. It was a lot of potential trouble for absolutely nothing. It had to be Beck's grief grasping at straws.

"Maybe nothing. I don't know. But it's the only thing I can think to use to compare what they all might have had in common, that would show why someone other than Engel might have wanted them dead."

"It's illegal to run those things for civilians, you remember. If Guess Who finds out, this could dump me in deep shit again."

"Why? These are all old records. There's no current case pending on any of them. And they're all normal, safe people to check on. No celebrities. No mob names. Nothing unusual."

"Except they were all murdered by Deathangel."

"Yes," Beck said. "Whoever he is. I have to find the truth. I owe it to Joe McCaslin, and to Kate. Hell, we owe it to our fathers."

Who the hell is we anymore, Allen wondered. "I'll see you tomorrow at five," he said. "No promises." He hung up the phone and relit his cigar.

Warden Richard Williams stood at his office window and surveyed the prison's perimeter towers. All eight of the castle-like cubicles were manned by seasoned guards with automatic weapons.

External control.

He turned to look back at the two TV screens: side by side images of Arthur Allen's office and the hall outside Engel's cell. The chaplain had just finished his phone call and now sat smoking that putrid cigar, unaware that he was being observed. Though Williams could not see or hear what went on in Engel's cell, he thought the microphone in the corridor light had picked up a measured scraping coming from that direction. Good old Tod must be carving again.

The warden aimed the remote, like a gun, at the sets. Both screens went black.

Internal control.

He smiled and picked up the phone.

Anne Demming turned onto Pierrepont Street in Brooklyn Heights. She ran her plastic security card through the slot to open the gate to the underground garage. The traffic down Sawmill River Parkway had been heavy for a Wednesday, and it was just after five in the morning. Getting more and more like Houston, she thought. Too many cars.

As an extra security measure after yesterday's events, she checked her rearview mirror and waited for the gate to close before pointing the Forerunner down the steep slope into the dimly lit opening. These garages weren't built for jeep-things, she complained to herself, carefully maneuvering the four-wheel-drive vehicle through the narrow tunnel to her level. She'd be better off in Matt's little Spider, but her aging daddy had insisted she drive something more like a tank to protect her from weather and muggers, in that order. The Forerunner qualified, and he could put her in any damn thing he wanted now that the money had come in. Actually, she could put herself in anything with her share of it.

By Texas standards, the 5,000-acre Demming ranch wasn't large, and it had eventually changed from running cattle to running dove and deer hunters. When the people in suits came to ask if they could try a new kind of drilling on the property, Anne and her parents thought they were nuts. They'd tried for oil before and found nothing but a hole in the bank account.

But new horizontal drills unearthed oil, gas, and mineral rights that filled that hole and would easily provide educations for grandchildren if sweet little Annie "would start squirtin' out the critters before she got too damn old." She felt too damn old right now, or tired, anyway. She steered around the circuitous descent. That was another issue she and Matt never talked about—her biological clock. She liked her lifestyle, even if that clock had ticked loudly in her direction a time or two, and even if friends sometimes gave her shit about living with a priest. If she had to describe Matt Beck, she often said, the last thing about him she would mention would be his profession. He was a lot more than what he did.

"What the hell was that?" she said as something ducked between two parked cars. It looked like a kid, a teenager. Great, all she needed was a gang member to confront her. But there was nothing now. What she really needed was to get upstairs, put on the coffee, and review her notes from the night's work, she thought, as she reached her parking level.

She expertly backed into the tight space and turned off the engine. She reached into the glove box for the LadyHawke. On the ranch, she had grown up with shotguns and rifles. She had only learned to use a pistol when she came to New York. Twitch had kindly taught her to hit where she aimed. Maybe she should use it on him, she mused, pulling her things together. His insistence that she keep trying to interview the victims' families was annoying, but then again chatting with the principals in the case might be exactly where she and Beck needed to be. If Rinski was any indication, they were right on target. Speaking of targets, she still had to make it to her apartment, and that shadow had spooked her.

Anne had been in enough tense situations to trust the goosebumps on her neck, whether they were inspired by lack of sleep or not. She cautiously unlocked the car door and slipped the gun into her coat pocket. Near the elevator, she electronically locked her car and stood with her back to the elevator doors. So far, so good.

The elevator arrived. She swiped her security card through the reader and pushed the button for her floor. It opened on the tiny corridor where 801 and 803 faced each other from opposite ends of the narrow, twenty-foot hallway. Automatically, Anne looked left to her neighbor's closed door and then right to her own.

Something was wrong. Cowering under the large antique umbrella stand in the hall was Abby, her cat. Unless the creature had figured out how to unlock the door and turn the handle, somebody was in her condo. And they had to have heard the elevator bell.

She could and probably should call the muscular front doorman, Alfonse Ciccilini, or the cops. But there was no phone on the hall stand and her cellular was in the SUV. Besides, if she left now, she'd lose the one thing that had saved her from bodily harm investigating similar situations—the element of surprise. She was damned tired of being on the defensive. With McCaslin dead and the two attacks they'd experienced, she didn't want to miss an opportunity to turn the tables. If there was no one inside, she'd phone Ciccilini and the cops from the apartment. If there was, maybe she'd finally force some answers or at least settle a score.

Her pulse quickened as she lowered her bag to the floor and gripped the LadyHawke. She twisted the knob and crouched through the open door. All the lights in the apartment were on.

The first thing she saw was the clutter. Everything lay scattered on the floor. The second thing she saw was the skinhead teenager with colored tatoos on his bare arms. He was bent over her computer desk, riffling through the drawers.

"Drop it all now, sonny," she yelled, holding the gun before her with both hands.

Obviously unafraid, he turned around. The cap he wore bore the symbols of a local white supremacist gang. He reached behind his back and Demming saw the glint of a blade in the lamplight. "What you gonna do, bitch? Shoot me?"

Without answering, she squeezed the trigger.

The kid yelped, grabbed his bloody knee, and hobbled backward.

"You history, bitch!" the skinhead screamed. His eyes looked past her.

She felt the sting on her neck and spun around to shoot. She heard the yowl of the cat. An acrid taste filled her mouth. She struggled to stay conscious, squeezed the trigger but did not hear the shot. The last thing she saw before she hit the floor was a small angel perched on top of her smashed computer screen.

Beck screeched the Spider to a halt in front of One Pierrepont. He jumped out of the seat and ran to the wrought iron and glass door. An electronic buzz sounded, allowing him entry. The doorman held the elevator and Beck tossed him the car keys.

"She's okay, Matt," the stocky, fiftyish man with curly black hair said. "I checked on her myself."

"Thanks, Al," Beck replied as the doors closed. "Do the car." He could not hear Alfonse Ciccilini's reply, but he knew the car was covered. What he couldn't understand was how the hell anyone had gotten up to Anne's apartment in the first place. A front hall doorman was there twenty-four hours a day, screening visitors and protecting the residents, who paid a lot for the service. If it wasn't Alfonse himself, it was somebody like him, a guard who would not let scumbags past the lobby and onto the front elevator. He wondered, though, about the service elevator.

If they came up this old front elevator, they would have had to start last week. The thing took forever. Its heavy mahogany interior, old gears, and iron grating added charm to the art deco building overlooking the East River, but right now he'd swap charm for speed. It hadn't taken him this long to drive here.

He'd had gotten the call at 6 A.M. from Grace Fanton, who, with her husband of fifty-five years, lived twenty feet from Anne in 803. She had heard the gunshots, called the police, building security and Matt before waking her soundly sleeping Jack to go see what happened. Beck had contacted the chaplain coming on at seven, asked him to take over early, and proceeded to battle incoming traffic for the last hour and a quarter. By the time the elevator reached the fifth floor, Beck had rehearsed his speech.

There had been break-ins in her other apartments over the years. It was a part of living in New York, like dirt and subway strikes. That was partly the reason for Anne moving to One Pierrepont three years ago—its security and relatively safe neighborhood. Alfonse and his crew could handle anybody at the door, and Grace and Jack watched after her like parents. With the other incidents, she had not been there to greet the intruders. This was different. This was the last time it would happen. It had taken him too long to drive here. They were too far apart. She needed to move up to Somers with him, where the mountain and his security system kept people like this the hell away.

Floor Seven. Enough of this shit, he thought, his anger rising with each floor. We've been together nearly ten years. I'm not losing you now. Not like this. Not like before. Not to the same murderer, the one we thought was locked up faraway from here. Hardly aware he was doing it, Beck started to speak. "Not again. Not ever. You've got to listen to me!" Floor Eight. "I love you." The doors opened.

"And I love you too, dear." Grace Fanton kissed him on the cheek and handed him a mug of coffee. "She told me to make it black and strong, so I did, but when you're ready Jack's got whiskey older than he is waiting for you down the hall."

Matt smiled and accepted the mug. "What I meant was—"

"I know what you meant, Matthew." She winked. Her makeup and graying hair was perfect, and dressed in a pink flowing dressing gown with a matching silk kimono robe, the seventy-year-old woman looked twenty years younger than she was. "Just be glad it wasn't a cop you said it to. Now drink that before your eyes drop out of their sockets."

"Where's Anne?"

"I'm right here and I'm fine." Anne stood by the apartment door in her mauve jogging suit, a four by four bandage on her neck. "And you can forget it. I'm not leaving."

Beck enclosed her in his arms, hugged her close. "How'd you know what I was thinking?"

"I thought the same thing until I came to my senses." She winced at the tight embrace and pulled away. "Come in. It's not that bad." She motioned to the apartment. "Twitch is around here somewhere, too."

Beck followed her through the open door. "And where are the cops?"

"Like a fart in the breeze," he heard Grace say from behind him. He took in the chaotic living room, glad Anne was not one more piece of debris left behind. Adrenalin-laden fear shot through him. He swore again he would not lose her to this.

"Shit."

"Calm down, Matt." The older woman patted him on the cheek. "This is not the norm in our building and you know it. Besides, our little Annie can take care of herself."

"So I see," Beck whispered.

"Matt—," Anne started.

"Now, now." Grace shook her head. "She's alive. She was outnumbered, but she nailed one of them."

"What?"

"I'll leave her to give you the details. If I go over them once more, I'll forget you're not a cop and I'll have to strangle you. Besides, I can't leave the old man alone too long this time of morning." She breezed through the door, coffee in hand. "It's when he's at his best, if you know what I mean. Bye, dears."

"Careful where you step," Anne warned as she led him through the living room. "I haven't swept up yet. Maybe when I do I'll find the cat. Abby's hiding."

The drawl from the next room startled him. "I found him," Jackson Twitchel said, joining them in the rubble. "He's under the bed in there."

"Some Texan you are," Beck said. "He's a she." His annoyance with Twitch was high right now. This whole disaster was his fault. "Guess you're pleased with the mess," he said. "It'll provide great background for the *CityMag* follow-up on Engel. Maybe Anne can take some pictures. If she can find her damned camera."

"Matt!" Anne broke in.

"No, he's right, Annie," the white-haired man said. Beck thought he looked like a cross between Charles Lindberg and Mark Twain. "But nobody could predict something like this would happen. We'll get you cleaned up and then discuss the next step in the story."

"The next step in the story is to call the damned thing off!" Beck said through gritted teeth.

Anne stepped between them. "Twitch," she said, "you need to go pick up stuff in the kitchen." She turned her boss in that direction. "And Matt," she said, taking his arm, "you come with me."

"Okay, okay. I screwed up." Matt knew he'd acted out of anger and fear for her. He'd apologize to Twitch, but not soon. "So tell me the deal from the beginning."

Beck surveyed the scene as Anne described what had happened. The computer screen was demolished, her desk disheveled, papers and computer disks strewn beneath overturned drawers. The emerald green couch, matching patterned side chairs, and divan were all gashed with broad knife strokes, as though the intruders were searching for items hidden inside. A large pool of drying blood circled a shadeless lamp on the wood floor and seeped slowly toward the rich oriental carpet and the wall. Beck knew the former owner of that blood would need medical attention, and that meant the police would very likely find him—unless he was considered expendable by his accomplices, in which case the East River would receive him instead.

"I can't believe the police left you like this." His fear for her increased with the assessment. "Did you tell them about yesterday? About McCaslin? What did they say?"

Anne picked up a towel and barricaded the blood from hitting the rug. "I didn't think it was a good idea to say anything, given our current distrust of their brethren in Westchester County. Besides, they all read each other's crime reports. They're all on the police intranet. They can put two and two together if they want."

Beck wasn't sure withholding facts would speed an investigation. If they believed there was a connection between McCaslin's murder, the attacks on them, and now this break-in, they might be more likely to pursue clues. On the other hand, Anne was right that they'd find out anyway when they cross-checked her name on their crime report web. "Maybe they'll be more interested once they learn you didn't tell them everything," he said finally.

"And I don't need to be wasting time down at their precinct house right now. So we'll let them believe just what they told me, that it was routine, and that there have been a lot of break-ins recently with increased skinhead gang activity in the Heights because of the money going into gentrification. And, of course," she pecked Matt's cheek, "that they'd get back to me. They took some photos and blood and fingerprint samples, gave me back my gun when I showed them the permit, and split. Out to catch druggies and traffic violators."

Beck pointed to the bandage on her neck. "What did EMS say?"

She touched the spot gently. "All they could find was a pinprick. But it still hurts like hell." She took a sip of his coffee. "Reminds me of the working end of a hornet I met at the ranch one afternoon."

"Can I look?" He lifted the taped edge.

"Sure." She winked. "I love it when you play doctor."

Around the tiny red dot was a bruised, reddish area. "Not deep enough for a needle. They know what it was?" He replaced the tape.

"Like I said—pinprick. They guessed a fast-acting barbiturate on a small ring spike. They hadn't seen this kind of thing with gangs before."

"Yeah, new territory," Beck said, trying to hide his shock. He had seen it before, but not with punk street gangs or even organized crime. In the years he'd been at Grasslands, he'd seen two foreign diplomats in the ER with identical markings. And the bitterness Anne reported, according to the doctors he had talked to on the earlier cases, could indicate anything from seconal to cyanide. She was either lucky to be alive or, more likely, they didn't want her dead. Yet.

"What?" Anne said.

"Huh?" Beck walked behind the couch to examine the debris. "I was thinking about what a nice job EMS did."

"No you weren't. What is it?"

She was too quick for her own good sometimes, Beck thought.

He told her and knew her reaction would be that of an investigative reporter, with little concern for her personal safety or reflection on what it all meant for herself.

"My God, look at the connections," she said, excitedly. "Rinski told me McCaslin's murderers were a young skinhead and an older foreign national."

Matt took her hand and sat on the edge of the couch. "That's what worries me. They killed McCaslin. What would have happened if they'd broken in when you were home?"

"They didn't want to be here when I was home." She waved her arms, gesturing at her scattered belongings. "They wanted to do this, to find out what else I knew about Deathangel."

Beck shook his head and stepped over the rubble to the window. "Anne, the diplomats I saw at Grasslands—they were victims of terrorist attacks. Whatever the hell a foreign connection with Deathangel could be is beyond me right now, but the stakes and the danger have just jumped to a new level. And it's one that we'd both better take more seriously."

"I hate to tell you this, Missy," Twitch said, returning from the kitchen with a cup of coffee, "but I agree with Matt here."

"About time."

"Sorry, Matt." Twitch put on his jacket to leave. "You know I wouldn't do anything to hurt this little lady. I love her damned near as much as you do." He headed toward the door. "Listen, I've got some contacts at Interpol. I'll make some calls. Can't hurt. And it might turn you up some new leads, tell us what we're dealing with here, or at least what that poison really was."

Beck watched Anne stand up and hug the older man. Part of him resented Twitch butting in, but he also hoped he could dig up something they could use.

" 'Night, Beck."

" 'Night, Twitch," Matt said as Anne walked her editor out the door.

Anne returned and curled up next to him on the couch. She fumbled for his hand. "Come on. They weren't trying to kill me, Matt, just scare the crap out of me."

Beck reached out and held her. "Well, they scared it right out of me."

"Okay," she whispered to his chest. "Me, too." He kissed her neck and she drew back. "Know what the scariest part was?" She went into the dining area and retrieved a handful of Polaroid shots the ever vigilant Grace had taken for insurance purposes, handing him the one on the top. "This."

"Shit." Beck frowned and examined the close-up of the top of her computer. A frilly white angel with a wire halo and wings sat on top of the monitor. It was the kind available at any toy store, though a Christmas store would be more likely to carry one this elaborate. It was not at all like the wooden angels placed in evidence at Engel's trial, angels that had sent the murdered victims to heaven and Tod Engel to a lifetime of hell in Weston Prison. But the message was clear enough.

"Stuck on with chewing gum," she said, pointing at the photo, "which might help the police if they can get a blood type from the saliva." She sighed and Beck knew her guard was coming down as reality set in, the reality of an angel staring at her from the machine that had produced the Deathangel story for *CityMag*.

"Damn," she said, leaning into him. "I thought I'd bought it. In that one split second as I was going down I only wanted one thing." Her voice cracked. "You."

Beck felt her tears on his black shirt and his protectiveness surfaced again. "Then come home with me now."

Anne reached for a loose tissue on the floor and blew her nose. "Hey," she said. "Did you set all this up to lure me to the mountain?"

Beck laughed. "If I had, you'd be in worse shape so you'd have to leave."

"Well, here's a surprise for you," she said, standing. "I'll play along this time."

Beck was startled. He had expected her to protest some more and tough it out. Maybe she did realize the danger she'd been in. Then again. "Okay. I'll bite. Why?"

Anne disappeared into the bedroom and Beck followed her. "Because Alfonse says it will take three days to have everything fixed in the apartment and a week to get my furniture back from the upholsterer."

"That's warp speed in New York."

"Al's really sorry about the break-in. He feels responsible for the breach of security. He thinks they must have commandeered the service elevator through an empty first-floor apartment, but he still should have somehow stopped them."

Beck agreed. And it brought him back to the question of how they entered the building. Even the empty condos had security systems that reported entry to the front desk and break-ins directly to the police. "He should have stopped them."

"Anyway, he's pulling in chits to get workers up here—and he knows who to pay." She folded clothes into two suitcases. "The magazine will buy me a new computer. I needed an upgrade anyway."

Beck would have felt better if Alfonse had spent his chits learning how the punks got inside and who had really hired them.

"Put my bags by the door and call Al to take them to my car. You might ask him to check the Forerunner for booby traps while he's at it and then bring it around front for me."

Beck shook his head. She looked like hell. A gorgeous hell with dirty hair and red eyes and a white bandage against the pale skin of her pretty neck, but hell nonetheless. At least she was conceding the need to stay with him a while. Maybe she agreed that now was when they needed each other the most. Now, when they were both vulnerable, might be the time to work their relationship through.

"So when will I see you?" he said, hoping she'd want to go straight to his house and crash. She could work on his computer from there if she had to.

"Gotta go into the office and retrieve my duplicate files on Deathangel and set up a couple more interviews, since Rinski's was so much fun."

Beck took her by the shoulders. "Are you absolutely sure about this, about continuing on, pursuing the story now?"

She touched his face. "I've been threatened and warned off stories before—and you've been through vast amounts of hate mail, pickets, and not a few threats your own little self for your liberal attitudes on death and dying, right?"

"That's different."

"Threats are threats."

"We give in, we give up," Matt repeated Twitch's favorite line. "Right."

He kissed her and clung to her for a moment. The meowing cat caught his attention. "What about the mouser?"

"Grace and Jack will take care of Abby for me when she decides to come out of hiding," Anne said, going to the kitchen to pour food into a bowl.

"I owe them double for minding you both," Beck said, phoning down for Ciccilini. He made the arrangements Anne wanted and told her he'd meet her on the mountain as soon as she finished in the city.

Anne appeared from the bedroom with her work bag. "I may not be there till late, Matt, depending on what I have to do. But I will get there. Today." She kissed him on the lips. "Promise."

The elevator bell dinged and Alfonse stepped into the hall with two sets of car keys. "A huge tank for you," he said to Anne, then turned to Beck. "And a little, unsafe sports car with no top for you to drive in New York City where they carjack even armored vehicles."

"I appreciate your concern, Al." Beck grinned. "But if you look in that apartment, you'll see why she's the one who needs the tank." Besides, who in their right mind would mess with a priest in a sports car?

"That shit'll be cleaned up by the end of the day, Miss Demming," the burly Italian said. "I got a crew here in an hour, trust me."

"Oh I do, Al," Anne said, stepping into the elevator with Matt. "Believe me, I do."

As the contraption descended to the lobby, Beck again wondered how the intruders had made it past security. He was not sure he trusted Alfonse Ciccilini at all.

Chapter 7

"Thanks for picking me up," Matt said. Anne directed the Forerunner down Post Road through Mamaroneck toward Rye. She had stopped by the hospital for him on her way up from the city. He felt bad. He should be the one at the wheel after the events of the morning. "I'll drive home when we're finished. Give you a little rest."

"That'd be great. I shouldn't tell you this while I'm driving, but I'm still a little light-headed from the knockout needle. I'll need a break after this interview. I'm just glad you could do lunch on such short notice."

"No problem," Matt said, though in fact it was a problem. He had hoped Anne would be at the mountain resting and waiting for him, but instead, when she went to work, she checked to see if any of her calls had borne fruit. The one from Langert had. He was returning from an out-of-town trip, coming into the White Plains airport around eleven. He could meet her at the Harbour Master in Rye at noon if she wished. She did wish. And he'd like her to bring Matt Beck, as well, if she wished. She wished that too. So here he sat on his way to what promised to be an excellent lunch wondering why he felt so reluctant about it.

"You okay?" Anne said.

"Yeah, I guess so." He pointed up ahead. "See that clump of trees? That's the restaurant. It backs, or fronts, rather, on the water."

"You've been here before?"

"Yeah." Beck stared out the passenger window as she pulled into the gravel lot and parked. "It's the bishop's favorite restaurant outside the city." He didn't move when she switched off the ignition. She took his hand and he turned to face her.

"Matt? What's going on?"

Beck shook his head. "I don't know. I'm just nervous about seeing Langert, I guess. Especially here." He gestured at the restaurant. "He used to bring Art Allen and me here when we were in seminary before he became bishop. It was a really big deal, the fanciest meal either of us would eat until the next time we went out on his tab."

"And?"

Matt leaned back against the door. "It was different then. He did it as a fluke, as a way to goose the establishment. We'd talk poverty programs and low-cost housing and universal health care, and we'd talk it loud enough to be overheard by people at other tables." Beck smiled, remembering. The three of them had been almost like family. Langert was someone they counted on to understand the trials and stupidities of seminary, someone they could talk with about the pressures of their own families, especially their FBI dads, who couldn't understand how they'd lost their sons to the church.

"And now, coming here years later, you feel like maybe he's become one of the people at the other tables?"

Beck frowned. "Or maybe I have."

Anne nodded vehemently. "Oh, right. That's why you work your ass off as a chaplain, why you've changed the hospital's protocols to help patients get what he called a good death—one with less pain and more dignity—in spite of the system. And why you're outspoken to the point of not being asked to speak at the diocesan convention anymore about health care and coverage."

"Yes, but—"

"Oh, and in case it slipped your mind, it's also why you and I are here interviewing Langert—the little matter of Tod Engel?"

"Yeah, okay." It was more than that for him, more complex. He looked away and Anne kissed him on the cheek.

"Listen to me," she said. "I've got one hell of a headache from whatever joy juice that little ring spike dumped into my system. I want to go in there, do the interview, have a drink and hurry home to the mountain with you and sleep it all off. Got it?"

"I got it." He smiled at her. "You want me to cut to the chase, right?"

"In a word, yes."

"Do my best." Still, he knew he had to be careful here, even with Anne. The emotional territory was still tender for them both. "You know how when you've been really close with somebody and then you grow distant and then you meet again and it's awkward?" He watched her nod. "Well, that's sort of what I'm going through now, especially with both of us here."

He knew Anne remembered as well as he did how Langert had dealt with the moral issue of their consorting together as singles, one a reporter and one a recently widowed priest. Publicly, he had remonstrated those in the church who were critical for their own hypocrisy, asking if their own relationships could stand up to the same personal scrutiny. Langert had argued that Anne and Matt were more obviously committed than most marriages he had seen and that marriage was more about relationship than ritual. His protective efforts had saved Matt from censure and the possible loss of his position at Grasslands. Privately, Langert cautioned Matt during the Deathangel trial to be less conspicuous about his relationship with Anne until the ordeal was over. An open involvement with the reporter covering the trial of his wife's killer could raise eyebrows that not even John Langert could lower. Matt might irrevocably jeopardize the only thing he had left after Kate's death—his career.

"You remember what he said to us during the trial?" Beck said. "When he was worried about the effect of the possible publicity on my career and your ability to be heard objectively about the case?"

"Who could forget that line?" Anne nodded. " 'Sex is one thing. Politics is another.' He thought he could keep you safe as long as we were discreet, but if we became a political liability in the Engel trial we were pretty much on our own."

Beck smiled. "He was right, too." He sighed. "I wonder how it happened that he and I drifted apart? I still see him at clergy meetings from time to time, but it's not the same."

"People go their separate ways. Different careers, different interests. The responsibilities of the bishop's office are immense, I'm sure. And you're no longer all that interested in diocesan politics. You were close once. Now you're not. That doesn't change the friendship you had back then."

Beck kissed her on the cheek. "Thanks." He felt better. He usually did when they talked, even though it was often painful to put words to emotions. Langert was yet another reminder of time passing before you knew it. Maybe he was also more shaken by the attack on Anne this morning than he realized.

"I guess I feel like I should somehow acknowledge all he's done for me, for us, and for Allen too, arranging the job at Weston." He turned to get out of the car, but Anne held him back.

"What you do—Allen, too— is your tribute to him. And if he's observant at all, he's proud."

Beck took Anne's hand as they walked down the gravel path to the stairs leading to the restaurant. There was one memory of Langert he had not shared with Anne. His mentor had not only known Kate; he had performed their marriage.

Beck stopped Anne at the top of the steps. He held her close and kissed her again. As they walked inside to Langert's table, he wondered if the bishop would be willing to do it again.

The maître d' escorted them to a private table by a window and explained that the bishop's flight had taken off late. Langert had called from the plane and taken the liberty of ordering the fresh catch of the day for them all, a nice baked Boston scrod. They should go ahead and he would join them soon. The maître d' vanished, and in his place a clone rushed across the room with a bottle in one hand and a silver stand in the other.

"Good afternoon," he said. He proceeded to show the bottle, uncork it, and pour a small amount into Beck's glass. Beck swirled the pale white-gold liquid in the goblet, sniffed it, and sipped a small amount, holding the glass up to the window to watch the swirl form "legs" and drip down the sides.

"An excellent white burgundy. Thank you."

"The bishop thought it would enhance your meal, Father," the man said, pouring two glasses. He put the bottle into the split and bowed politely. "I am Victor, and I will be attending you this afternoon. If there's anything I can do to make your experience more enjoyable, please let me know." He looked at Anne. "And you as well, madame."

"Thank you." She nodded, and the man stiffly walked away.

Anne leaned over the table. "Do these guys not like women or just not like women with priests?"

"Maybe both." Matt picked up his glass. "Who cares about the sexual preference of the person bringing your wine?"

She raised her glass to his. "I only care about the sexual preference of the person drinking it with me." She winked.

"My sexual preference is you." He clinked her glass and looked out the window at the blue water and wispy clouds. "Great view of the sound."

"What I want to know is, how do all those people have enough money to be out in their sailboats at noon on a Wednesday?"

"Life is unfair," Beck said sardonically, gazing at the boats slipping by in the distance. "That's why it's important to do what we can to even the odds." He looked back at her. "You do it at the magazine, I do it at the hospital."

Anne pursed her lips. "Been nice if somebody would have evened the odds for the lady in the Chevy yesterday, even if she was ready to shoot at us. I think it's real coincidental that the one person who could maybe lead us anywhere became one with the pavement."

"Ably assisted by the police captain, who works for James Rinski. Still," Matt said, shaking his head, "it's hard to believe that Rinski, even back then, had a hand in those murders."

"You wouldn't say that if you were a woman. You'd wonder why the creep slimeball wasn't the prime suspect."

Beck withheld his comment as the waiter returned with salads, bread, and freshly ground pepper. He watched Anne dive into her salad and wondered how long Langert would take getting there. The sooner, the better. He could only hide his anxiety behind small talk and wine for so long.

"I'm still playing around with the hit theory," she continued. "I'm sure this occurred to you, but what if Rinski himself was Deathangel?"

"He may be capable of it, but somehow that doesn't seem possible," Matt said, knowing it wouldn't be the first time the impossible turned out to be true. "What reason would he have to execute all those people, especially Kate? She had no ties to the police, to Rinski, to Engel, or anyone else for that matter."

Anne sipped her wine. "Unless there's a connection between the victims we haven't uncovered yet."

Beck shook his head. He wondered if he and Anne might discover some unknown link when they received the BCI sheets from Art Allen. "Right now, all we're certain about is that Rinski has some vested interest in keeping the case closed."

"Which makes me curious to find out what it is."

For a second, Matt was aware of how much he desperately wanted Engel to be Deathangel, despite the circumstances of the last few days. It would make things so much easier, validate his grief, allow him to move forward. He was about to make a comment to that effect when he heard a familiar voice and turned to see a tall, gray-haired man nearly fly into the room. "Maybe this gentleman can help," he said, standing to greet the Right Reverend John K. Langert.

"Good afternoon, Bishop," Beck said, holding his hand out. Langert ignored it and clasped him in a back-thumping hug.

"How good to see you, Matt." Langert was slightly taller than Beck. The older man's grasp was firm and strong, as though taut muscles carried a sturdy frame under those black and white trappings.

"You remember Anne?"

"Miss Demming is unforgettable, Matthew." Langert took her hand and gently squeezed it as he smiled. "I always read and enjoy your articles in *CityMag*. You are quite an adventurous woman, and an excellent writer."

"Thank you, Bishop. I like to see myself as a good reporter who tracks down reasonable leads."

"But what I like about you is that you also track down the unreasonable ones, Miss Demming. That's what makes you a cut above the rest."

"Thank you, again. And it's Anne, please."

Matt pulled out a chair as the wine steward made sure the glasses were appropriately filled.

"I would have been here earlier, but my regular driver, Earl, got his dates mixed up and is off with his family today. I've had to use a substitute," Langert said, closing his eyes, "who drives like an old lady. An old blind lady. He gives new meaning to slow."

Beck couldn't tell if the instant familiarity he felt was engendered by the wine or the bishop's good humor. His anxiety seemed to have disappeared. It was as though they had just been here together a few weeks ago.

"Really wonderful to see you both," Langert said. "It has been far too long. I know we've all gotten busy with our lives, but that's no excuse. Perhaps this will be the start of more occasions like this."

"I hope so too, Bishop," Matt said, and he meant it.

"I'm only sorry our meeting has to be over such a gruesome subject—though Anne, I believe, may have come over to my side of the argument regarding Tod Engel. Is that right?"

Beck let them eat while he explained that Joseph McCaslin had contacted him shortly before his death, claiming to have information that exonerated Engel and might prove that the Deathangel murders had not been random acts at all.

"A terrible tragedy, McCaslin's murder. I'm doing the funeral tomorrow, you know," Langert said. "You'll be there?"

Matt said he would. He was pleased to hear Langert was conducting the service. Beck's father had always said to play your cards close to the vest, however, even with people you thought you could trust. He kept the advice in mind, leaving out some important details about the search of Anne's apartment, her difficulty pursuing a follow-up investigation, and the incident with the blonde in the blue Chevy. Nor did he tell Langert about the attack at McCaslin's house or the discovery of the journal.

Langert looked stunned. "After all you've been through and you still made it here today?" He touched Anne's hand. "I am honored!"

"Job's a job, Bishop," Anne said. Beck motioned to the waiter to bring their steaming plates of scrod.

"This looks great," Langert said.

"I told her you would reschedule," Beck continued, "but she's trying to interview all the principals of the trial and didn't want to let the opportunity go."

"They're all in prominent positions today as a direct result of that case," Anne said nonchalantly, nibbling a piece of fish. "Including yourself."

Beck had waited for this. He knew she would slip it in at the end of something innocuous. He wondered how Langert would take it and found he'd guessed correctly.

"Absolutely true, Anne. My chiseled profile on the evening news certainly raised my stock, not to mention the clever shot you took of me jumping to my feet to lecture the jury on Engel's innocence. With those two bits of luck, my name became a household word in the Diocese of New York just around the time of the diocesan convention that would elect the next bishop."

Beck jumped in, "But isn't it also true that, given your track record, you were already the leading candidate, based on your previous activities and service?"

Langert paused to swallow his food. "Yes, but Anne is correct in assuming that Engel propelled me into the office, hands down."

"You saw him recently, didn't you, Bishop?" Anne asked. "About a week after you arranged for me to interview him. Which, by the way, I really appreciate."

"You're welcome, of course. Sometimes it just takes a little ecclesiastical pressure to get the politicos to do the right thing. And it didn't hurt Engel to have another visitor, either."

Matt watched them talk and wondered why he felt compelled to defend the bishop against the same questions Anne would ask of any interview subject. Hell, Langert hadn't come this far by avoiding the press; he could probably handle any question Anne threw at him. Or so it seemed so far, as she queried him on background information.

Langert turned to Beck and raised his wine glass. "Before I forget, this celebration is on my tab."

"Celebration?" Matt asked.

"Certainly," Langert said. "First, to celebrate our reunion, Matt. But then, even though it comes with horrible news about McCaslin and the attacks on you, I must say the other reason is equally wonderful. Something has happened! It confirms what I've said all along, that Engel had no motive. He may have had opportunity, and the evidence apparently proved he had the methods at his disposal, but the missing element has always been motive!"

"Retarded, delusional people don't usually require motives, Bishop

Langert," Anne said quietly. "At least that's been the argument we've heard so far."

"That's what they said then, and that is what they continue to say." The prelate sat back in his chair, composing himself. "But I will tell you," he said, shaking his finger, "that someone covered up the truth then and is still trying to do so today."

"Like what?" Beck raised his eyebrows.

"That I have been unable to discover, though, as you know, it is something about which I have continued to be vocal all these years." He set his glass down and spoke more calmly. "I hope you have gone to the police with this new information?"

"Not yet," Anne said. "It's all speculation at this point."

Beck leaned forward. "We've thought about trying to find some common denominator among the victims, on the chance that the killings were deliberate executions. The death of the woman who attacked us has us concerned about the possible involvement of the police, and Anne's assailants used a device on her that's known to be a favorite with foreign terrorists."

"With terrorists, all things are possible, to coin a phrase," Langert said, finishing his glass of wine. "Or so my brother European bishops tell me. In this country we have no idea of the kind of threat they and their parishioners live under all the time."

Langert was silent as the waiter filled their glasses one last time and took away the bottle and stand.

"You might ask former prosecutor Martin Ehrhart's beloved spouse about such things. I understand her family is quite prominent in manufacturing in Germany. There was some controversy in the last election over his receiving campaign support from her family's business. It was largely kept out of the papers, but in political circles it was something to talk about."

Matt finished his meal and pushed his plate to the side. He made a mental note to check on Ehrhart's German supporters and what else they might be supporting.

Anne set her glass down. "I did have one more question, Bishop, if you don't mind?"

The prelate nodded.

"The police weren't clear on the religious affiliation of the victims," she said. "Now I know it may seem silly, but, even though the police didn't believe there was any possible connection, given the population of the county, I was wondering if you had any information about that."

The bishop's face brightened. "As a matter of fact, I do." He leaned forward on his elbows and put his chin on his hands. "I checked into that very early on, as a possible clue to—I don't know what. I was grasping at straws, perhaps as you are now. Anyway, they all turned out to be Roman Catholic—"

Matt looked up at him and he returned Beck's stare.

"Except for Kate Beck. Correct, Matt?"

Beck sighed and straightened in his chair. "She was Jewish, as I'm sure you recall. Raised in a Reform Jewish family, anyway, a nonpracticing one. She became Episcopalian when we got married." He avoided Anne's eyes. "For the sake of my career and because, quite frankly, it didn't make much difference to her."

"So Kate was the only non-Catholic?" Anne said.

"Looks that way." Beck watched them both. While they were asking simple factual questions, his guts were churning.

"Though you could make the argument that she was also Catholic—Anglo-Catholic or Episcopal as opposed to Roman Catholic." Langert looked at Anne. "Does that help or just confuse things?"

"I don't know. But it's one more thing to go on," she said.

Vincent approached from the bar. "Excuse me, Bishop. You have a call at the front," he said.

Langert pushed back his chair. "Be right back. I'll ask them to bring dessert. If you don't like crème broıllæe, order something else, but it is incredible here."

When the bishop was out of earshot, Matt spoke to Anne. "So, what do you think?"

"I think the boy likes to be in charge. Wine, food, dessert."

"He's just being generous," Beck said, feeling uncomfortable again.

Anne looked at him. "I wonder how generous he is if you don't do what he wants?"

"Order something different for dessert and see if he explodes." Matt smiled. Hell, the guy was getting old. He was entitled to a few idiosyncrasies. Besides, it had saved time and allowed Anne to ask more questions. And the food was good. Including the dessert, which had just arrived.

"He's certainly convinced Engel is innocent," Anne said, picking up her spoon. Matt liked to watch her eat desserts. She took very small bites from the sides and worked her way to the center. "But that's his job, isn't it?"

"You've spent all this time with me and you still believe that? And with your Baptist background!" Matt said. "His job is to run the Diocese of New York, and he didn't get there just by being a soft-hearted liberal. There are rumors of his being nominated for presiding bishop—the highest office in the church, though the arch-conservatives are fervently against it. He's actually received death threats." Beck picked up his spoon. "But smart as he is, I think he's certain of Engel's innocence because he misunderstands retardation. He believes Engel was incapable of planning the crimes, but the level of M.R. varies greatly, sometimes even in the same person. He could seem totally incompetent one day and capable the next— or any combination of both. What if he had the capacity to do the crimes, but not to plan them?"

Anne cocked her head. "That would mean that Engel could be the killer, but others, the ones who set him up for whatever reason, still have everything to lose by opening the case."

Tears suddenly filled Beck's eyes. He felt scared and overwhelmed, with no place to run. "Damn it," he said, grabbing his napkin and standing away from the table to look out the window at the sound. He appreciated Anne's sitting there, letting him do this without getting up and rescuing him yet. Not here. Not now. "I'm sorry. It's just being in this place, facing all these feelings again," he said, wiping his eyes.

"Maybe that's not a bad thing for either of us," she said, reaching for him.

He took her hand and came back to the table. "Maybe not." He leaned down to kiss her. They had talked at the beginning about ripping the scab off the Deathangel case, but he hadn't counted on the scab of his own festering wound being torn off, too. He imagined his blood pouring out over six wooden angels.

Langert rounded the corner with a frown. Time to go, Matt thought, still holding Anne's hand.

"Please enjoy your dessert," the older man said, signing the slip of paper by his seat. "Crisis du jour at the office, so I have to hurry back to New York. And with this driver I may not make it till next Thursday."

Beck rose to accept the bishop's embrace, stifling tears that he feared would overflow forever. He stood back as Langert graced Anne's cheek with a kiss.

"Next drinks are on me, Bishop," she said. "And they'll be Texas shooters, knocked back with salt and lime, if you figure you can take it."

"You're on," he said. "Would you mind if your significant other walks me to the car? I need to chat with the boy about his career choices."

"Long as you send him back here to drive me home, I'm fine." She winked at Matt.

Beck grimaced. He was already feeling vulnerable. Now was not the moment for advice about his ministry, however well intentioned. Would it be premature to bring up the idea of Langert performing a second marriage? "I may have a few things to discuss with you as well," he said, taking his superior's arm and heading out the door.

Through the picture window by their table, Anne watched the two men walk down the long wooden stairway to the back parking lot by the sound. They seemed to be speaking vehemently, both waving their hands, ultimately laughing together. What were they talking about? As she queried him at lunch, Langert had been forceful and convincing about his beliefs, yet smooth as a baby's bottom when it came to questions of a personal nature. He was, indeed, the master politician. He seemed to be in the right place at the right time in terms of what Matt had told her about issues tearing at the church.

The two men stopped and Langert hugged Matt again, then shook his hand. Was it in congratulations or parting?

Anne watched the sleek black limo slink around to the bottom of the stairs. Langert said something to Matt and took the last steps to the car as Beck headed back up the stairs to the restaurant. She squinted to try to see the driver the bishop had complained so much about. Something strange caught her eye.

"What in God's name is that?" she said, staring at the car, which was turning an odd, light blue color on the inside that had nothing to do with the window tinting. She saw the driver convulse and slump over the wheel, heard the horn sound, and watched Langert rush toward the front of the limo.

"No!" Anne shouted. She searched about her and, finding no other way to halt the bishop or get him to look up at her, she grabbed her chair and shoved it through the plate-glass window with all her strength. She covered her face with her arms as shards of glass showered around her. Customers shouted in alarm as she looked down to see the chair crash on the asphalt two stories below.

Teetering on the edge of the huge open space, she leaned out and screamed, desperate to be heard above the blaring horn, "Gas! Deadly gas!"

Helpless to stop him, she watched Matt race across the lot to the black limo as Langert opened the driver's door and collapsed in a choking blue cloud.

Anne sat impatiently in the waiting room of the Grasslands ER. Why the hell were they taking so long in the crash room? Along with all the other emotions of the last three days, she tossed in irony. Ten years ago she had met Matt Beck in this very spot. Now she was waiting to meet him again, and for the identical reason—Deathangel. She felt as though the fickle finger of God had hit the rewind button. Everything from the last decade was being replayed, reexamined in slow motion so that what had seemed logical and true now looked flawed and corrupt.

Outside, two men got out of a black van, flashed badges, and entered the ER. Five minutes later they escorted a narrow gurney with a sheet loosely wrapped around a body through the automatic door. Anne could see the outline of the toe tag. Presumably, that was the chauffeur going to the coroner's office for a postmortem. Now somebody was driving him.

For a second, she let herself imagine it was Matt. She visualized Robert's body in the flag-draped casket at the funeral home, his lifeless, rigid features echoing the stiff, formally dressed honor guard at the service. That's what this reaction was about, wasn't it? Her fear of losing Matt. Not just of losing him, but of his leaving her first, of her being left behind again. What would she do if his was the next body rolled out? Could she ever feel as much as she had for Robert?

Shit, she thought, watching them lift the gurney into the van. It feels like we're in a race for who leaves who first. She grinned and a familiar voice jolted her.

"I hope that smile means Matt is okay."

She looked up to see Twitch towering over her. Beside him stood a dark-haired man with a bushy moustache. They looked like Mark Twain meets the Monopoly Man.

"He's not sporting a toe tag," she said, "if that's what you mean. EMS insisted on bringing both him and Langert here in ambulances with oxygen and drugs diluting the noxious gas in their bodies. Langert was cooperative but weak. He sucked in a pretty good snoot-full of gas. Matt thought it was silly to come in when he was perfectly alert and awake, but when they told him they surmised, from the color, that it was hydrogen cyanide, he changed his mind."

"Hydrogen cyanide?" the short man said. "Are you sure?"

His German accent was thick. She kept waiting for him to tell her she'd won the Community Chest or not to pass Go. "And you would be?"

"I'm sorry, Anne," Twitch said. "This is Friedrich Baumschen. He's—"

A nursed tapped her shoulder. "Mrs. Beck? You can come back now."

"Thanks," she said, taken aback by the name, but not as much as she might have been only a few days ago. Maybe that was the answer to her question about Robert. She turned to Twitch. "Shut up and come with me," she said. Not certain what Matt's condition would be, regardless of what he had said, she anticipated the worst. She walked toward the bright lights of the crash room.

Beck sat on the white gurney, naked to the waist. It was not his usual view of the Grasslands Emergency Room. Though he didn't like it, he was grateful to be in one piece, attended by people he knew and trusted.

"You're a lucky man, Chaplain." Doug Jonsby, the attending ER. doctor, patted him on the shoulder. "And so is your bishop friend in the next room. He only got a whiff of that stuff before you yanked him away from the car." The doctor tossed Matt his clergy shirt. "If you hadn't, he'd be on his way to the coroner, like his driver. Hydrogen cyanide gas is lethal, you know."

Matt tucked in his shirt and slipped the tab collar into place. "So how much would you have to inhale to kill you?"

Jonsby answered, his eyes on his notes. "If you're asking whether the gas bomb was meant just for the chauffeur, the answer's no. The police said there was enough gas in that car to take out this whole ER. and then some." He closed the chart. "Whoever did this might even have counted on you rushing in to help." Jonsby winked. "Your sermons been pissin' people off again, Matt?"

"His sermons don't intentionally piss people off, Doctor," Anne said from the doorway. "It's just that some folks have no sense of humor." She came over to the gurney and hugged him. "He's going to be all right, right?"

"What was your name again, lady?" Matt said. And who are these other people you brought with you? And why am I wearing this black shirt?"

"So now your excuse for everything will be, if only I hadn't inhaled that gas. Right?"

Jonsby chuckled and left the cubicle. Beck kissed Anne and then turned his attention to Twitch and a short man who had come into the room with them. "What's going on?"

"Father Beck, I am Friedrich Baumschen, with Interpol." The man shook Beck's hand. "Your Mr. Twitchel called some mutual friends and they told me about your case. I was already in New York in regards to a terrorist ring based in Austria and Germany that is believed to have a sister cell in this area. I am interested to know more about the drug used on Fraulein Demming this morning and about the woman who attacked the two of you yesterday."

"The bad news is that you'll have to check with Westchester Police Commissioner James Rinski about the woman," Beck said. "The good news is you're wearing pants."

Baumschen looked at him, clearly puzzled.

"Rinski likes to intimidate women," Anne explained. Beck nodded.

"I have already attempted to look into the matter," the man said, "by contacting the Westchester County morgue, but it seems the woman's body has inexplicably disappeared."

Matt glanced at Anne and looked away.

"What a coincidence," Twitch drawled.

"Let me guess," Matt said, as he leaned against the stationary gurney. "The bodies of Joe McCaslin's murderers are also nowhere to be found."

"That's right," Twitch said. "I called this morning to see if they'd I.D.'d anybody. Nada. Nada. Nada." He folded his arms across his chest. "I believe they said they had temporarily misplaced them."

"How convenient to have the Hudson nearby for disposable waste," Anne murmured.

Matt pulled the tape and cotton ball from his arm and buttoned the sleeves of his shirt. "Have we gotten the lab results from Anne's blood work yet? I would think Mr. Baumschen would need to see that."

Again Twitch answered. "Takes a few days to run the chemical analysis—or at least that's what they told me last time I checked."

"So we have to wait on that." Matt was ready to leave, but Baumschen was getting a fair amount of information from them. Maybe he would return the favor. "Is there anything you can tell us about your investigation, Mr. Baumschen?"

"Another of what Mr. Twitchel calls an interesting coincidence." He tugged at his moustache. "I have most recently been investigating your county executive, the superior of your Commissioner Rinski—a Martin Ehrhart."

Beck's jaw clenched. The circle kept narrowing. "I believe Ehrhart has European connections through his wife."

"It is a little more complex than that, Herr Beck. It seems Frau Ehrhart's family are quite wealthy industrial chemists. They own factories near Hamburg and just outside Munchen—Munich, and they are known to have certain sympathies." When he shrugged his shoulders his whole body seemed to wrinkle. "It may be nothing. Often these things look worse than they are. But it is worth pursuing."

It still didn't show them how or why terrorists would be connected to a ten-year-old murder case. "Pursuing separately or in relation to Deathangel?" Beck asked.

"Not sure and both," Twitch answered for Baumschen. "Lots of politicians have well-laundered campaign support from overseas companies and corporations—for obvious reasons. If Ehrhart gets to Washington he can help affect the flow of billions of dollars, not to mention the various defense capabilities of the European nations—and others. There's a lot at stake for Ehrhart here, and it may depend on his real role with Deathangel."

"That is true, Herr Twitchel," Baumschen said, frowning. "This man Rinski, his name sounds familiar to me for some reason as well. Do any of you know why that might be?"

"Excuse me, Chaplain." A nurse broke through the group and handed Beck a clipboard. "Sign and you're outta here."

Matt scribbled his name and asked about the bishop.

"That old guy's quite a character," the nurse said. "Got a body like a fifty-year-old. But he's still going to be woozy for a while this afternoon. He's sleeping now, but we'll probably let him go home today. Jonsby doesn't think we'll admit him."

"Thanks." Matt put his arm around Anne and walked to the crash-room door. Baumschen stopped him and held out two cards.

"Here is a number where you can reach me, day or night. Use it when you need it. And in the meantime," he saluted them, "be careful. Be very careful."

Outside, in the Forerunner, Matt leaned back in the passenger seat and looked over at Anne through half-closed eyes. "What did you think of Baumschen?"

Anne answered, "Not sure yet. How do we know we can trust him?"

"We don't," Beck muttered as Anne pulled onto the main highway and headed north. Something disturbed him about the conversation with the Interpol investigator. He squeezed Anne's hand and she returned the motion. "Did you hear what Baumschen said when he handed us the card with his number on it?"

Anne yawned, then replied, "He told us to use it if we need it."

"No," Matt said softly. "That's what bothers me." He lifted Anne's hand and kissed it. "He told us to use it when we need it."

"No more for me." Art Allen held up one bony hand. "I should have left after the third one. It's hard to drink my favorite Kentucky bourbon without smoking a cigar."

"This house hasn't had cigar smoke in it since I moved here. But the previous owner was a cigar and wine connoisseur." Beck was enjoying the banter and the bourbon. Like McCaslin, Art had been a good friend in difficult times. When their fathers got too macho about their jobs or too demanding of their only male offspring, the two had turned to each other to hang out and commiserate.

"I remember you showing me the wine vault in the basement," Allen said. "Still there?"

Beck nodded. He regularly took guests on a tour of the cellar, the main one anyway. Only Anne knew about the small private one the previous owner had built behind it, accessed through a section of revolving wall. Supposedly, the reputed Mafia chieftain had stored his expensive bottles there, but Beck and Anne had found evidence of other things when they discovered it, shell casings and pieces of jewelry.

"Humidor still there, too, or did you take it out?" Allen gestured with his drink up at the glass bookcases lining the living room walls.

"I left it there," Beck said. "Piece of history. Besides, I can hide stuff in it when I go on vacation. On really wet evenings, when it's rained all day and the water hangs in the trees, you can still smell a hint of the old Don's cigars." Beck sipped the whiskey. "Some people leave an imprint beyond their lives."

"You thinking of your dad?" Allen asked, almost politely.

"Actually, I was thinking of Tod Engel."

"I still don't understand why you're doing this. The police closed the case years ago. Nobody can benefit by bringing it up again."

"Not even Engel?" Beck said.

Allen shook his head and frowned. "Least of all Engel."

"Why? If he didn't do it, he can go free."

"Free to do what? Where's this guy going to end up? At least at Weston he's got three hots and a cot and a roof over his head, not to mention continued notoriety with reporters coming to check on him to see if he's dead yet, which is more than we can say about most people." Allen fingered the cigar in his pocket. "No, I've seen it a million times. Tod Engel couldn't make it on the outside. He'd be in a mental hospital or another prison inside of three months, if he lasted that long."

Beck pressed his defense, though he wasn't convinced of it himself anymore. "He seemed to do okay before."

"Before what? Before he went around randomly offing the citizens of Westchester County?" Allen bent forward and looked intently at Beck. "Just what makes you so damned sure he's not Deathangel? Are you willing to take the chance you're wrong and let this guy loose again?"

Beck stared at Allen, waiting for the next question.

"Yes, I'll ask that, too. Do you believe Engel didn't kill Kate?" He put his drink on the table. "Shit, Matt, I loved her too. I loved her because she loved you. And it by-damn pissed me off when that son-of-a-bitch killed her. How the hell easy do you think it's been for me, locked up in that prison with Engel, becoming the only person who sees to his rights, the closest one to him, the one he comes nearest to trusting, if he trusts anybody. I carry that crap with me every day I walk into the place. And I admit I've thought of a thousand ways to take the bastard off the count."

"But you haven't," Matt said quietly, surprised, not at the depth of Allen's emotion, but that this was the first he'd said of it since Kate's murder. Allen stood and walked to the window.

"Hell no, I haven't." Allen turned back to Beck. "He's not evil, for God's sake. He's mentally frigging retarded."

"But you said yourself at one point even you weren't sure," Matt reminded him.

"I've reconsidered." Allen sat back down on the couch. "I flipped through those files before I brought them over here." He pointed to the stack of brown folders on the coffee table. "They're too random, Matt. The killings don't make a damned bit of sense. The have the M.O. of someone who doesn't really understand what he's doing, whether he's M.R. and delusional or just one can short of a six pack, and Engel certainly fits that description."

Matt pondered his next request and rubbed his tired eyes. He needed someone on the inside monitoring Engel's moves. "Listen. I don't want this to be true any more than you do. But, unfortunately, I have at least two good reasons to suspect that Tod Engel did not commit those murders."

"And those are?"

Beck hesitated. "A dead priest and a scar on my neck."

Allen squinted at him. "What does that mean?"

"It means Joe McCaslin was not murdered by passing muggers."

"Jesus. You're more paranoid than I am. You're more paranoid than our fathers were. And they had good reason."

Beck ignored him. "Whoever arranged McCaslin's death tried to off me—as you so colorfully put it—when I went to McCaslin's house to look for a diary." He leaned forward and pulled aside the collar of his sweatshirt. "Here's the knife cut."

"Jesus." Allen reached over and retrieved his drink. "But how do you know it wasn't just a burglar?"

"A burglar who was interested in the exact same computer disk of McCaslin's that I wanted? A burglar who waited for me to find it, then came out from behind me, tried to knock me out, and, but for some timely intervention, would have added another kill to his list?"

"McCaslin's death was the result of a robbery. The fool resisted and was killed. It was stupid. He should have let them have whatever they wanted."

"Oh, they got what they wanted," Beck said, leaning back in the chair. "They wanted McCaslin dead."

"Stop right there, Matt." Allen placed his drink on the coffee table and stood up.

Hoping to break through to Art's emotions once again, Matt hammered on. "If it was a simple mugging, why the hell have the bodies of the muggers disappeared from the county morgue? Along with the corpse of a woman who attacked Anne and me yesterday before being flattened by a police car? Does the word conspiracy have any nostalgic meaning for you?"

"I don't want to hear any more of this shit."

Beck took a deep breath. He had pushed too hard.

Allen headed for the door. "I live a nice, quiet uninvolved life at Weston. I've got ten more to go for retirement in the state system. I have no desire to be an accessory to anything that would jeopardize that."

Beck followed him. "At least hear my argument. There was a time when you would have gladly joined the cause."

"That was a hell of a long time ago," Allen said, opening the front door. "It's like we finally learned from our wonderful, dedicated, foolish fathers. It's all about money and power. There isn't any cause here, so quit searching for one. Engel's been happy as a pig in slop for ten years. Let him be. He's already been transferred to solitary. Keep juggin' with him and you'll get him killed. If he doesn't deserve to be where he is now, he sure as shit doesn't deserve that."

Matt had nothing to lose. "I was hoping you'd keep an eye on him and call me if—"

"If what?" Allen snapped. "If he wakes up dead? No, Matt. Brothers or not, I'm out of this." He started to leave, then turned back. "And don't give me too much grief here," he said, pointing toward the coffee table. "I did bring your friggin' BCI runs." He put his hand on the doorknob. "That in itself may be more dangerous than I know."

"Bye, Art," Beck said, as the door slammed shut. "Thanks for the files," he whispered.

"Y'all come back, now," Anne said from the top of the stairs. She yawned and stretched, the top of her pink sweatsuit rising to reveal her slim belly.

"How much of that did you hear?" Matt met her at the bottom of the steps and escorted her to the living room couch.

"Most of it, I'm afraid," she said. She poured a small glass of bourbon and sat beside him, resting her head in the crook of his arm. "The doorbell woke me the first time, but then I dozed off. I thought I was dreaming about Engel when I sort of resurfaced and heard Art mention his name."

Beck sipped his drink. He liked it when she was sleepy and soft like this, more vulnerable than the cowgirl who rode bulls and stories for the full count. He had let her nap when Allen arrived partly because she needed it and partly to keep the conversation with him focused on Engel rather than the past.

"Too bad about Art." She snuggled closer.

"I wouldn't be too critical," Beck said. "He's been through a lot these ten years, especially with all the changes at Weston under Williams. And then there's his great relationship with Langert. Art won't return the bishop's calls and arranges to be out when he comes to see Engel."

"It still wouldn't have killed him to agree to watch Engel."

Matt kissed the top of her head. "That's the point. It did kill McCaslin, damned near got you in Brooklyn, and almost slit my throat, not to mention the dead blonde on Old Mamaroneck Road and the bishop's poor chauffeur. In a way, I don't really blame him for not wanting to become involved, though he already is involved by doing the BCI runs. We had to have them or we'd be nowhere. I think." They had very little cooperation from the few families of the victims, and that information was not reliable. The Bureau of Criminal Information files, however, were cross-referenced with other law enforcement agencies like the FBI and DIA.

Anne sat up and swirled her drink with her little finger, putting the tip into her mouth and sucking on it. "Allen said he'd looked through the files. Did he identify anything?"

"I don't think so. And despite his appearance, Art Allen is smart. If there was something to find, he'd have spotted it." He glanced at the folders. "Unless, of course, he wanted me to think there was nothing worth seeing in them. But I don't believe he'd do that, not on this one. He knew McCaslin, too. And Kate." Beck picked up half the pile and tossed them on the couch beside her. The rest he put in his lap. "I thought if we took a few minutes and went through them, we might hit on something that was overlooked."

"Or purposely ignored," Anne said. "Especially if Rinski had anything to do with it." She placed four files, each open to the cover page, on the couch next to her, side by side. "Put your four on the coffee table, all near each other." She watched as Beck complied. "We'll take them category by category, in good computer order. If you'd thought of it, you could have asked him to push a few extra buttons and save us time."

"I was damned lucky he'd even do this much, Anne."

"Sorry." She kissed his cheek. "It was a thought, not a criticism."

Beck sighed and sat back. "Sorry," he said, taking her hand. "I'm really on edge with all that's happened. And then there's McCaslin's funeral tomorrow."

Anne held him and gently kissed his face. "Not to mention that you'll have to open Kate's folder in a minute."

Matt returned her kiss. His sleight of hand in arranging the folders was busted. He had to steel himself to look at Kate's folder with the same objectivity as the others and he had to do it now. The stakes were too high for them all.

"Maybe I should have put her folder in your pile."

"No, you did the right thing." Anne fanned out their files. "You have your ghosts and I have mine. I guess we're confronting them together now."

It was like starting from scratch ten years ago to find Kate's murderer. How would it affect his feelings for Anne? Would determining the truth make him freer or shut down his heart even further? There was only one way to find out. He touched his glass to hers. "Okay. Here's to the family. Yours, mine, and ours."

Anne nodded. "Maybe we can cajole their spirits into helping us concentrate on the data here and see whether the wrong man has been in

Weston Prison for ten years—while the right man was laughing at him."

Beck froze at her words. "Concentrate longer," he said. "That's what Engel keeps saying. Concentrate longer." Maybe it was an admonition, a pleading command, directions for someone to help him.

Matt opened the first file. "Let's see what's so funny."

The police commissioner punched a button to ask Charlotte to retrieve a number for him, then thought better of it. What if she was keeping track of his calls? Logging them? That log was a paper trail. Phone records could be messed with by computer, but a secretary's memory and her log sheet were indisputable to a jury.

He looked up the number and dialed the private line. The phone rang five times before anyone picked up.

"Ehrhart here."

"This is Rinski. I believe we have our little problem taken care of for the moment."

"I don't know how you could have been so stupid in the first place, James."

"Do you mean now or ten years ago?"

"Shut up, you idiot!"

Rinski smiled. "Calm down, Mr. County Executive. I thought you said these phones were clean as a whistle."

"They were. But a lot has happened since then." Ehrhart's voice tensed. "Nothing, Rinski, nothing is above suspicion. Never assume anything."

"Yeah, you're probably right. Just for the record, in case this is being heard over the county office building P.A. system, the event ten years ago I was referring to was taking the promotion that got me where I am today, working for you."

"We'll have to be very careful, if we want that career to continue."

Don't threaten me, asshole, Rinski almost said. They knew too much to do this to each other. He'd humor him for now. "I know, Marty. I know. One thing at a time." Rinski lit a cigarette and sat on the desk.

"I learned something, right after I talked to you, that may continue to complicate our situation."

Rinski blew a cloud of smoke in front of him. Whatever it was, he could handle it. "What's that?"

"I was informed by, shall we say, an interested party, that someone has requested and received copies of the BCI sheets on a certain group of murder victims."

Rinski stood and crushed out the cigarette. "Shit," he swore. He could take care of external meddlers, but internal connections worried him. Sometimes they kept records they shouldn't, like Charlotte out there. "Who the hell was it?"

"The same man caught snooping through your property room, I'm afraid," Ehrhart said.

"Beck? I may have to deal with him directly."

"Again?" Ehrhart's voice was sarcastic. "Your little plan didn't quite work out last time, did it?"

"I never gave orders for her to fire on anybody." Rinski aimed his punch at the jaw. "Did you?"

The line was silent. Point scored. "What are you talking about?" Ehrhart finally said.

"I want to know if the blonde chick was on your dole." Maybe the silence meant Ehrhart had been humping her too.

"No," Ehrhart said. "She was not. She came highly recommended from an out-of-state source."

Rinski heard the change in Ehrhart's voice. "Out of state or out of country?"

"I can't talk about this right now. We have other problems to discuss, and it doesn't help to have us at each other's throats, not trusting each other." Ehrhart sighed. "I don't want you messing with Beck and Demming until we talk."

Rinski would take it all under advisement, including Ehrhart's reaction—and evasiveness—just now. He would have preferred to kill Beck—after he asked him how the broad was in bed. Of course it would cause more trouble than it was worth to do it now, though it would still be fun. Through the phone he heard the sound of pages turning.

"Can you come to my office tomorrow at noon?"

Without looking at his own calendar, the police commissioner answered. "No," he said. He didn't want to waste any more time listening to orders from this man. "I've got a meeting with all the local chiefs of police tomorrow."

"Cancel it. Put Steiner in charge. We haven't much time to decide how to dispose of our problem. These inquiries must stop—and soon—if we are to continue our plans." Ehrhart paused. "Do you understand me?"

Rinski tossed his calendar on the desk. Though he hated to admit it, he agreed with Ehrhart. Further disclosures could ruin them all. They had to be done away with. "I'll be there at noon. But have some lunch ready, will you? And not that rabbit food shit you eat, either. I want a steak."

The phone went dead.

Rinski wished Ehrhart would do the same.

Anne stretched her arms over her head. "God, these reports are thorough," she said.

Matt closed a folder and rubbed his forehead. "Even Kate's." He sighed. He had started with hers to get it over with. The pain he felt was less than he had anticipated, partly because there was little information in the file and partly for another reason. As he had often told others who were grieving, the anticipation of the event—holiday, anniversary, birthday—was usually worse than the event itself. That had happened to him now, and he was thankful. It was a clear sign that he had healed more than he knew.

"In her case, 'thorough' means only half a page long. Basic data and a couple of parking tickets. Short file, short life. And the information in all the files is routine."

"That's what I find interesting," Anne said, leaning toward him. Beck had long since stowed the bourbon and added ice to his Bushmill's. She retrieved her glass of wine. "The criminal records aren't extensive, even on the prostitute and the dwarf, Melin. I assumed there would be more busts to both of their credits."

"Prostitutes only get busted when there's an election coming up." Beck flipped through the folder with Melin's name on it. "Melin's minor scrapes weren't enough to warrant surveillance. He was a small fish in a big sea." Matt looked down the column under Arrests. "Nope. I don't think there will be anything on any of them under this rubric. So much for the police hits theory." He looked up at Anne. "Take it a category at a time."

"What about date of birth?"

"That doesn't help. The victims' ages were quite different according to my notes here." He glanced at the scribblings on the legal pad in his lap. "Well, no—maybe they weren't. The first couple was young."

"So was the prostitute—and Kate. That's one grouping. The other grouping would be around the other end of the age spectrum, wouldn't it?"

"Not exactly," Beck said. "Melin and Connie Bartus were around the same age, early sixties. Then the old couple were somewhere in their seventies or eighties weren't they?"

"She was eighty-two and he was seventy-nine." Anne sighed. "Lousy deal for them."

"Yeah, it was," Beck said, pensively. He wondered if he and Anne would live to their old ages together. He pictured them for a second, together in this house. It was a long way from where they were now. And yet, life was short. "Lousy deal for all of them."

Anne frowned at the files as if she had suddenly remembered something important. "You know who we're missing?"

Beck shook his head.

"Joseph McCaslin. Where does he fit in the age profiles?"

"He doesn't fit anywhere, Anne. Why should he? He's not one of the original murder set. He's after the fact. A spectator. Killed because he knew something he shouldn't have, or someone thought he did."

Anne sat back on the couch. "It was a thought. Grasping at straws, maybe."

Matt reached over to rub her neck. "So there aren't any age correlations. Correct?"

"Correct. And you can stop that sometime next week." She ran down her list. "Now, we also checked religious affiliation, and Langert was right."

"All except Kate were Roman Catholic. But, as Langert said, there's really no correlation. If a sniper went nuts in downtown White Plains or New Rochelle, the chances of hitting seven Catholics are about ninety to one in favor." He looked at the yellow sheet in his lap. "Next category. Birthplace."

He took a swallow of liquor while Anne went through the names and places they'd compiled.

"Wait a minute," she said. "Check this out."

"What?" Beck peered over her shoulder.

"According to my list, the prostitute was from North Dakota. The first couple were both students, the boy from Westchester County, the girl an out-of-state student from Florida. And Kate was from Ohio, right?"

Beck nodded.

"Now look at these four, the older subset," Anne said. "They have a different kind of printout."

Beck examined the folders. "INS records. But just on Melin, Bartus, and the Reids." He laid the three sheets side by side. "All four of them came through Ellis Island."

"That's right," Anne said. "They have an Immigration and Naturalization Service record. Makes interesting reading, don't you think?"

"Maybe not." Beck put the documents on his lap. "It's not unusual for people to change their names when they enter the United States. Sometimes they want to sound more Americanized and less foreign. That seems to have been the case with these people."

Anne pointed to the line for names on each. "Melin was Melindorf, Bartus was Bartenburg, and the Reids were Rittenwald."

"Again, not that unusual an occurrence, but it is a tie that connects those four people and separates them from the rest." Beck slid his finger over to the section marked Birthplace. "Look at this. Another crosshair. Country of origin."

Anne stared at the entry. "Write them down for me," she said, and got up to leave the room.

"What are you doing?" Beck called.

Her voice reached him from the den. "Locating that road map of Germany and Austria we used the last time we were over there."

"Third shelf from the bottom, about halfway from the right end."

The silence was broken by an enthusiastic "Got it!" Anne rushed into the living room and spread the map on the carpet. "Read off the towns one at a time," she said.

"Okay." Beck smiled at her enthusiasm. It countered his general cynicism. "Melin is listed as having been born in an Austrian town called Feyregg." He spelled it for her.

She flipped the large, yellow road map over for the index, then put her fingers on the two cross-coordinates. "Give me a second," she said. "It's in this square somewhere. Spell it again."

"F-E-Y—"

"Feyregg! Found it." She circled the town with a red pencil. "Next one."

"Connie Bartus." He scanned the sheet. "This one is easier. Enns." He spelled the name. "Wonder if they justify the means." He grinned.

"Enns! It's easier on the map, too. It's a larger town and in bigger letters." She looked up at Beck. "And it's just south of Feyregg."

Beck joined her on the floor. "The next one is—" He showed her the name on the report.

"Langenstein," she pronounced. "Whose is that?"

"Garnet Reid, a.k.a. Garnet Rittenwald." Beck looked on the index, then flipped the sheet over and searched the same square green area.

"I think I may have seen that one already," Anne said. "Here! I was right."

"It's due north of Enns," Matt said, his eyes intent on the map. "Circle that one, too."

"And Mr. Reid?"

"Arnold," Beck said. "Arnold is from—" He took a second to pronounce the word. "Schwertberg."

"Very good," Anne said. "Let's not even search for it on the index. It has to be in this area somewhere."

Beck focused on the map's small printed names. He made a mental circle around Enns and searched each quadrant systematically. "There it is," he said, putting his finger on the upper-right section of the circle.

"Northeast of Enns," Anne said, underlining the town in red.

They squatted on their heels and stared at the map.

"Well." Beck reached for his drink. "There you have it."

"But what exactly is it?"

He circled the entire area with the red pencil. "What we have is one hell of an interesting coincidence."

"And none of it came up at the trial." Anne looked at him. "This connection—whatever it means—is totally new information." She sipped the wine. "I remember a lot about the trial, Matt, my first major murder trial in New York. I paid close attention to the details, and I've reviewed them all again. The prosecuting attorney swore there was no connection between the victims whatsoever."

"The prosecuting attorney who is now county executive with relatives in Germany."

"Rinski said the same thing when I interviewed him the other day. Even Arthur Allen said so, and he had just looked at the files."

Beck picked up a folder. "So you're wondering how they missed the INS sheet?"

"Aren't you?"

"Well, to begin with, it's a very small document, attached to the back of the papers. And, it wouldn't be unusual for immigrants to end up in this area of the state."

"But wouldn't you think the prosecuting attorney would check out the names of the towns, just as we did?"

"No, not at all," Beck said. This was one place where his cynicism was on target. "They weren't looking for any connection. They were convinced that the murders were the work of a delusional retarded man who'd confessed. And even if they did find it, it wouldn't have given them anything to correlate with the others. Remember, there are four other victims who were U.S. natives and had nothing to do with the immigrants from this region of Austria."

Suddenly he couldn't breathe. Shock grasped his throat. His heart raced.

"Oh, my God!" Anne looked at him, her eyes wet with tears.

"That means," he said in a choked whisper, "that four people were murdered at random to cover up the deaths of these four."

The truth washed over him, overwhelmed him with its immensity. He could not carry the crushing weight of it, reprocess ten years of certainty crumbling to lies in front of him. Not only had Kate's death been senseless, it was a mere ruse by an insidious killer, a gruesome means to a horrible end. He broke the grip at his throat, gasped to fill his lungs.

"No!" he yelled. "This cannot be happening." He hurled his glass against the wall, shattering it.

He felt Anne's arms around him and dropped his head to her neck. He wept wrenching tears as he released dormant emotions held in check for years.

"Stupid," he whispered. "Senseless. She didn't have to die."

"I understand, Matt." He heard Anne sob and somehow realized his grief had grasped hers, pulled it to the present. "I feel the same about Robert. Stupid. Senseless. For what? Like Kate."

But it was not the same. Robert had died trying to free hostages. The best that could be said of Kate's death was that she took the place of another innocent victim. "He died for country."

"Bullshit, Matt." Anne cried even more. "All about power and money. Politics."

Beck drew her closer. They both cried until they were so empty they could cry no more. He kept his arm around her. They moved to the couch and he handed over her glass.

"Nice arm," she said, nodding at the wall.

"Yeah." He poured himself a drink in another glass. "I particularly like the way the whiskey dribbles through the paint, changing its color permanently." He sat down next to her, blew his nose, and tossed her the box of tissues so she could do the same. "Who says grief can't be creative?"

Anne sighed. "Why didn't we ever do that before?"

"Never had to." He echoed her sigh. "We both had our losses packed away, supposedly understood, accepted." He pointed to the folders. "And now this. It rips us open, especially given everything that's happened, when we've nearly lost each other and are terrified it will happen again. Meaningless, random, useless death."

"As if murder were ever anything else."

Matt sipped his drink and propped his feet on the coffee table. "There are two things we have to do," he said.

"I'm listening."

Matt kissed her. "The first is to love each other in spite of it, knowing one of us will die before the other."

"Unless we're lucky the next time we're confronted with a blonde in a blue Chevy with a gun. Then we could go together." She kissed him back.

"I'm serious."

"So am I. What's the second thing?"

Matt picked up the folders of the four murder victims from Austria. "These make it clear that Tod Engel could not have planned these murders." He gently touched Kate's folder. "So the second thing is, we have to find the real murderer."

Anne retrieved the map. "Well, we suspected that would be the case. I suppose we should turn this information over to Baumschen, don't you?"

Matt sipped the whiskey and thought for a minute. He was exhausted, empty, floating near sleep. The booze was definitely sinking in. "I don't know. I'm not sure I trust the man. It's just a little too convenient that he happened to show up right when this burst wide open. And he wasn't exactly effusive with information about his investigation." He closed his eyes and listened to Anne's breathing. He stirred when she pulled away.

"I know what I have to do."

"Huh?"

She held up the map. "What we don't know is what these four towns have in common."

"And not much of a way to find out, either."

"Maybe," she said pensively. "Maybe not."

"Meaning what?"

"Meaning I need to go to these places and dig around. There happens to be an international mayor's conference in Vienna this time of year. And since the mayor of New York will be there, it seems only fitting that someone from *CityMag* cover it, don't you think?"

Beck squirmed at the idea of her going off without him. "Are you sure Twitch will let you go?"

"He knows a story when he smells it. He'll let me go, especially if I tell him I'm hooking up with Baumschen over there."

Matt cupped her chin in his hand. "Listen, Anne. This is serious business." His voice lowered. "If we're right about these connections, we're dealing with something that's scrupulously been kept secret for more than a decade."

"Something that some people would do almost anything to keep secret," she said. "Like breaking into my apartment, killing McCaslin, and the woman tailing us. And nearly killing you and Bishop Langert."

Matt pulled her back to him. "I don't think I want to be separated from you just now, especially after what we've learned." He felt closer than ever to her. He didn't want her to go to Europe when questions of terrorism were in the air, when the real Deathangel was still out there somewhere, maybe even in Austria. Who the hell knew?

"I'll be fine," Anne said. "Or I won't be. Either way I have to go and look. There's no guarantee of anything. You and I know that better than most people."

Why was it that as soon as he grew truly close to someone, they left? "Can you go later this week?"

"Sure," she said, grinning. "Tomorrow is when I had in mind."

"Great."

"My only problem is I'll have to go without the LadyHawke. Too difficult to explain on the plane."

He didn't like it. "What if we both went. Too suspicious?"

"Especially after our little visit to Rinski and the property room at the County Courthouse." She took his hand. "No, Matt. The conference is a good cover. If there is anyone watching us, they'll think we've dropped the whole issue. You'll be here at work, and I'll be there at work. I promise I'll be careful."

"You're going regardless of what I say." Beck knew he'd be disappointed if she did anything else. She wouldn't be the woman he loved, for the reasons he loved her.

"It's the only way we'll discover what those four people had in common."

Beck corrected her. "Five. The four victims and Deathangel."

The house was dark except for the bathroom light in the master bedroom. Anne lay beneath the cool sheets. She listened to the reassuring sound of Matt brushing his teeth.

The light went out, and she watched his shadowy outline move from the bathroom door to the other side of the bed.

"Matt?" she said, as he pulled back the covers.

"What?"

"Before you get in?"

"Yes?"

"Would you close the bedroom door?"

He turned away and put his hand on the knob. Anne spoke softly again from the bed.

"And Matt?"

"Yes?"

"Just this once—lock it."

Chapter 8

M att Beck stood behind Art Allen in the line at the entrance to St. Jude's Episcopal Church, the gray morning drizzle dampening his clothes as well as his spirits. Protocol demanded that Bishop Langert conduct the service, and Matt was glad Langert had the sensitivity not to ask him to assist. The emotional memories were too overwhelming, especially now. He would sit toward the back with the rebellious Art Allen, who would provide some distraction from the intensity of the service.

Matt moved forward too quickly and missed a step, bumping into his friend. "Jesus, Art," he said, making a face. "When was the last time you cleaned that sport coat? Smells like sweat mixed with moth piss."

"Nineteen eighty-five," Allen said. "You don't like the odor, don't wear it. In fact, don't even sit by it."

"Gives new meaning to the phrase 'church pew,' " Beck mumbled. He wondered if Allen would have a whole bench to himself.

They were about to enter the church when Beck poked Allen and pointed to the street. They turned to see an awed vestryman lift away yellow cones, allowing a long black limo to park behind the hearse.

The Right Reverend John Langert slowly emerged, his gray hair accenting his pale skin.

"Looks like Jesus coming out of the tomb," Allen said.

"Jesus had a better complexion," Beck responded. "That gas attack really knocked him flat."

"Not for long," Allen looked away. "He's got to put on a good show here so everyone can see he's fit for presiding bishop. It helps that he's such a health fanatic."

"Yeah, I can see that from the smoke following him out of the car." Matt was surprised that Langert hadn't kicked the nicotine habit.

Allen stared at the ground. "The guy works out twice a day. He's got muscles better than yours and a cardiovascular system second only to Bill Rogers."

"Who is dead, you know." Beck remembered reading that the running enthusiast had died on the trail.

"Like I said."

Matt watched the bishop stop in front of several reporters who had formed a virtual wall with microphones and cameras. The bishop of New

York conducting the funeral of a murdered priest made for sensational news. It might even make the network link in the evening. Beck wondered why Langert took so long answering their questions.

"The boy never misses an opportunity to grandstand," Allen said, turning back to him. "You watch. This is just the beginning, setting the stage for when he gets elected PB. Then he'll be on Nightline once a month about some issue or other."

"Maybe there's nothing wrong with that if it's the right issue, Art."

"Sure."

Beck smiled and shook his head. He watched Langert nod to the reporters and push through the crowd, up the steps toward himself and Allen.

"Good morning, Matt. Good to see you again so soon. Sorry I had to leave lunch like that yesterday."

"Hello, Arthur." The bishop stuck out his hand.

Allen nodded and shook it.

"Close call the other day," Beck said. "How're you feeling?"

"Too close for comfort." Langert frowned, stepping under the canopied doorway to get out of the drizzle. "Thanks entirely to you pulling me away from the car, I'm much better. Sitting up, taking nourishment. I'll be fully back on my feet in a week or so."

"So why would anyone try to off you, Bishop?" Allen said.

"Lots of reasons." Langert sighed. "Most having to do not with reality, but with the fantasy that I either could or should be doing something other than my job." He handed his cape to a man who appeared to be his regular chauffeur. Beck thought he was either a brave soul or a fellow desperate for work. "There are a lot of people out there unhappy about the stands I've taken."

"Including the one on Deathangel?" Allen asked.

"Yes," Langert said. "As a matter of fact I talked with Matt and Anne about that just yesterday." He took Allen's hand. "I know you think I catapulted into office on the back of Tod Engel and that I have given up my commitment to the things we talked about as a threesome—you, Matt, and I—so many years ago. All I can tell you is that you cannot see behind the scenes, and I would urge you to look deeper than the ten o'clock news bytes I just prattled off over there." Langert released Allen's hand and turned to Matt. "You must excuse me now. I have to go vest for the service. Give my regards to Anne." The chauffeur cleared a path for him to enter the church, and they vanished in the crowd.

"Why do you do that?" Beck asked Allen. "Why do you dislike him so much?"

"Never trust anyone in authority," Allen said. "Machiavelli was right. 'Power corrupts. Absolute power corrupts absolutely.' That's why I have studiously endeavored to remain on the bottom rung."

"Doesn't that depend on how you use it?"

"Not according to our boy J.C.," Allen said as they walked into the church. "Jesus eschewed power at every opportunity. In the wilderness, that's what the devil kept tempting him with, three times, and Jesus rejected it every time."

Matt pointed to empty seats in a back pew. "That's because the devil, like the rest of us, didn't pay any attention to what Jesus said about power—that none of us, including his apostles, understood what power was, understood what glory was. If we did, we wouldn't find the devil's suggestions so enticing."

"Thank you, Reginald Fuller, renowned professor of the New Testament."

"At least one of us remembers our seminary classes," Matt chided, as they sat down. He had more to say but didn't want to argue during the service, which was about to begin. Allen whispered that the front three pews of clergy looked like rows of crows waiting to be first for refreshments.

Matt shifted uncomfortably in his seat. From this view, in the right rear corner, he could observe most of the congregation. He pretended to read the prayer book and tried to scan the backs of heads stoically lined up in the dark mahogany pews. Who had returned to the scene of the crime? Who was here out of curiosity? Occasionally, he could make out a familiar outline of clergy or laity. As the congregation stood and the bishop solemnly led the casket down the aisle to the altar, Beck began to locate profiles of people he had guessed might show up at this particular event.

Martin Ehrhart was the first. The county executive sat in a prominent position directly behind the clergy. It was a senate election year, with Ehrhart the leading candidate. Stooping to coming to funerals.

As the congregation sat down, Beck saw the big, unkempt man just behind Ehrhart—Police Commissioner James Rinski. He figured Westchester County's top cop would put in an appearance. McCaslin was killed on Rinski's watch, after all. Beck crossed one leg over the other. Or maybe he had more than professional responsibility at stake today. Nothing was out of the question. Rinski might be here to hold political hands with Ehrhart. He wondered what else they shared. Hell, maybe Rinski just came to ogle the female priests.

Allen nudged him. "What's he doing here?"

"Who?" Beck said.

"Three rows in front to the right of the stained-glass window of St. Sebastian. The guy in the out-of-style blue suit with the uniforms on either side. My favorite Martian, I mean warden. Richard Williams."

Beck wrinkled his brow. What connection could Williams have with McCaslin? Joe had never mentioned him. And there was no way, presumably, that Williams could know of McCaslin's revelation regarding Deathangel. Or could he? Was that the reason the warden had slammed Engel into solitary, as Art had said?

Matt watched the bishop climb into the pulpit but forced himself not to listen to the words. There was nothing conciliatory to say. McCaslin's death was horrible, tragic, and untimely, and he, Matt Beck, had been the decision-maker to end it. The only grace was that the death was peaceful, a quiet end to a violent assault.

"See what I mean?" Allen said when Langert began reading the litany.

"Huh?"

"The sermon, or weren't you listening?"

"Actually, I'm afraid I spaced out," Beck whispered.

"This is a perfect opportunity for Langert to talk about social issues, crime, compassion, forgiveness, violence. And instead it sounds like a canned funeral speech he's given a hundred times."

"Maybe that's how you get to be presiding bishop," Matt said.

"Unless somebody takes you off the count first."

"Just don't let it be you," Beck said, patting Allen. "At least it's over now," he added as the prayers ended and the casket was rolled back down the red-carpeted aisle to the hearse. The crowd moved like sludge through a straw into the parish hall for a reception with the bishop. There would be no trip to the graveyard. What little family McCaslin had in Pennsylvania had made arrangements with Matt for cremation and subsequent interment there. Beck and Allen's line of sludge oozed its way toward the door to the parish hall.

"Excuse me," a voice from behind said. Matt twisted to see a hand on Allen's shoulder. It was Richard Williams. "Was that standard procedure or did the deceased do something so particularly heinous that his very name ought not to be mentioned?"

Allen answered, "Unfortunately, it is standard procedure with this bishop to follow the Episcopal tradition of focusing the burial office on the gospel rather than mentioning the name of the person in whose honor the party is being given."

Beck drifted with the flow of the crowd, trying to stay even with the other two. He decided it might not hurt to turn up the heat a little. "The only heinous crime I know of that Father McCaslin committed was raising the question of the Deathangel murders." He looked at Allen.

The warden's response was immediate. "What question was that, Father Beck?"

"The question of whether or not Tod Engel is really Deathangel."

"Who else could it be?" Williams smiled a controlled smile. "It seems to me that question was answered ten years ago. And I can assure you that his behavior since that time has consistently reinforced that guilty verdict."

And warranted isolation? Beck wondered. "How did you know Joe McCaslin?" he said instead.

"I didn't. But a lot of my men did. The state prison system is connected by officers who transfer around. Many of the men at Weston were once assigned down the street at Sing Sing and used to come to this church before shift. Some are here today. I heard them talking about it in the mess hall this week and decided I'd come along for a show of support."

Beck saw that Art Allen had "how thoughtful" written all over his face. "Since you see Engel so often, Warden, I'd be very interested," Matt said, thrusting a business card into the man's hand, "in knowing if you ever hear him say anything about the case. As you are aware, Bishop Langert has always supported him, and, since the Demming article in *CityMag*, there seems to be interest in opening up the case again." That should increase the temperature, he thought, right under your collar instead of mine.

"That would be a very stupid thing to do," Williams snorted. "It would waste taxpayer money and be cruel to the man himself, don't you think?"

"Not if he was innocent," Allen chimed in.

"You think everyone is innocent, Chaplain."

"Not everyone, Warden."

"I'll see you back at Weston," Williams said, abruptly turning away. "Father Beck, I'll keep in mind what you said."

"I'll bet he will," Allen said. "I think I'm going to head back to my nice prison full of ax murderers, rapists, and cannibals, where it's safe. I'll catch up to you later." He wrapped his scarf around his neck and started to leave, then paused. "By the way, any of that BCI stuff useful?"

Matt decided it was better to keep the answer between him and Anne for the moment. "Some of it, maybe. Thanks for getting it." He watched Allen walk out the door and wondered if the man would ever find something to live for. On the other hand, maybe he had. Maybe there was something to staying on the bottom rung, siding with the emotionally or economically downtrodden and spending your life with them.

He saw the bishop enter the parish hall. On the other hand, he mused, there was the path Langert had taken to positions of ever higher influence. And that influence had a great effect on many more people than Beck or Allen could have. Besides, if men and women like Langert didn't hold those positions and use them wisely, others of less savory natures would. And here was one of them now, watching the women intently.

Beck grabbed some coffee and wandered up to the man. "Looking for the usual suspects, Commissioner Rinski?"

"Everybody's a possible, Reverend," Rinski said. "Even you."

Beck wondered if he was referring to the incident in the property room. "Sounds like something Captain Steiner would say. Just before he ran over a suspect."

Rinski was unmoved. "The way I hear it, he saved your butt from death by Chevrolet." Beck watched the commissioner's eyes follow a bosomy woman in a low-cut black dress. "For which I am eternally grateful, of course. Too bad we didn't have the chance to interview the woman, though. Might have been interesting to learn who she worked for."

Rinski put his hand on the pack of cigarettes in his shirt pocket as if to signal his exit. "Maybe somebody didn't like you sticking your collar into their business." He nodded in the direction of Langert. "Just like the bishop. You shove your neck out far enough, Reverend, somebody's gonna take a slice at it. You know what I mean?" He took out a cigarette and placed it between his lips. "You take care of yourself, Reverend. And that Demming chick, too." He turned his back. "Yeah. You take special good care of her."

So much for turning up the heat, Beck thought, putting his hand to the scab on his neck. Was Rinski's comment a warning or a confirmation?

"Excuse me, Father Beck?" Matt swung around to face Ehrhart, neatly dressed in a dark gray suit and maroon tie. The man did not smile except when he was scanning the room, acknowledging people with a nod or a wave. He looked older and heavier than when he had prosecuted Engel. "I just want to offer my condolences." It was the same line he had expressed to Beck about Kate a decade ago, and Matt was a little taken aback by the comment. "I am sure this death is quite a blow to you, considering your long friendship."

How did he know that? Of course, it could be discovered with very little checking. But why would Ehrhart bother? Had Rinski tracked down the information after Steiner found Beck in the property room? "Yes, it is quite a loss. How is it that you knew Father McCaslin?"

Ehrhart graced Beck with a cold stare and an icy voice. He had evidently heard the underlying accusatory tone. "Father McCaslin came to the county on many occasions for block grants and other governmental assistance for this community. I worked with him on several projects through the years, even before I become county executive." Ehrhart paused. "Why? Did you think I was simply here to politick for the upcoming election?"

Beck ignored the parry. "Did you ever attend services here? Come for the sacraments?" Like confession and absolution, you asshole. Ehrhart seemed to ponder the question as though it were a trick, which it was.

"Actually, I have from time to time, when my schedule was rushed. I find the smallness of St. Jude's quaint, and McCaslin's services were always short and to the point." He glanced at his watch. "Which reminds me, appointments call." Ehrhart shook Beck's hand. "Stop by if I can ever be of help, Father Beck."

"I'll take you up on that, believe me, when it comes to reopening the Deathangel case."

Ehrhart performed a one-eighty. "I would advise strongly against that." He pressed close enough to speak softly and still be heard over the din of the crowd. "As you know, I prosecuted that case. It was air-tight, a full confession. No questions remained to be answered. It would be a tragedy to all involved to stir up things that have settled after all this time. I would think you would prefer to let your wife's memory rest in peace."

Matt held his rising anger in check and slammed the ball back to Ehrhart. "There is one question that hasn't been answered, however, and that is why Joe McCaslin was murdered."

"I know nothing about that, Father, except that Commissioner Rinski and his team tell me it was entirely random, the result of an attempted robbery."

Random. Like the four other victims of Deathangel.

"I'm sure Father McCaslin's murder has nothing to do with the Deathangel matter."

Beck looked straight at the County Executive and said, "Doesn't it?"

"No, it most assuredly does not." Ehrhart turned away again. "Good day."

For somebody who doesn't know anything about the McCaslin murder, he sure is opinionated about it, Beck thought. He'd managed to light a small fire there, though, and maybe he could do the same with Rinski. He wondered what the effect of all this heating up would be. These people, whoever they were, whichever ones were involved, played for keeps.

He'd have to be especially careful from here on out. As he was about to search out McCaslin's relatives, he heard a familiar voice.

"Matthew," John Langert said.

"Yes, Bishop?" Beck looked with curiosity at the man in the purple shirt, which gave color to his wan complexion. "What is it?"

"I hope this isn't a bad moment to ask this, but your question fascinated me the other day at the restaurant, and I pondered it the whole time I was at the hospital."

Beck expressed his puzzlement.

"The one about the religious preferences of the victims of Deathangel." The Bishop lowered his voice. "Have you learned anything more about that connection?"

Odd that the bishop should ask at this particular time. "As a matter of fact," Beck said, "Anne and I may have turned up something useful, or at least interesting, not about religious preference but about another issue entirely."

Langert's bushy gray eyebrows arched like caterpillars. "And what would that be?"

Not a chance, Beck thought. Not even with you. "I'm afraid it has to be under the stole for now," he said. "We're still poking around to see if what we found means anything. I don't want to get your hopes up for nothing."

"Well, it sounds like good detective work on your part, I must say. Did any of the information you uncovered come out at Engel's trial?"

"It did not, because nobody thought to ask, or, perhaps more to the point, it may have been purposely overlooked by those with motives other than the execution of justice."

The Bishop placed his hand on Beck's arm, and he was struck again by how hard his grip was. "That is essentially what I've been getting at all these years. Perhaps with your new connection, we will have enough evidence to reopen the case."

Beck patted his hand and smiled. "I'd be careful who you say that to around here, Bishop. The last person who suggested it is now on his way to the crematory. And you were almost not far behind him. You might want to consider tightening your own security now. You can't advocate for Engel if you're one of the real villain's victims."

Langert thanked him for his concern and said, "When I feel better, maybe next week, we must talk. You must come to my place in the city and we will discuss this further. It's very exciting." He motioned across the room for his chauffeur. "I tire too easily right now. I really have to get home to the comfort of my living room."

The chauffeur, a short stocky man in black coat and driver's hat, who Beck thought seemed vaguely familiar, brought out the bishop's coat. Langert introduced him as his usual driver. "Lucky for Earl, he wasn't in the car yesterday, don't you think? He was off visiting his mother in Jersey."

"Incredibly lucky," Matt said, wondering how to check on Earl's story and his background. "Good day, Bishop. And take care of yourself."

Langert disappeared into the crowd of reporters and cameras again. Matt caught sight of Ehrhart exchanging what appeared to be angry words with Rinski. Unable to eavesdrop, he meandered outside, near the bishop's limousine. Despite his supposed exhaustion, Langert had stopped to talk privately with Warden Richard Williams. Were they discussing Tod Engel? Probably so. Matt bet the conversation was a lot different from the one between Rinski and Ehrhart.

Later, Beck drove the black Spider with its canvas top flapping beneath the pouring rain on the interstate. He recalled a comment about the car's safety in New York and realized where he had seen the bishop's chauffeur. He was one of many men of similar description who occasionally filled in for the doorman at One Pierrepont in Brooklyn Heights. He worked for Alfonse Ciccilini.

Jackson Twitchel pecked his way through the piece on the computer screen. Absorbed in editing the article, he lent only half an ear to the conversation of his staff. He liked to sit out in the bullpen sometimes and take the temperature of the place. He hated hierarchies, and when his employees saw him hard at work, it tended to improve their own performance.

"County Desk, Brady speaking. No, Anne Demming's not in at the moment."

Anne's name caught his attention, but he kept stabbing at the keys with his two forefingers, wishing like crazy he had learned to type forty years ago like his parents told him.

"Important? Just a sec." Brady's voice carried across the room. "Anybody know where Demming is?"

"Haven't seen her."

"Don't know."

"I think she's out of the country, but she doesn't want anyone to know she's gone. Burglars and shit."

"Burglars" did it. Twitchel looked up and saw the phone dangling in Brady's hand. Whoever was calling could hear everything that was said in the press room. He stood up hastily as one of the secretaries yelled from her cubicle.

"She's in Vienna at that stupid mayor's conference, isn't she? I processed her ticket yesterday."

Twitchel strode across the office and snatched the phone from Brady. "Who is this?" he said to the monotone buzz of the empty line.

Beck zipped his jacket against the cool dampness of the late September afternoon. He sat on a bench on the Brooklyn Heights Promenade, looking out at one of his beloved views of New York. To his left stood the Statue of Liberty and the Battery, to his right the Brooklyn Bridge; straight ahead the lights of Manhattan twinkled in the dusk. It would be about thirty minutes before the sun set and the landscape turned black and white.

Black and white, he mused. It would be nice if things were that clear cut. Maybe they would be once he talked with the man he was meeting here. He stared at the boats leaving the harbor, passing the statue, whose lights were now on.

A gruff voice startled him. "Father Beck?"

Matt looked up to see the imposing frame of Al Ciccilini standing over him. He got up and shook hands. "Want to walk or sit?"

"Sit. Been on my feet most of the day at One Pierrepont, you know."

Beck opened a brown bag and handed him a large paper cup, then took the other out for himself. He wanted this meeting to seem like they were on the same side, against whoever it was that broke into Anne's condo. "Brought us coffee. Assume you take yours regular?" he said as they settled on the bench.

"You got it. Thanks."

"It's the bribe for information on your employee." And maybe about yourself, as well.

"Yeah," Ciccilini said, popping the lid off the cup. "Turns out there's some shit to tell about him, too. Excuse the language."

"Forget the language. I've heard it at least once before in my life and use it regularly." He sipped the steaming coffee and stared past Ciccilini to the bridge. The lights had just come on there, too, creating that famous outline. "So. What's the story on your friend Earl?"

"First off, Earl Eslin ain't my friend, right?"

Beck nodded.

"Okay, so I hired the guy right out of prison, to give him a break, you know?"

"Which prison?"

"Rikers. But it ain't what you're thinkin'."

"Correct me."

"He wasn't an inmate, he was a hack."

"A guard?"

Ciccilini nodded. "Worked there nearly ten years. Guy's a fitness freak and black belt with muscles like hams. Seems he got a little too close to the inmates, if you get my meaning."

Beck shook his head.

"Well, he was kitin' shit in for them—drugs, chicks, whatever. As long as his bank account expanded, he didn't care. So some pissed-off inmate he probably shook down rats on him and he gets busted, but his record at Rikers is so good—no write-ups the entire time—that he plea-bargains a deal. Somewhere he heard Bishop Langert was needing a general all-around gofer, driver, and bodyguard. The judge let him go to work for Langert under strict conditions of probation, and that's who he's been with for, hell, I'd say the last twelve years."

It was growing darker and colder. Beck wrapped his hands around the hot cup. Time to cut to the chase. "So how'd he find his way to you?"

"Some nights he's off and don't feel like getting into trouble. I had a job open at One Pierrepont watching the door and he took it. He don't work all the time, but if I'm in a pinch or he has time to kill, he picks up extra money here. Been real reliable, too."

The words "kill" and "reliable" hit home. "Do you know what Eslin was doing the night of the break-in at Anne's apartment?"

"Sure do. He was driving for the bishop that night. I remember, because he specifically told me that's why he had to be off."

"I don't think so." Matt gazed out at the Statue of Liberty.

"What?" Ciccilini said, putting down his coffee.

"Langert was out of town that night."

"No offense, Father Beck, but how do you know that for sure? Maybe Earl isn't the one lying about his whereabouts."

"No offense taken," Beck said. It was a perfectly good question, and not one likely to be asked by someone involved in the break-in. Unfortunately, he had the answer. "Anne and I had lunch with Langert the next day and he was delayed because his plane back to town was late landing." Beck drank his coffee. "And Eslin would know the access code for the freight elevator, wouldn't he?"

Ciccilini nodded and downed the last of his coffee, then tossed the cup and lid into the wire basket beside the bench. "One of 'em's lying. Should be easy enough to check out, right?"

"Can you roust Eslin? Find out what the deal is?"

"Listen, Father Beck," Ciccilini said, a serious look falling over his face, "I been around enough to figure you think I might have had somethin' to do with this mess. But I'm tellin' you straight and swearin' on my mother's grave, I'm damned near as fond of Anne Demming as you are. She's good goods as far as I can see. If I hired anybody who put her in danger of any kind, I'll take care of it. Believe me."

"Okay." Beck stood and thanked him. "Let me know what you find out as soon as you can?"

"As they say, No problemo." Ciccilini turned and walked away.

Matt leaned on the fence and finished watching the sun edge down over the city. Twenty minutes later, he was speeding back to the mountain. The Spider's top was down and he had the heater on full blast, just like where he felt he was—between heaven and hell. But he had cleared up one thing. Alfonse Ciccilini was no longer a suspect.

So far, he was the only one who wasn't.

Beck was nervous. It was one thing facing the bad guys, even with Anne's gun. It was quite another breaking into the bastion of supposed good guys. The former justified any action he might take; the latter supported any action they would take. He had parked his car three blocks from the county courthouse, and now he was on his own. It would take every memory of the things his dad had taught him to get in and out without being caught. If D'Angelo had done his part, at least access was provided. The old Italian had really gone above and beyond, but he trusted Beck and disliked Steiner, who had been promoted over the sergeant. Anything that might incriminate the captain and leave the post open again D'Angelo seemed happy to do.

Street lights cast a dull glow, illuminating pockets of sidewalk as Beck walked down back streets toward the White Plains police property room. The movements of scantily clad women on the opposite corner reminded him that ten years ago in this same area, perhaps the same street, Deathangel had viciously killed one of them—for nothing. What if he was still here?

There was no other way to do this. Anne had to travel to Austria and he had to go here. Somehow, he'd feel safer in Austria. He knew D'Angelo could not return to the property room for him without attracting suspicion. And Beck could not bring in a group of Boy Scouts, as he had originally planned, to attempt another look. By the time they managed it, the property would probably be missing or he would be under such scrutiny that he could never get close enough to obtain the answer he needed. A court order was possible, but it would also take time, and he understood the police system well enough to know that time would be spent tampering with evidence. He only hoped what he sought had not already been altered beyond usefulness.

He approached the street at the rear of the courthouse and gathered his dark jacket around his neck, obscuring his white collar. If necessary—that is, if he got caught—he hoped to unzip the jacket, show the collar, and beg off with an excuse of being locked in a stairwell and not knowing how to exit. Flimsy, he thought. Very flimsy. He would have to come up with something better—or not get caught.

The green lighted numbers on his watch read 11:30, the time D'Angelo said to enter the door by the dumpster. Shift change was over; the night shift was still settling in with unfinished paperwork, fresh coffee, and stale doughnuts. They would think any noises were stragglers from the three-to-eleven.

Beck slipped on the latex surgeon's gloves he had acquired from the hospital O.R. and crept through the shadows to the dumpster. The stench nearly made him puke. Why was it he could handle the hospital smells of vomit, feces, urine, and necrotized body parts, but the stench of rotting food turned his stomach?

He waited to make sure there was no activity, as D'Angelo had told him to do, for as long as he could stand it, then quickly made for the door.

As promised, it was open.

Beck removed the tiny piece of wood from the latch. He would retrieve all the items D'Angelo had used to allow entry. He would not need them on the way out. He had learned from his dad that buildings were designed to get out of; getting in was the hard part. But not now, he thought, as he worked his way up the darkened stairwell, using the laser penlight Anne had given him last Christmas. He stopped at the third floor and listened to the conversation in the county police patrol room.

Sergeant D'Angelo was right again. Talk centered on questions about paperwork. Radio transmissions from patrol cars taking their assigned routes for the night were the only interruptions to the mundane chatter.

Beck tried to put the penlight in his pocket, but he dropped it. The clatter sounded like the clanging of a church bell from the distance of two feet.

He stood motionless, listening, waiting. There was no noise from inside. He imagined them sitting like bird dogs, waiting for the next sound to go on point. A small sound. Any sound.

But he did not oblige them. He crouched in the darkness, knowing he could wait them out. If only they would let him. If only they would not barge through the exit door into the stairwell.

One minute passed. Then two. Suddenly a Code Three came across the radio, and their talk resumed.

Beck breathed deeply for the first time in minutes. He bent over and felt on the floor for the light. His clammy hand nudged it, and it began to roll toward the stairs. At the last second he caught it in midair. Then, even more slowly than before, he rose and located the first step again.

When he reached what he thought was the fifth floor, he flicked on the light. There, on the fire door, was the number 5. In the lock was a small piece of wood, which he stashed in his pocket as he shut the door behind him. Ironic, he thought, shavings of wood leading him closer to the killer, just as they had done with Tod Engel.

His heart beat wildly as the outline of the steel cage became clear. D'Angelo said budget cutbacks meant the property storage room wasn't manned on the graveyard shift. Any property that came in overnight was held downstairs in the property check-in room. Anybody who needed access to the storage area could wait until the sun was up.

Street lights through the dirty windows provided enough illumination for Beck to see his way around the corner to the door gate. There, too, D'Angelo had done his job. The lock, from a distance, seemed closed and secure. But as Matt gripped the gate and pulled, it opened.

The tiny squeak the gate made sounded to him like the brakes of a subway train. He was sure his dad could have done this silently. He felt like a novice, setting off every loud noise in the building. He entered the steel cage and used the laser in the inner areas of the shelving, trying to remember which row contained the evidence from the trial.

He went to the third row, walked to the end, and stooped to look at the bottom shelf. He was certain this was where D'Angelo had led him before.

But this time the tray was marked "Stanser Trial."

Someone had replaced the tray and hidden the Engel evidence.

Frantic, Beck flashed his light on the labels in the aisle. Moving to the aisle in front and behind it, he hoped he had simply miscalculated the correct area in the dark.

But he was sure it had been the third aisle—the last basket at the end. He looked again at the labels on the other boxes. And then he noticed the difference.

The other labels were worn and dusty, just as the one for the Engel case had been the other day. But the Stanser label was new. Too new.

He returned to the carton and hauled it into the aisle. It was the Engel evidence with a new name tag.

He held the light in his mouth and focused it on the contents of the carton. He removed the plastic bags containing the six carved wooden angels and examined them again, one by one. His heart beat faster when he came to the one with Kate's name on it, but something was different. Maybe it was the fear of being caught, maybe it was the pressure of time, but he put it beside the others and moved on. He found the envelope containing the piece of hair that had added convincing fuel to the fire that sought to burn Tod Engel at his trial. Stuffing the small packet under his jacket and into his shirt, Beck understood that this was a break with the law. He would have a hell of a time explaining it if he was wrong.

He removed several other pieces of evidence, including the telephone from Engel's apartment, and spread them on the floor. Then he heard a noise at the door.

At first Beck did not move. He sat still, his heart pounding, and he listened for the next sound.

It never came. But he was out of time. He tossed the plastic bags back in the tray, but he put the phone in another basket on the opposite row. As he replaced the angels, he counted them again, mentally tagging them with each set of murders.

One, Umbrella Point couple. Two, New Rochelle dwarf. Three, Katonah woman. Four, White Plains prostitute. Five, Pelham old couple. Six, Kate Beck.

Six incidents. Six angels.

Beck stared at the box. Something wasn't right. There was no time to think about it now, as he looked at his watch. He hoped it would surface later, maybe with Anne's help. As he slid the tray back into place, Beck heard the sound again, only this time it was directly behind him.

A footstep.

And then he could not breathe.

Chapter 9

The last thing Matt remembered was the image of a wooden angel. The first thing he saw when he forced opened his eyelids was James Rinski sitting behind a desk, expressionless. When Beck stirred in his chair, Rinski handed him a cup of coffee and sat back in his seat, hands behind his head, like a large cat that has just captured and toyed with the hopeless mouse. A large cat with a cigarette.

"You're a fortunate man, Reverend," Rinski said.

Beck didn't feel very fortunate. He felt like a flattened cartoon mouse. His head throbbed and he thought the pressure behind his eyeballs might pop them out onto Rinski's desk. He squinted through the coffee steam at the commissioner. "And how is that?"

"For openers, you're damned lucky you didn't get your ass shot off in that property room." Rinski reached for a mug on his desk and held it in both hands. Beck noticed it was the shape of a pink breast.

"And you're lucky they called me instead of dragging you down to booking to press charges and spend the night in jail, like they should have done."

Matt dragged the chair opposite him over and propped up his feet. "What hit me?" he whispered.

Rinski pointed to a lipstick-sized container on the desk. "New kind of stun spray. Paralyzes the lungs. Real experimental. Not on the market yet." He picked it up and uncapped it. "Still some bugs to work out. Causes cancer in rats."

Great, Beck thought. He hoped Rinski used it as breath freshener. "Next time, just shoot me," he said, sipping the coffee.

"Deal," the police commissioner said, unsmiling, as he unscrewed the cap of a Four Roses bottle and poured a shot into the breast mug.

"That help?" Beck asked, holding out his cup. If you drank with a person, he couldn't arrest you, could he?

"Never hurts." He doled out a shot into Matt's coffee. "That spray should wear off soon. At least, according to the guy who loaned it to me." Beck noted that the man spoke in a monotone, not exactly calm but not threatening. Should he tell him everything to watch his reaction and give him enough rope to hang himself? Or should he say nothing and risk charges? The commissioner was not going to let his prey just escape.

"You were out for forty minutes, long enough for Captain Steiner to call me and bring you here." Rinski poured more coffee for them both and perched on the desk. "Feeling better?"

Beck nodded.

"Good." Rinski lit another cigarette and glanced at his watch. Beck wondered who he had left in bed. "Then let me frame the picture for you, Reverend. It's late. I'm tired." The commissioner leaned over and blew smoke in his face. "And you are in a shitload of trouble here. Mostly felonies." His lips tightened and Beck could see the stains on his teeth. "So tell me just what the hell you were doing in my property room."

Beck coughed and considered tossing the coffee in the man's face and running. Rinski was too fat and slow to catch him. But he couldn't outrun the radio—or the gun.

"And while you're thinking of a good lie, remember that one more whiff of that shit," Rinski tapped the spray, "and you're found back on the floor upstairs, maybe not in such good condition."

Maybe with a bullet in me, Beck thought. This slimeball would do it. "Why should I tell you what you obviously know?"

"If I obviously knew it, Reverend, I wouldn't be asking. You wouldn't be here and I definitely wouldn't be wasting my time in this place at this hour of the night. So talk, damn it."

What if he didn't know about the Austrian connection between the victims? And then there was what Matt had figured out in the property room, but he would save that trump card till last. What if this was all a sham? The only way to tell was to spin it out a piece at a time and watch.

"Deathangel," Beck said.

Rinski exhaled smoke slowly. "Good start. You've got my attention."

"I'll give you the Reader's Digest version. My head can't take the full novel." Beck drained his coffee and described McCaslin's call and subsequent death.

"Coincidence," Rinski said. "A theft got out of hand when he resisted."

Matt studied the man's baggy, impassive face and described the attack on him at McCaslin's house. He thought it odd that the commissioner didn't ask what he wanted in the house, unless he already knew. Or had the disk.

"You surprised a burglar who heard the priest bought it and knew nobody was home. Big deal." Rinski leaned his elbows on the desk and crushed out the cigarette. "We're still not at the property room."

"I'm on my way, Commissioner. But the ride takes me through the little incident with Captain Steiner and the blue Chevy." Beck looked at

Rinski. "She worked for you, didn't she?"

Rinski stared back. Clearly he was considering how much to tell Beck. Apparently the decision was easier to make than Matt had expected. Either that meant Rinski believed he already knew what he was going to say or it didn't make any difference, because Beck wouldn't be around to pass along the information.

"Used to work for me." Rinski said. "But let's say I did want you tailed and employed a private expert to avoid a warrant and a court order. After Anne Demming's little tryst in here Tuesday morning and your first visit to the property room, I'd have good reason to do it."

Beck watched him light another cigarette. The stench of the unfiltered brand would be embedded in his clothes, like the stench of the man's demeanor in Anne's mind.

"If the two of you have new evidence about the Deathangel case, I want to hear about it first so I can make sure justice is served and no mistakes occur." He drank his coffee. "Hell, I was the arresting officer on the case."

"For which the grateful citizens of Westchester County rewarded you with promotion to your current position of power."

Rinski's voice tightened. "I have no provable connection to the woman who tried to kill you, Reverend Beck. So if you're implying that I purposely caused her death, you had better have stronger evidence. The actions of Captain Steiner saved your life."

And saved your ass, Beck thought. "You want to know what I was doing in that property room? Well, put this together. McCaslin is murdered, I'm assaulted at his house, your tail gets killed by your man, and then there's a gas attack on Bishop Langert."

Rinski sneered. "And your paranoid brain thinks I had something to do with that?" He shook his head. "Sure. And I was on the grassy knoll, too."

For the first time, he smiled. It was the smile of a man who had been overestimated—or wanted Matt to believe he was. That was good. Matt wanted him relaxed and overconfident when the shit hit the fan.

"Motive?" Rinski stated. "Including Langert?"

"Motive is the same in all of it."

"Deathangel." Rinski screwed up his face, as if considering the possibilities.

"Deathangel," Beck repeated. "Maybe somebody—like you—thought Langert was meeting us to share information about the case."

Rinski stared through heavy lidded eyes.

Matt decided to play the trump card, but very slowly, and watch

Rinski's face for the reply. "So either someone has a lot to lose and doesn't want the case reopened because it would mean a fall from power, or the real Deathangel is still loose in Westchester County."

Rinski, looking bored, shook his head. "The real Deathangel is in Weston Prison. The evidence presented at the trial was conclusive beyond a reasonable doubt to twelve jurors." But the muscles in his jaw tensed. He stood and walked over to Beck. "Now get to the damned point on the property room."

Matt pushed further, hoping Rinski would make a mistake. "That is the point." He leaned forward. "Not all the Deathangel evidence was presented." He paused. "And I think you know that."

Neither man spoke. Beck kept every nerve pinned on Rinski, ready to make whatever move was necessary. But Rinski returned to his seat, obviously forcing himself to calm down and regroup. He pushed forward in his chair. "I don't like you, Beck."

"I'm shattered. What's the bad news?"

"The bad news is that I could call down the full force of the law on your little escapade tonight." His cheek muscles clenched as he talked. "I could arrange it so that you never leave here, that you spend the next few days in the drunk tank at the jail, get lost in the paper shuffle, maybe end up in a cell with someone who doesn't like priests or likes them a little too much." Rinski frowned. "The bad news is that you're messing way over your holy head, and, as that head can feel from tonight, your white collar isn't going to help you out of this one."

"Listen to me, Rinski." Beck's anger flared and his eyes narrowed. "I don't like you, either. And I don't like the bullshit politics you stand for. Now I don't know exactly all that you did to help get Tod Engel convicted. I'm pretty sure you suppressed evidence or tampered with it." He pushed his chair back, his eyes focused on the unmoving Rinski. "But now I'm going to put you under an ethical obligation—as if that means anything to you any more. I'm going to tell you why you have to reopen the Deathangel case, regardless of what it means to your lazy, worthless career."

"There's nothing about that case I don't already know," the commissioner said, almost to himself. "There's absolutely no reason to screw with a solid conviction." He stared at Matt. "And no reason to screw with my lazy, worthless career, either."

Matt saw Rinski reach for the stun spray. With one sweep of his arm, Beck cleared off the desk, knocking the spray and the breast mug to the floor.

The commissioner jumped up. "You dumb shit! Look what you've done!"

Beck stood and spoke with as calm a voice as his agitated pulse could muster. "No. This is about what you've done." He gulped air to steady himself as he played the trump. "I recently learned that there was a connection—and a logical one—between some of the victims. They were not random murders."

It was as though Beck had punched him in the face. Rinski looked sobered. "Where did you discover this supposed connection?"

"In the records of the victims, of course. But then, we were motivated to find it, unlike yourself and the rest of the prosecution."

"That's crap." Rinski collapsed in his chair. Matt scrutinized his red face. He looked convincing. There was a possibility, although small, that he really did not know. "But if you don't tell me what it is you think you've got, you're withholding evidence. I can have you—"

"You can have me what, Commissioner?" Beck said sarcastically. "Let's cut the bullshit. If you were going to do anything, you'd have done it by now. You want to find out what I discovered in that property room?"

Rinski stood again. His voice was much too controlled. "I think it doesn't much matter what you found, Reverend."

Matt raised his eyebrows. Something had happened while he was out cold. "It seems that, following your break-in, some property was missing."

"Like what?"

"Like the telephone, for one thing. But we'll turn it up. You couldn't have hidden it too well in such a short time."

"What else?" So far, Rinski was fishing.

"Why don't you tell me, Reverend Beck?" Rinski came out from behind the desk. "Since you were the last one to see those items."

"Well, if I were to guess which pieces were most incriminating to you and which ones you would most like to see vanish, I would put my money on the angels."

"Now that you mention them," Rinski smiled, "those things do seem to be misplaced. Which confirms my suspicion that you're the one responsible for their whereabouts."

"Nice try. But if you pinned that on me, it would raise the whole issue for the press, wouldn't it?" Matt backed toward the door. "And besides, it still doesn't change the evidence, does it?"

"I think it does, if the evidence is gone."

"But there's still a property list that confirms what was in that box, isn't there?"

The commissioner looked puzzled.

"And somewhere in Engel's file is a certified copy of that document. Even if it were somehow to be altered, the certified copy, not to mention the transcript of the trial, would list the evidence exactly as it was presented to the jury, wouldn't it?"

"And your point would be what?"

Beck turned the doorknob. "The point is that I came back to your property room to count how many angels could stand on the head of a killer." Let Rinski believe he'd been after something specific.

Matt knew from the rage on the man's face he was on target. "Let's figure it out together, shall we?" He said, opening the door to leave. "Exactly how many angels were there in that evidence bin?"

Rinski glared back at him. "There were six occasions and eight murder victims," he said. "So we have six angels."

"Correct. That's exactly how many there were." Beck walked out the door. "But there should have been seven."

The elderly, ruddy-faced Austrian bartender waddled across the mahogany planks of Der Schwartzer Lowen with a liter stein of frothy dark beer. Anne Demming, sitting alone at a table, thought he looked like a wind-up doll. When she first entered the Black Lion to recoup from her seemingly endless search, he had been friendly on the tourist level, as had everyone in the town of Feyregg. But it was clear that the "gemutlichkeit"—conviviality—was a way to maintain distance, to avoid unpleasant topics from the past, like the people she had asked about all day.

"Ein Bier, Fraulein?"

"Danke shon," Anne said. Her college German served her well enough.

"Sind Sie allein hier?"

"Yes, I am here alone." She had not expected the question. "Why do you ask?"

"Please excuse my...broken...English, Fraulein."

"It's better than my broken German." She motioned to the seat opposite her, hoping for her first lead of the day. "Nehmen Sie ein Platz, bitte. If you have the time."

The old man motioned to a waiter to take charge of the bar and sat down. "You have a look of, I do not know, here we would say angst, on your face. That is why I asked if you were alone, or waiting for someone who did not come."

"It's more like I've been looking for someone who's supposed to be here but isn't." Maybe if she began in generalities he would be more likely to help.

The bartender clasped his hands. "Ich verstehe nicht. What do you mean?"

She took a long drink of the beer and wiped the brown foam from her lips. "I mean, Herr Oper," she said, addressing him with the formal term of a waiter, "that I have spent the entire day looking for people who are supposed to have been born in this village and other villages nearby and there are simply no records on them to be found."

"But that is not so unusual, Fraulein—"

"Demming." She was surprised and pleased at the contact. "Anne Demming." She extended her hand. Whatever he was up to was not apparent, if he was up to anything. Maybe he was just being friendly. Or maybe he had heard of her questions through the short village grapevine and sought to discover her real reason for searching out these people. In either case, she would play along.

He shook her hand politely. "Ich bin Herr Kremsbach. I own this restaurant."

"And your English?"

"From the Americans during the war. They helped us in the Resistance."

Why was it that every Austrian she met was in the Resistance? With all that opposition going on, it was a wonder Hitler lasted a week. Or maybe they changed sides—and memories—after the war. "You must have worked closely with them. Your pronunciation is nearly perfect."

"Jaja. Those were years of meaning and struggle. Not like today. The young, they have no sense of what those times were like."

Anne nodded and drank the beer. She could not imagine what they were like either, though she had felt her loss at the hands of war, a senseless, egotistical war that would effect the rest of her life, too.

Herr Kremsbach smiled, "But I was telling you, Ich glaube, about the lack of accurate records. During the war, the Nazis controlled this entire country. They either destroyed records or severely altered them to suit their purposes. The only records they were unable to touch belonged zu den Kirchen."

Matt had told her that was true in other countries as well. When official records were lost or destroyed, those painstakingly kept by the churches remained, logged by hand, for generations. "How did the church records escape?"

"Because the people would not permit it. It was one thing to destroy a birth certificate or alter a name on such a document. It was quite another to destroy or alter a baptismal certificate. Also, die priester—the priests—often hid the documents in tombs in the catacombs."

"What about grave markers?" They often confirmed church records. She knew that from a case she had investigated in Austin.

"Those should still be intact, unless the Nazis had some reason to—how do you say it—obliterate them?"

Pleased that she seemed to be receiving some assistance, Anne tried to maintain her academic interest. "But I checked the graveyards also, and I still can't find any sign that these people existed."

"Vielleicht—perhaps—kann ich Ihnen helfen," he said. "But before I help, I must, out of courtesy, of course, join you." The man lumbered from his chair and returned with a smaller stein of beer.

"Is it only the tourists who order liter steins?" Anne asked when he sat down again.

"Nein. Not the tourists only. But they order them more than we do, at least here in Feyregg." He looked at her half-empty stein. "You have done better than most, already. Many tourists cannot drink even half the amount."

She clicked her stein to his. "I believe the word is 'prosit.' " She liked this rotund Austrian with red cheeks and black moustache. She wondered if the state paid him to look like this so tourists could take pictures.

"To your health," he replied.

She opened her zippered bag and took out a folder. "Here are the names and their towns," she said, handing him the list. "All I've gotten from the folks in Langenstein and Enns have been cold stares and silence."

"That is most unlike—" the old man began. He stopped when he saw the names.

"What is it, Herr Kremsbach? Why won't anyone help me find these people who are not here?"

The man finished the small stein of beer and motioned to the waiter to bring him another. "It is I who should have had the liter, Miss Demming." He did not speak to the waiter. "Errinern sie sich—excuse me. There is much you must remember about this part of the world, Miss Demming."

"If you're talking about the war—that was fifty years ago." If you're talking about something else, tell me what it is, she thought.

"But many of us still have horrible memories that will die only when we do." He swallowed a drink of the dark brew. "We can only pray to God that we have not passed on too many of those feelings to our children and grandchildren. Although, if you read the papers here, you will see that there is a resurgence of the hatred from those ugly times."

"But what has that to do with these names?" She pulled a sheaf of photographs from another folder. "And these pictures."

The blood drained from Kremsbach's face. "Please, Miss Demming. Sagen sie—tell me—why do you want to know about these people?"

Pay dirt, she thought. I've got you hooked now. "Will you tell me what you know if I do?"

"Jaja. Though you may not wish to hear it."

She decided to level with him. If she fabricated a story, he would bolt. "I work for a magazine in the states. About ten years ago there was a series of murders." She pointed to the names and photos. "All of these people were killed by the same person. No one knows why. They still don't. Recent evidence has emerged indicating that perhaps the wrong man has been imprisoned for the murders. My friend and I are trying to reopen the case."

She paused for a moment to drink the beer and thought of Matt. Whether it was the alcohol on an empty stomach or jet lag or both, she felt a split second of yearning for him. She wished he was sitting in that booth with her, instead she was sitting across from Heidi's father.

She put down the stein and spread out the photos. "Part of the new evidence is that these four people were all from the same area and emigrated at about the same time. Their exit visas from Austria all show the exact same date, in fact—May 25, 1945.

"Genug. Das is genug. Enough, Miss Demming." Kremsbach was obviously shaken. "I only wish I had not promised to tell you what it is you want to know."

Anne's heart beat faster. "Why? What is it?"

The big man leaned over his bulging, intertwined hands and whispered to her. "I know these names. All of us in these villages—we know these names." He was so close she could smell the beer on his breath. "These people all worked for the Nazis during the war." He sat back a little and looked again at the list. "I cannot speak for all of them. I have only heard stories of some of these names because I have relatives in two of these other villages, in Schwertberg and Enns. But I can speak about Melindorf, or Melin as you call him. He was from here, from Feyregg."

Anne found herself matching his quiet tone. "His name was shortened when he emigrated to the states."

"Yes." He looked at her intently. "He and the others here—you said they are all dead?"

She nodded. He was winding down. Ending. She had not uncovered all she wanted, but it was more than she had heard all day. Maybe it was best not to push Kremsbach further. "All of them. But what did they have in common? Was it what they did for the Nazis?"

"Ich bin—I am afraid that is all I can tell you." He heaved his bulk out of the small booth and stood. "Except to leave well enough alone. These people do not deserve to be remembered. That is why their records no longer exist. If they are now dead, so much the better. One can only hope they died violently and painfully."

"But what—?"

"No more, Miss Demming." The man cut her off. "Please accept the beer and my advice with compliments from the house." He bowed politely, smiled briefly, and waddled back to his place behind the bar.

Anne finished her beer and returned the folders to her bag. What had they stumbled into? Things were becoming more complex and interwoven. She absently touched the place on her neck where the pin prick had delivered the poison. She remembered what Baumschen had told them about the hydrogen cyanide attack on Langert—a gas used by the Germans in World War II. Combined with what she'd just heard from the jolly barkeep, all signs pointed to a sensational story. Assuming they lived to tell it.

She had had this feeling before and she liked it, excitement mixed with fear, like slinging a leg over the back of a rodeo bull just before the chute opened. You didn't know what the ride would be like or if you could stay on for the count, but you were sure you were in for one hell of a trip and the bragging rights were worth it.

Anne placed some coins on the bar in front of Herr Kremsbach. "I won't take the advice, either." She smiled. "But thanks for offering."

She walked outside and looked up and down the quaint street where she'd left her car. Perhaps there would be time to pick up something for Matt before locating a place to stay the night. A woodworker's sign caught her eye, and she headed toward the shop. Matt liked wood, and he needed a new jewelry box. Maybe she could also find one of those nutcrackers with the tall hat and bushy whiskers, or one that looked like Herr Kremsbach.

She peeked into the store window at the dozens of carved items. If Matt were here he would check to see if they were made in Taiwan. Always the cynic, though he would swear he was a realist. She scanned the different nutcrackers, but there were also jewelry boxes, cuckoo clocks, ballerinas, crèche scenes with tiny wind fans run by heat from small candles, little trains, alphabet blocks, and miniature animals carved in great detail. A window filled with so many things that her eyes skipped from one to the next.

Then she stopped, her gaze riveted on two objects in a back corner arranged as part of the display.

Two hand-carved angels. The small sign in front was lettered with "Circa 1940" and "Nicht zu verkauften"—not for sale. The angels were identical to the ones she had photographed a decade ago, held, no, caressed in the palm of James Rinski as he arrested Tod Engel, lifted high by Martin Ehrhart as macabre symbols of senseless death, tossed on the bleeding bodies of terrorized victims.

Death angels.

The dark lacquered wood was crudely carved, not polished like the newer pieces in the window. But the workmanship was intricate, the wings carefully angled, the expression on the tiny faces mournful, plaintive; the chubby arms reached out mercifully, beckoning. Anne felt them call to her, supplicating, begging her to notice, to convey their story and end their sorrow.

She blinked and took a deep breath. For a moment, she felt the tentacles of that great war engulf her, immobilize and mesmerize her. In this small town she had found the link to murders thousands of miles away.

Anne entered the shop. A tinkling bell at the top of the door summoned a squat man from a carving desk behind the counter. He wore traditional Austrian lederhosen, green leather shorts with a kind of halter top over a dark green shirt with a feather pin over one pocket. His wrinkled skin and thick gray goatee made his bald head all the more noticeable. He wiped his hands on a towel and spoke the customary greeting.

"Gruss Gott!"

"Gruss Gott, mein Herr," Anne Demming replied. "Ich wurde die zwei Engel im Fenster sehen, bitte."

"Vielleicht. Perhaps we should converse in your language instead of mine?" the man said, his eyes twinkling.

"That would be better for us both, I'm sure," Anne smiled at the elf-like man. But she was on her guard. A man exactly this size had left his knife mark on her thigh in Houston. That story and seventeen stitches had gotten her a raise.

She walked toward the front window and pointed. "I would like to see these two angels, please."

The man reached into the window-well and retrieved them. "You may of course examine them, but," he said, ominously, "you may not purchase them. They are for display only."

"Why are they not for sale?" Anne said. This trip was all on *CityMag* anyway. She could afford whatever it took. "They are lovely, and they must be antiques, are they not?"

"They are sehr interresant—very interesting pieces, but I do not think they are, what did you call them, lovely? In fact their story is anything but lovely."

An opening. "Just what is their story?" She asked.

He hopped up on the stool behind the counter. "A sad one, I'm afraid." The man was suddenly distracted by a large figure staring in the window. Anne looked over and saw Herr Kremsbach slowly shake his head and walk away.

"What was that about?" she asked.

"It is Herr Kremsbach."

"I know. I just came from his restaurant."

"He is a man who is very angry. He wants to bury the past, to forget and never to forgive. Like many of us, he has his reasons."

"I don't mean to pry," Anne said, prying like crazy, "but could you tell me what those reasons are?" She held an angel in each hand. "It may assist me in clearing up a mystery that has kept a man in prison for many years."

She watched the battle on his face as his wish to help was overcome by his need to protect something deep within. "No, Fraulein," he finally said. "I really cannot. There are certain secrets of small villages that should remain secret, that must be buried with us in the ossuary by the church."

"Including the secrets of Josef Melindorf?"

The man stared at her. She could see him weigh his thoughts. This boy should never play poker, she said to herself. If he did, he should play for big stakes with her. His face was a neon sign for his brain. She knew he would talk.

"Is that why you show interest in these angels? Do you know their meaning?"

"I know something of it," she lied. "Most importantly, I know that Josef Melindorf was killed, violently murdered ten years ago in New York. I have traced him here, to Feyregg, where he was supposedly born and raised. But his records have vanished, his life erased."

The shopkeeper sat at eye level with her, the greenness of his eyes matching his outfit. "I presume you have good reason to want to know these things?"

"Yes. I'm a journalist with a magazine. I believe that the man convicted of Melindorf's murder is not the man who committed it."

"There is a person unjustly imprisoned on account of Josef Melindorf?"

"For the last decade. Actually, several people were murdered."

"Of course." The man sighed. "It would be several."

Anne controlled her eagerness. "What are you talking about?"

A tapping noise on the window interrupted them. They both looked up to see Kremsbach again shake his head, though this time his frown seemed angry, his clenched jaw foreboding.

"He will stay there now until you are gone, Fraulein." The man shook his head sadly. "And he can very likely hear our conversation since the glass is quite thin and acts as an amplifier in the window."

So close. Don't let go now. "Then you will not come to the aid of a man who may be unfairly imprisoned for the death of this Josef Melindorf?"

"I must live in this village for the rest of my life, Fraulein. You will leave tonight, perhaps never to return. That puts us in very different positions, does it not?"

"Yes, but—"

"Let me finish," the man said. He reached under the counter and retrieved a small box filled with tissue. "I will sell one of these angels to you, but at a very high price. That is my prerogative. I have had them in the window long enough." He looked at her. "But I cannot tell you their story. That will be your job." He took them from her hands and laid them on the tissue paper. "Choose one."

Anne examined the angels. One had a near smile, and the other, a pouty lip. "This one," she said, indicating the second one. "It reminds me of a friend of mine." Beck would argue with that, too.

The man wrapped the angel in tissue and placed it in the box. "You should never buy just one angel, you know," he said. "It will be very lonely."

"But you wouldn't sell me the other."

"Not at this time, Fraulein," the man said as he wrote up the bill. "But I sell you this one on the condition that you promise to return some day to purchase the other." He looked up at her and grinned. "At which time you will tell me how your search ended and whether the wrong man was in prison."

"I will do that, Herr—"

"Grundich," he said. "Here is my card."

"I'm Anne Demming." She shook his hand, then stared at the bill. "Five thousand marks?"

"I told you it would be expensive." He grinned. "But I think you will find the purchase well worth it."

With a sigh, she handed him the money and turned to leave.

"Oh, Miss Demming!" the man said. "Let me put my residence number on that card, in the event that the shop is closed or I am not here when you return."

She gave him the card, and he scribbled on the back of it.

"Good," he said, returning it. "That will provide what you need." He smiled again as she left. "Wiedersehen, Fraulein."

"Auf wiedersehen," she said, shutting the door behind her. She turned to her left and spoke to the man standing there. "And a good auf wiedersehen to you as well, Herr Kremsbach."

"I hope you have a safe journey home, Miss Demming," Kremsbach said, as politely as he could.

"I intend to do just that," she replied. "But I will need a place to stay the night. Wo wurden Sie emphelen?"

"I can recommend nothing in Feyregg, I am afraid. But in the town of Enns I believe you will enjoy excellent lodgings at Der Goldener Hirsch. It is only a twenty-minute drive from here. I will call so they will expect you."

"Thank you, Herr Kremsbach." She turned to go to her car. "Wiedersehen."

Kremsbach grunted and walked into the wood carver's store.

Two hours later, Anne sat propped up on her bed at Der Goldener Hirsch. She drank a warm beer from the minibar and chewed on the bittersweet Austrian chocolate left by the maid. A yellow Michelin map of Austria was spread out to her right, and she began to plott her next move, which would be on the way back to the airport in Munich. Perhaps if she went next to Schwertberg to check on Arnold Reid, she could backtrack to Langenstein to trace his wife, Garnet. Now, with the angel in hand, maybe people would be willing to add to the story.

She reached into her bag and pulled out the small cardboard box, unwrapped the angel from the paper, and looked at the carving. The wood seemed darker still, the brown ebony and the pouty lip more like an expression of pain than anger. The intricacies were deeper, more pronounced, as though made with crude tools and even cruder deliberation.

The angel felt odd to her. It sent chills up her arm, and she placed it on the map and stared at it.

"Who are you?" she said. "What do you mean?" She picked it up again and felt eerie, even frightened. "Where did you come from?" And then, as though the piece had spoken to her, she said, "My God! What have you seen?"

"That's it, isn't it? It's what you've seen!" This was worth one more trip back to the man in the wood shop. In fact, she would go tonight. She had his home number. Kremsbach wouldn't see her and they could talk about what this angel had seen.

She fished the card from the box. On the front was etched, in European script numerals, the address and phone number of the store, but Herr Grundich had penciled in what appeared to be his home phone number. So what had he written on the back of it? She turned the card over. There were two words.

"Antwort: Mauthausen."

"Answer: Mauthausen," she repeated softly. She vaguely recognized the name. She had come across it looking on the map for the other villages in this area.

She leaned over the map and scanned the tiny print.
"Yes!" she said, underlining the name with pencil. It was nearly equidistant from the other marked villages where the people she had searched for were born. In fact, Mauthausen was the center of a circle, with the four towns—Enns, Feyregg, Langenstein, and Schwertberg—on the circumference.

Anne retrieved the Green Guide from under the map and flipped to the description of Mauthausen.

It was not just a town.

A chill rippled through her again. Slowly, she read, "Mauthausen concentration camp was the Auschwitz of Austria."

She sighed and put the book down. There would be no call to Herr Grundich. She knew what the angel had seen.

Matt Beck waved at Switchboard Betty on his way out the door. He had come to the hospital after too few hours of restless sleep with a horrible headache from Rinski's spray. The Four Roses hadn't helped his stomach either. At times like this it was good to work at a hospital. Jonsby was able to supply the appropriate medicines to overcome the lethal feeling of spray and booze, thankfully without asking a lot of questions. As he popped yet another antacid, he felt like the Four Roses was the more deadly of the two substances still lurking in his body. He walked out the sliding doors and was grateful for the crisp cold of the night filling his lungs and clearing his head.

But he wondered just how clear he was when he looked into the lighted parking lot at his Spider. He could have sworn someone was sitting in the passenger seat. Pretending to go to another part of the lot, he glanced up again and saw the same shadowy outline slumped in the seat.

Not sure what to do, Beck kept walking, circling behind the car. He could call security and they would check it out for him. But then he was putting them at risk, too. He would get close enough to make his own determination and, depending on what he found, he could always double back for help. It could be anyone from a hospital employee who knew his car and wanted to talk with him to a homeless person seeking temporary shelter. Or it could be someone else.

As Matt moved close to the passenger window, he saw that the car was now empty. Suddenly, he glimpsed motion to his right. His heart pounded and he readied to strike the first blow.

"Take it easy, Father," a familiar voice said, chuckling. "It's only me."

Matt's pulse slowed and he sagged against another car. "God, Alfonse, next time light a flare, will you?"

"Sorry." The big man thumped Beck on the shoulder. "I spotted someone circling behind the car. Instincts told me to watch it." He smiled sheepishly. "Sorry. But you know, you really should be more careful, considering the ragtop and all."

"No problem," Beck lied, thinking he might have to make a bathroom stop before he got home. "So why are you here?"

Ciccilini lit a cigarette. "I had to tell you this in person. I don't trust phones, especially them new cell phones. Shit, anybody could be listenin' in by radio, if you know what I mean?"

Beck nodded, rubbing his hands together. Home was looking better and better. "Is this about Earl?"

"Yes and no." He took a deep drag. "I nosed around like you asked, and I found out that old Earl had a partner in the black market stuff he was kiting into Rikers."

"Let me guess," Matt said, trying to hurry him up. "It was Bishop Langert."

"No, but you're in the ballpark." Ciccilini flicked away the ashes of the cigarette. "It was another guard by the name of Williams. But he wasn't around to be busted when Earl got his. This Williams character left the prison under some kind of cloud before Earl's little racket was exposed. I'm still checking on what exactly went down."

Bells sounded in Beck's head. "And what happened to this Williams?" As if he didn't know.

"Not long after the incident, whatever it was, he resurfaced as a guard at the nuthouse prison. Word on the street is that Ehrhart was his protector and arranged the job."

"You mean Weston Prison. The man who is now Warden Richard Williams."

Ciccilini nodded. "Figured you ought to know."

Beck thanked him and watched him leave for his own car. Ciccilini would contact him again with any further information he came upon. And Matt was to tell Anne Demming that her apartment was ready for her to return any time she felt like it.

So Earl and Williams knew each other in a previous life. The bishop's driver and the prison warden. It didn't mean anything beyond coincidence right now. Matt would speculate on the possibilities on his drive back to the mountain, and he would leave the ragtop up all the way home.

Beck braked the Spider to a stop halfway up the road to the mountain. He killed the engine.

It was the curtains. He always left them open one inch, a trick he had learned from his dad's stories of surveillance. If intruders broke in to steal or to wait, they would either shut the drapes for privacy or open them slightly wider to be able to see approaching cars. In either case, no one would put them back exactly right. Like now.

Beck grabbed Anne's LadyHawke from the glove box and checked the clip, glad she had left it with him. Though he did not particularly like guns, his dad had taught him to shoot at an early age. He climbed over the driver's door and slipped off his white collar. The deep dark of evening would conceal his movement through the thick woods to the house.

He thought about calling the police, but if the intruder was still there he might escape before they came. Whoever it was, Matt didn't want to lose him. Fed up with half-answers, he sought information he'd never pry from Rinski and his minions even if he were able to drag them into a courtroom. Hopefully this was the same guy who had tried to knife him at McCaslin's house, back for a rematch. Good. This round, he had the tactical advantage.

He crouched down and crept to a back door. Beck turned the key in the doorknob and stepped into the gasoline smell of the empty garage, flipping the safety off the .38 and slowly turning the door knob. No light showed from the kitchen. Another sign. He always left the light on over the sink, and he'd just replaced the bulb last week.

Someone was there.

Of course, there might be more than one someone. McCaslin had been killed and Anne attacked by teams of at least two men. He hesitated only a moment. He owed too much to too many. It was time to play for keeps. He opened the kitchen door.

Nothing. No one. He ducked down and inched toward the thick wood doors that separated the kitchen from the living room.

From beside the refrigerator he heard a voice.

"Don't move, Beck. Or you're a dead man."

Beck did move. He whirled around, fired two shots and rolled across the floor to avoid return fire. Breathing hard, he quickly came to his feet beside the sink cabinet, where he had a clear view of the rest of the kitchen. He saw a form dart away from the fridge and heard a voice shout, but he squeezed off two more rounds before he paid attention to the words.

"Matt! Stop it, Matt!" the voice yelled. "It's me! Stop shooting! It's Art Allen!"

Beck slid out from the small space. It did sound like Allen, but he wanted to be sure before ending up a trusting corpse. "Switch on a light!" he ordered. "And keep your hands where I can see them!"

The fluorescent ceiling light blinked on to reveal an obviously shaken Allen looking more pale and gaunt than ever.

"Geez, Matt! Lighten up. Can't you take a joke?"

"Joke, hell! You crazy damned sonofabitch!" Beck tossed the .38 on the table like it was molten hot. Adrenalin rushed through his body. He wanted to kick the shit out of the man for scaring him. He stomped on the floor. "Drop your damned hands. You look stupid."

"Better stupid than dead," Allen said. "Do you always come home and shoot your houseguests?"

"Only when they break into my house, you idiot."

"Well, you weren't here and I needed to use the bathroom."

Beck shook his head. He looked at the splintered boards in the far wall and the two slug holes in the refrigerator door. "Next time I'll aim better."

"Next time I'll dump in the woods." Allen grabbed a chair and caught his breath. "Okay," he said, "I'm sorry. I should have sent a telegram first. You'll forgive me when you see what I've got." He gestured to two folders on the kitchen table.

Beck read the names on each. "I may not shoot you, after all." He sat down at the table. "Depending on what these little gems reveal to us."

"My mother would say you're forgetting your manners."

Beck reminded him that his mother was dead and that he had nearly joined her.

"After you try to kill someone, you're supposed to ask them if they want a drink."

"Right," he said, suddenly very tired and missing Anne. He put a bottle of whiskey and two glasses on the table.

Allen poured, took a big drink, and poured again. "Better," he said. "Now if I can just clean up the mess in my underwear."

Despite the scare, it was good to hear him joke again. "Welcome back to the human race."

"I'm only here for a short visit." Allen opened the first folder. "Check it out. I had these run by the Bureau of Criminal Identification this morning. I'm relatively sure word has gotten back—at least to this first person— that his record has been accessed."

"Martin Ehrhart?" Beck smirked. He imagined the County Executive when he found out that his BCI file had been pulled from the Big Brother computer. "I thought his would have been vacuumed spotless at this point in his career, considering the media can also gain access to it."

"Right," Allen said. "So we assume he knows and isn't too worried. Except that he's not going to know what we uncovered."

Beck swallowed the searing whiskey and peered at the small type as his friend flipped through the report. "There was nothing of interest from BCI," Allen said. "Vacuumed, like you said. A few tickets, some notes about lawsuits against him when he was the assistant D.A. years ago. Those things are fairly standard for people in public office, especially the D.A.'s staff." He yanked a sheaf of paper from the back of the file. "Here's the good stuff."

"You look like the cat that just ate the canary," Beck said. "What is it?"

"You want the bottom line or the gory details?"

"Line first, details later."

Allen sat back in his chair. "Martin Ehrhart—contrary to popular belief and, I might add, to sworn testimony—knew Tod Engel before he saw him in the courtroom for the Deathangel trial."

Beck was stunned. He picked up the paper. "Let me see that."

"And he knew him under a different name."

This changed everything. "Wait a minute, wait a minute. Slow down!"

"You wanted it all at once." Allen grinned.

"Back it up and run it past me frame by frame."

Allen took a slug of his drink. "It occurred to me this morning that you only wanted files on the victims. So I wondered what would happen if I pulled the two major players in the drama. Ehrhart." He opened the second folder. "And Tod Engel."

Matt scanned the documents. "Where's the part where Engel changed his name?"

"Here." Allen showed him the paper. "That much came out at the trial, remember? Engel was so obsessed with whatever character his mind had taken on that he actually effected a legal name change. As you can see from the records, his real name was Edward Clopton. But he changed it to underline the designation of his deeds. Tod Engel, which of course in German means Death Angel."

"And everyone at the time," Beck said, "simply thought that added to the evidence, both for his craziness and his guilt."

"Correct. But there are two interesting sidelights."

"I'm listening."

"The first is that Ehrhart lied under oath when he said he had never seen Engel before."

"No wonder he doesn't want the case opened."

"That's just the beginning." Allen thumbed through the record in front of him. "Check this. It's a record of all of the cases Ehrhart tried before he joined the D.A.'s staff in Westchester County."

Beck looked down the printout. "He worked in New York City?"

"Yes. Did a lot of minor prosecutions, the kind of crap you're handed straight out of law school. Cuts their teeth on the tough stuff so when the big cases come along they'll have had some experience."

"There it is. People v. Edward Clopton. Looks like a P.I. charge."

"Right," Allen replied. "They all are. I counted a total of thirty public intoxication charges over the two years Ehrhart was with the New York office."

"So there's no way he can claim that Engel, or Clopton, was just another pretty face in the crowd."

"Not hardly. Now they weren't exactly bosom buddies, but Ehrhart had to have known his face and his record. He had just seen Engel, according to this sheet, eighteen months before the Deathangel killings."

"But why would he lie?"

"I'm getting to that," Allen said. "Given the volume of cases he'd handled and the fact that he mostly related to them as file folders instead of faces, he could probably claim that he didn't recognize Clopton. Besides, nobody wanted to know about Edward Clopton anyway. They were so focused on Tod Engel that Clopton's rap sheet wasn't ever mentioned in the court records except to say that he'd done time on public intox charges."

"This is wild," Beck said.

"There's more."

Matt smiled and poured another round. This was the Art Allen he remembered. The one who hated unfairness and would kick butt to even scores. Maybe he had returned to the human race for more than a visit. Funny how death sometimes brought life around.

"Squint your beady little eyes and look carefully at who the arresting officer was—the flatfoot who repeatedly hauled Edward Clopton to jail so he could be prosecuted by Martin Ehrhart."

Beck turned over each record and studied the name scrawled on the bottom.

"Oh, my God!"

"No, but someone who thinks he is."

"James Rinski," Beck said, staring at the page. "So when Rinski made the bust of Engel's apartment that night, it wasn't their first meeting."

"Not by a long shot, apparently." Allen unwrapped a cigar and chomped down on it. "Now, to be absolutely fair here, which you know I hate, it is technically possible that Rinski really did not know Deathangel was Clopton before he banged down the door with the cameras rolling." Allen took a sip of whiskey. "He could have been as surprised as anybody else."

"And Laurel didn't know Hardy, and Stanley didn't know Livingston," Beck said, excited. "I'll bet if we went back over Anne's photos from the bust, we wouldn't see astonishment on either face."

Allen set his unlit cigar on the table. "There's one more thing that's not in these papers. Engel did some of his public intox time—as Clopton, of course—at Riker's Island. Small bids, but enough to get known there too—by some people."

Beck took the hint. "Like the chaplain?"

"Catholic. I've known him for years." Allen nodded. "I called Father Kelly over there, and it turns out Engel always got assigned to his block area." He leaned forward and folded his hands. "About the fifth time around, Kelly had him tested."

"According to the trial records, Engel was certified M.R."

"Agitated M.R.," Allen said. "Kelly told me Engel had one hell of a mean streak, that he could be violent at a moment's notice if he felt threatened or in physical or emotional danger."

"Unlike us, of course."

Allen smiled. "Right. But it does support the claim that he was at least capable of doing the murders—still leaving the question of whether his mental retardation would make him capable of planning them."

"How in Sweet Jesus did he manage to go through all the red tape to get his name changed?"

"I was wondering when you'd come to that." Allen stared at him.

Beck felt a chill of anticipation. "Somebody helped him?"

Allen nodded and waved a faxed copy of a cash receipt.

"You know who it was?"

"The name change was effected in a courthouse in a small Pennsylvania town to ensure there were no immediate New York or Jersey records available." He took a drink. "What they didn't count on was the compulsiveness of the county clerks in those little burgs."

"And that's the cash receipt for the transaction?"

"Yep. When I pinpointed from the BCI records where it was done, I called and asked them to fax me copies of what documents they had. The lady I talked to was Episcopalian and was most helpful—as you can see." He spread out several papers. "They were very careful to have Engel sign everything himself, as best he could. But Engel didn't have the money to pay the fee for the legal papers, and that's where they screwed up. They thought they were being smart paying cash, but the old clerk there just had to write a receipt for the money, including the person's name and license number, with a carbon copy."

Matt looked at the signature and felt his heart pound.

It was John Langert.

"I can't believe this!" He took a deep breath and shook his head.

Allen smiled. "I sure as hell can."

"So Engel was definitely set up?"

"Looks that way to me."

Beck's head whirled. "What if there's another explanation?"

"Like what?"

Matt tried to think of something logical, but too much was happening. His whole life was being rearranged. His relationship with Langert seemed to be falling into the same dark hole that Kate's death occupied. He desperately wanted Anne to be upstairs in the bedroom when he got there later, to talk to, to hold.

"I don't know." Beck said, "What if someone like Earl, that driver of his, forged Langert's signature and used his driver's license?"

"Photo I.D.?"

"Not ten years ago," Beck said, trying to calm down, trying to reconcile his memories of Langert with the sight of the man's signature on the receipt.

"Point for you," Allen said. "Maybe we can ask him about it next time we're invited for tea."

"Or consult a writing expert. Besides, why would Langert do this? And how does this fit in to the attempt on his life? It makes no sense, Art."

"It does if, as my paranoid mind imagines, there are more players in this story than one."

Matt sipped the whiskey. It was too much to believe—the bishop, the man who had defended both Beck and Engel, could do harm to the man in Weston Prison. "Does that mean Engel did the murders for someone or just took the fall for them?" He glanced at Allen. "And do all these people in your paranoid mind know how much we know?"

Allen held his drink in midair. "Excellent question. We have to be really careful now, or your trick in the kitchen will look like a B.B. gun."

Both men jumped at the sound of Beck's pager. He hit the squelch button and read the digital number. "This is a stat call," he said.

"I gotta go, too." Allen grabbed his jacket from the counter. "But I need a ride into town. I had car trouble and left it at a gas station. They dropped me out here."

Beck started to open the front door. "Wait a minute." He hurried back to the kitchen. "Give me the files—and that fax sheet." He bundled the folders into a plastic bag and stuffed them in the freezer behind two boxes of ice cream. If Allen was right, it might sufficiently fool intruders. He folded the fax and put into his pocket.

"Don't worry. I made copies of everything."

"That's not what concerns me."

Allen looked puzzled.

He patted the receipt. "I'm worrying about who set up Langert."

"I like that," Allen said. "It's even more paranoid than I would have thought."

"And who may be setting up us." Beck's beeper sounded again. "Shit," he said, hurrying them toward the door. "They don't page twice unless it's bad." He grabbed an extra phone battery. "I'll call from the car."

Fifteen minutes later, Matt almost ran past Betty at the switchboard on his way to the ER. He would have to be attentive to the mangled patient and the terrified family he would meet. But his mind was on whether Art Allen could pull off the final task he had asked him to do, without getting caught.

Chapter 10

Anne followed the signs from Route 3 into Mauthausen. Other than a couple requisite tourist shops, little was there. Only a few people milled around the vacant town square in the middle of the morning. It was as though the heaviness in the gray, overcast day had pervaded their very souls. Unlike the other Austrian villages Anne had seen, the directional signs were also few. Usually, a drive through the center of town resulted in reorientation, at least to the main road. But Mauthausen seemed intent on remaining hidden, hoping outsiders would drive away before finding the thing they had come to see.

The one clue to the existence of the monument Anne sought was a small, badly weathered sign under the one for the U.S. Military Museum. The sign's white paint was chipped, and the black letters seemed thin and emaciated, embarrassed to point to its destination.

Anne found the road up the hill similarly unwelcoming. It was only one lane wide, grown over with grass that brushed the underside of the car as she slowed for the sharp bends. There were no signs to tell her she was headed the right way. If you missed the first one, you might be discouraged enough to turn around.

Suddenly, there it was. The building at the top of the hill nearly made her stop in the middle of the road, so overpowering was its size.

Now the road broadened and became well paved, all the way up to the large parking lot at the front gate. The Austrian government, Anne thought, had maintained the facility and their part of the property. The town, like much of the rest of the world, would just as soon forget the concentration camp existed and clearly resented its status as a memorial and museum.

Nobody likes their id on display, Anne thought. She got out of the car and walked through the gate. Especially a national one.

She climbed the stone steps to the front gate of the inner complex, but she could not go straight inside. She knew that she would find the answer to something horrible within those gray stone walls. The journey would exact a toll from her, and the answer would be as devastating as the reason she had come.

"Antwort: Mauthausen." She spoke softly, remembering the shopkeeper's message.

She delayed her entrance by a detour through the tiny tourist cafe, stopping to find the "Toiletten" sign with "Damen" on the door. Emerging from the cafe with a large coffee, she paid her hundred marks at the ticket booth and entered the compound marked "Konzentrationslager Mauthausen."

Anne had seen prisons before. She had toured Sing Sing, Greenhaven, Attica, and, of course, Weston in New York. She had interviewed prisoners in federal penitentiaries in New York and Texas. This one looked much the same. Same walls, same turrets, same gray darkness. Since it seemed smaller on the inside, it was somewhat less foreboding than most.

She consulted the map to get her bearings. On the left were the prisoners' barracks, most of which had been torn down. Some had been reconstructed to show the size of the accommodations. North of those were the ruins of the "experimental" buildings. On the east, the typical facilities: laundry, bakery and kitchens, repair shops, processing units for new prisoners, complete with showers. And—she would put it off until the last—the crematorium with its gas ovens. The thought made her flesh crawl. What was it like living here, knowing this was where you would eventually go?

A lump formed in her throat. There was too much sadness here, too much sorrow. She fought off tears, but would not let herself be distracted by them. She sucked in a deep breath of the cold camp air, just as she imagined the prisoners had done.

She pushed herself on. The barracks took only minutes to tour. There were the usual bunks, desks, and toilets, the latter used for torture as well as hygiene for the hundred or so people assigned to each. Is this what Robert would have faced had he been captured instead of killed in Iran? How could she have stood knowing it?

How could people do this to one another, she wondered, until she reminded herself of her reason for being here. What did the angels have to do with it? What was the antwort, the answer to the Deathangel puzzle? Would it find her first, scream out to her in the agonizing cries of the dying or the stench of burning flesh? Or would she be forced to view its bloody ugliness?

Anne headed for the plaques cemented onto the K Buildings. But she walked more slowly now, waiting to be shocked. She felt as if she were being pursued, imagined voices murmuring in the background, directing her, calling her closer. Her cold flesh crawled with fear and anticipation.

The plaques described, in six languages, the function of the buildings.

She shot close-up photographs of the ones in English to save time writing long descriptions Besides, she could not bear to copy the words.

> Block 20, was originally a newcomers' block, then a sickroom, then an experimental unit for Soviet officers and other NCO's. These prisoners were allowed to starve to death, under close medical and scientific supervision, to determine the effects of various nutrition regimens.

Anne winced at the conclusion of the story.

> Just three months before the camp was liberated by the Americans, 500 prisoners escaped from K Building, Block 20. All were recaptured and killed.

She kept reading and photographing.

> In Hut 19, weak and old prisoners were housed. They stood in front of the hut from morning to night and, completely debilitated, died either on the spot or on the gas-car, a moveable gas chamber.

She swallowed hard. There was one more plaque to capture. She snapped it, then read it again.

> In 1968, 9800 exhumed corpses from the Marbach mass grave and the prisoners who died after their liberation in the surroundings of Mauthausen were buried in this place. May they rest in peace.

Mass death, like the eight murders in Westchester County. Right now those eight seemed to pale beside the millions who died in camps like these. Yet she must understand how they were linked.

Revolting anger raged inside of her. She was determined to see the rest of the camp, every detail, until the answer became clear, regardless of the cost. Nothing could compare to the agony of the souls who had walked on these stones. She owed it to them and to the Deathangel victims.

Stolidly and quickly, she visited the other buildings. She descended into the showers next to the laundry. Here, prisoners were processed and tortured with high-pressure hoses of hot water or forced to strip and get into mass "shower" rooms where lethal Zyklon B gas poured from the nozzles. Zyklon B—an insecticide containing cyanide. Zyklon B, a pale blue gas.

For a moment she was paralyzed by the tremors rippling through her body. She felt stifled by the sense of terror around her. She heard the gasps of women, saw frightened children crying, clinging to each other, men coughing and sucking in the gas the Nazis had developed for just this purpose—to exterminate people like pests. She hurried upstairs and into the open air, leaned against a railing to steady herself for the next descent, the one into maelstrom.

She made her way slowly down the stairs and she recognized the words for "the final solution" above it: Die Endlosung. It was a separate museum. A pretty woman in her twenties sat in the ticket booth, smiling. "Guten morgan, Fraulein," she said.

"Guten morgan," Anne said, handing her the admission fee. The woman's dark hair and fair skin reminded her of herself at that age.

"You are from the United States, yes?"

"Is it that obvious?"

"One has little to do here but play such guessing games with visitors, though I take my post much more seriously than most." Anne glanced at the book she was reading. "I see you do," she said, nodding at the copy of Mein Kampf.

The woman blushed. "It is not what you think. I have made it my goal to read all of the documents in this museum, and in my five years here I have gotten to nearly all of them. My generation understands so little of this. Some of us must learn all we can, to remember. It is my mission."

"That's very good," Anne said. The woman was certainly proud of the accomplishment. "I wish I could read all the documents in there. The English translations are so succinct, I'm afraid I'm missing important material."

The young woman looked around. "I am Fraulein Schirmer," she said, coming out of the booth. "Lisa."

"Anne Demming." She shook the Austrian woman's hand.

"There are no other visitors today. You are the only one. If you like, I could take you through and translate for you."

"I would be very grateful, Fraulein Lisa," Anne said, deciding she would hand this angelic-looking young woman a large tip when they finished.

"Then follow me, bitte, and feel free to ask any questions you may wish."

They went into the first room, an antechamber that looked like a hospital surgery. Lisa described how prisoners were forced to desecrate the half-alive bodies of people they knew, removing gold fillings, shaving and storing hair for furniture, saving particularly deformed or unusual physiotypes for further torture and experimentation, and sending the others to the next room. To the ovens.

"Wait a minute," Anne said, breathless in anticipation of what she would see. "How bad is it in there?"

"It is not bad now, Fraulein."

"Anne."

"Anne." The young woman nodded. "It is not bad now. But it is in imagining the pictures of the horror that occurred here that the badness comes." She turned toward the portal and entered. "As it should."

As she entered the room, Anne had the feeling that she was being led onward, and not by Lisa Schirmer. It was as though the souls of the victims murmured at her, carried her forward on their tendril arms, flashing images before her of the evil still vivid all around her.

And then she saw it.

There, in a square, obviously handmade glass case, just above the hideous round oven, was an angel, a small, hand-carved wooden angel.

"Just a second," she said, catching her breath. She snapped a picture of it, and this time she wrote down the word on the sign beneath it.

"Todengel," she read. "Tod Engel." Her mind sped to the man in the cell at Weston Prison. "My God," she said, sinking down on the bench in the dank, musty room. It was one thing to hear the translation at the trial, to hear the prosecution state that his name conclusively convicted him. It was quite another to see the name in this place of torture and death, confirming that fact atop a rusted iron oven.

"What did you say, Fraulein? Anne?"

"This angel, this Deathangel—" she said. Was this the answer she had come so far to see face to face? Had someone found four Austrian emigrants and murdered them, with four others, taking on a name identified with the most heinous crimes in recent history?

"You would like to know the story of it? This angel?"

"Yes," she whispered.

Lisa Schirmer took a seat beside her. Anne listened, but she focused on the carved object above them.

"These small wooden angels were carved out of scraps of wood by the haftlinger— the prisoners in the camp. As people died or were killed, the angels were passed on to new prisoners as a sign of hope and luck. The angel was symbolic of their prayer to flee the prison one way or another, of their hope for liberation by God or the Allies, whoever arrived first." The guide paused. "Are you hearing me, Fraulein?"

Anne spoke solemnly, holding in her emotions. "The ones who were gassed seem like the lucky ones. Those left behind were starved, worked to death, tortured, or used for experiments." She stood and went to the glass case. "May I?"

Schirmer nodded as Anne removed the angel from its box and held it up.

"The Nazis hated Der Todengeln," the guide said. "At first they tolerated them, but then the angels became a sign of defiance and hope. One of the things the rulers of the camp learned was that they had to destroy hope. It is not those who are downtrodden and have nothing to lose who revolt, but those who have a glimmer of hope to sustain them.

"Prisoners started tossing the small objects onto bodies about to be cremated, or into the mass graves they had been forced to dig, and on the dead bodies of the elderly and deformed who were forced to stand until they fell were shot."

Anne cradled the tiny angel on her lap like a doll. She could imagine the scene as Schirmer described it. In fact, it was as though she was there, as though those murdered so many years ago imparted their visions to her. She felt her eyes begin to tear again as she looked at the guide. She coughed and gulped a bit of her cold coffee.

"When officials tried to stamp out the angels, even more appeared and the camp was on the verge of either uprising or being decimated by systematic slaughter to regain control. Neither would have endeared the Kommandant to Der Fuhrer, so the decision was made to again ignore the angels, to tolerate them until the idea died out. But it never did. Some believe the angels—Der Todengeln—were responsible for the camp's ultimate liberation, that they led the Allies here, that they continue to lead people here, people who can understand and help."

Anne put the angel back on the shelf. Had she been led here by the angels? She frowned. Why had Mauthausen not come out before this? What was the link between Engel and the camp? She stared directly into the gaping mouth of the oven. The prosecution sensationalized the man's name to connect him to the acts of murder. But had no one discovered the source of that name and those angels? Or did they know about Mauthausen and suppress it for other reasons? Or consider it irrelevant? Could Deathangel be a camp survivor or a relative, a descendant, taking revenge on four people who had been complicit in their incarceration, or who had perhaps even worked here? That changed everything.

Anne took one last picture, then gazed at the ovens. She said a silent prayer for those whose bodies had been incinerated but whose souls haunted the grounds. Unsettled, she felt someone take her hand.

"Fraulein, you are upset?"

"No. No. I'm sorry. I got distracted. Please, go on."

The woman looked at her with a deep sense of understanding. Maybe you could not work at this place and not be affected by it.

"This is more than a story for you? This is, somehow, personal for you?"

"Yes, it is." Anne explained why she was there, the connection with Tod Engel, the four victims from the area, her experience in Feyregg at the inn and the wood shop.

"Ich verstehe. I understand now, Fraulein."

The woman was silent a moment. Anne wondered what she was thinking, then watched her remove a large skeleton key from her pocket.

"So. I must take you to the private archives then. We only permit serious researchers to enter these—as well as those who are dedicated to preserving the story of the Reich."

Anne followed the guide through the museum to a small door behind a glass case. She walked in to an immaculately kept library with what must be original documents on the wall, cases of memorabilia, photographs, and intricate descriptions of events and prisoners. Whoever maintained the library, possibly the guide, was obviously proud of the material.

"Take your time and look carefully, Fraulein, to see if anything is of use to you here."

"Danke shon," Anne replied. She wondered how she would figure out where to look, what to search for. She could only trust that the deathangels who had led her this far, the ones at the crime scenes in Westchester County, Kate's angel, and the ones at the scene of the crimes here, would continue to bring the things she needed to know to her attention.

Anne scanned the pictures on one side of the room, then on the other. She looked again. "This man." She pointed to a fairly welldressed man. "Over there he is in a picture of prisoners, is he not?"

The guide smiled. "You have a very good eye for photographs, Anne Demming. Not many would have put the two together."

"He went from inmate to administrator, or vice versa?" She took pictures while the guide explained.

"He was a high-ranking Polish Communist prisoner, Eduard Czahallerynsky, originally a supporter of the Nazis in return for promises of safety for his country. He acted as a liaison for prisoners with the guards and kommandant. It was a very sad story when you see how he ended up. It is in his file here." She opened a steel file cabinet and retrieved a photo-copy.

"This was written by him?" Anne frowned, startled.

"Yes. We have had many former prisoners return to tell their story. We save copies on file so the world will not forget them or the ones that kept them prisoner." She pointed to a floor-to-ceiling glass gallery of photographs. "This is a wall of photos of such people, the guards."

Anne studied the fading black and white pictures. There were ten columns and maybe twenty-five rows top to bottom. Most were men, but a few were young women. As she looked them over she said: "Do you happen to have a complete prisoner list?" She was sure this was a rhetorical question. Of course there was such a list. They were Austrians.

"Naturlich." Lisa Schirmer opened another cabinet and flicked on a computer. "We put the names on this compact disc. Between August 8, 1938, and May 5, 1945—the day of liberation—over 206,000 prisoners were processed here."

"Can you look up some names for me?" Anne asked as soon as the screen set up. "The names of the Deathangel victims in New York."

"Certainly. What are they?"

She handed Schirmer a scrap of paper with the names of Bartenburg, Melindorf, and the Rittenwalds.

As the guide read them, a change came over her face. It was as though Anne had named the devil four times under four aliases. Lisa Schirmer was clearly shaken.

"Gott im himmel," the guide whispered. "You will find none of these names on the computer list, Fraulein."

Anne felt her flesh crawl again, the spirits of the dead raising their voices in crescendo around her. She steeled herself. "Why?" she asked, wanting and not wanting to know. "Why is that?"

Schirmer took Anne's hand and led her to the pictures on the wall. "It is because they were not prisoners." She pointed. "Look here in alphabetical order for the names while I retrieve the biographical information for you."

It didn't take long to pick out the names under the photos. "Holy God! They were guards!" Anne shot pictures of them and wished like crazy Matt was here now. Her legs barely held her up. She felt nauseated. "They were the guards," she repeated.

Lisa Schirmer handed her four pages and a cover sheet overlaying it with a strange title. "They were more than just guards, Fraulein Anne, they were called Wechseljuden."

Anne thought a second, then translated. "Changed Jews?"

"Sehr gut, yes. Jews who, through an interesting route, became guards here." She glanced at her watch. "I'm afraid I must be closing the museum very soon for the midday rest. The paper on top will explain about it." The guide headed toward the door.

But something was incomplete. Anne stood still, the voices stopping her again. Don't go. Not yet. "Is there anything else I should know about the camp? Anything that was different or distinguishing about it?"

The guide removed the key from her pocket. "This was a quiet camp, but quietly hideous. All of its special history is in the little booklet you received when you came in the front gate."

Anne looked at her. Surely there was something more. "This is extremely important, Fraulein Schirmer. A man's life may depend on information only you can give me from your study here. Information I suspect is not in the tourist booklet."

Schirmer sighed and turned to her. "Yes. All right. There were two things for which the camp was known. There are brief descriptions—and these are in the tour book—of both the Viennese Grave and the Stairs of Death, areas of the camp where prisoners were forced to work under tortuous conditions in the nearby stone mine until they died."

Anne took hurried notes, asking her to say the names in German and to spell them. The voices were yelling now. Her breathing quickened.

"That is only the first thing. The second is this man." Lisa Schirmer went over to a small shelf that held a charred, faded photograph, an officer's cap, and shoulder bars next to a leather journal. "His name was Karl Helliger. He had the distinction of being the youngest camp commander in the German system. This photograph was rescued from the pyre where his body was burned. You can see him here with Goebbels and Himmler and Mengele, who all look old enough to be his grandfather."

Anne tried to take a photo of the picture, unsure whether it would come out.

"Helliger's family was close to Hitler's inner circle. They wanted high honors for their son and swore allegiance to Die Endlosung—the Final Solution. Like a kid getting a new car, Karl received the camp commission after working there only a couple of months, when the kommandant unexpectedly died. There were rumors that Helliger was responsible for the death so he could use his family's influence to move up, and it is possible.

He was renowned throughout the camp system for his brutality, his hatred of Jews, and his habit of strutting through the camp killing at whim."

"May I examine this?" Anne picked up the leather journal.

The guide nodded. "It is the journal of the first American officer to enter the camp upon its liberation. It is quite an emotional record of what he found, including the funeral pyre of Karl Helliger, who supposedly shot himself when he realized the Americans would arrive the next morning."

"Supposedly?"

Schirmer returned to the archive door and opened it. "That is the official story in all of the camp brochures. But in that journal a different tale is proposed from the personal interviews the officer did with prisoners." She returned and opened the book to a page marked with a ribbon.

Anne read a moment, then looked up. "Escaped?"

"Read more carefully. He is clear that it is a rumor of an escape. The prisoners believed that the night before the liberation, Helliger and several of his guards fled to Switzerland after piling the body of another guard on the pyre with Helliger's belongings. It could never be proven, so it is not the official record."

Anne snapped pictures of the pages and put the journal back on the shelf. "As much as it makes a good story," she said, "and as much as it might help my investigation, it's the same tale that's always told in events like this."

"What do you mean?" Schirmer glanced again at her watch.

Anne followed her out of the library and watched her secure the door. "It's always the same when some infamous person dies by suicide or fire or is destroyed beyond recognition. Those who had suffered much under the person's rule or command always believe he did not really die. The top guy always vanishes into the wind. It was the same with Hitler." She followed the guide through the crematorium and again gazed at the todengel over the oven. "People swore Hitler had not died in the bunker and claimed to have seen him in South America for decades. It's the stuff of which novels and movies are made."

"Veilleicht. Perhaps." Schirmer led her to the museum entrance. "But we cannot really know, can we? Perhaps he is dead. But perhaps somehow he lives again in another time."

"Or a part of him does." Anne remembered her musings about how evil disappears only to show up later in another place. She thanked the woman for the special attention. "You have been a much greater help than you realize."

Lisa Schirmer switched off the lights in her booth. "We owe them the truth, nicht wahr, do we not?"

Anne nodded and turned to leave, then looked back. She wondered if the guide heard the wailing voices? "We owe them more than that."

The woman stared at her.

"We owe them the assurance that we will not let it go unpunished again," Anne said. She ascended the stairs into the cold pale afternoon, wondering if that was possible.

She crossed the barren central grounds, like walking down the aisle of a grisly cathedral. Outside the camp, she turned to take a final photograph of the sign over the entrance gate. It read, "Arbeit Macht Frei." "Work will make you free."

As she got into her car, she realized that the man in the Feyregg wood shop was right. Beside her, in photographs and words, lay the clues to unravel the Deathangel mystery.

She started the car and drove slowly down the hill to the main road. Her mind was filled with the unspeakable.

She decided to call Matt as soon as she reached the airport. She would have to speak carefully, but she wanted to tell him the news. She had found the antwort, captured on film beside her, and forever in her soul.

She wiped away her tears, and looked in the rearview mirror. A small gray car following her much too close behind.

Beck left the family in the ER waiting area. "I'll see what I can find out for you," he told them.

In the crash room, a five-person team worked feverishly around the still body of a young girl from a motorcycle wreck. Matt took his place on the periphery. "What's it look like?" he asked.

"Looks like another pair of kidneys, compliments of a donorcycle," Jonsby said, picking up the phone. "Would you approach the family about donating this kid's organs, Matt? I'm calling the procurement team to come evaluate the damage."

"Just kidneys or everything?" Beck knew her age made the victim a good total donor. Corneas, bone, skin, major organs, ear bones could be sent across the country to a wide range of people who would see, hear, and live because of her death. Organ donations were the only miracles he'd ever seen. It was what he had done with Kate, knowing her wishes.

"Start with kidneys. The team will go from there." Jonsby gazed at the twenty-two-year-old body on the table. "Why the hell won't they wear their damned helmets?" he mumbled.

Beck had started to return to the family when he felt a familiar vibration at his waist. He looked at the digital display on his pager.

New York City area code. Who was calling from New York on a Saturday afternoon?

He smiled. Anne. Maybe she had arrived early and had some news. Maybe the pieces would start falling into place now. Maybe she could still make it to the mountain tonight.

He headed back to the waiting area, then decided that a two-minute delay would not make that much difference in breaking the news to the family. Once he had started the process with them, it would take the better part of the day to work out the details.

He picked up the phone at the nurse's station, got a WATS line, and dialed the number. It rang several times before a man's voice answered.

"Hello?"

"Hello? This is Chaplain Beck, calling from Grasslands Hospital. I received a page to this number."

"Matt?" The voice was familiar. "This is Bishop Langert."

"Sorry, Bishop." He wondered what crisis would make Langert call. "I didn't recognize your voice right away."

"My fault, not yours. I've had a little laryngitis today, Matthew. Are you in the middle of a situation, or can you talk?" He sounded self-effacing. Not his usual self. Something was up.

"Actually, Bishop, I have to break some news about a possible organ donation." Whatever the problem, this family had to be first priority.

"Then I don't want to keep you, of course." Langert paused and Matt wondered if he was taking a drink of something or considering what he would ask. "But I would appreciate it if you would come by when you finish there."

Matt glanced at his watch. "I can do that, Bishop, but it's likely to be well into the evening."

"It is important, Matthew. It concerns our recent discussions about the Deathangel affair."

Beck hesitated. He was caught between his professional obligation to tend to the family and his burning curiosity to know what the bishop had to say and ask him some questions. Maybe thirty more seconds. "Can you tell me briefly what this is about?"

"Just come and see me." Beck heard a sigh on the other end of the line.

"It seems," the bishop said, his voice despondent, "that I have a confession to make." He hung up.

Beck was stunned. Coming on the heels of Allen's discoveries, the bishop's call seemed doubly ominous. What did he have to confess? More importantly, what did this have to do with Deathangel? Had John Langert actually helped Tod Engel change his name? He remembered McCaslin's first phone call and the fear in his voice—fear from hearing words in a confession. Words that led to his death.

Matt's pager jolted him back to the present. He had to halt this speculation, rein in his imagination. He slowly walked to the family in the ER waiting area. Their hopes would soon be destroyed by the words he must speak to them.

He wondered if Langert might be about to do the same to him.

Anne loved and hated driving the Autobahn. One of Hitler's greater achievements, it was built to move large numbers of troops quickly and land planes in a pinch. The lack of speed limits reminded her of driving the vast, flat stretches of West Texas at speeds her daddy would have had a fit over, except that she learned them from him. She smiled as she glanced at the needle resting on 150 kph. He wouldn't like this woozy little VW Golf either, but it held the road better than the used pickup he'd given her at sixteen, especially in this drizzle. She flipped her headlights on as the gray clouds rolled in with the misty dusk from the mountains. She gripped the wheel and glanced in the rearview mirror. As much as she loved the unlimited speed, she hated the trucks that crept up behind her, flashed their high beams, and harassed her until she managed, at speeds even she thought dangerous, to shift to another lane and let them by.

Just as one was doing now.

She had entered the A1 on the other side of Enns late in the afternoon, and followed the signs for Wien. She had just gotten up to her fastest cruising speed when the huge truck came from nowhere, blinked its lights, and demanded passage.

The road was slick from the on-again, off-again showers that had accompanied her ride from Mauthausen, and she could feel the tires hydroplane on the thin layer of water and oil on the surface. If she went much faster she risked losing control of the car and crashing into the guardrail, possibly ending up under the wheels of the 18-wheeler. And yet she had to get around the speeding cars in the slower right lane.

Suddenly, the road opened up into a flat plain, and she floored the accelerator. The Golf slowly responded as she straightened her arms on the steering wheel, pushed the speedometer to 160 kph, then 170 kph, and now, as the car vibrated, to 180. She felt the front tires momentarily lose contact with the slick pavement. Up ahead she saw the road curve to the right. Her jaw tensed and her heart pounded. She had to move now or spin out.

The truck behind kept pace with her, lights blazing, bearing down, only a few feet from the rear bumper of her car. As the curve approached, Anne saw the chance to cut between two cars on her right.

Gently she eased over, barely turning the hydroplaning front wheels, forcing the second car to slow down and give her space to enter. As the lorry raced past her, she slowed back to 150 kph just in time for the curve, regaining control but causing the car behind her to flash its lights in anger.

Her heart had no time to recover from the adrenalin surge and strength necessary to guide the Golf. Even as she made her escape from the truck, she had seen another vehicle in her mirror—again. The two-door gray Mercedes had stayed behind her since Mauthausen, as she navigated her way through the narrow streets of Enns, across the river, and up to the Autobahn. It would not be unusual, she told herself, for tourists to be on the same route to Vienna, to pick up the A1 in the identical spot.

But this car was different. Others had sped up to pass her, and this one maintained its same distance behind her. When she changed lanes, it changed lanes. Even now, when she narrowly maneuvered her way out of danger, the Benz had followed dangerously close behind the truck, apparently not wanting to lose sight of her. Their first mistake.

Because now, with more trucks pushing from behind, the gray car was stuck in the left lane, directly beside her.

"Assholes," she snarled, the fury she'd experienced over the attack in her apartment somehow combining with her outrage at Mauthausen. She kept her car steady and rolled down her window for the best shot in the short time she knew she had. You don't wait till the snake strikes to see what it is. You move or get bit.

She moved.

Anne watched the two men in the gray car, but they would not turn their heads. She honked her horn. The passenger tossed her a menacing look, and she smiled sweetly and flipped him the bird. She was certain he could read the three words coming from her lips in any language.

The man yelled something to the driver as the passenger window gradually lowered. She saw the rising tip of an automatic weapon. Timing was everything. She honked the horn again to make sure she had both men's attention. Then she quickly raised the high-intensity photographer's flash from her lap, aimed it out the window, and pressed the button.

Ultrabright light lit up the Benz, temporarily blinding both passenger and driver. The driver slowed the car and Anne swerved hard into the Benz, forcing the huge vehicle into the center guardrail. She saw the gun drop from the passenger's hand as she careened away, hearing a loud sound that she hoped was their front tire and not hers. The rebound sent her out of her lane onto the paved shoulder. She hit the brake to regain control, then accelerated, assuming they would be right behind her. But when she checked in the rearview mirror, she saw the stalled Benz blocking both lanes of fender-bending traffic.

"Mark one for our side," she said, breathing deep with relief. When her adrenalin finally subsided, she became aware of the damage to her own car. It was difficult to steer, and the engine seemed to miss or skip or whatever the crap it was called. She saw signs announcing the St. Polten rest stop in three kilometers and the Schwechat Airport in fifty. She guessed the Golf could make the former but not the latter, and she pressed down on the gas pedal to get there quicker.

Who were her trackers and why did they seem willing to kill her? Could jolly old Herr Kremsbach have alerted them? For what reason? For what she might have learned at Mauthausen? Maybe. No wonder they didn't want her to see the death camp. The connection was there all the time. The language. The names. The pictures. Did these men seek to hide the proof she had recorded on film? If so, there was something much larger at stake than a few murders, something that stretched not only across the Atlantic but across the last fifty years, that meant these people would not stop at a missed shot on the Autobahn. They would try again, and she would need to be ready.

What should she do? She could outrun their car but not their cellular. If they were serious about capturing or killing her, all they had to do was to phone ahead for reinforcements. She wished Matt was here. It was what she wanted most of all—to see him. Not that he'd have any more of a clue what to do than she did. But she feels safer with another set of eyes, an alert mind disciplined by his father's special training. Someone she could trust as a stranger in a strange land. Someone she loved.

She shook her head to clear her thoughts. Cell phone. Phone. Should she call the Austrian police? And notify them of what? Of her paranoia that seeing a man with a gun meant he was going to use it on her so she smashed his car into an accident on the Autobahn? Unlikely that they would rush to her rescue.

The rest-stop sign read "Gaststatte 1K," and it had the symbols for gas and food on it. This must be one of those huge things where the restaurant was built up over the highway. The thought of food reminded her of the starving prisoners at Mauthausen, forced to work in the stone quarry, to build the camp, to carry huge granite blocks in back harnesses up the Death Staircase—Der Todsteige.

The Ausfahrt sign to exit appeared up ahead. But what would she do when she got there? Who could she— ?

Baumschen.

He knew the case and he was the expert on terrorists. He wouldn't think she was crazy, and he had told them to contact him when they needed help. At least she should let him know where she was and what had happened—assuming she could trust him. She would have to.

The light was fading when she swung off the Autobahn into the large parking area by the restaurant and gas station. Just to be safe, she circled the lot and parked in a distant spot with the damaged side of her car to the forest. She hunkered down in the car for twenty minutes, pretending to read a map and tour book. Anyone watching would think she was resting, determining her route instead of watching for the gray Mercedes. From behind the map she used her cell phone to call Baumschen's number. The scratchy quality of his voice mail made the message in German even more difficult to understand. She briefly described what had happened and her present location and asked him to send someone out to meet her. If she could manage to leave the restaurant in one piece, she'd call again and arrange an escort to the airport.

Feeling safe for the moment, she finally emerged from the car with her camera and purse in hand, locked the door, and walked to the restaurant, which perched like a glass bridge high above the road. From its many tables, one could see cars streaming underneath, as well as spectacular views—in weather other than this darkening drizzle—of the Vienna Woods, Der Wienerwald.

Wienerwald.

Todsteige.

Todengel.

Why hadn't anyone searched out these connections before? She stood staring out the window, surveying the parking area in case there was something she had missed before. And there was.

Anne spotted the gray Benz near the repair bay of the gas station. Empty. Her heart raced as she rushed from the window. She wasn't sure whether to return to her car or risk encountering the men in the restaurant. But she knew there was one place they would not be.

She located the door marked Damen and went in.

Fifteen minutes later, she emerged from the rest room, having unsuccessfully tried Baumschen again. She walked by the window and saw one of the men next to her car. He glanced up just as she looked down, but she didn't think he saw her amid so many people. She quickly entered the crowded restaurant and chose a booth in the back, invisible from the entrance station. They would not risk coming up here, given the numbers of people seeking refuge from the rain, including families with children. And if they did, they would not easily find her. They would think she had escaped or was down in the petrol area trying to hitch a ride or steal a car.

She pretended to read the menu and looked up to realize she had not seen the mirror extending across the length of the back wall. In it, she could view the entrance station—and the man holding his automatic weapon could see her.

She cursed but did not move, waiting to see what he would do. Surely they would not start shooting. She dropped her hand to her purse as the man motioned to his nearby partner, who fired an Uzi into the ceiling. Shrieks went up from the patrons as the man yelled in German—and in English.

"Everyone down on the floor! Now! Take out your valuables!"

As the screaming people complied, Anne grabbed the heavy glass sugar container on her table and flung it into the mirror a few yards away. It crashed to shards and, in the confusion of noise and people, the gunmen missed her crawling toward the kitchen through the shuffling crowd. She prayed that there would be a rear exit.

Suddenly, a uniformed security cop rushed out of the kitchen firing his Glock. Anne saw the gunman take a step back from the force of the bullet to his chest but continue to stand. A vest, she thought, hoping the guard knew where to aim next. But she knew he would never get the chance. She crouched behind a table as bullets riddled the man's body and he dropped a few feet away.

Anne slithered to reach the cop's gun, checked the clip, and, trembling, rose on one knee to aim above the screeching people throwing themselves to the floor. She targeted just below the vest, fired, and watched the gunman's thigh explode in a gush of red.

His partner fired in her direction, but she had already fled behind the safety of the same swinging door the guard had used from the kitchen. If she could draw the remaining terrorist to chase her, she could distract him from hurting the others and maybe buy time for the police to arrive. Why hadn't Baumschen sent someone for her? Or—she wondered in a moment of real panic—had he?

She had only seconds. She shoved at a large service door, but it was locked tight. The kitchen staff had disappeared. She stowed her camera in her purse and skidded it across the floor toward a pile of spilled produce. If she didn't make it, maybe her notes would. Then she ran to the only hiding place she saw.

Hunched down beside a huge stainless steel cooler, she heard the kitchen door slam open and a fusillade of shots burst from the Uzi. She cringed as bullets careened off metal everywhere, pinging by her as they ricocheted. She had two choices—wait for him to work his way back to her and try to squeeze off a shot before he killed her or try to surprise him. There was no decision. Never wait for the snake.

She grabbed a metal skillet from the counter and tossed it toward the opposite side of the room. As the hail of bullets followed the pan, Anne jumped up and unloaded her gun at the terrorist.

She did not see where she hit him. The wound in her side and the slam to her leg made her dance like a marionette with cut strings. In those brief moments of silent slow motion, Anne saw Robert, arms reaching for her, smiling and kissing her, welcoming her back to him. She felt safe, comfortable, so at peace. When the horrible staccato came again, she was in the middle of a swirling vortex of pots and pans, knives and steel. She called out desperately for Matt as she flailed at the air and collapsed in a blood-smeared pile on the floor.

Unable to move, she could barely hear the sound of distant sirens. She watched a blurred figure limp past her, grab her purse, and, after some seconds of searching—take her camera. Then he vanished amid more distant gunshots.

Pain. Everything was pain. Anne frowned in confusion as tall blurs gathered around her. An old man picked up an object that had fallen from her purse. He leaned down and placed it by her hand, just outside the widening pool of blood beneath her.

It was the hand-carved wooden angel.

"Todengel," he murmured, as if in prayer. "Todengel."

It was the last word she heard.

Chapter 11

The death had taken less time than Beck expected. The girl's family would not sign for organ donation. They wanted her body intact, the way it had come into the world. They abhorred the thought of disfiguring her any more than she had been by the accident even though the procurement team assured them there would be no signs of such surgery at the funeral, that her death would save five people's lives and restore the sight of six more. It was too much for the Parents. They signed the funeral home papers, said their good-byes, and left.

For the last hour, Matt had driven the Spider from the county to the city, his mind changing lanes more often than the car. The girl's organs were wasted, he thought, as another pair of kidneys passed him riding a donorcycle. What did the bishop have to confess? Maybe somebody Matt knew could have used those organs. Maybe the bishop? Anne? God forbid! Himself? He remembered Ciccilini's comment about the car's open top in the city. Why was Langert's driver working for Ciccilini? Coincidence or something else?

Matt jumped when his cell phone rang in the seat beside him. He clicked it on and held it to his ear. "Hello?"

"Father Beck?"

Speak of the devil and up he pops on your phone. "Ciccilini?"

"You know I don't like these cell things, but I tried you at home and work with no luck. I got some information you might need right away."

"It's okay. What happened?"

"Turns out you were right, Father, about Big Earl Eslin. He claims he just got the dates wrong and forgot Bishop Langert was out of town the night he told me he had to drive for him. His friend who also works for me backs his story a hundred percent."

"What do you think?"

"I think they're both lyin' bastards. You should forgive me, Father."

So Eslin, Langert's employee, probably broke into Anne's apartment, but what was his connection to terrorists or Deathangel?

"I was also thinkin' you'd want me to fire their sorry asses, Father."

He was taking a chance involving Ciccilini further, maybe even endangering his life. On the other hand, Alfonse was probably pretty well connected himself. "Not yet, Al. Watch both of them for me and see if they go near Anne's apartment while she's out of town. But be really careful. He may be a lot more dangerous than either of us knows."

Beck heard a loud snort.

"Nothin' me and my family can't handle, Father."

Matt smiled and changed lanes to head toward the bishop's mansion on Morningside Heights. "Thanks for checking."

"Somethin' else I need to tell you."

Beck was silent, concentrating on taking the right exit and dodging pot-holes.

"While I was checkin' on Eslin, I got talkin' to some Polish cops in the local gin mill and they were braggin' on that Rinski guy up where you are in Westchester? How he's gonna be First Polack once his boss is elected to the Senate. They say he's gonna get some security post or something. Said he should, seein' how his old man was some kinda Nazi hunter or something."

Beck nearly dropped the phone. The European connection again. What was Anne facing over there? He'd have to contact Twitch and see how to reach her. "Sorry," he said. "Did you say Nazi hunter?"

"Yeah, after the war, but they didn't really know much about it. You know how this younger generation is. They hardly know anything about anything. Could be it's just rumors, like things are most of the time. But I thought you should know what I heard, about Rinski, I mean."

"Thanks. That's really good information, Al. Call me if you hear anything else, anything at all."

"You got it."

"And keep an eye on Eslin."

Beck heard the snort again. "Hell, I got more than that lookin' at him, I can assure you. This is a long way from over."

Matt told him again to be careful and clicked off the phone. He was not surprised about Eslin lying, but the Rinski details didn't seem to fit. If his father really was a Nazi hunter, he was probably about the same age as the Austrian Deathangel victims. Perhaps he had known them. Where was all this going? Beck felt like he had downloaded a picture off the Net and the resolution was too fuzzy to tell what it was.

He pulled onto Morningside Drive. He would have to consider it later, hope the resolution filled in more completely after his talk with Langert. Otherwise it would distract him from what he had to say to—and hear from—the bishop of the Diocese of New York.

He braked the Spider to a stop in front of the mansion, and the gray-haired uniformed doorman approached.

"I have instructions from Bishop Langert to put your car in our secure garage, if you will permit me, Father Beck? The neighborhood, you know."

Matt slid the car key off the ring and handed it to him. That way, if anyone stole the keys or wanted to make a copy, all they could get into was the car.

"Thank you very much," he said, handing the man a five dollar bill. It would be a start on the chiropractor fee when this old guy pried himself out of the Spider.

"I cannot accept that, Father, but thank you for your generosity," the man said as he slipped into the car and drove away.

It occurred to Beck that he had just handed over his Fiat to someone who provided no identification and could just as easily be a con in a rented uniform as the doorman for the bishop.

He smiled. Interesting what trust we give and expect in this world, based solely on attire. Had the doorman been dressed in jeans and a T-shirt, Beck would certainly have questioned his employment and probably verified it with the bishop. If Tod Engel were dressed in a blue shirt and tie, he'd be mistaken for the warden. Put the warden in a Sing Sing suit and he'd look like a convicted mass murderer.

Clothes, titles, appearances—warden, county executive, bishop, police commissioner, priest, journalist—the worst ways to judge character were always the first methods used in society, which was why so many people were conned. And also why the church eschewed normal attire and dressed its religious and clerics in common black or gray. That way clothes could not confuse or mislead; the focus was on words and actions, not on appearances. It also made his wardrobe choices a lot easier every morning.

Funny, Beck thought, as he ascended the steps to the front door of the large, three-story brownstone, how that idea had backfired. Now people looked at clerical attire and automatically assumed trust and openness, which often paved the way for temptation and deception—and worse. It reminded him of his dilemma. How would he raise the issue of Engel's name change and Langert's signature on the receipt? He had to do it, but it would make or break their relationship. His thoughts were interrupted by the Bishop's tenorous voice.

"Is that you, Matthew?" The words came through the small speaker by the door.

"Yes, Bishop."

"Come to the second floor."

The lock buzzed and Beck pushed the door open. He wondered if Langert would be wearing the traditional purple shirt and pectoral cross of his office. And he wondered what that attire concealed, what was about to be brought into the open.

On the second-floor landing, John Langert welcomed his guest. The purple and pectoral had been replaced by a plaid sport shirt and white cardigan.

"Thank you for coming this evening, Matthew," he said, shaking Beck's hand and leading him into the parlor. "I know it was a long drive from the hospital, and I hope you will forgive the urgency of an old man's worries."

The two priests sat down across a round, wooden coffee table with a glass mirror top. The room reeked of strong tobacco, and Beck was surprised that Langert did not ask if he could smoke. Perhaps he assumed better, and rightly so.

"I remember the last time I was here," Beck said, "right after you became bishop." In better days. Closer days.

"I know, and I am sorry for that. Our careers, our interests, they seem to rule our lives for a time, don't they? We presume that our jobs are so important, the issues are so pressing, the moments so few." Langert looked contrite. "I hope that will all change after we talk tonight and that you will be a more frequent visitor to this place."

That remained to be seen, Beck thought, glancing around the room. "It's elegant. Did you do the furnishing?"

"I am afraid there is a guild for everything in our beloved Episcopal church. The Diocese has a group of people, men and women in St. Gertrude's Guild, whose job it is to decorate and outfit the living quarters." He took two glasses from a small side cabinet. "Can I offer you a drink?"

"Whiskey, if you have it."

"Of course. Black Bush." He used silver tongs to remove ice from a glass container. "They did let me approve the plans for the remodeling after Bishop Mayfield retired, but I must admit that it was pretty much a rubber stamp." He surveyed the study. "Victorian may fit my personality, but not my tastes. I did prevail in my office area, however. It is more modern, quite a contrast to this—" He raised his hands in a sweeping motion. "This nineteenth-century French whorehouse look."

Matt raised his eyebrows. "I was thinking it but not saying it."

"Everybody does." the bishop smiled. He raised his glass of whiskey. "Salud."

"Cheers," Beck said. He drank, the Black Bush warming the back of his throat. "For a man who describes himself as anxious, you seem more relaxed than I expected. Perhaps it's the shirt and sweater."

Langert laughed. "I'm not the bishop twenty-four hours a day, Matthew, just as you are not a priest when enjoying the company of your friend Miss Demming."

Beck was not certain whether the comment was meant to put him off guard and make him nervous or an attempt to garner affinity, a reminder that they knew and understood each other's needs and the reality of their profession.

"How is Anne, anyway?" Langert asked. "She looked well, and you both seemed happy at the restaurant—before the, what shall we call it?"

"Attempt on your life seems appropriate." Beck wondered if Langert was taking his time leading up to something or just working up the courage to talk. "Are you recovered from that?"

"Almost completely. But we were talking about Anne."

Yes, but why? "I assume she's fine, Bishop. She's off on some assignment for *CityMag* for a few days, buzzing around the world interviewing people. It's not a bad job."

"It certainly isn't. And I must say your relationship beats the hell out of any of my own." Langert glanced around the room. "It's very lonely here sometimes, in this big house."

"I always wondered why you never married."

Langert stared at him. "I called you here tonight to hear my confession, Matthew, so I suppose I may also tell you about other details of my life, details that few, if any, know about me." He poured another glass of whiskey for himself.

"I was married once. It was a long time ago, even before I came to the seminary in Ohio."

"Bexley Hall?" Matt queried, trying to hide his surprise.

"Yes, that was it." He settled into the overstuffed chair. "I had graduated from a small college in Ohio—Otterbein—and decided to work a while to determine what I wanted to do with my life. I was, believe it or not, quite a shy person, and so the first girl I fell in love with I married. To make a long and very painful story short, she left me after I had been at Bexley for two months." He smiled ruefully. "Ran off with another seminarian. I received annulment papers about six months later in the mail from a judge in Spokane."

"And since then?"

"Since then, my romantic liaisons have been few, especially in the last ten years as bishop. As you know, things are possible in a local parish that would never be permitted at this level of visibility." He sat up a bit. "And now they must be severely limited—or very discreet—for the remaining years of my tenure."

Beck looked at him. Here it came. "Why is that?"

"Because I learned today that I have been nominated to become presiding bishop of the Episcopal Church."

Matt also sat up. He had assumed it from all the church and clergy rumors, but having it confirmed was another story. It was a quantum leap in power and authority, not entirely unexpected of this man, who had led the Diocese of New York through difficult financial and social times. "Are congratulations or condolences in order?"

"A little of both, I'm afraid. I must admit that I've secretly hoped for this chance. There is so much to do at the national level, and I believe my influence could effect sweeping changes in the social action agenda of our denomination."

Beck put his drink on the table and propped his chin on his hand. "It may be time for a liberal leader again, in the tradition of John Hines and Roger Blanchard. But you'll face stiff opposition. There's a conservative backlash in the Church that would like to hitch its agenda to the national politics of the Right."

"I didn't become bishop by ignoring what I see, Matthew. You seem troubled. Do you have some objection to my running for P.B.?"

Beck chose his words carefully. If he was wrong, if he cast unjustified aspersions on Langert, and if the bishop got pissed at him, his career was over, former friendship or not. "I have to tell you the truth."

"I would hope you would."

Beck took a deep breath and launched in. "I recently heard something very disturbing, if it's true. It's about Tod Engel." Matt paused. "Or rather, Edward Clopton."

Langert raised his eyebrows.

"Your name, your signature, is on a receipt that paid for Tod Engel to change his name from Edward Clopton to the equivalent of Deathangel." Beck watched the other man carefully. "I need to know how you explain that."

Langert folded his hands and placed them in his lap. He stared in silence a moment.

"I believe you are here to hear my confession, Matthew. And I would like to begin that sacrament right now."

Beck tried to restrain his nervousness. "Formally?" He removed the small stole and oil from his pocket.

"Semiformally," Langert said, waving them away. "It is formal in the sense that it is said to you in priestly confidence. It is informal in that I do not intend to use the ritual of the prayer book. I simply wish to talk."

Matt nodded. "That's fine," he said. "But, to be frank, I don't understand. Why me?"

Langert sipped his whiskey. "You are a priest who knows me but is unlikely to prejudge what I'm going to say—at least I hope that is true, given what you've asked about Tod Engel. It is important to me that the confessor be fair minded. But the main reason will become obvious as I talk."

"About Engel?" Beck ventured.

The bishop nodded.

Beck leaned back, trying to rein in his eagerness to push. "I'm listening."

"Let me say first," Langert began, "that I appreciate your concern for Tod Engel. You seem to be the only person, other than myself, who shows an interest in the man these days."

That was not entirely true. "A lot of people are interested in him, Bishop, but for different reasons. Most of them want him to remain right where he is."

"I'm sure that's correct." Langert's tone turned solemn. "We are under the stole now, you understand?"

Beck nodded, slipped the small stole around his neck, and braced himself for a shock.

"Good. Then what I have to confess to you is that a part of me sides with them. If Tod Engel is quietly kept in Weston State Prison, my future is almost assured. On the other hand, if the case is opened up there is a good chance that I will not be elected Presiding Bishop."

Matt took a swallow of the Irish whiskey to stall his response. Whatever he had expected, this was not it. Langert, the long defender of Engel, claiming it was in his best interests that Engel stay incarcerated? "Continue," he said quietly, trying to control the gasping sensation in his lungs.

Langert took a deep breath. Beck could see that this was hard for him. "All candidates for presiding bishop are carefully screened, as you know. A private, independent investigating agency does a background check, leaving little unearthed. And that's a good thing. It would be quite a public embarrassment to the church if the person elected turned out to be—I don't know—a violent criminal or an embezzler or a bigamist or something."

"Embarrassing but entertaining." Beck grinned, trying to lighten the situation.

Langert's voice remained serious. "In my own case, none of the above is true. But there is one item you alone must know. I can only hope that, by telling you, I can pursue the office with a clean conscience."

Beck fingered the stole. Only his commitment to what it represented instilled the necessary calm to sit and listen. Everything in his life, it seemed, had been damaged by Deathangel. He prayed to forestall his anger at his mentor for keeping secrets about the case, secrets that might throw new light on Kate's death.

"It's a matter of public record that I have avidly supported the innocence of Tod Engel in the decade since the murders. I made something of a spectacle of myself at the trial to the point of being charged with contempt for one too many outbursts in the courtroom. But you don't know why, do you?"

"You knew him from his hanging around your church. You'd given him food a few times, and you always had some intuitive sense that he was not a killer."

"No," Langert said, sitting forward. "It's more than that."

Matt looked at him.

"The truth is—and this is said under the seal of the confessional—that I now confess to you I knew Tod Engel much better than I admitted in court and long before the murders were committed."

Beck's head spun from more than the alcohol. "You what?" he said, before he realized his tone. "Sorry."

"It's all right." Langert smiled. "It's as much a shock for me to say it as it is for you to hear it." He sipped from his glass. "I knew Tod Engel very well. That's why I'm certain that he couldn't have done the killings."

"But how?" If this information surfaced now, it might appear as if the bishop of New York had withheld evidence in a homicide case, maybe even conspired against the man. "You admitted enough acquaintance with him to testify to his character at the trial, and to vociferously defend him in the courtroom." Beck stared at his superior. "What the hell did you hold back?"

Langert folded back into the chair. "It's actually quite a simple story, as Engel is a simple man," the Bishop said. "When I was first made rector of St. James in Hastings-on-Hudson, a man named Edward Clopton appeared at my door one night."

"How did he choose St. James?"

"Just let me ramble. I'll get it all in, I promise."

Beck added ice to his drink. This could be a long night.

"Clopton, or Engel as we know him now, was a drifter. He'd been living in doorways and under bridges in New York City until, like many people more prosperous than himself, he decided to reside in the plush regions of Westchester County.

"The first place he came for a handout was the church. At that time the rectory was right next door—it's been replaced by an education building and a school now—so Engel, I guess it was his first night in the county, knocked on my door and told me his story."

Must have been some story, Beck thought, watching the man who would be king bow before his own memories.

"Engel said he had traveled a long way, was hungry, and would work for food." Beck watched Langert cup the drink in his hands. Clearly it was hard for the bishop to relive this, but his future depended on it. "I was underfunded, with no staff in what was a poor parish then, and the church needed someone to do sexton work." Langert held Beck's gaze. "So I decided to help. I invited him in, and he spent the night in the basement of the rectory. After breakfast the next morning, I set him up in an old hotel down by the river where a lot of older people lived on small pensions.

"The deal was that I would help him and he would keep a low profile. He cleaned the church when no one was around, late at night, and he wore a ball cap and glasses so that even if someone did see him, they wouldn't recognize him a second time. The church was so small that it was easy to do. If he had been discovered, they would have run him off. He was—abnormal—in some ways. But he seemed to understand that. Mentally retarded, possibly brain damaged. I had lots of odd jobs for him. He was the perfect person for them. He spoke very little, was good at following directions, and had a knack for staying out of sight."

Matt was puzzled. "So what was the problem? So far, I see nothing to prevent you from acknowledging all this."

"No, wait." Langert sat forward again. "Something happened. He was working in the church yard one day when the neighborhood bully started harassing him. He ignored it as long as he could, but when the kid pushed him, he pushed back. Hard. Defending himself. He knocked the kid to the ground and accidentally split his head open on a rock. I heard the commotion and ran outside." The bishop's voice tensed. "I panicked, too, not knowing what would happen if people found out I'd been hiding Engel, paying him on the sly. What would my congregation think? So I sent him away and called the ambulance, telling them the injured boy was vandalizing the church and fell when I ran out to stop him."

Matt guessed what happened next.

"The kid died in a coma. His family tried to sue the church but couldn't win, given the boy's rap sheet in juvenile court." Langert buried his head in his hands. "So I have covered up the death, the murder really, of a young person by Tod Engel."

"Self-defense, maybe involuntary manslaughter at the most, but not murder," Beck said. Though he knew any review committee for presiding bishop would not see the cover-up that way.

Langert perched on the edge of the chair. "But I must tell you, Matthew, that despite this incident, there wasn't a violent bone in that man's body. He was just pushing the boy away. He couldn't have committed those murders." His voice become fervent. Matt wondered who he was trying to convince. "And that leads to the answer to your original question."

"Your signature on the receipt?"

"Yes. After the boy's death, the police constantly harassed Clopton. They'd drag him in on vagrancy charges or whatever they could think of to get him in a lineup. Edward came to me one day saying he wanted to start over and asked me to help him change his name. He had some notion that he wouldn't be bothered as much, or that the police records would show no priors on an Engel and would let him go if he was detained. I knew it was silly, that his fingerprints would link him to his real name, but I also assumed it couldn't hurt anything and that he couldn't make the change himself."

"So you did help him?"

"Of course I did. Wouldn't you?"

"Why Pennsylvania?"

Langert replied, "He didn't want to do it in New York or Jersey. He was afraid the clerk would look up his record and not allow him to do it or that they might notify police of the change and it wouldn't make any difference."

Beck asked carefully: "And where did Clopton come up with that name? Why did he choose that name in particular?"

Langert looked genuinely puzzled. "I imagine he must have known some German, but I'm not sure. I do remember he had it written down on a piece of paper. Maybe it was some odd reference to his killing the boy."

And an odd, very coincidental reference to the later murders of eight people, Matt thought. "The name was written down?"

Langert nodded. "Though, now that you say that, Clopton can't really write. He only makes block letters. And I'm almost certain the name was in cursive."

Beck wondered about the bishop's sudden revelation about a piece of paper long vanished. "So someone could have given him that name and suggested he change it to avoid the police? Someone who was setting him up for a future fall?"

"I hadn't really considered it until recently, but yes, that seems possible. All I know is that Clopton seemed happy after we went to Pennsylvania and signed the papers, and he was grateful to me for helping, in addition to loaning him money for the processing fee."

It was all plausible, especially if Rinski was in the picture. Beck would discuss the issue with Anne as soon as he saw her. "And Engel's behavior toward you now? How does he react when he sees you?"

"Tod always hated being confined. I'm sure being in Weston these years has taken its toll on whatever restraining reflexes he had."

"So he's violent with you?"

"Not exactly. He has never hit me. I don't believe he would, either. But he is always agitated and upset with me. I'm not sure if he blames me for his incarceration, for not coming forth at the trial and admitting I knew him back when the boy was killed, testifying not just for his reliability, but for his docility."

That indeed was the question. "So," Beck said gently. "Why didn't you?"

"You will think this weak of me, but I was frightened. I was afraid that I might be forced under oath to answer a question about whether or not Tod Engel had ever hurt anyone. That answer would not only have underscored their conviction, it would have resulted in my own prosecution, as it would today."

Beck shook his head. Oh, what a tangled web we weave.

"And all the evidence, including Tod's own confession, pointed in the direction of his guilt. The murders did stop when he was apprehended." Langert rubbed his face. "I'm ashamed and embarrassed to say this, but it's true. I confess to you that I feared no one would understand my relationship with Engel. And, of course, that I would be at all associated with such a horrendous murderer—other than in the mode of an occasional food or clothing handout from the church—would have meant the end of my career, just when I was about to reach a position where I could really make a difference."

Beck understood. "As it would now," he said.

"As it would now," Langert repeated, staring at him, "should the information ever become public."

Matt placed his glass on the table. The inference was clear, and he didn't like it. "I see," he said. "So you would also find it to be in your best interest if the Deathangel case were not reopened."

Langert nodded. "I am, in a sense, at your mercy. If the case is started up again, there's a better than decent chance that the investigators will discover my long-term connection with Tod. And," he said, looking intently at Beck, "that would mean the end of my dream to become presiding bishop." He put his drink aside. "I know this is hard for you, because of, well, Kate. But that was ten years ago. You have to think of the greatest good for the greatest number now. You have to consider what will happen if a conservative bishop is elected—the direction the church will take."

Matt stared back at him. His impulse was to throw his whiskey in the man's face and storm out. So this was why Langert had chosen him for the confession. Not only was it all "under the stole" so Beck couldn't repeat it, but the bishop was asking him to retreat from the issue entirely. Ultimately asking him to hide the truth about Kate's death.

Beck stood to go. "Let me see if I've got this straight, Bishop. Are you asking me to drop my inquiries, let McCaslin's death—his murder—go unpunished, and allow Tod Engel to rot in Weston Prison without ever finding the real murderer, just so the obviously greater good of your personal career and, of course, the church's national agenda, can go forward unimpeded?"

He was surprised that Langert did not blink at the verbal assault. Instead, the bishop answered calmly, as though he had anticipated the reaction and sought to soften it. "The only thing I have asked you to do is to hear my confession." Langert rose from his chair. "Nothing more," he said, bowing his head. "Do I have your absolution?"

Matt made the sign of the cross. "For not coming forth at the time, you do. For your protection of the man regarding the accident, you do also." His voice deepened with anger as he removed the stole and stuffed it in a pocket. "For the present situation and the request you are intimating of me, you will have to go to a higher authority than myself."

Langert crossed himself. "In the Name of the Father, and of the Son and of the Holy Spirit. Amen." Beck saw him press a button on the phone to alert the old guy in the uniform downstairs. He turned and led Matt to the hallway. "Please keep in mind, Matthew, that upon my election to presiding bishop there will be many top positions, influential positions with social clout, that will need to be filled with competent, capable people. People such as yourself."

Matt was furious at the offer. "Assuming you're elected, of course." Asshole. It took incredible gall for Langert to presume that Beck would work for him after this. Allen had been right about the man all along.

Langert smiled. "I have done my homework, Matthew," he said. "The votes are counted before the convention begins."

"They may do a recount when the Deathangel case is reopened." Two can play this game, Beck thought, and Langert had seriously miscalculated his latest move.

"If it is reopened," the bishop said sternly. "And that depends a great deal on your influence with Anne Demming."

Beck descended the stairway to the ground floor. He decided discretion was the better part of valor. It was time to get the hell out of there. "I'll be in touch."

"I'm counting on it." Langert raised his hand in blessing. "Thank you again for coming tonight."

Matt spun around, about to reject the blessing, the booze, and the slimy political offer. He checked himself and said only, "Good night."

Outside, Beck was relieved to breathe the brisk night air, the first clean smell he'd inhaled in the last hour. It cleared his buzzing head, calmed his anger, and brought him back to the reality of where and who he was. It would take time to process what he'd just been through, and he wished he was simply going home to Anne. God, he missed her.

The smiling doorman rounded the block in Matt's car and nimbly climbed out. All Beck wanted was to be gone, and he forgot to even offer a tip to be refused.

As he drove away in the open Spider, he glimpsed John Langert watching at the curtains of the second-story window. Beck thought of Joe McCaslin lying in ICU, breathing his last. For the first few miles Matt continually tested the brakes.

Even after he reached I-284 north of the city, Matt's fury still had not abated. Unfortunately, Langert was correct in his assumptions about who would be elected presiding bishop. If the other candidates were archconservatives, as they likely would be, or even progressive moderates, the impact of the Episcopal church in the twenty-first century could be determined by this election. If Langert and his liberal social agenda were taken out of the running, social progress would be delayed, impoverished people would suffer even more at the hands of the conservative political trend, and the powerful resources of the church would be restricted for at least another decade.

He checked the vibration at his waist and saw the phone number for Anne's office at *CityMag* on his pager. Great, he thought, for the second time that day, maybe she's back sooner than she planned. He punched the number into his cell phone and heard only a series of beeps indicating a low battery. But he was just ten minutes from the mountain and could call as soon as he reached the house. Beck pressed the accelerator, anxious to talk to Anne, wishing she was home to greet him at the door, just as he had once felt with Kate.

Kate. That was what was really eating at him. Langert had clamped him in a vice between the church and Kate. A decision not to pursue the case, or to attempt to dissuade Anne from continuing her investigation, was a decision to let Kate's killer go free. The alternative would mean exposure of Langert's earlier involvement and his probable withdrawal from the nomination for presiding bishop—an enormous setback for the church, even if its prime servant was morally bankrupt.

His pager repeated the same number a second time. Matt switched on the heater to dull the chill seeping in around the ragtop. Got to be Anne, he thought, and got to be important. He turned off the main highway and argued the moral dilemma both ways in his head. Did the potential for good inherent in the church supporting a social agenda for issues of moral justice outweigh the bad of the real murderer being allowed to escape? But their efforts to discover that killer, even reopening the case, offered no guarantee that they could find the real Deathangel. Indeed, the heavy hitters with whom they were playing might be able to ensure that Engel was convicted again. Evidence could disappear, files could vanish. People could vanish or die, too, as he and Anne well knew. And what of Jesus' injunction to leave the dead to bury the dead? Did that mean it would do no good and greater harm to pursue the case just to find Kate's killer? Would she even want him to do that, given the stakes? Was that what sacrifice meant in this situation?

Beck cursed as he felt the vibration at his waist a third time. Maybe this would teach him to carry the phone cord and the plug in the glove box with him, as Anne had suggested about a million times. At last he raced up the drive to the mountain, pulled into the garage, and hurried into the house to the phone.

"Matt, is that you?" the voice answered, without greeting.

"Twitch?" Why wasn't Anne on the line? Beck didn't like the tone of Jackson Twitchel's voice. The chief at *CityMag* was used to stress, and it took a lot to flap him. "Where's Anne?"

"What the devil took you so long?"

"I was on the road," Beck said. "What's going on down there? Is she back? Did she find something?"

Silence met his question.

"I'm afraid I have some bad news for you."

Beck's mind spun. Flashing EMS lights. A crowd around Kate's body. It was happening again. Deathangel.

"First of all, she's still alive."

"Alive?" Now he truly panicked. This could not be. This could not happen to her. "Where is she?"

"She's in Europe. She went there—"

"I know why she went there. What happened, damn it?"

"There's no easy way to put this," Twitch said. "She was involved in a terrorist attack."

Beck collapsed into a chair. For a moment, the breath was knocked out of him. He saw her in the apartment with a bandage on her neck. Why hadn't they been more cautious? Was this the answer to his dilemma of Langert versus Kate? He could not lose two women he loved to Deathangel. He would make her drop everything. Leave Langert alone. Go off by themselves and stay away from danger. He clutched the phone.

"Matt? You there?"

"Yeah. Okay. Tell me what happened."

"She was at a rest stop on the Autobahn—I guess she was on her way back to the Vienna airport—when two terrorists busted into the restaurant and started shooting."

"Oh, my God." Not again. "How bad is she?"

"Details after that are sketchy—except to say that she reportedly killed one of them."

"How? She didn't have her LadyHawke."

"She took a gun from the security guard when they wasted him."

Matt shook his head. Vengeance is mine, says the Lord. But Anne had helped the Lord out a bit this time. "What's her condition?"

"Her condition is damned lucky," Twitch said. Matt did not like the hesitation in his voice. "She took one slug to her side, but it was a clean wound, if there is such a thing. It did break a rib, but they tell me that heals pretty quickly. The others—"

"Others!" Beck said, standing up. He had known Twitch almost as long as he'd known Anne. It was unlike him to hold back unless the news was very bad. "How many others?"

"Twelve in all."

Again Matt could not breathe. He sagged against the table.

"It was an assault gun. An Uzi. But listen."

Beck could not listen. He dropped the phone on the table. Tears filled his eyes. He couldn't stand thinking of her in pain. He couldn't do this again. He would have to join her if she died. From a distance he heard Twitch yelling through the phone.

"Listen to me, Matt! I talked with the doctor. She was pumped with twelve hits, but the majority were flesh wounds. She looks like shit, according to him, beat up mostly, but the one side wound was the only truly invasive one."

Beck sat on a kitchen chair and tried to regain control. He picked up the receiver. "I'll leave immediately. When can I bring her back?"

"Not necessary." Twitch's voice was firm and Matt knew the man would not bargain. Decisions had been made. He would have to comply for the moment. "I knew you'd want to go, but I've arranged with the state department for her to be on the next military flight from Vienna to Kennedy. She'll be home before you could possibly get there, just as soon as she's stable."

"Can I call? Talk to her?"

"The doctor said no, not right now. She's pretty sedated, and they need her to stay that way, mainly for the trauma."

"What trauma?" Beck felt anger flood over the fear. "Damn it, Twitch, what else happened to her?"

"She took a graze wound to her head. They did a CAT scan and are assuming no damage was done, but they won't know until she wakes up. The doctor said she could have some memory damage—or there may be no problems at all. They're keeping a close watch on her—the doctors and the police. I talked with Baumschen at Interpol. Remember him?"

"Yes."

"Apparently she tried to contact him just before it happened. He had his agents on the way. But by the time they arrived, they found one dead terrorist and the other escaped, though it appears she put a few mementos in his body, too."

Matt smiled tightly. "Don't mess with Texans, she always says." She was going to be all right. He was sure of it, even though the chaplain side of him, the side that imagined her coming into his ER, would not be so optimistic. She had to be all right. Had to be.

"Damned straight. I'll call you when I'm sure what time the flight comes in. Should be another twenty-four hours at most."

"But I could get there in that time."

"She's under constant medical observation. Just sit tight and I'll let you know when I have definite information." Twitch paused. "There was something else, Matt."

Beck took a deep breath, ready for more bad news. "Tell me everything."

"It's not about her medical condition. It's about how Baumschen said they found her."

"What?" The nightmare of Kate's body on the stretcher with Anne's face flashed before him.

"Remember those angels that were always left at the murder scenes by Engel?"

Beck couldn't answer. His heart pounded.

"There was one beside her on the floor."

Matt swallowed hard. The quest begun with the break-in at her Brooklyn condo had ended in a rest stop on the Autobahn. She had found the connection she sought and they had tried to kill her for it. A connection beyond New York. Beyond Tod Engel. Right back to Deathangel. "Call me as soon as you know more."

Beck hung up and forced back the fresh tears from his eyes. He shouted at God, furious, scared, worried, shouted as he would at a friend, like Art, who would listen and love him anyway; prayed for her safe return to him, prayed to find the killer, prayed for God to wreak vengeance on him—on them—or to use him as the instrument to do it. Soon.

He walked to the living room and opened a hidden drawer in an end table. He lifted out the LadyHawke and checked the full clip.

As he lay in bed that night, the hand that was used to caressing the soft flesh of Anne Demming now clung to the cold steel of a .38.

The tower guard poured his fifth cup of coffee that morning. "God, I hate this stuff," he said, frowning.

"Yeah," the other guard said. "You'd think we'd get used to it after all the years we've spent at this joint."

"I got this theory." The first guard grinned. "This shit is like some kind of potion. It's what keeps us sane and the bozos behind the walls there crazy."

The other guard smirked. "Maybe it's what makes us think we're any different from them." He dropped three sugars in a ceramic mug with "Sea World" emblazoned on it. "I mean, hell, Hank, be honest now. Wouldn't you like to have done half the stuff these psychos have gotten away with?"

"Now that you mention it, the wife and I were talkin' just the other night about how these bums get to rape and steal and kill, and all they get is locked up and fed and pampered. Damn, Bill," he said, looking out over the feeder roads to the prison, "you and I ever tried that shit, they'd shoot us for sure."

Bill nodded and said, "Our wives damn sure would, anyway!"

Their laughter filled the office of Richard Williams. He poured himself another cup of coffee, watched the oily, black substance flow into the plain brown mug marked "Warden"—a gift from a prisoner in the art therapy class—and wondered if what they said was true. He went back to his desk and sat down.

What was the difference, anyway, between the keepers and the kept? Instinctively he had always known the answer. The difference was control. We exercise it and they don't, he thought. So when they're caught, we exercise it for them. This whole prison was their external control. The rest of us had the prison on the inside, controlling or at least limiting our impulses, our deepest hidden desires to do bodily harm, to steal, to cheat, to rape and plunder and kill.

The "vandal impulse," he called it. Civilized people and civilized nations generally kept it in check. Others, both people and countries, needed to have someone control it for them. The world was quite simple, really.

Williams cradled the warm cup in his hands. He had long ago determined how to inhibit his own personal vandal impulse. He had let it slip out a few times, and he recalled each occasion vividly, especially the last one. But no one would ever find out about those. Or so he hoped. He would not like to have people talking about him the way the tower guards did about the inmates, imagining him a crazy person capable of breaking the law without remorse, keeping him locked up for his own good.

A shudder went down his spine. He would do anything to prevent that. Anything.

The warden looked at the silent monitors and continued to listen to the banter from Tower One.

"Car on feeder road three." The voice came through the speaker.

"Who is it, Bill?"

"How the hell should I know, Hank? You've got the binocs. Check the plate."

The guard looked through the glasses, then punched at the computer. Instantly, the name flashed on the screen.

"Nothin' to worry about," Bill said. "Just one of them do-gooder preachers here to try and save another wall-walker. Name's Beck. Matthew Beck. I'll call the gate."

Williams set the coffee aside and picked up the phone.

"Isolation Unit, Petokis speaking."

"This is the warden, Petokis. How is the prisoner?"

"Engel seems to be deteriorating in there, sir. He's more lethargic, except that he's periodically severely agitated."

"Double the thorazine."

"But, Warden, I think if we just let him out in the yard for a while, maybe with some other people, he would—"

"Did you hear my order, Petokis?" As an EMT, Petokis could legally give the injection, and he'd better not refuse his superior's command. Williams had positioned EMT's in the isolation areas for just this reason.

"Yes, sir."

"Then call me when it is carried out."

"Yes, sir.

Williams watched the monitor as the guard went to the drug box, drew up the required amount in a syringe, and carried it into Engel's cell. Moments later he returned and dropped the spent needle in the sharps box for disposal. Finally, he picked up the phone and notified the warden.

As soon as Williams hung up, the other phone rang. "Front gate, Warden. Someone for Engel. I told him he had to see you first."

"Tell Father Beck I look forward to talking with him."

"Yes, sir."

"And do a search, Sergeant. A thorough search." Williams turned off the monitors. Maybe the tower guards were right, he thought, glancing at his cup. Maybe it was the coffee.

Chapter 12

B eck stood still and tolerated the pat down, though he knew clergy were seldom made to do this. Even at maximum security prisons like Weston, they usually had the standard wand passed over them after they went through the metal detector. It was a way to show him who was in control, a pissing contest to put him in his place.

But Matt knew if anyone was in control, it was him, and it took everything he had to maintain it. Worried to his soul about Anne, every time he had awakened last night he had expected her to be there. Her absence had shocked him back to the present, hour after dark hour, like a splash of cold water. Was she on a plane yet? Was she awake? Did she hurt? What did she find that was worth her life? Finally, he got up at four and put on coffee. The only thing that held him together now, that kept him from venting on the guards by throwing a civil rights fit here in front of all the other visitors, was Twitch's call at eight saying the plane would probably leave sometime today—tomorrow at the latest. He would stay in control until he saw Anne. After that he made no promises.

"This way, Father." A guard escorted him out of the intake section and down a long corridor. "Warden wants to see you first."

As they approached the dark wood doors of the warden's office, Beck hoped he could avoid contaminating his meeting with Williams—and with Engel—with these raging feelings.

"Sit down, Father Beck," the Warden directed when the guard closed the door. They shook hands. "Coffee?"

"Thanks, but I'm coffeed out." If he had any more caffeine in his system, he would fly. He watched the warden fill his own cup. "Our paths seem to be crossing a lot these days, first at McCaslin's funeral, now here. You were supporting your guards by attending, I believe you said."

"Yes, that was partly the reason I went. But I am also a lifelong Episcopalian, and I enjoy any contact I can have with our bishop. He's a good man, even if he is a little off in his unwavering defense of Tod Engel. But I suppose that's a professional hazard, is it not?" Williams waved his cup over the desk. "My business is to restrain humanity's dark side, and yours is to believe in the light."

"Not exactly," Beck corrected. "My business is to make people aware of both sides and then help keep them in balance. Sometimes that means bringing light into overwhelming darkness—ferreting out the truth of an injustice, for instance. Other times it means siding with the darkness to restore the balance. We're made up of both, Warden. You, me, and everybody in your charge here."

"Nice sermon, Father Beck." Williams smiled a little too condescendingly. "Bishop Langert would be proud. I did have the chance to talk with him after the service, which, by the way, I thought he did well."

"He gives a good funeral," Beck said, his voice flat.

"You do not care for John Langert?"

Before last night I did, back when I believed he had integrity, Beck thought. "We're fine," he said.

Williams smiled curiously. "So what prompts your visit to our most infamous resident at this time?"

Beck debated how much to tell him, then figured Williams would not ask questions if he didn't already know the answers. "A series of recent events seem to point in the direction of Engel's innocence."

The warden laughed. "I'm sorry, Father Beck. I'm sure you're quite serious. But after ten years, when the man has remained basically the same, spouting the same nonsense, having been duly convicted by a jury based on his own uncoerced confession—excuse me if I find that a bit amusing."

The image of Anne, hurting and terrified, stoked Matt's resentment at this pompous-assed buffoon who pontificated over his prison like the Wizard of Oz. Maybe somebody should yank back the curtain. "Why else," Matt said, "would so many people not want the case reopened?"

"Perhaps they view it as a waste of the taxpayer's money?" Williams waved his arms. "Like so much of what we do right here for prisoners like Engel, who have no quality of life and are merely being warehoused until they die." He smirked. "You of all people should know about that, Father Beck."

"Why is that?"

"It's your mission, death and dying. It's what you do. Our work here is just like at the hospital with patients on ventilators. We waste millions of dollars a year keeping them alive, warehousing them in ICU's, do we not? In fact, there are even ventilator hospitals now, crammed full of such people, if you can call them that. How is that any different from this place, warehousing those who have been psychotic and delusional for twenty, thirty years, wasting identical millions on people who are mentally terminally ill?"

Beck lowered his voice. "Some of us might argue that the ones holding office who climbed there over the back of Tod Engel are the waste of taxpayers' money. Coincidentally, they may have the most to lose if the case

Deathangel 217

is reopened. Especially those with higher political aspirations."

"A cynical picture of politics, Father Beck." Williams blinked.

"A realistic assessment of human nature." Beck stared at him, unsmiling. "Take yourself, for instance. Your career advanced rapidly thanks to your new best friend, Martin Ehrhart, who got you your job here and supported your rather meteoric rise."

Williams waited, silent.

"And now you're in a very powerful position regarding Tod Engel. You control access to him. You oversee his stability. You can help or inhibit the reopening of the case." Beck paused, watching the warden's stoic but reddening face. "You have the ability to assist or end some very important political careers, including that of Mr. Ehrhart, who would like to go to Washington next year."

For a moment, he thought Williams was going to halt the conversation and refuse the visit. Then Matt would have to use the collar to demand access. If the warden ignored the comments, maybe he had nothing to hide. In either case, Beck had put him on notice that Engel better not wake up dead any time soon.

"You have quite a vivid imagination, Father Beck," Williams replied slowly.

"Oh, it's even more vivid than that, Warden. Suppose, just for a moment, that you yourself were the real Deathangel. You would be in the catbird seat regarding Engel's life and death, to cover up your own crimes. How's that for vivid?"

Matt could tell the man didn't like confrontation on his own turf. Tough shit. Beck didn't like anything that had happened in the last week. The warden came around the desk to face him.

"Very entertaining, Father Beck. Total fantasy, and may I add somewhat delusional, even a bit paranoid. How about my own vivid imagination seeing you in here as a prisoner? Perhaps you lost it for whatever reason, took momentary leave of your senses and murdered someone. You could be in the cell next to the man you came to visit today."

"There but for the grace of God goes any one of us, Warden."

"So what do you possibly hope to gain from a man who can hardly think straight, who has shown violent outbursts when Bishop Langert has given him only the utmost kindness, and who, I might add, has been in isolation for the last week due to our suspicion that he may try to kill himself?"

Beck looked into the warden's eyes. "I thought I might gain the truth, which is more than I've gotten from anyone else so far."

Williams ignored the inference and reached for the phone. "Send Chaplain Allen to my office immediately." He turned to Beck. "Your friend will escort you to Engel's cell. Though if you are looking for the truth, Father Beck, I suggest you search elsewhere than a prison for the criminally insane."

"People didn't think they'd find a king in a stable, either," Beck shot back.

"Spare me the religious delusions."

"I thought you said—"

"I said I was a lifelong Episcopalian. You should know that has nothing necessarily to do with religious belief. Church attendance, like other required social indulgences, has its personal and political benefits. Men like you and Chaplain Allen and Bishop Langert are useful for the singular purpose of controlling the masses. Opiates, as Marx said."

A knock at the door broke the tension, and Allen entered the office.

"Morning, Warden," he said. "Matt." He reached out his hand to Beck.

"I want you to escort Father Beck to the cell of Tod Engel." Williams looked at Beck. "I'll tell the guard to accommodate whatever arrangements you wish. I would never prevent access to a prisoner by a man of the cloth. But I will warn you to keep your distance and to limit the length of the interview. Unless, of course, you wish to contribute to his diminishing state of mental and physical health."

"Of course not." Beck imagined Williams had already done quite enough in both areas. "Thank you for your kind consideration," he said, remembering that his mother had taught him to be especially polite to assholes.

"What was that all about?" Art Allen said when they were outside in the courtyard between cell blocks.

"Your friendly neighborhood warden seems to be more than a little involved with the Deathangel case."

"How?"

"I thought you didn't want to know anything about it."

Allen looked like he was going to snap back, but then he grimaced. "You're right. I apologize for being such a shit about this." He glanced at Beck. "And about a lot of things these last years."

Matt patted him on the back. "Careful, Art. You may screw up a long, perfect record of reticence and hostility."

Allen shook his head. "I deserve that, but when this mess is over, I want to talk with you again, maybe get together with Anne."

"Why? What happened?" Matt was glad to reconcile, but nobody turned around for no reason.

"I've been thinking about what you said about McCaslin, about how you believe he was killed for what he overheard about the Deathangel case."

"It's a little more complicated than that."

"I know. I know. But it sort of got me stoked like I was—well, before. I was surprised at how good it felt to have a cause again, to be pissed off about something worthwhile." Beck watched him retrieve keys to the outer door of the isolation block. "Besides which," Allen lowered his voice, "there's some prison grapevine on Williams." He dug out a cigarette and lit it, stalling. "A trusty cleaning the outer office—very quietly, I might add—overheard a phone conversation."

Beck leaned against a rough stone wall. The outside yards could be viewed by camera, but the constant brisk wind off the Hudson probably made microphones useless. "About?"

"About the county executive offering Williams a position on his soon-to-be Washington senate staff."

Like a computer receiving data too quickly, Matt was overwhelmed with names and connections. Ehrhart running for U.S. Senate, Rinski backing him, surely for some position. Langert becoming presiding bishop, Williams chummy with Langert and his chauffeur and also riding on Ehrhart's coattails. An angel on Anne's smashed computer in Brooklyn, an angel by her broken body in Germany. All of it connected with Deathangel.

Matt finally spoke. "In exchange for watching over Engel. What better way to shut the case tight than to cut a deal with the one who controls him?"

"Controls Engel?" Allen laughed and crushed out his cigarette. "Nobody controls Engel but Engel."

"Let's go find out." Matt pointed to the door and Art opened it.

"The warden has had Engel in isolation for almost a week," Allen said, "on high doses of psychotropic medication. He thinks Engel is apt to kill himself."

"What do you think?"

Allen stopped and stared seriously at Beck. "I think nobody understands Engel around here the way I do. He'd be the last person to commit suicide. In some weird way he likes being Deathangel, or at least he accepts that it's his identity. It gets him lots of strokes. He probably doesn't understand the isolation bit, though, so he might hurt himself fighting out of it."

"Are you suggesting I shouldn't interview him? Would it be more than he could handle right now?"

"I'm suggesting that this may be your last best shot at him, Matt, unless I can convince more of the guards to hold back his medications—like I did this morning."

Beck smiled and shook his head. "The old Art Allen reemerges. Watch, out world."

"Question authority at every turn. They're all sneaky, power-hungry bastards out to get us—as even your father ended up admitting." Allen grinned. "Some of the guards are sympathetic to Engel. Some will do anything to gig the warden. When I heard you were coming today, I asked the morning guard to waste whatever psychotropic drugs were ordered, to have Engel as clear as possible for you."

"And in touch with his anger, hostility, and love of clergy, I'm sure." A little Thorazine wouldn't hurt, Matt thought. Maybe he should wangle some for himself.

"You can't have everything, buddy."

"Will I be in there alone?" Another mixed blessing, but Beck wanted the privacy—and the cover of isolation.

"Yes and no. The guard will be at the door, and so will I." Allen spoke softly. "And remember, Williams has as much of this place wired as he can—but not all of it. Anything you say may be overheard by him. I don't think the isolation cells are live. Hell, I can't receive any beeper calls down there, so if he tried to transmit TV images, I don't see them slamming through those eight-foot thick walls. And he can't use cable because it keeps getting cut somehow." he smiled. The two stepped inside and approached the door to the isolation unit. "I think you're safe, but I'd assume anything I said was being heard by half the world, just in case."

Allen caught him by the shoulder. "One more thing before we go in there."

Beck saw his friend's look reaching out to help.

"I've known you long enough to tell when something's not right. I trust your decision not to let me in on what it is, based on the way I've treated you lately. But I want you to know I remember farther back than that—to when we were young, stupid seminarians and pledged to fight off all the bad guys for each other." He smiled and tapped Beck on the chin with his fist. "You just need to tell me who they are."

Matt considered him for a second before responding. "The bad guys got to Anne," he said, a lump forming in his throat. "She's supposed to be okay, but she's been shot." He stopped Allen from speaking. "If I say anymore, I put you in jeopardy too. Don't worry. When I figure it out, I'll tell you who to go after first."

Allen hugged him. "Call me when you see Anne," he said, and led them to the end of a long corridor. Guards on both sides of a thick door blocked the entrance to the row of cells. One guard banged on the door and inserted his large key. The guard on the other side did the same. Both keys turned and the door swung open, revealing the men to one another.

"Welcome to paradise, gentlemen," the second guard said.

"Nice to see you too, Petokis." Allen introduced Matt.

"I know who he is. Warden called for me to prepare Engel for him."

Matt understood what that meant. "How is he today?"

"He's been a bit under the weather lately." The guard glanced at Allen. "More medication was ordered this morning."

Allen nodded his head. "I see. Father Beck will remember not to disturb him unnecessarily or to stay too long."

Petokis marched them to the last cell on the right. All the cells were small, undersized due to age and design. The hallway was a dim tunnel with no external light. The steel doors had locked panels through which food and slop cans were exchanged, often at the same time, it appeared. The place smelled like a disinfected urinal.

Petokis tapped his key on the cell door to alert Engel. He inserted the key in the lock, turned it twice, then back once, a preventive measure, Beck assumed, to be sure the door was not being rushed from the inside.

"You goin' in alone?" the guard asked.

Beck nodded.

"Fine," Petokis said. "It's your funeral."

"How long?" Allen asked.

"I'll come out when I'm done." Matt pulled the door shut behind him.

As it closed with a hard metal clang, he heard Petokis say to Allen, "Unless we have to drag him out."

Beck thought the scene surreal. Tod Engel—the man convicted but not guilty of killing Kate, the man he first encountered in the emergency room at Grasslands, the man over whom he met Anne Demming—sat on the lone bunk with his head down, looking at the floor, his fingers interlaced, a mop of brownish hair hanging over his high forehead like a kid from Our Gang. Was he apprehensive? Was he frightened? Was he even aware of the presence of another person in his cell? Matt could decipher nothing from the silence, and he was afraid to touch the man who would tower over him if he stood up.

Where to start?

"Tod?" Beck said softly, in case Engel had not realized he was there. "I'm Father Beck, Tod." He debated saying he was a friend of Bishop Langert for two good reasons; if Engel hated Langert, it would be a bad association, and after last night Matt wasn't certain the designation still fit.

"Tod, can you look up, or is it okay if I sit on this chair here?"

Still Engel sat silent and Matt was unsure what to do. If he were at the hospital and the patient was comatose, dying, or stroked out, he would grab a chair and talk as if the patient could hear every word. Maybe that was what he should try now. He had to do something, had to enable Engel to speak with him. Even though this man had not murdered Kate, he had still been somehow involved with her death, even as a scapegoat. He was the key to the real killer, the key to everything. But the key lay trapped inside a retarded man, locked inside a maximum security cell, buried deep within a maximum security prison. A riddle inside a conundrum, wrapped in mystery. Unlikely as it seemed to him, maybe just talking would begin to unravel it.

"As I said, Tod, I'm Matt Beck." He extended his hand, just in case, then pulled it back when Engel did not acknowledge it. "I'm a chaplain at Grasslands Hospital a few miles down the road. I first met you there when the police brought you into the ER." Try a little orientation. "You may remember, Kate Beck was one of the victims of the Deathangel murders ten years ago. She was my wife."

Matt sat back when Engel raised his head, frowned, and stared as though memories were desperately trying to force their way into his consciousness, like a TV signal moving from lines to blurry to clear.

"Do you remember any of that, Tod?"

Engel sniffed and wiped his nose on the arm of his shirt. Beck handed him a tissue from the small wooden table and Engel held onto it, still looking through, rather than at him.

Now that I've got his attention, or think I do, Beck thought, let's determine whether he really hears me. He leaned over and spoke directly into Engel's face.

"I don't believe you killed my wife." Beck waited for a response, but Engel sat still, barely breathing. If Matt were at the bedside of a comatose person, he would keep going. "In fact, I don't believe you killed any of them."

The silence continued. Matt allowed it to hang there longer this time. Just as he was about to speak again, Engel reached under his pillow, pulled out a dirty rag, and unwrapped a small, sharp penknife.

Matt did not move. He was transfixed by Engel's stare. Would he lunge at him, try to slit his throat before Beck could call out for help, stab him in the heart before he could reach the door? What was the man doing with a knife anyway? He was supposedly in maximum security isolation, for God's sake! Another setup to give the poor prisoner an opportunity to kill himself, Beck supposed, or to attack and injure visitors like Langert, Allen, or Beck, who might come searching for the truth.

Matt jerked back with fright when Engel bent to retrieve an item from under the bunk. It was a small angel emerging from a block of wood, as slivers were stripped off by the knife. Beck's heart thumped at the sight of Engel carving it. He wondered if the man was trying to tell him something; if he couldn't communicate with words, maybe he could with actions. But what did he mean?

"What is it, Tod? Is there something you want to tell me?"

Another long silence. Maybe nothing he said was being heard, although Engel occasionally watched Beck as he carved.

"Do you remember any of it?" Matt continued doggedly. What did he have to lose now? Nothing ventured, nothing gained. "Do you remember what you were doing, where you were at the time of the Deathangel murders?"

Engel used the knife with a little more energy, or was it anger? He seemed to squint, or was it a grimace of pain or annoyance? Beck wanted to give him the maximum time to process without overloading brain cells that were probably soaked with psychotropic meds.

Matt checked his watch. Any minute now, Warden Williams might pick up the phone and pronounce the visit over. Either that or Art and Petokis would grow worried about the quiet and break this terrific rapport he and Engel were building. Regular chatterbox. Hard to shut him up once you got him going. Shit. Maybe some dynamite would help.

"So, Tod," Matt said, "would it be better if I called you by your real name?"

The inmate cut harder, bearing down on the block of wood with the penknife and pursing his lips.

"Edward? Edward Clopton?"

Engel stopped.

Matt's heart leapt into warp speed as he watched the man gently place the knife and the angel on his pillow. What was going on now? Was he about to explode? Or was this the breakthrough Beck had hoped to accomplish? He knew one thing—he had to keep his mouth shut.

Engel whispered through lips that seemed tightened by drugs. "Concentrate longer. Concentrate longer."

Beck matched his whisper, leaned toward him but still did not touch him. "We're trying, Tod. We're trying to concentrate longer, but we need your help here. Can you give it to us?"

Again the words slipped out, almost forced from his mouth through spit and drool. "Toad sticker. Toad sticker. Matthew's son's a toad sticker."

Matt shook his head. He really did feel for the man, bound by the dual straitjackets of mental disability and layers of hardened drug barriers. And still Engel tried to force his way through them, to do his best courageously, Matt thought, to say something, maybe to help. "I'm sorry. I know these phrases mean something to you, but I just don't understand them. Believe me, I wish I did." He touched the huge ham of a hand.

Engel looked up at him, but was it with pleading or distress or hatred? With medication flattening the affect, it was hard to tell.

"Grabbin' wieners. Grabbin' wieners. Death comes to grabbin' wieners."

Then he paused. It was as though a clock had wound down. Engel's face was a mass of sweat, watery eyes dripping tears down his stubbled cheeks, saliva dribbling from his downturned mouth. It occurred to Matt that the man might be dying. Not this exact second, but soon. His years of dealing with patients at the end of life had taught him the look, even the smell. Engel had both.

Matt took a wad of tissues and wiped the man's mouth and forehead. "Listen to me, Tod. Listen to me carefully." He stared into the dull gray eyes and spoke as if he were giving orders. "You have to stay alive. Do you understand me? You have to stay alive until we find the real killer." Beck thought of Kate, attended by EMS. He was near pleading now, beyond ordering. "We're almost there," he said. "Just a few days longer and we'll have you out of here, out of this cell, out of this prison. Once we free the key from you, we'll unlock it all. And if you can't give us the key, then you have to stay alive until we discover it, until we make them give it to us." Nearly in tears himself, Beck knew he was asking as much for himself as for Engel. Again, he brushed the man's hand. "Do you understand me, Tod?"

Engel stared, wrinkled his forehead, squinted as if about to say something more. Then he sagged against the bed. Matt sighed and leaned back. He was ready to give up and leave.

With unlikely speed, Engel lurched forward, knocked him off the chair, and hauled him up by the shoulders, pinning him against the steel door. Beck felt the vicelike grip of the huge man's fingers crushing him. Too shocked to fight back, Beck also realized such resistance would only lead to more damage to them both. He heard commotion outside. His best bet was for Petokis to get in and rescue him.

Beck stared into the huge contorted face edging closer to his, moving to the side of his head. He was suddenly irrationally afraid the man would bite his neck, vampirelike, but instead Engel held his mouth to Beck's ear and whispered three words, spit them like bullets into his brain.

Matt felt the door shift behind him. At the same time, Engel dropped him and stepped back as Petokis and Allen crashed through. Allen pulled Beck out of the cell and Matt caught sight of the guard spraying Mace into Engel's screaming face. His massive form doubled up on the bunk, crying in stinging pain, desperately trying to wipe off the chemical with the sheet.

Allen helped Beck to a chair. Petokis slammed and locked the cell door.

"Nice way to end a pastoral visit, Matt," Allen said. "I'll be sure and learn from your masterful technique."

"You all right, Father?" Petokis asked.

Matt checked his disheveled clothing. "Other than feeling stupid. I don't think anything's broken." He took a few deep breaths and put his hand to the back of his head where he felt his damp hair.

"You're bleeding there," Allen said. "Better have the prison doctor take a look."

"I'll be fine. I just reopened a recent wound."

"You get slammed against doors often in your line of work, Father?" Petokis said. "You know you lead a pretty rough life, for a priest."

Matt looked at Allen. "We learned it from our fathers."

"What were they, prizefighters?"

Allen answered, "Something like that."

Petokis laughed. "Just what did you say in there—if it's not too personal?"

"Sorry," Beck replied. "I'd like to tell you. But it's all under the stole." If the camera was on in the hallway outside the cell, he wanted to leave the impression that it had been a very informative visit. Beck stood and held out his hand to the guard. "Thanks for getting me out of there."

"It's what they pay me for, Father."

Matt nodded toward the cell. "Can you give him something that will take away the pain?"

"They pay me for that, too. I don't want him to suffer any more than you do. He suffers enough just being himself."

Allen banged on the outer door and the two guards released them.

"Let's get you out of here, " Allen said. He took Matt's arm as they walked through the gate.

"Thanks again, Petokis," Beck said with a knowing look. "For everything." If the guard had drugged Engel as he'd been ordered to do, the interaction would not have been possible, including the violent conclusion.

Petokis nodded. "Put in a good word for me with the man upstairs."

"I'm afraid I have no clout with the warden." Beck grinned.

"I meant a little higher than that." Petokis slammed and locked the door behind them.

"You got it," Matt replied through the glass. He leaned heavily on Allen. He was more shaken than he first thought. When they had exited the isolation building, he stopped to rest.

"I guess I took a harder hit than I thought."

"You want me to drive you home?"

"No," Matt said. "I'll be fine—just need some air. It was so confining in there. Cramped, no breathing room. I don't know how you work in a place like this."

"Oh, yeah," Allen said. "It's a lot easier to work where there's blood and puke and disease and death."

Beck smiled. "Anyway, thanks for the assist."

"Did it help? What really happened?"

Matt glanced around the courtyard. "Can he hear us out here?"

Allen pointed to the door they were about to enter. "I'd say so."

Richard Williams stood stoically, his arms across his chest, flanked by two of his men. "I hope your pastoral visit with the murderer was satisfactory, Father Beck?" he said, as they entered the area.

"Excellent, Warden," Matt said. "Couldn't have been better."

"So I heard," Williams said. "Of course, I will have to alter your visiting arrangements, should you wish to return. Any further contact will be in an open visiting room with Engel in shackles and two guards nearby, one in attendance."

"You know the ACLU and I won't permit the one in attendance." Church and state arguments were still useful.

"We'll see, Father Beck."

"Actually, Warden," Matt said, shuffling toward the exit door, "I doubt any further visits will be necessary."

"Really?"

"Yes," Beck said, without smiling. "I obtained the information I need."

"Indeed!" Williams snapped. "And did you get that truth you were looking for?"

Matt nodded. "That and more." He studied the man's face. Underneath the facade, Williams had to be worried about what had transpired in that cell. It must be the only dead spot in the prison. Appropriate term.

"Would you mind sharing a little of it with us before you vanish into the sunset?"

"Certainly, Warden." Beck noticed a small line of sweat on the man's upper lip. "But I'm sure he's mentioned it to you before."

"And that truth is?"

Beck glanced at Allen, then looked back at Williams. "Toad sticker, Concentrate longer, and—my favorite and I'm sure it's yours, Warden—Grabbin' wieners."

Allen and the guards suppressed their instinct to laugh. Williams was stone-faced.

"That's right," Beck said. "He didn't say shit. He became hostile when I mentioned the names Rinski, Ehrhart—even Langert. And he really got pissed when I suggested he might not be Deathangel." He straightened and walked toward the gate, waved at Allen, and nodded at the silent warden. "I'll be in touch."

As Matt left the prison, he felt certain Williams didn't believe a word he'd said. Sometimes the truth was the biggest lie of all.

"Ich verstehe nicht, Fraulein," the nurse said. "Sie mussen. You must lie still now. It is the doctor's order."

"Listen to me," Anne Demming pleaded. "This is very important." She lay flat in a hospital bed with two IVs and a catheter, too weak to protest, feeling like she would fade out again at any moment.

"I cannot understand." the nurse repeated. She smoothed Anne's hair and tried to comfort her. "You must rest, Fraulein. You must."

"Damn it!" Anne said. "Get me someone who speaks English! This is very complex—and urgent! Kann ein man hier Englisch sprechen?"

"Jaja, Fraulein. Herr Baumschen kann Englisch."

Anne breathed a sigh of relief. "Then get him. Or have one of those Austrian cops guarding my door find someone!"

The puzzled nurse hurried from the room. A few minutes later the small, bald man with the enormous moustache appeared at her bedside.

Anne thought she was dreaming. Was she in New York with Twitch and Matt? Did Baumschen know what had happened? Then the dream spoke.

"Guten tag, Fraulein. I am very glad to see you are alive."

"Listen. No time," she said, struggling to keep her eyes open. "I need you to do something very complicated and very specific—and it must be done immediately."

"I will do whatever I can to help find the people who did this to you, Fraulein Demming, and, perhaps more importantly, the reason for it."

"Fine," she said, closing her eyes. It was a mistake. Each time she closed them, the medication took over. When she opened them again, the man was still there, reading a book.

"What happened?"

"You went to sleep for half an hour. You are under much medication. If you did not have it, you would be in great pain." He put his book down. "If you wish to give me information, you must try to stay awake, I am afraid." He held a straw to her mouth for water.

Anne sipped just a bit, then coughed and grimaced from the searing pain breaking through the drugs. "Yes, yes. I understand. Thank you." She struggled to prevent her eyes from shutting. "I have to tell you before—"

Again, sleep overtook her. When consciousness returned, she looked to her left and saw the little man still reading.

"What? Did I do it again?"

"Yes, Fraulein, I am afraid so, for an hour this time." The man's moustache parted and his brown teeth showed through in a grin. "Perhaps if I go on talking or wake you when you next leave us?"

"Yes." Anne paused and the room whirled, pulling her down. She forced the spinning to stop. "Please do that. Do whatever it takes. This really is a matter of life—" Her heavy lids fell over her eyes.

But Baumschen took her hand and jostled it. Immediately, she awoke.

"Thank you—thank—you. Do you think I could have another sip of water? Perhaps that—"

"Of course." The man placed the straw at her lips. She sucked in a small amount, nearly choked again, and swallowed hard.

"My throat is so sore."

"Yes, Fraulein. You had lost much blood when they brought you in, and you were going into shock. They had to—what is the English word?"

Anne knew the word. But she never thought she would use it in reference to herself. "Intubate?" she offered.

"Yes, that is it. They inserted a breathing tube until you started on your own again. But you are fine now, relatively speaking."

"Fine—now," she repeated in an echo, starting to drift again.

"Fraulein?"

Anne roused. "Oh—yes—quickly," she said, rallying her strength, trying to pull together the words she had to say. "Please listen to me."

"I am listening, Fraulein Demming. What is it you want?"

"When they brought me in, it was from a rest stop on the Autobahn, wasn't it?"

"Yes. I was there, but too late. I am sorry for that."

"Then—my car. What happened to my car?"

"I do not know. I can find out for you. Is that all you want me to do?"

"Yes," she said wearily.

"I will be back as soon as I have an answer," the man said, rising from his chair.

But Anne could not reply. The drugs had again stilled her conscious thought.

It was as though someone was calling her from a long way down a dark alley. The voice reverberated, sounded silly, demanded she come away from her floating and settle. It knew her name, kept calling her, bringing her closer and closer to the surface, growing clearer and clearer, until finally the voice was next to her ear, and she awoke.

"Miss Demming," the voice repeated.

She looked into Baumschen's moustache.

"Gute nacht, Fraulein Demming," he said. "I hope you may remain awake for somewhat longer intervals now."

"How long?"

"A few hours."

"And now?"

"Now it has turned to night—twenty two hundred, ten o'clock. You have been asleep while I have been out doing your bidding."

Anne yawned and tried to stretch one restrained arm. "And just what was that?" Immediately, her memory of the event came screeching back to her. The narrow escape with the car, the shots exploding in her mind, the searing pain. "Oh, my God," she said, as tears pooled in her eyes and fell into the marshmallow sheets. "Oh, my God."

"It is frightening to remember, Fraulein." The man gently grasped her hand. "Before you drift off again, I must tell you I did exactly what you asked me to do."

"You found the car?"

He nodded his head and smiled through his moustache. "It was no trouble, really. It was in the lot where you left it."

"And was it intact?"

The man nodded. "I discovered what you wanted me to find."

Anne opened both eyes wide. She tried to sit up in the bed, but the pain snatched her back like an electric shock, slamming her down to the mattress.

"Do not try to move, Miss Demming," Baumschen said. "You will be transferred in good time. Perhaps as soon as tonight." The inspector shrugged off his jacket. "But first," he said, "we must talk."

"Of course," Anne said faintly, as she floated back into the solemnity of darkness.

The lush, rolling hills of the Taconic Parkway stretched out in front of Beck's Spider like an airport runway, welcoming speed and power. Given his emotions the last two days, he accepted the invitation to exercise both and pressed on the gas. The last time he had glanced at the speedometer, the needle rested on eighty-five.

What the hell, he thought. He had a lot on his mind, including a knot on his head. He was in a hurry to reach the mountain. He was worried about Anne. He was seriously pissed at several people. And he hadn't seen a cop for miles.

A siren interrupted his musings.

Beck looked in the rearview mirror and told himself the state trooper did not want him. Then he thought of excuses for speeding, all of them weak. He slowed to see if the car would pass. But the black and white trailed behind him, its red and yellow lights flashing.

Shit, he swore to himself. He hoped the man was of a denomination that deferred to collars.

"License and registration, please."

From the expression on the trooper's face, Matt could see that he only deferred to badges. Oh well, he thought, as the cop handed back the documents. Get the ticket and go home.

"Would you mind stepping out of the car?"

Wrong question. Beck frowned as images of Anne flashed through his mind. Was this how it started with her attackers? Whoever this clown was, nobody had briefed him that standard procedure on a high-speed parkway was for the driver to remain in the car. And that was exactly where Matt wished to stay, within reach of Anne's .38 in the glove box.

"Could I ask what this is really about, Officer?"

"You could, Reverend. But I would like you to do so outside the vehicle," the trooper said, stepping back and resting his right palm on his holstered Magnum.

Beck realized his options were limited. He could pretend to get something from the glove box and grab the .38, but not before the cop drew his own gun. He could start the car and hope the guy was a bad shot. Or he could play along to buy time and wait for a better opportunity. Whatever he did, he had to stay alive—just as he had told Tod Engel. He couldn't help Anne if he was dead.

He slowly walked to the rear of the Spider, aware that the other man stayed just beyond striking distance. "I know I was speeding. Just write the ticket and we'll both be on our way."

"We both know I can't do that, Reverend." The trooper closed his ticket book and plucked the radio from his belt. "County One, this is Trooper Five Seven. Over?"

The small, hand-held unit responded immediately.

"This is County One. What's your twenty?"

"One mile north of Valhalla Exit." He kept his eyes on Beck as he spoke. "ETA?"

"One minute. Out."

"Five Seven out." The trooper replaced the radio and continued to rest his hand on the pistol.

If these were the same people behind the attack on Anne, staying alive meant striking first. "Company coming?" he said as he edged back along the other side of the Spider toward the glove box.

The cop unsnapped the holster strap. "Just stand still for a minute, Reverend, and you won't get hurt. Black don't look nice with dark red on it. Besides, if my employer wanted you hurt, you would have been hurt by now. Consider it a stroke of fortune that all he's after is a chat with you."

"Didn't he ever hear of voice mail?"

The cop grinned. "Ask him yourself," he said, as a limousine appeared on the horizon.

Matt decided to play it out and see who would go to all this trouble to talk. If things got out of hand, he was actually better off in a smaller space than outside the limo. His dad had taught him about spots like this, about how he had to assess the area and use it. A car interior had hard objects to smash someone's head against, and it wouldn't take much at this point for Beck to do it.

The limo rolled to a stop in front of the Spider, and a uniformed chauffeur opened the center door for Beck.

Glancing back at the cop, Matt greeted the gray-haired man lounging in the blue, crushed velvet seat.

"Phone calls are cheaper than thugs," he said to Martin Ehrhart. "But then you must have a large campaign chest."

"Just get in and sit down, Father Beck," Ehrhart said. "I went to a great deal of trouble to locate you in unobserved territory. If we act civilized here, we'll both be back to our business shortly."

The car felt like an isolation booth. No outside noises could penetrate the steel and glass container, and no internal conversation could be heard outside. Matt looked over his shoulder through the black glass.

"No," Ehrhart began, "the driver can't hear anything unless I turn on the speaker."

"Not even a gunshot?"

Ehrhart laughed. "I don't really think you believe—"

"After this week, I'd believe anything," Beck said. He felt the car start. "Where are we going?"

"Just driving while we talk. Your car is safe until we return."

Though Ehrhart's voice sounded conciliatory, Beck felt as incarcerated as the inmates at Weston Prison. It was technically possible to overcome Ehrhart with one slam against the window, but it seemed unnecessary now. These were not urban terrorists, except in the sense that all politicians were, and the danger was over. Instead, he would listen.

"Drink?" Ehrhart unlatched a panel revealing a fully stocked liquor cabinet.

What the hell. It would help with the pain in his head. "Bushmill's."

"I apologize for the unnecessary drama, Father Beck, but I could not simply phone and ask you to drop by the office."

"Why not?" Because it wouldn't have the effect that strong-arming me would? Regardless of the reason, the clear message was that Ehrhart could wield power wherever and whenever he needed it.

"In the first place, there was no guarantee you'd come, and this meeting had to happen immediately. Also, since my ratings are growing higher in the polls, there are reporters watching my office and my home like hawks—make that vultures—and your arrival would have stirred up interest and unwanted questions."

Beck sipped the drink and shrugged. "So what do you want?"

"I'll be blunt. I want you to stay away from the Deathangel case and let the authorities handle it."

Get in line, Matt thought. He recalled Allen's admonition never to trust authorities. "I'm listening."

"I'm concerned about you and Miss Demming. I can see that you've been attacked recently, and I understand she was critically injured yesterday."

Matt clenched his jaw. His anger rose again. How did this man know about Anne? Did he have information Twitch didn't have? "What can you tell me about her? And how do you know?"

"I have only sketchy details, that she was injured in a terrorist attack and had several wounds, and that she is resting comfortably in an Austrian hospital under close guard."

Where the man in front of him may have put her. Matt watched Ehrhart sip a glass of mineral water.

"It is quite typical of police to share information regarding people in their area. I received a fax from the local polizei over there when they found her driver's license."

Beck finished the Bushmill's and jammed the glass on the sideboard with a rattle. "Maybe. Maybe not," he said. "Maybe you got your information from your own connections in Munich." Matt waited for a reaction, but Ehrhart was as steely as his German inlaws. "Or are they more than connections? Are they operatives?"

Ehrhart looked out the window. His face flushed as he turned back to Matt and crossed his legs.

"I receive campaign contributions from interested parties all over the world, Father Beck. And why not? We live in a global village. Someone sneezes in New York and a person in Munich says Gesundheit. You have probably preached this very thing. There is no such thing anymore as the national interest. We are far too intertwined with the politics and economies of the world. Some participants in those economies believe in my platform and wish to support my candidacy."

Nice speech. Let's see how you do with a little more pressure. "That's no problem except when that candidacy happens to be linked with repressing information about the Deathangel case, like the fact that you knew Tod Engel before you prosecuted him ten years ago."

Ehrhart pursed his lips. "Did Rinski tell you this?"

Bingo, Beck thought. "Not that, he didn't. But, considering all that we've already dug up on Rinski, he had no choice but to play ball with us." That should worry him.

Ehrhart maintained his composure. The guy was German carbon steel if nothing else. He wondered what it would take to bend him.

"The BCI files," Ehrhart murmured.

Beck nodded. "That's how we learned you were the prosecutor for Engel's PI's." Here we go. "But Rinski offered me something in addition to what's on the legal record."

The constant onslaught must have chiseled through a vulnerable spot. "That double-crossing Polack handed you the print, didn't he?" Ehrhart growled.

Shit, Beck thought. Pay dirt. He must not show his surprise. He wished he had a better poker face. Sweat dampened his black shirt. He leaned back and folded his hands. "About which your explanation would be what?"

Unsmiling, Ehrhart sat his glass on the counter. "What I did may have been wrong in one sense, but it was the right thing to do at the time."

"This must be some story," Beck said. The trick would be to ferret out the information without revealing too much ignorance.

"Listen to me." Ehrhart swallowed. "I did not want that case, Father Beck."

Whose print had Ehrhart been hiding and what did it have to do with Deathangel, Beck wondered. "Go on."

"I tried my damndest to get out of it, to refer it to another assistant district attorney, to be absent when the decision was being made." Ehrhart shifted against the blue velvet, clearly agitated. "But my boss, the D.A., didn't want it either. He thought it would be political suicide if it was lost, and he believed he couldn't prove the case beyond a reasonable doubt, even with the confession from Engel. He was a very conservative man, and he'd been in that office for nearly twenty-five years. Frankly, he was lazy. By bestowing the case on a younger assistant, he appeared to be coaching from the sidelines and allowing the bright young faces to shine. And if that face lost—too bad for it."

"You thought you couldn't handle it?"

Ehrhart smiled. "You don't know me very well, Father Beck. I've never turned down anything in my life because I thought I couldn't handle it." He shook his head. "That's probably what has driven me this far—and placed me in this much difficulty."

Where was this going? Beck tried to get ahead of the details, but he couldn't.

"No. I knew damned well I could prosecute the case and probably win the full sentence—life imprisonment with no parole. I would end up looking good, garner a promotion, and have my career off to an incredible start at an early age. But to do so," Ehrhart lowered his voice and his head, "to do so, I would have to withhold some evidence, just as you have said." He looked at Beck. "Not evidence that would convict or exonerate Engel, mind you, but evidence nonetheless."

"About the print," Beck said, as if the connection were obvious.

Ehrhart nodded, seeming penitent, though Beck doubted he ever was about anything. Steel seldom is.

"The print of the man who was in bed with Connie Bartus when Engel killed her."

"Is alleged to have killed her," Beck corrected.

"No, Father Beck. I am still convinced, as was the jury, that Engel murdered those people—all of them, including your wife—with a vengeance only his strange mind could have invented. I would prosecute the case the same way all over again, and I would win again. But this time I could offer the one bit of testimony that would corroborate the time and method of the killing of Connie Bartus."

"From the man who was there with her?" Beck guessed.

"From the man who was there with her." Ehrhart paused and took a long swallow of water.

Matt braced himself for the unknown as well as he could. It was unclear whether he was supposed to know the owner of the print or not. He would do his best to be neutral.

"As Rinski undoubtedly told you, the man was my wife's brother. His name was William Ingleman."

Using his skill at hearing bedside confessions, Matt picked up on the verb. "Was?"

"Yes. At the time of the murder, Bill had been diagnosed with a rare neurological disease similar to ALS. Lou Gehrig's disease. He was rapidly deteriorating, and the one pleasure remaining in his life was his relationship with Connie Bartus. It kept what was left of him sane."

Beck weighed the possibilities. It was fairly elaborate for a lie. The facts were easily checked out—something he would do if he ever got out of this traveling coffin alive.

"Bill's affair with Bartus had been going on about six months. That night, he met her in the city for dinner and they went back to her house in Katonah. The rest you know."

"About him finding her?" Matt said, risking everything if this was the wrong track.

"Exactly."

Internally, Matt breathed a sigh of relief. But where was this leading? So he protected his brother-in-law, who he did not believe was the murderer.

"It was simple, really. Engel drugged them both as they slept, then murdered Bartus. Bill awoke dazed, discovered the gruesome sight beside him, and became hysterical. He had the presence of mind to call me first. I told him how to cover his tracks in the house and gave him an hour's head start before I notified the police that an anonymous call had just come into the office."

"But being an amateur, unlike yourself, he screwed up and left the print."

"I wanted to save him—and my wife—from enduring the rigor and embarrassment of the trial in the last few weeks or months of his life."

Not to mention the demise of your future in Westchester politics, Beck thought. Just like now. "But the police reports never indicated the presence of anyone else in the bed with her. You must have had a plant in the department to pull this off." With chills running down his spine, Beck knew who it was.

Ehrhart emptied his glass as if it contained a magic potion that would strengthen him to continue. Either he was a good actor or this was hard for him. The man's sweaty forehead indicated the latter.

"That is quite correct. I contacted a certain policeman who I knew would do the investigation and file the report the way I suggested."

"A policeman you took with you to where you are today?" Beck said.

"Correct again. And that man—James Rinski—will follow me to the senate when I am elected."

"Even though he gave up information that could severely damage you?"

Ehrhart took a deep breath. He seemed calmer. "None of us is perfect, Father Beck. You know that well from your profession. Different people bow to different pressures." He smiled. "One wonders what pressures might cause you to bow, to hold this information to yourself and avoid unpleasantness."

Matt thought of Anne in the hospital, imagined her in pain. How willing he had been last night to bury what they'd learned if it would only keep her safe.

"You can see," Ehrhart continued, sounding more confident, "what would happen if any of this became public now. It would be embarrassing, but eventually my spin doctors would make it understandable. The public might be shocked, even disappointed, but a thorough investigation would confirm that no real damage was done. The facts of the case remain the same." Ehrhart seemed to relax. "Engel, after all, is still the murderer."

"Assuming nothing else was altered or covered up," Beck ventured.

Ehrhart recoiled. "What do you mean by that?"

"Just what I said." Beck stared at him. "Your story's touching, but maybe it's all a red herring to avoid anyone discovering something far more damaging."

"What could that possibly be?"

Big mistake, Beck fumed. "Let me count the ways," he said. "Bartus could have been involved with your wife's family's chemical business in Germany. Maybe she knew too much about your dealings. Or maybe you found out something about her you didn't like." So far, no reaction other than shaking his head. "Maybe your brother-in-law killed her over something stupid and lied to you about it." There was, of course, one final possibility. But Matt was not ready to pronounce it, not locked up in a car with the man who might be the real Deathangel.

"I suppose you would have to think of all of those things—and more," Ehrhart said. "But my main point still stands. What could you possibly gain by pursuing this? Engel is a retarded, delusional man. He confessed to the killings."

"That's just what worries me." Matt could tell Ehrhart was unnerved. Things had not gone exactly as he had planned.

"Look, Beck." Ehrhart had dropped the term "Father". "Be reasonable. Even if, just for speculation, Engel was not the killer—though I would stake my own life on the fact that he was—but if he was not, then what? The best that might happen would be that he would be released and a fruitless search opened. But in the process, my career and several others would be ruined."

Ehrhart's tone was somewhere between pleading and threatening. Matt didn't like either one.

"I urge you not to pursue this, regardless of what you think you've found." The man leaned forward, only a few inches from him. "I don't know why your friend McCaslin was murdered, or why you and Langert and Anne Demming have been the objects of violent attacks, but I give you my personal assurance that if you leave this alone until after the election, I'll see that it is pursued with all the law enforcement and investigative power I can command. I believe you know that power is considerable—both here and abroad."

Beck was uncertain how to respond. Ehrhart had just admitted several things that everyone else had skirted or denied. He sat in silence, trying to order his thoughts as the man continued.

"Listen to me. I realize this is personal for you, but I can assure you that, however things may seem, Tod Engel is Deathangel. I can also assure you, again regardless of what you've come to believe, that reopening the case now will result in a severe setback for what is currently a minority liberal voice in Congress."

Beck remained silent as the car eased to a stop.

"Don't do this, Father Beck. Think of the consequences if you are wrong."

The car door opened like the lid from a pressure cooker. Matt could almost hear the rush of escaping steam. "I'll be in touch," he said, starting to extricate himself.

But Martin Ehrhart was not finished. "Contact me soon, Father Beck. Time is of the essence."

"Tell that to Tod Engel," Matt said as he exited the limo. They had returned to the spot where he'd been forced to leave the Spider.

"Be careful," Ehrhart said as the chauffeur closed the door.

The County Executive smiled as he watched the priest through the rear window check under the hood of his car. His smile vanished when the phone at his side beeped.

"Hello? Yes, Warden. How are things?"

Two minutes later, he slammed down the phone and stabbed at the intercom button.

"Bring mich schnell nach Hause!"

"Jaja mein Herr," the chauffeur responded. "I will take you home. Quickly!"

Ehrhart snatched up the phone again. There was one more call he had to make.

Chapter 13

Friedrich Baumschen stalked down the hospital corridor with a frown hidden under his moustache. It was not the only thing he was hiding. As he opened the door to the room, he rearranged his features into a bland but encouraging smile.

Anne Demming lay on the hospital bed, fully clothed. She looked tired and drawn, but there was still a certain vitality about her that he had noticed when he met her in New York. Her packed suitcase was on the wooden chair beside her, looking pathetically small. A uniformed nurse swabbed her arm with an alcohol pad and injected a syringe of pain medication. The smell called up unpleasant memories.

"That should prevent discomfort until you get to the airplane," the nurse said, patting her hand. "Once you are aboard, you may take the tablets I put in your purse. The directions are in English."

If you get to the airplane, Baumschen thought as he approached them. "Guten Morgan, Fraulein Demming," he said, smiling also at the nurse. "Are you ready to go home?"

"Yes," Anne said. "Especially after our conversation last night. There are many things that need to be attended to quickly there."

"And I will continue to help in any way I can." He took her hand and helped her stand by the bed. "All you need do is call—or have Herr Twitchel or the authorities contact me here in Vienna." He glanced out the window to the street.

"What's wrong?" she asked.

"Nothing, Fraulein," Baumschen said, realizing she was far too alert for him to have made such a mistake. "We are simply taking extra precautions this morning to assure your safety on your way home."

She glared at him and he felt the skeptical lens of the journalist focus tightly.

"I feel much better, regardless of how I may appear, and I don't like not knowing what the program is."

"I promise that we will keep you informed. For right now, the program is to get you to the elevator." He gestured toward the door. "Shall we?"

He grasped her hand and helped her take a few uncertain steps across the gray tiled floor. He was surprised at how hot her skin felt.

"I'm a little shaky," she said. The nurse put one arm around her waist and the other on her arm. "Thank you," she said. "Strange." She blinked her eyes a couple of times. "I felt much stronger before that last shot of med—"

Baumschen opened the door to a waiting white gurney and two orderlies.

Panic filled Anne's voice. "What the—?" She looked at Baumschen through heavy-lidded eyes.

"I am sorry, Fraulein," he said. "But we think it best." He spoke quickly to the others in German.

The nurse caught her head as one orderly cradled her limp body in his arms. Together they placed her on the gurney and pulled the white sheet over her face.

"She makes a lovely corpse, does she not?" the nurse said, and Baumschen barked at her.

"There is no such thing," he growled. "Especially in this case." He pointed to the room. "See that her bags are taken first to the ambulance. Then proceed according to plan."

The nurse vanished and Baumschen escorted the gurney to the elevator. He knew his charge could possibly still hear him and leaned down so his mouth was next to her ear.

"You will be fine, Fraulein," he whispered as they descended. "You will be fine. This little deception is necessary to move you out of the hospital and into the ambulance. No one would question the transport of a corpse, so that's what you must be. It would not be convincing for the corpse to groan or react to light or sound."

The elevator came to a halt at the basement. The doors opened to the morgue sign marked "Leichenhalle," and Baumschen unholstered his Glock, peering into the hallway before allowing the others to emerge. He held the .9mm at the ready as the orderlies rushed the gurney through the dimly lit room of tented sheets. Even ventilated and cooled, the room reeked of bodies and death. He hoped the woman was so far under sedation that she could not smell it. It would not help for her to be agitated now.

"We are almost there, Fraulein," he said when they arrived at the loading dock. They stopped and signaled to the ambulance idling nearby. Baumschen reached under the sheet and squeezed the cold, clammy hand. "If you can hear any of this, Fraulein Demming, I wish you the best of journeys."

His moustache twitched with nervousness as he supervised the two orderlies loading the collapsible gurney into the back of the ambulance. An armed officer sat next to the motionless body.

Baumschen slammed the rear door of the van and patted it in a final gesture of blessing. The orderlies departed, but Baumschen stood and watched the ambulance move slowly down the long driveway of the hospital. After the van turned onto the main highway, he sighed and went back inside to the morgue.

It was then that he heard the explosion.

He ran to the dock and saw a blazing inferno where the ambulance had been. Flames engulfed the ambulance, and a pillar of black smoke spiraled into the afternoon sky. Like a Mauthausen crematory.

Sirens blared, covering the sound of Baumschen's cursing.

It was not supposed to happen that soon.

"You have to do something, and I mean now, James." The smooth voice blasted through the line like icy air-conditioning. Rinski knew it was equally artificial.

"And just what would that be, Marty?" The police commissioner propped the phone against his shoulder and lit a new cigarette off the butt of the old one. "Should I have him picked up and summarily executed? I wanted to nail him for tampering with evidence, but you said that would bring too much attention to the case. Now you kidnap him on a major thoroughfare, hold him captive in your own car at gunpoint, and think you can keep him from talking by giving—giving—him information that he would never have obtained otherwise."

"He said he already had it."

"Not about your stupid brother-in-law!"

"He acted like he did. He said you gave him the print!"

"And you believed him, you idiot!" Rinski blew smoke through his nose. "That was just plain stupid, Marty, whether you trust me or not. And you had better start trusting me or you'll never get where you want to go." And the more you trust me, the more I have on you, the further I go, Rinski thought.

The County Executive snorted, his temperature and his voice sounding a bit higher. "I'm not the one who allowed Beck to break into the property room and play with the Deathangel evidence."

Rinski had hated telling Ehrhart about Beck's little maneuver. "Funny thing about that, Marty," Rinski said without a smile. "All those wooden angels seem to be missing after that break-in and there's no way to tell the exact count now." He drew a deep drag on the cigarette. "At least I know how to cover my mistakes."

"Not all of them. You'd better make that evidence list from the trial disappear as well."

"Already working on it," Rinski said, jotting a note to have Miss Incompetence call Steiner when this conversation was over. Assuming she could dial the number. He grinned. Of course, she had dialed his number pretty good last night.

"We have to dissuade him before the election or you and I will be permanently and quite uncomfortably unemployed."

Rinski was growing more annoyed. Beck was the least of their worries. "How do we know he's found anything that would hold up in court?" It was one thing to guess and take pot shots and quite another to have viable evidence.

"I talked to Williams today. Beck was up there snooping around, visiting Engel in isolation." Rinski heard ice cubes clink on Ehrhart's line. "Williams said Engel told Beck something so significant that Beck claimed he didn't need to see Engel again. God only knows what the man said. Sometimes I think he's not quite crazy enough. I wonder if we need to help him along a little."

"Anything can be arranged, Marty."

"Then we should fix that problem once and for all."

"You'll have to do it fast." Rinski inhaled and blew the smoke toward the ceiling. "Although Engel dying now might raise more issues than squashing them."

"True, but we don't have the luxury of time anymore. Williams has him in strict isolation and he's already not faring well. It wouldn't take much."

Rinski leaned forward on the desk. "They have an infirmary in that joint, right? So maybe the prison doc, or better yet, one of our choosing, like a specialist, has to treat him until the election is over. And then if things get too hot, Engel could have, how do they put it, an unfortunate occurrence? Of course, it'd be difficult for him to have any visitors while he's ill, wouldn't it? Him being so frail and all."

Ehrhart paused and ice rattled. "That's more like. But it still doesn't solve the problem of Matt Beck."

Rinski crushed out his cigarette. "It's late." He yawned. "I need to think about that overnight. You take care of the situation with Engel."

"Right. No problem. Call me first thing in the morning."

"Yeah. And next time you're in a limo with a creep, Marty, remember who covers your back." Rinski hung up the phone and cursed Martin Ehrhart. He popped the tiny cassette from the audio recorder and tossed it in the bottom desk drawer next to the disk containing his current journal. He locked the drawer and lit another cigarette. "I'll take care of Beck all right," he said to the silent phone. "But I ain't about to take the fall alone."

The small fireplace burned its one somber log as the bishop of the Diocese of New York lifter his slippered feet on a cushioned stool.

"Yes," he said into the phone. "The convention is to be assembled in two weeks. I'm the favored candidate, and I've made most of the proper arrangements to win on the second or perhaps the third ballot. I do not wish to prevail on the very first. That would be unseemly. I must maintain the proper humility at this point in the game."

John Langert sipped his sherry. "Yes, that's true. I don't know what I will do about Matthew Beck. I've enlisted his assistance, but I cannot be certain he'll follow the suggestion I made to him."

He listened intently to the voice on the line and shook his head. "No. I think that's premature." He paused. "But gather the proper resources together in case we're forced to proceed in that direction: Photos of him with Demming, tax documents, copies of his charge card bills. If he chooses badly, it will be too late for a mere warning. He must be delayed in his pursuit until the convention." The bishop considered a moment. "And possibly after that."

He looked at the intricate gold clock over the mantelpiece.

"You must end this conversation. Phone me tomorrow at the same hour—on this line." He hung up the phone in the middle of a sentence. One could not be too careful. Not now, when he was so close. He could not let anyone stand in his way. Not Matt Beck, not Tod Engel, not even the heretofore innocuous Arthur Allen, who suddenly seemed to have grown balls. Not anyone.

He examined the list in his lap. There were five more bishops to contact to assure the exact number of ballots in his favor. Three were in western time zones, so he'd waited until now to call.

Langert watched the log in the fireplace break in two. At first the fire burned low, but then it flared, each half providing a brighter light than the whole had before.

He smiled. It was a good omen. The break that would soon occur would produce many small fires, each of which would burn more brilliantly than the whole had ever dreamed.

And he would be the force that caused it, that dragged the church kicking and screaming into the twenty-first century.

He took another drink and punched the numbers on the phone.

"Yes, that is correct." Warden Richard Williams spoke with a steady, measured voice.

Control.

"I understand it will delay the visitations, but we must keep this prison secure. There have been too many instances of contraband leaving this institution."

"They're not gonna like it," the gate guard said. "They're gonna scream to their Congressmen and the press."

"Refer all such calls to me," Williams replied. "Just do it. Search everyone leaving the facility with the handheld metal detector and examine all bags and briefcases. If you find anything suspicious, including prison property, write up an incident report and send it directly to me."

The officer stopped his protestations.

"Do you understand?" Williams had to ensure there were no mistakes. Everyone was to be checked, including himself, the cooks, the volunteer teachers, and especially the chaplain. "Keep me informed."

That should prevent Allen from taking any more documents out of here without his knowledge. Now if Engel would just cooperate by deteriorating enough to be hospitalized, as Ehrhart had suggested only minutes ago. Unfortunately, Engel had regressed to a quieter level in isolation; more hostile, but calm. Perhaps some event was needed to prod him.

Like a visit from the warden.

Williams flicked on the monitor for the isolation area. The guard was reading a book and the cells were silent.

He punched in the extension and watched the guard pick up the phone. "Petokis, this is the warden. How's Engel?" he barked into the speaker.

"He's getting weaker all the time. Eating less and less."

"Is he still receiving the same dose of medication?"

"Yes. But, Warden, if you don't mind me saying so, I think it's the drugs that're causing the problem, along with the isolation."

"Uh huh."

"And I was wondering, sir, if I might take him out for some fresh air tonight. I mean, there would be nobody else in the exercise yard."

Williams hesitated, then said, "Certainly. I think it may do him good. Let me consider it for a couple of minutes and get back to you. Maybe I'll come down to your area."

"Oh, that's not really necessary, Warden."

Williams bristled. He resented Petokis's attempt to protect Engel from him.

"I mean, you know how he reacts to you. Your visit might make him too agitated to go out."

"He will have to conduct himself well, even in my presence, if he is to warrant any time in the yard." Williams settled on two decisions, one about Engel, the other about the guard. "You might try to tell him that, Petokis."

"But, sir."

"I'll be there in twenty minutes. Have him ready."

"Yes, sir," the guard said dejectedly.

Williams punched another button on the phone.

"Captain's desk, this is Stratham."

"Stratham, this is the Warden."

"Oh. Hello, Warden. Whatcha doin' here so late on a Monday?"

"My work, Captain," Williams said icily. "And what I notice here late at night is that some rescheduling needs to be done."

"What are you talkin' about, Warden?"

"How long has Petokis worked Isolation?"

"Oh, God, he's been there for years. He loves the place. We all think he belongs there himself, that's why he likes it so much."

"He's been there long enough. I want you to reshuffle all the assignments in Isolation, starting with his. People stay in a position too long, they grow careless, too attached, too accustomed to the routine."

"But, Warden."

"I want it done by third shift tomorrow."

The captain's reply was clipped. "Yes, sir."

"Have a good night, Stratham."

Williams stretched his cramped muscles. He really must start exercising again, he thought, as he drank the last bit of the coffee he had made earlier. Maybe when all this was over. He left the office and walked into the bowels of the prison. In minutes, he stood at the door of Engel's cell.

Ehrhart would take care of Beck, or so he had promised earlier. He himself had countered the surreptitious movements of Chaplain Allen. Now, if all went well, or badly as the case might be, Williams would precipitate the beginning of the end of Engel. Williams smiled. He had planned to take Engel off the count sooner or later anyway. Now he had the added advantage of having it appear as though Ehrhart instructed him to carry out the task. And Ehrhart would owe him for it because the naive County Executive thought it was his idea.

Petokis looked sullen when the warden arrived. Perhaps he already knew about the reassignment. Too bad, Williams thought. He must learn not to stand in the way of progress.

As Rinski entered Engel's cell, the guard closed the door behind him with an especially loud clang. Engel stirred in his bunk and gazed at the warden through hazy, drug-blurred eyes.

Williams approached him. He felt no pity for this sorry broken hulk that stood between him and the future. In the old days, in places he had visited, this travesty of humanity would not have been allowed to live this long. Things were better then. Clearer. Cleaner. It made no sense to incarcerate men like Engel, keeping them alive in this dungeon, using food and money that could be spent on deserving people.

"Hello, Tod," Williams said, wondering if the man even understood his name. It was moments like this, these close encounters, that validated everything Williams believed. If he had his way he would clear out the prison tomorrow, rid the world of insects like Engel.

"Tod, wake up. Sit up here and look at me." Williams spoke like he would to his dog. He walked over to the bed and stood over the prisoner, watching Engel's eyes widen as he approached. "On second thought, you just stay there." He leaned down and touched Engel's hand. "Maybe we can chat about the old days."

The deafening roar from Engel's mouth shocked the warden. He jumped back as the convicted killer rose up from the bed, swaying over him. Williams knew a cadre of guards would rush to open the cell, though he heard Petokis fumbling the key in the lock, a purposeful act for which the man would pay later. Though Engel did not reach for him, Williams yanked the blackjack from a back pocket and sapped the huge man twice until he fell to his knees, then twice more until he hit the floor. He started to raise his arm high to hit the prisoner again, but the squeal of the key twisting the steel lock caused him simply to stare through narrowed eyes at the bleeding, unconscious hulk collapsed like a supplicant at his feet.

When the guards burst into the cell, the warden ordered them, in his most solicitous voice, to take the prisoner to the infirmary.

Art Allen cursed as he listened to the sound of Beck's answering machine. He had wanted to speak directly to him, and he couldn't safely page him to the prison number.

The tape beeped.

"Matt? Art. I did what you suggested and the digging paid off in a gold strike. I need to talk to you as soon as possible. Call me at home. I'm at the prison now and will be on my way in twenty minutes."

As he was about to hang up he heard a click, as though the phone had been disconnected. Someone was listening. "Shit," he said. Busted. Maybe dead, like Joe McCaslin, if they were in as much trouble as Matt suspected. He tried to calm his racing heart. Okay, fine, he told himself. If he didn't make it out of the prison, he would have to make damned sure the latest documents he had uncovered did.

He thought a second and sat down to smoke what was left of a cigar in an overfilled ashtray. The folder on Williams was thick, about forty pages, containing all his work history, some biographical information, and the critical reports Beck had asked him to research. First he had to get this data to Beck. Then he had to protect Engel. And to do both he had to stay alive.

Unfortunately, the only fax machine in the prison was in the warden's office, for security reasons. Allen put down the cigar and smiled. He imagined knocking on the office door, asking if he could please fax the warden's BCI file to Matt Beck. Fortunately, some months ago Allen had grown tired of the hassle of requesting permission. He had bought his own fax, a small, cylindrical model that he could hook up to the phone in his office. He risked discovery if he used the machine right now, he surmised, puffing vigorously on the cigar. Being technologically challenged, he didn't know what happened if someone was listening in on a fax transmission. Was the transmission stopped? Could the listener tap into the fax and have it delivered or copied to his office? That would be dandy. Here Warden, in case you missed a few things on your resume.

The other problem was the length of the file. If he did fax it and the person monitoring him—presumably Williams—realized it was the sound of a fax transmission, the warden could have guards in the chaplain's office in minutes. There would be no time to send the entire thing safely.

Allen stuffed the cigar in the tray and went through the file page by page. He pulled out the most significant pieces and placed them in a small pile. It came to seven pages. If luck held out he'd send more.

He put the portable fax device on his desk and connected it to the phone line. Dialing Beck's fax number at Grasslands Hospital, Allen nervously fed in the papers one by one, watching them curl slowly through the cylinder. Time froze with the insertion of each page. He was sure the warden was sending armed Marines to retake the Chapel at any moment. Every noise in the corridor caused him to sweat more. Finally, two decades later, he tore up the pile of documents and flushed them down the old toilet in his office bathroom. Then he paged Matt, sending the hospital fax number to alert him to look there, and prayed that all the pages had gotten through. It was the first time he had prayed in years.

The smart thing now was to get the hell out of Weston. If Williams suspected anything, Allen could easily meet with a little accident in a dark corridor. But the chaplain was through being smart, especially after perusing the warden's file. In fact, he thought the smarter thing to do was to spend time with Tod Engel. He called Petokis in Isolation.

"What's the matter with your phone, Chaplain?" the guard demanded.

"I'm not sure. Been having some problems with it. You know this old prison junk. Why?"

"I've been tryin' to call you for a head's up on Engel."

"What happened?" Allen asked, worried that somehow the man was already dead.

"Williams came down and paid him a visit."

Allen listened, his breath nearly gone. They both understood they had to assume their conversation was being overheard.

Petokis continued, "I just took Engel to the infirmary."

"On my way," Allen said. He raced out the door, hoping he could manage to be a guardian angel to Deathangel.

"Which bed, Lo?" Matt said to the ICU nurse as he entered the unit. The patient had been described to him on the phone as a corpse with a steering wheel in his brain.

"Still coding." She pointed down the hall. "They've been working on the guy for half an hour and still can't get anything going. I think Doctor Cain's been waiting for you to arrive, actually, because the family—and there are lots of 'em—are all going nuts."

"Got it." Halfway down the hall he saw a white-jacketed doctor surrounded by what appeared to be half the population of China.

"Excuse me," he said, wading into the crowd. "I'm Chaplain Beck. Is there some way I can help?"

Forty minutes later, with the assistance of a Chinese nurse from Labor and Delivery, Beck had helped the doctors explain why they had to stop coding the young man and communicated to the staff why the family had to sit in the room with the body for a full two hours after the death was pronounced to comfort his spirit. After condolences and thanks were exchanged in several dialects, Matt gratefully accepted a cup of coffee from Loraine as he charted the event at the nurse's station.

"Stick around, Matt," she said. "Busy night on the interstate. We have another one coming in, direct admit to ICU. ETA thirty."

Beck felt his pager vibrate. "May have to go to the backup chaplain," he said, punching up the number. At first he did not recognize it, though it looked familiar. Then he remembered.

"There's a first," he said to the nurse. "My fax machine just paged me." He smiled. "I'll go see what it wants when I'm through here."

Beck finished charting and was headed out the ICU door when Loraine called after him.

"What? They here already?"

"No." She handed him a piece of paper. "Betty at the switchboard called and said to track you down personally for this one. Very mysterious, she said. You are to contact a Mr. Baumschen at this number. Make any sense?"

It was all Matt could do to answer her in his rush out of the unit. He located a private phone in the doctor's dictation room and called the number.

"Yes?" the deep voice answered.

"Baumschen? This is Matt Beck. Is Anne all right? Is she there? Put her on the phone."

"Pfarrer Beck." The voice sounded strained. "She is here. I accompanied her on the plane from Austria."

"Where are you? I'll come immediately."

"Actually, I am in your hospital."

"Here! My God, why didn't you say so? What room?"

"Yes," the voice lowered. "You may come and view her in room five sixty-eight."

Matt dropped the phone and hurried around the corner to a stairwell. Elated, he bounded up the stairs from the second to the fourth floor. Then he slowed, suddenly wondering about Baumschen's choice of words. The man spoke excellent English, and Beck knew the man meant "see her," so why had he said "view her?" That was something you did to a body—in a casket.

"Oh, my God. No!," he shouted, his voice echoing in the green stairwell. He reached the fifth floor and ran to the end of the hall, tears already brimming in his eyes.

Without knocking, he flung open the door to room 568 and barged into the room where Friedrich Baumschen waited with a gun, standing over the still body of Anne Demming.

Chapter 14

Beck watched the sun rise over Grasslands Lake. Wispy pink and gray clouds reflected in the surface of the calm water, broken only by the bubble rings of fish coming up for breakfast. Having been submerged all night in data and emotion amid snatches of sleep, he too was about to surface. He pulled the blind to let the first rays of light flow through the large window of room 568. He rubbed his gritty eyes and cracked open the glass to inhale the clean air of morning. It was colder than he thought, and he shut the window so the draft would not chill Anne, who slept on the bed behind him.

He turned and touched her hand. The initial image of their reunion would never leave him. He was certain of that. When he saw Anne's unmoving body under the white hospital sheets, his heart sank and he nearly collapsed with despair. Certain she was dead, he had ignored Baumschen and rushed to her lifeless side, holding her as he had held Kate long ago, wanting revenge on whoever had done this to her. Then he heard her sigh, and his soul returned to his body.

"She will live, Herr Beck," the Interpol man said. "But she will need your assistance in her recovery."

"You don't know Texans," Beck said. "When she wakes up, she'll get up."

Matt had talked most of the night with this strange man whose bald head and Carioca moustache belied the expertise he brought to this case. He learned from Baumschen why Anne had been attacked, what she had found, and how he had arranged her secret transport across international borders.

Right now, the Interpol investigator was sacked out on an uncomfortable cot by the bathroom. Matt smiled at the thought that he was snoring in German.

In the wee hours of the morning Baumschen explained the near disaster with the ambulance in Vienna. "We switched the gurneys when we went through the morgue so that we put a corpse in the ambulance. I was not totally certain the vehicle would be targeted, but I was worried enough to ignore the orders of my superiors, who were convinced otherwise. When the driver reached the main road, I thought I had plenty of time to remove Fraulein Demming from the morgue and into a van I had waiting at another entrance. Then the ambulance exploded, nearly on the hospital grounds, and we were barely able to make the transfer and exit unobtrusively, knowing the terrorists had to be observing their handiwork close by."

Beck glanced over at Anne. He was about to lean down and kiss her when the bedside phone rang. He grabbed it as Baumschen bolted up from the cot, scowling.

"Beck here." He waved Baumschen back down, but the man got up anyway.

"Matt?"

Beck didn't need caller I.D. for that voice. It was Jackson Twitchel.

"How are you holding out? How is Anne?"

Matt explained that Anne was coming off the narcotic medications, waking periodically and starting to ask angry questions: But she recognized him, or at least she smiled through the morphine blur at whoever she thought he was.

"Anything you need done? Bring you some food?"

Matt looked at Baumschen. "I don't think we require anything right now." The German nodded in agreement. "But stand by the phone for the next couple of hours. We may need some clout, or the threat of it, as the day goes on."

"Whatever you want, you got," Twitch said. "Kiss that lady for me, and tell her we're ready to kick butt and take names."

"Thank God for reinforcements," Beck said as Grace Fanton waltzed into the room with two shopping bags.

"What?" Twitch's voice rose.

"Oh, Anne's neighbor just arrived. Call back later today and Anne should be awake."

He hung up as the older woman heaved the bags onto a counter and withdrew a stainless-steel thermos with all the theatrics of a magician pulling a rabbit out of a hat, including the bow. "I just knew you two boys would need some fresh coffee first thing this morning." She took out two porcelain mugs and poured them full, handing one to Baumschen. "And this isn't that store-bought crap, either. I brewed it at home in my own Italian coffeemaker, with fresh beans I made Jack go out and buy last night after you phoned, Matt." She kissed Beck on the cheek and handed him his mug. "And no styrofoam. Poisons the taste, if you ask me. Bad for the environment, too."

"Good morning, Gracie," Beck said, grinning as she clucked over Anne's sleeping form. "She's actually been up twice to the bathroom, and I believe she's coming around again."

"What do you think, Mr. Baumschen?" the older woman asked.

"I agree with Father Beck, Frau Fanton. And thank you so much for the excellent coffee. It does help."

"Well, I can't stay. Just brought over some food for you, and the other bag has the clothes you asked for from Anne's apartment. Things you boys would never think of, I'm sure."

Baumschen pulled a silver flask of liquor from one bag.

"Oh, that's from Jack. He sent it to tide you over and to make you bring it back so we'll be sure to see you again."

Matt watched her pat Anne on the shoulder like you would a small child, for reassurance and love. Grace smooched the bandaged forehead and almost broke into tears, then hurried from the room.

"Quite a lady," Beck said, lifting his coffee mug in salute to Baumschen. He rubbed his eyes again. "Listen, would you mind watching the store while I jump in the shower to wake up?"

"Not at all," Baumschen said. "I have to make some calls to Europe, and now is a good time of day to do that." He sipped the coffee. "We will talk more when you are done."

Matt grabbed his small bag of spare clothes and stumbled into the bathroom. The only time he had left Anne's side all night was to run to his office to retrieve the faxes from Allen. They had been stunning in their detailed implication of Williams as a major Deathangel suspect. Even though he had suspected it of the man, he had been surprised at what Allen had uncovered.

He stripped down and moved into the thin stream of steaming water. Between the two of them, Matt and Baumschen had pooled their information to answer many of the questions. Using the Interpol agent's notebook computer and access codes, along with the data Anne had gathered and the incredible photographs she'd taken at Mauthausen, they had traced and printed phone records, airline and credit card slips, paper trails that led convincingly back to the four men most involved with the case—Rinski, Ehrhart, Williams, and Langert.

Ironic, he thought, that it boiled down to these four. But could they be missing someone? What if it still was Engel somehow? Matt let the hot water roll over him, relaxing taut muscles. With all that they knew, they still had no proof that any of the men was the real Deathangel, nor could they say for certain why the killer had struck.

They had determined the connection between the victims, that all four were Wechseljuden, Jews who hid their identity by becoming baptized

Christians and then were offered jobs they could not refuse at the camp—jobs as guards over their own people. The four had escaped, along with many others who ran the camp—the Konzentrationslager—just before it was liberated, and eventually found their way to Westchester County, where they lived quietly for decades.

The angels, symbols of hope at Mauthausen, had obviously been left at the scene of the crimes to terrorize anyone else who might be linked with the victims and their past—a prisoner, a guard, or perhaps a family member or friend of either group. The carvings could have been meant as a sign of someone completing unfinished business from the camp, killing off the remaining Nazi guards. But the murders also could have been the work of a neo-Nazi group ferreting out the remaining Jews from Mauthausen, in particular, those Jews who had used subterfuge to survive the war. Due to his lengthy pursuit of the terrorist group whose trail had led to New York, Baumschen favored the latter view.

Anne had unlocked the mystery of the nonsense phrases Engel had been spouting all these years. All of Engel's words were bad pronunciations of German terms he must have heard, words that described things from Mauthausen. But was he repeating those phrases to ask for help or defy it, to provide the clues that would lead to his exoneration or to affirm his guilt? In either case, how could he know about the death camp?

Mauthausen, Beck thought. His mind replayed Baumschen's description of the events Anne had endured, and again his heart sank for her. The elation at finding the pieces of the puzzle, the fear she must have experienced in that restaurant, the pain of her wounds.

Matt soaped his hair. The hot water washed over his whole body, cleansing him as he hoped they would both soon be cleansed of the evil they had touched. He knew it would take more than the scent of soap to rid the stench from his nostrils.

He and Anne had believed from the beginning that there had been incredible negligence at the trial, but evidence was mounting that it was much more than that. Whether he played a role in the killings or not, Engel had been set up to take the fall for someone or a group of someones. Still, there was no flashing sign pointing to Deathangel's true identity—Ehrhart, Rinski, Langert or even Williams. Baumschen had no hard evidence that any of them were involved in terrorist activity, though circumstantial connections for each man had emerged from the paper trails.

Beck dried himself, shaved, and got dressed. His nerves tensed with anticipation of what he had proposed to Baumschen. He was more awake now, from the shower and from Grace's high-test, leaded coffee coursing through his system. In any case, he could not sleep until the task was accomplished. His anger at the injustices done with official blessing would fuel his energy for the remaining hours.

"You look like a different man," Baumschen commented as Beck returned from the bathroom. "In fact, I almost shot you." He smiled.

Beck liked the man's sense of humor as well as his tenacity and sense of fairness. In some ways, Baumschen reminded him of his dad, except maybe this man was a bit more realistic about the forces he was fighting.

"Have you thought further about the gathering?" Matt asked, pouring another cup of coffee.

"I have done more than think about it, Herr Beck," Baumschen said. "I have discussed it with my superiors and with a colleague at Interpol in New York."

"And?"

"And they all believe it is not only very foolish, but personally quite risky. They think that we could lose our case against them and that the lives of many could be endangered if we are not extremely careful."

Matt stifled a retort. He could not carry out his plan with just Anne, especially in her current condition. If Baumschen was not on board with his professional resources, they were stuck, at least for now.

"And?" Beck said again. He would have to come up with an argument that would punch through Baumschen's resistance.

The man smiled. "And—for all of those reasons I say we proceed."

"What?" It was not the answer he had anticipated. For a second, he thought Baumschen had convoluted his question into a double negative.

"I agree that we must go forward and we must do it quickly, Herr Beck. There are forces at work that would like to have us delay, even for hours, our counterattack on them. But we will need outside backup from your CIA or DIA. My authority in this jurisdiction is limited to detaining. I may only stop and hold perpetrators for the authorities.

Beck immediately defined "stop and hold" in the broadest possible terms, from cuffed to coffined. "Since we can't trust anyone with local authority, like the police commissioner and the county executive, we'll also have to get some help from the state attorney general." He glanced at Anne. "I'll call Twitch about that. You confer with Interpol and alert the feds."

An hour later they had extracted what they wanted from a reluctant attorney general and an eager CIA assistant director. They were ready to begin.

Beck picked up the phone to make the first move, but he stopped when he heard a whisper from the bed.

"Who—calling?" Anne said, almost too softly to hear.

Matt took her hand. "Hey. You waking up?"

"Awake. Off and on," she said, her eyes still closed. "More on now."

"Etwas—anything you require, Fraulein?" Baumschen offered.

"Listening," she said.

"That's good, Anne," Beck said, kissing her cheek. "We'll put the phone on speaker so you can listen and so you'll know your part when we get to it."

"Good," she said. "Water."

Beck gently placed a straw to her lips and she drank nearly the entire cup, more than she had all night. She seemed to be coming back, but it remained to be seen how much she could participate in what he and Baumschen had in mind.

He synchronized his watch at 0600 with Baumschen. By three that afternoon, if they were lucky, it should be finished. Damn you, Joe McCaslin, he thought, as he considered Anne, looking small and hurt beneath the crisp sheet. Damn you for noticing, for refusing to back away, for telling me. Damn you for dying. And damn everyone else who had anything to do with this godawful travesty of cover-up, conspiracy, and murder. Damn them and bless them for bringing it all to light.

"Let's do it," Beck said, reviewing the list of phone numbers.

A busy signal beeped over the speaker for the first one.

"Not surprising." Matt spoke partly to Anne, who was breathing softly in the bed beside him. "He's known to be an early riser." He held out his cup for Baumschen to pour a warm-up. "I'll bet we wake the other ones out of a deep sleep." He looked at Anne. "At least I hope so."

He tried the same number again. This time it rang.

"Williams residence." Sounded to Beck like a servant, possibly a trusty. "May I help you?"

"Get the warden," Beck said. "There's been a prison break."

Instantly, Williams was on the line. "Who is this? What happened?"

"Matt Beck, Warden. There's been no break except the one about you."

"Just what is that supposed to mean? Is this some kind of sick joke?"

"Only sick joke here is the one I'm talking to." Matt imagined the man getting red in the face. "Before you hang up, pencil in your calendar a meeting at Weston at two today with Tod Engel."

"Why should I arrange such a thing?" Williams snapped.

"Because if you don't, the next time your phone rings it will be the A.G. ordering you to do it." Matt wondered whether the lengthy silence on the line meant Williams was evaluating the reality of the threat or composing himself to answer. "Warden?"

"If what you say is true, and I will believe it when I receive a call from the attorney general, then I apparently have no choice in the matter." He paused again. "However, I may not be there myself, due to other duties."

"You have to be present, Warden."

"And you are giving me orders now because—"

"Because Engel has been in your charge."

"I see," Williams said, and Matt did not like the confident tone of voice. "Well, perhaps he will not be in my charge, as you put it, for much longer, Father Beck." Matt could almost see the man's satisfied smile. "Perhaps he will soon be in yours."

"What happened?" Beck had not counted on losing their star witness. They'd have to punt fast if Engel had been incapacitated.

"Oh," Williams taunted. "You didn't know? But, of course, how could you know everything? It seems that you are partly to blame, Father Beck. After your visit the other day, Engel became quite agitated. He had to be severely subdued and moved to the infirmary. He's under heavy sedation. It's a delicate situation. As he has been ill lately and generally run down, we risk the problem of further reducing his respirations with the medications. If he is not watched night and day, who can guess what might happen?"

Beck stared at the two words he and Baumschen had written beside the warden's number. Playing these cards might buy the time to save Engel's life.

"Tod told me about your secret from Rikers, Warden." He threw in the second card immediately. "And we know the meaning now of his so-called nonsense phrases."

The line was silent.

"You will be at the meeting or you will read Engel's words once again in *CityMag*, only this time they'll be about you, in detail." Again, nothing. Matt persisted. "Two o'clock today, Warden. Have a room ready to accommodate—"

"Go to hell, Beck." The line went dead.

"Shit." Matt slammed down the phone, irritated as hell at the man's intransigence.

Baumschen grinned behind his moustache. "I will call your attorney general on my cell phone," he said, retrieving the small black phone from his case.

Matt nodded and hit the second number on their list. It rang a dozen times before a sleepy, annoyed voice growled from the speaker. Just what he wanted. "Fine way for a future senator to answer his telephone, Mr. County Executive."

"Who is this, damn it? What are you doing, disturbing me at this hour?"

"Rise and shine, Ehrhart, it's truth-telling time."

"Beck! Is that you? How did you get this number? What the devil do you want?"

"I want you to come to Weston Prison at two o'clock today to meet Deathangel."

"What? What is this about? Give me one good reason why I shouldn't hang up on you."

Matt breathed deep and laid his hand on Anne's arm. "Your brother-in-law, Ehrhart. If you don't appear at Weston this afternoon, his name will be on the front page of *CityMag* tomorrow, with a detailed story inside."

"You can't do that, Beck!" Ehrhart fumed.

"I can do any damned thing I want, Ehrhart, now that I've learned the meaning of Engel's phrases."

"Beck, wait. Be reasonable."

"Like you have been with Tod Engel?" Beck spit back. "Be there or your senate bid is over."

"Beck, let me ask you something," Ehrhart whined. "If I come, it's also possible that Anne Demming could use the magazine for whatever, uh, damage control, I might need, is it not?"

"Show up and we'll see."

"I will be there at two." Ehrhart spoke quietly, giving the impression of being subdued, but Beck understood it was part of the game. He doubted the man had any humility left after all these years in power. Power and humility seemed to be mutually exclusive except in people with deep spirituality, and Ehrhart was far from being one of those. He punched off the speaker.

"Two," Beck heard Anne say.

"Two o'clock this afternoon, that's right." Beck checked his watch. "And it's about six thirty now."

"Better by then."

Matt smiled at Baumschen and shook his head. They'd see how much better she was and whether she could play a part in the final show. He knew how important it was to her, and to them, to finish this together.

"The attorney general has promised to contact Herr Williams and command the meeting. I also took the liberty of arranging our own safe passage from here to the prison with a federal escort, since we cannot trust all of the local gendarmes."

"Good job. Thanks," Matt said as he punched in the third number. It was answered on the first ring.

"Morning, Bishop. This is Matt Beck."

"An early call for you, isn't it, Matthew?"

"Not when I've been up all night, it isn't."

"I'm sorry to hear that. I hope it wasn't due to a bad outcome."

Matt looked at Anne. "It has had a very good outcome, actually." He glanced at Baumschen, who was pouring himself more coffee and listening intently. "But the reason I'm calling is to reply to your offer of the other evening."

John Langert did not respond.

Matt frowned. "Are you there?"

"Continue."

The bishop's tone was suddenly austere. Perhaps he sensed the aggressiveness in Beck's manner. "It seems your concern with my knowledge of your previous association with Tod Engel is a moot point."

"What do you mean?" The bishop spoke more softly now. Beck could nearly hear the man's heart pounding over the phone.

"I mean that I had a long conversation with Tod Engel. The new medication they're using on him is working. It's as though the delusions have disappeared. He had moments of amazing clarity, Bishop. That's the good news."

The man whispered, "And the bad?"

"The bad, for you anyway, is that he seems to remember you from that previous time, saying, as you have always said, that he did not do the murders. But now he's also claiming that you know who did."

The bishop remained silent.

"I want you to come to the prison this afternoon at two o'clock so we can talk to him together."

Langert seemed to regain his composure. "I am afraid that will be impossible, Matthew. I have an interview with the Standing Committee of Bishops. As you know, they screen the candidates and it is a compulsory—"

Beck interrupted. "Be at Weston Prison at two today, Bishop."

"That sounded like more than an invitation."

Beck's voice became terse. "It was."

Langert's tone matched his. "What is the meaning of this? What are you insinuating?"

Matt struggled to respond calmly. Anger would not work with this man; it would only alert him to danger. He had to be persuaded. "You have to come today because we have to put the right spin on this if we're going to get you elected presiding bishop."

Langert hesitated. "It sounds as though you've accepted my offer, then?"

Thank God, he took the bait. "Let's just say I'm real tired of hospital work and I'm ready to move on in my career. We go back a long way, to far better days than these, both personally and nationally. I agree that it's time for a different direction for the church, and I want to be a part of that with you."

"I must admit I'm a bit surprised to hear you say this."

"I just decided it was important to live in the real world, Bishop, and quit complaining about not having an ideal one. I have to let go of the past. I believe this meeting is just a formality, but one we both must accept if things are to proceed as we intend."

Langert sighed. Matt and Baumschen shot each other a nervous glance. This was the critical moment.

Langert became businesslike, and Beck knew the hook was in. "I may not be able to get out of that interview with the standing committee."

"If you aren't there, John," Beck pleaded as if he had an equal stake in the issue, "Engel may see to it that there is no need for the standing committee meeting." He held his breath as Langert paused again.

"Very well. I see your point. And I'm very grateful for your decision. I believe it's the right one for both of us."

"I'll meet you at Weston at two," Beck said. He punched off the speaker phone and breathed a huge sigh of relief.

"You are a convincing liar, Pfarrer Beck," Baumschen said. "If your present position does not work out, call me for a job anytime."

The priest touched Anne's hand again. "Sure thing," he said quietly, watching her.

"Can always tell," Anne murmured, and Matt thought he saw a slight smile.

"Not fair, Fraulein," Baumschen said. "You have had more practice listening to him."

"This next one's for you, Anne." Beck grinned and dialed the final number, which rang repeatedly before the angry voice boomed through the speaker.

"What?"

"Haul that fat carcass out of bed, Rinski. It's Matt Beck."

"Go to hell." Click.

"He hung up on me." Beck looked at the buzzing speaker. "I'm shocked." A smile appeared on Anne's face.

The phone rang seven times before Rinski picked up again.

"Is this Beck?"

"We know the meaning of the phrases from Engel, Rinski," Beck said quickly, sure he was about to be cut off. "And that's only the beginning."

"Good for you. Now go screw yourself." Click.

Eight rings.

"Wake up, asshole," Beck said. "Next call is to the attorney general."

There was a long pause. "What the hell are you talking about?"

Matt could tell that the police commissioner's eyes had fully opened. He would do his best to keep them that way.

"Not on the phone, Rinski. Not even your phone."

"You're full of shit, Beck," Rinski said, hacking his smoker's cough. "You don't have anything or you wouldn't be calling me up to bust my nuts about it. You'd be marching into my house with the feds and a warrant to indict my ass."

"There's more than one way to skin a fat cat, Rinski," Beck said, "and to skin your senatorial buddy right along with you."

"Spell it out for me, Beck. I'm kind of dumb about those things."

"The news media would be an interesting place to retry this case, don't you think, Commissioner?"

"Even idiots like your bitch with the nice tits have to have more to take to the public than some wacko phrases you think you now miraculously understand from a case ten years ago, Beck." Rinski snickered. "It won't wash."

Matt bristled. If Rinski was in any way responsible for Anne's pain, he would deal with him personally. "I wasn't talking about the phrases, Rinski. I was talking about your famous, or should I say infamous, relative." He heard an audible gasp on the other end of the line. "A little publicity with the wrong slant would send you right back into the rat hole you crawled out of, wouldn't it?"

"You're bluffing, Beck. You wouldn't do that."

"Like hell I wouldn't."

The police commissioner said softly, "How much you want?"

"A quaint—if Neanderthal—idea, believing money can buy silence. I'm after much more than that."

"I'm all ears."

"Good, because I'm only going to say this once. If there is any hesitation—any—I hang up and it's over."

"So talk, damn it."

"Be at Weston Prison at two this afternoon."

"What for?"

"Good-bye."

"No! Wait, Beck!" Rinski sounded panicked. "I'll go. I just want to know why."

Beck's eyes met those of the man across the room. "I want you to have a little chat with a considerably more lucid Tod Engel, a Tod Engel who remembers a few details that were conveniently left out at his trial." Beck looked at the bed beside him. "You will sit face to face with Engel. And then we will watch the real Deathangel emerge."

The commissioner laughed. "You're crazier than he is. It's been ten years and he's been on every drug they make. That loony con can't remember a damned thing."

"Then don't show." Beck hung up, certain Rinski would call back.

Ten seconds later the speaker rang. He let it go for seven rings for payback.

"Beck." Rinski's voice sounded strained and angry. "I'll get you for this. And it won't be pretty."

"I'll lay awake nights worrying about it."

"Count on it."

"I assume that means you'll be there?" Beck took the dial tone as a yes.

Baumschen set down his coffee cup. "Are you certain this is the correct method?" he asked.

"I'm not certain about anything right now." Beck motioned to the bed. "Except her. And it seems the only way to know for sure what happened—or what we surmise happened—is to bring them all together, as we discussed last night.

"What is the expression?" Baumschen said. "Putting all the eggs in the same omelette?"

Anne spoke slowly, "Breaking."

"What?" Matt frowned.

"Breaking—all your eggs—in the same basket."

Matt squeezed her hand and dialed one more number. At the beep, he entered the hospital room number.

Two minutes later the speaker sounded.

"Art?"

"Matt! Thank God you called. I'm at Weston, on my own cell phone. Engel's in the infirmary and—"

"I know. Williams told me."

"But he's changed the guards on Engel. They're men loyal to Williams. They'd just as soon kill the inmate as look at him, and get bonus pay for it. I've been sleeping in my office, waking up to check on him every two hours through the night since they stuck him in there. Knowing Engel's being watched has held them off, but he's getting worse, and I don't think it's from natural causes."

Beck wondered if he'd sealed Engel's fate by calling Williams's hand earlier. He explained about the meeting and asked if Allen could stay with the prisoner until they arrived at Weston that afternoon.

"That's one hell of a lot of time to kill," Allen said.

"I know it is," Beck replied. "But you have to stall them. Do whatever you have to. Just keep Engel alive."

"Right," Allen said. "But get here as soon as you can."

The line buzzed and Beck punched it off and stared out the window. The pinks and grays had turned to stunning reds, the sweet dampness of night giving way to what would become an Indian summer day. He leaned against the wall and sipped his coffee. "One more thing," He said to Baumschen. "I need you or one of your agents to call Sergeant D'Angelo at the Westchester County Courthouse station for me." He paced the room, coming to rest at the side of the bed, looking at Anne.

"I could call him," she said, her eyes closed.

Matt leaned over and held her, thanked whatever powers had transported her back to him. "You think you're ready for that so soon?"

"Here's my list." She opened her eyes and squinted with a mild grimace. "I want coffee, my camera, and you." She kissed him. "Not necessarily in that order."

"That can be arranged," Beck said, his voice unsteady.

"Welcome back, Fraulein."

Anne scowled at them. "Will you two quit gawking and help me get out of this damned bed? From what I just heard, it's time—as my esteemed boss likes to say—to kick butt and take names."

Matt lowered the bed rail. "Not necessarily in that order," he said. He mentally added one further item to the list.

Her .38.

Chapter 15

Arthur Allen dutifully read Scripture to the patient who lay in the steel-frame bed with white enamel bars. A stained sheet was pulled up to the inmate's ears, nearly covering his head, as if portending his imminent demise. The man faced the wall, and the priest imagined the words bouncing off his back like water off a duck. Indeed, Allen felt his task was just as futile.

"And from the eighth chapter of Paul's Epistle to the Romans: 'For I consider that the sufferings of the present time are not worthy to be compared with the glory which will be revealed to us.' "

The patient did not move. His breathing remained as steady as it had since Allen had taken up his position. The chaplain glanced for the hundredth time at his watch. One o'clock. Damn it Matt Beck, he thought. Hurry up and get here. I can't hold out much longer.

Allen had already claimed religious privilege several times that morning. He had requested to be left alone with Engel before the warden arrived and, when Williams rescinded that request, he demanded to remain at Engel's bedside "for comfort and support in the prisoner's time of need, as state law permits." But state law and spiritual deference were about to be abandoned in favor of what Williams had termed "medical necessity." And that medical necessity had just entered the infirmary, needle in hand.

"I'm not quite through with this section, nurse," Allen said. "Do you think I could have another twenty minutes? I'm sure I could be—"

"You're through now, Chaplain." The male nurse in the white short sleeve-shirt and matching polyester pants strode across the room to the bed. "Warden's orders."

The man's tattooed biceps were as big as Allen's thighs. Obviously hired to maintain order in a nonsecure area, he was about to impose that order in spite of all the stalling Allen had managed.

"I don't believe you understand the legal implications of a breach of this inmate's right to spiritual guidance."

The nurse smiled. "You can guide him wherever you want after I'm done with him, Chaplain. I really don't give a shit." He lifted a small glass bottle from his shirt pocket and plunged the needle into the milky liquid.

Allen had seen the results of enough prison fights to know what it was. "Morphine?"

"Just a little bolus to keep him comfortable. This amount would put you out for some time, Reverend," the nurse joked. "Maybe I should save some for you."

Allen wanted to tell him to shove the needle where the sun don't shine, but he held himself in check to keep the nurse talking, running down more seconds on the clock. Even this small of amount painkiller might push Engel over the edge, given his frail condition and the medication he already had on board. "If you make him any more comfortable," Allen looked at the nurse, "he'll be dead."

"That's not my problem, Chaplain," the nurse said. "And I wouldn't make it yours either, if you know what I mean." He held up the syringe and squirted the excess out the top.

"The fountain of death," Allen said.

"That's just what the warden thought you'd say," the nurse said somberly. "That's why he asked me to have you leave the room before I give Mr. Engel here his injection. That state law you so self-righteously quote works both ways, you know."

"What?"

"It seems you are an impediment to this inmate's health care, Chaplain Allen. So I must insist that you—now—go back to the chapel or wherever else it is you sissies hang out."

Allen stood by the bed, unmoving, between the two men. Despite the few tricks his father had taught him and the skills he had learned from college wrestling, he judged he was no match for this nurse. Besides that, if he tried to intervene, the warden, whose camera equipment wouldn't work in the depths of the infirmary but who could hear in the outside office, would fill the room with guards and have him ejected from the prison.

"You've made your point, buttface," Allen snarled. "Now let me make mine."

The nurse maneuvered around him. "Later, Chaplain," he said, blocking Allen's attempt to buy a few more minutes with a standoff. "Unless you'd like to join this sucker—and we could certainly arrange that."

Slowly, as sluggishly and annoyingly as he could, reciting the Twenty-Third Psalm, Allen walked to the door of the infirmary. When he left the corridor, he made sure other guards saw him head toward F Block. Then he doubled back, by darkened hallways, to his office.

Twenty minutes, he thought. Twenty minutes left to go. Sweat broke out on his forehead. "Damn it Matt," he mumbled to the cold, dank walls, "hurry up and get here."

In the infirmary, the nurse lifted the patient's wrist without disturbing the rest of the sheet. He inserted the needle into the Heparin lock, drew back blood, and slowly pressed the plunger down the barrel of the syringe. He looked at his watch, then remembered to check the patient's vitals for the documented medical record before leaving him to fall into a deep sleep and beyond.

The nurse threw back the sheet and cursed.

The smiling face was not that of Tod Engel.

"Thanks for the free drugs, asshole," the happy inmate slurred as his drooping eyelids fell shut. "Nighty night."

The nurse ran to the outer office, where his panicked voice boomed over the warden's speaker. "Engel's gone!"

"Find him, damn you!" Williams yelled back. "Find him now!"

The Right Reverend John Langert reclined in the back of his stretch limo, and reached for his second pack of unfiltered cigarettes. The bright turning leaves of the Taconic valley contrasted sharply with the stale, dry smoke in the car. It was the way Langert viewed the entire world in relation to himself. Everything outside seemed to grow, to prosper with warmth and light and happiness. Everything inside him seemed dark and barren, desolate and cold. That was why he focused on the one thing he did well, the one skill that provided him great pleasure and made life worthwhile.

That one thing was manipulation. It had taken him years to develop, but almost against his will, as if the plan of a willful God, he had become the master of arranging and rearranging, coaxing and coercing, forcing and intimidating, planning and executing. He knew he was one of a handful of people who were not afraid of power and its concomitant risks. He smiled, reflecting on the upcoming presiding bishop election. In fact, he actively sought power, bathed in its perilous electricity that could energize or kill.

"Can I say somethin' to you for a minute, Bishop?" Earl's voice blurted through the speaker, interrupting his train of thought.

"Certainly," Langert said, dropping the window between them. "What is it?"

"I just gotta tell you, I think this going to Weston is a bad idea. It's like your support for Engel over the years is coming back to bite you, to bring you down. I been worryin' about this all the way up here and I finally had to get it out of my craw."

Langert blew smoke into the front compartment. "Thank you, Earl, for your concern. You really are good to me. I don't know how I'd manage without you running, shall we say, interference for me." He sucked in a final drag from the cigarette. "But there will be no problem today, not with Beck cooperating. In fact, with his help, it will be an exercise in strategic success. Another one."

"I hope you're right."

"And if we play it right," Langert said, "this time we may even arrange for Tod Engel to be set free at last. After all these years."

He stared out the window and lit a final cigarette from the butt of the used one. He would leave the beauty for God to tend and accept his own talent for manipulating the power that really changed the world. After all, there were only so many heartbeats.

"I'm afraid this latest development may adversely affect our proposed arrangement, Warden." Martin Ehrhart's silky voice slithered through the warden's speakerphone until he switched it off and picked up the receiver. This conversation should not be echoing through his office.

"But I told you there was nothing I could do to stop it!" Williams was teetering on the brink. The most important thing in his life was rapidly eroding under the stone walls of his own private bastille.

He was losing control.

"You could have stalled him, Warden. You could have taken the position that to have such a gathering of persons of this magnitude posed a severe security threat to your institution and to the lives of the people invited, make that commanded, to attend."

The man was an idiot. "You don't think I considered that?" Ehrhart's condescension infuriated him, especially after all Williams had done over the years. All he had done. "It was the first thing I told the attorney general when he called. I informed him that we were short-staffed, that the meeting would interfere with regular visiting hours, that we had men out of the building on special training leaves, and that we could not guarantee anyone's safety. But not even you would argue with the chief cop in the state."

"Stop talking a minute," Ehrhart said, suddenly far too confident for

Williams's liking. "That may be just what plays into our hands."

"What?"

"It may be perfectly fine that our security is not guaranteed," Ehrhart said. "It may be that what we need is a major disruption—something totally out of control—to accomplish what we could not do otherwise."

The warden smiled. He had already considered the idea, but he hadn't expected the county executive to agreed so easily. There was more at stake for them both than the election. "You mean orchestrated chaos?"

"Exactly."

"I have a scenario in mind for just that."

"Then you may be the man for the job, after all."

Williams heard Ehrhart's voice relax and knew he had countered the panic once again. But now he had to divert the conversation away from Engel. "Where are you now?"

"According to the last sign we passed, we'll arrive in ten minutes."

"That should be sufficient. See you then," Williams said, trying to hang up before the inevitable question.

"Oh, and Warden?"

Damn it. There it was. "Yes?"

"What is the status of our most prized and valuable inmate?"

"As you already know, he was transferred to the infirmary and has been kept totally sedated. I'm afraid his condition is worsening. He has been attended by the chaplain the entire morning."

"What?"

Williams tightened his grip on the phone. "Yes, it has been difficult to arrange time alone with the inmate—even to perform his routine medical care and to provide the medication he needs for—for comfort."

"In that situation, can't you expel the chaplain for a time?"

"We've done that." Williams debated his next move. He decided a first strike was better than an embarrassing question in front of the entire group. "And it seems that neither the chaplain nor the inmate can now be found."

Ehrhart's voice exploded. "What kind of shit are you feeding me, Williams?"

The warden pictured him red-faced and glassy-eyed, leaning forward in his limousine. His kind always erupted in anger that ultimately blew their cardiovascular system. They understood little about control.

"Do you mean to say that in your own institution, you cannot find two prominently identifiable men?"

Williams drew a deep breath. Stay in control. "We will locate them by the time you arrive. There are, as you can imagine, only a certain number of places they can go."

Ehrhart snapped, "You have seven minutes."

The car phone switched off. Ehrhart would soon arrive at Weston Prison, the turf of an increasingly angry Williams. After the guards tracked down the two men—and they would—the warden would demonstrate to the County Executive and wannabe senator from New York just what control and power were about.

After all he had done.

The smell of thick smoke and new leather mingled in the black Mercedes. James Rinski had purchased it with money he had hoarded. He'd paid cash for it. It was his one concession to personal luxury. Top of the line throughout. He could listen to discs, have a drink or two from the hidden compartment under the teak dash, and let the cruise control carry him to his destination practically on its own.

But today was different. There was no music or bourbon, and Rinski's hands gripped the leather steering wheel like pincers. Today the air-conditioning blew cold air onto his tense body. Eventually he turned it off and lowered the window. Even so, the car felt like a tomb. And in that tomb he was nervous, murderously angry at everyone and everything.

How much could Beck know? More importantly, what could he prove? Rinski had not been able to reach the County Executive before leaving the house. Had Ehrhart decided to go it alone? To jettison his police commissioner after all this time? No. That couldn't happen. Ehrhart and he had come too far together, even as unwilling allies.

Allies. Like Beck and Demming. Rinski's mind wandered over the woman's body a few moments, then returned to the present. It was too late for pleasure. The knot in his stomach tightened at the sight of the green sign for the prison.

He had to stop them. Soon. All of them, he thought, naming the list in his head. Beck. Demming. Engel. He added one more name.

Ehrhart.

Martin Ehrhart.

Abruptly, the knot in his stomach loosened and his brow unfurrowed. Of course. That was the key. If Ehrhart was out of the picture, Rinski could maintain his empire as it was, work even less than he did now, retire early, risk no exposure on Deathangel, and do Charlotte for lunch.

He put up the window, turned the air-conditioning back on, and lit a cigarette. He would go to this meeting and, regardless of its outcome, execute his fail-safe plan.

Rinski popped a CD in the player and decided he had time for one short drink before he arrived at Weston State Prison for the Criminally Insane. With eleven bodies down, why not make it an even dozen?

Beck thought the prison conference chamber could have been a throne room in a European castle. Its high stone walls retained the must and moisture, making the air cool and heavy. There were no windows, not even barred ones at the top of the high ceiling, with the black iron chandeliers that had been forged by inmates long forgotten.

"You would think we might have progressed beyond all those things," Baumschen said, pointing to the array of tools formerly used for isolation and interrogation, now fastened to the walls for visitors to see.

"Frankly, Herr Baumschen, a part of me would like to employ those on our honored guests this afternoon." Beck winked. "In a Christian manner, of course."

Beck wandered around the room, checking the arrangements. Ten chairs surrounded a dark mahogany conference table at one end of the room. A loungelike arrangement was set up at the other table near the door, complete with plush, overstuffed chairs around a large Indian carpet. Beck imagined the four suspects sitting there and wondered what their reactions would be to the afternoon's events. How would they deal with each other? Hopefully, the confrontation would cause one of them to slip or to turn on the others. As Baumschen pointed out, there was no true honor among thieves. The threat of exposure might be sufficient to force Deathangel into the open. His heart began to beat faster with the anticipation of ending the mystery once and for all.

"My guess is that the A.G. put the fear of God into your Warden Williams," Baumschen said.

"That remains to be seen," Beck replied. "A chat over a cup of coffee does not the fear of God make."

Baumschen shook his head and took a seat, as Beck paced. At five minutes before two, the wall phone rang.

"Beck here."

"Father Beck, I have four people down here at the front entrance ready to be escorted to the conference room, including Warden Williams. He asked if you are ready. If so, we'll bring them up."

Matt recognized the voice of Officer Petokis and wondered why Williams had put him on this assignment. Was it just coincidental that the man had been transferred to front office duty and happened to be the escort? Or did the warden want him present for a reason?

"Come on in," Beck said, and a fast few minutes later he watched them file into the room. Rinski was first, ignoring him and gazing at the implements of inquisition as though choosing the one he'd like to use.

"Good afternoon, Father Beck," Langert said, reaching out to clasp Matt on the shoulder. Clearly, he was establishing pecking order this way. Beck thought he could have handed out church leaflets saying, "I know this man better than anyone else and this is not about me. It is about you, because one of you is a serial killer and he'll prove it."

"Bishop." Matt nodded and returned the gesture. He didn't mind the pretense of familiarity. It was, after all, partly true, and maybe Langert would be relaxed enough to react in ways he might not otherwise.

The County Executive seemed more nervous than the other two. Beck caught him glancing over his shoulder several times as he came in the door. He headed straight for the coffee. Beck spoke to him, and the man merely nodded in return.

"Are there particular places you want us to sit?" Williams asked Beck. Beck thought his tone of voice was that of a parent whose kid has temporarily taken over the living room. He knew someone would ask, and he had planned for the Interpol inspector to do the honors.

Baumschen, having introduced himself to each of the four as they entered, showed them to their assigned seats at the carpeted end of the room. Beck watched them react to the Austrian and to the name of Interpol.

"Where do you want me, Father Beck?" Petokis asked, standing at the door.

"You stay in here, Petokis," Williams ordered.

Beck nodded at the guard as if to say, Fine for now. He smiled broadly. This was it. They were all here. As he had told Baumschen, all the omelettes were in one basket. Now they had to keep a damned close eye on that basket.

Beck watched the men shift anxiously in their seats. In a loose circle, Langert was at his left in the upholstered fabric chair. To Langert's left, with a small table between them, sat Rinski in the matching swivel. The leather chair was occupied by Williams, who, from his position, could see the entire room. Finally, on Beck's right, Ehrhart perched in the straight-backed, hardwood chair probably fashioned in the inmate shop. The long conference table stretched perpendicularly in front of them.

Matt walked casually back and forth before the group. "First of all, I want to thank you for coming today."

"As if we had a choice," the warden mumbled.

"True," Beck admitted. "There was a bit of arm-twisting. But many arms have been twisted over the last decade, have they not? So what are one or two more now, at the end?"

"The end?" Langert said.

"Yes, Bishop. This is the completion of the Deathangel story."

"That story was finished ten years ago," Rinski threw out. "And you know it, Beck."

"And you know that it was not, Commissioner Rinski," Beck shot back. "But," he said, composing himself, "I'm getting ahead of myself. As I said, today we will bring an end to the Deathangel mystery." He looked at each person as he talked, hoping to raise their anxiety. "In a few moments, I'll describe how each one of you contributed to the Deathangel case. And to begin," Beck turned to the warden, "I would like Warden Williams to ask Officer Petokis and the guards just outside the door to leave this area."

"I'll do nothing of the sort," Williams said. The other three appeared a bit alarmed. He started to stand when Beck signaled to Baumschen. The inspector left the room and quickly returned with four Interpol agents.

"We are in good hands here, as you can see, and we have the blessing of the attorney general," Beck said to Williams.

"I don't see why we should require any guards," Langert said. "I certainly know I don't."

Martin Ehrhart pushed up from his seat. "I think I won't participate any further in this farce without benefit of counsel."

Rinski stood and faced him in a way that could only be interpreted as threatening.

"Sit down, Marty, and don't be such a buttwipe. I'll protect you if things get out of hand." Rinski glared at Beck. "Which they won't."

"Perhaps you could wait a few minutes, Herr Ehrhart," Baumschen said diplomatically, "to listen and determine whether or not legal counsel is really necessary. Unless, of course, you are convinced you need it right now."

Rinski and Ehrhart returned to their seats at the same time, the first with a satisfied look, the second even more worried than before.

"Warden?" Beck inquired, with raised eyebrows.

Williams nodded sharply at Petokis, who dismissed the correction officers at the door and followed them out.

"Leave the door open," Beck commanded. "I'll close it when my assistants arrive."

"Your assistants?" Ehrhart's eyes narrowed.

"Yes." Matt turned to him. "They will help me tell the tale of the Deathangel murders from the very beginning to the very end. Only this time," his gaze shifted to the warden, "it will be told truthfully."

He felt the tension in the room jump a notch. Rinski frowned as the first of his colleagues came through the door.

"I'd like to introduce Police Sergeant Vincent D'Angelo, who works in the county courthouse."

D'Angelo pulled a chair from the table and sat down, exchanging glares with the Police Commissioner. He positioned the small cloth bag he carried on top of the table in front of them.

Beck continued, hoping the momentum would play on their fear of exposure. "Next, we have an especially important participant in this game of murder and deception."

"Wait a damned minute here, Beck," Rinski began. "You got a lot of balls to drag us all here and accuse us of bullshit like that."

"I'm not aware of accusing anyone of anything yet, Commissioner. Though my associates might have other ideas."

All eyes focused on the doorway as Arthur Allen entered the room. "No," Allen said to the group. "It's not me he's talking about." The chaplain turned and coaxed the man behind him. "It's okay to come in. No one will hurt you here. I promise. Please."

Slowly, his head hung low, an unshackled Tod Engel shuffled into the room.

"You are ape-shit crazy, Beck," Rinski growled.

Matt saw Langert's hand drift to his pocket. Williams jumped up. "Where have you kept him? We've been searching since—"

"Since what, Warden?" Allen asked. "Since you tried to have him killed this morning?"

"That's enough," Beck said. "Please take your seat again, Warden. And bring Mr. Engel up here to the table with Sergeant D'Angelo, Chaplain."

Engel sat down compliantly and lit a cigarette.

"Don't smoke in here," Beck said.

The others tensed, ready for the man to leap. Instead, Engel pinched out the lighted end with wet fingers and folded his hands to listen.

"Thank you," Beck said. "And now, the final member of the group, the one who has unraveled the secret of Tod Engel, the one who will assist me in telling the untold story behind the murders. And the one who will enable us to know who in this room is the real Deathangel."

The men looked at each other, then watched in stunned surprise as Anne Demming walked through the door. Matt knew the effort and the medications it took to bring her here looking as good as she did, with pain under control and lucidity high. Her face was thin and hollow, reflecting the death she had stared in the eye. Yet she stood steady in her dark green slacks and jacket, unsmiling, with the demeanor of a woman who desperately held her feelings in check. It was clear that the least provocation could vent her fury at the person—or people—responsible for the pain of so many, including herself.

She reached Matt's side and unzipped the leather case she carried under her arm. She handed the photographs to him. The notes she kept for herself.

"And finally, so that it's just us and no one will feel inhibited to say what is on their very soul." Beck nodded at Baumschen, who ordered his astonished men to wait just outside the room. Beck couldn't tell if the four suspects were relieved that the Interpol agents were gone, afraid that they were in the same room only a few feet from a volatile, unshackled, convicted serial killer, or stunned that Anne Demming was still alive.

Matt pulled the thick door closed, bolting it shut from the inside.

"Let's begin," he said in a monotone. As he watched Anne take a seat at the table and looked into Engel's blank eyes, he wondered if they were seeing the same image he did.

A small wooden angel. Crimson. Poised, as if ready to speak.

Chapter 16

Beck paced as he addressed the group. "The Apostle Paul said, 'Now we see through a mirror darkly, then we shall see face to face.' For the past ten years, the Deathangel murders have been viewed through a dark mirror that has reflected lies, half-truths, and deceptions." He stopped and made eye contact with each of them. "Now we shall see face to face."

"Wait a minute, Beck," Ehrhart protested. "Who appointed you judge and jury in this case?"

"Joe McCaslin's murder did that," Beck snapped. "Along with the death of the blonde woman in the blue Chevy who tried to shoot Anne and me and the chauffeur gassed in the attempt to kill Bishop Langert."

"But you have no right."

"I believe we all know he has every right, considering his own loss," Langert offered.

"Shut up, both of you," Rinski said. "Let the man talk. He's already very interesting."

Ehrhart glared at Rinski and then at Tod Engel, who was intent on picking a scab on his hand.

Beck started again. They would begin with the facts and hammer at emotions. They had to force the murderer to show his cards, make a mistake, or say something incriminating if they were to assure a conviction. While they had a plethora of circumstantial facts, they had little concrete evidence that would hold up in court, most of it at least ten years old and subject to faded memories and disappearing clues.

He held up the *CityMag* issue with the headline announcing Deathangel's capture and waved it in front of the group. "A decade ago, eight people were murdered over a three-month period by what was thought to be a serial killer Deathangel." He paused and nodded in Engel's direction. "Supposedly this man."

Engel sat inert, looking down at his lap. Beck stepped aside to allow Anne to speak. They had agreed to do it this way. Actually, Anne had insisted, once she knew she could stand and walk with the help of some powerful meds. It gave Beck a chance to observe the players and Baumschen time to react and order his men inside if push came to shove. More importantly, it let Anne return some of the anguish inflicted on her. What goes around comes around, Matt thought. Just not often enough.

"But it was not Tod Engel who committed these crimes," Anne said. "In order to understand who the real killer was and why he murdered, you have to know who the victims were and how they were connected—and not connected." Her voice was strong, though occasionally she needed to lean on the table to steady herself.

"They fall into two groups of four each. The first victims were purely random murders, totally unrelated to each other. Two students parked on a darkened street in Larchmont were shot and killed with the same bullet. A White Plains prostitute was sedated with a drug that kept her conscious while her finger was forced to pull the trigger of the gun that blew her brains out."

Matt broke in on cue. "The fourth, as all of you are aware, was my wife, Kate Beck." He felt emotional but surprisingly steady as he spoke. It was as though he were describing a dream from a distance. "She was shot point-blank in the chest behind a shopping center in Mamaroneck." His mind, again, started to replay the scene. His gaze then met Anne's and the memory faded. Matt knew he had just passed a milestone in his struggle with grief. He nodded, as if handing her the baton. Beside her, Engel gazed at the ceiling, seemingly entranced by a fly on the chandelier.

"But these murders, as vicious as they were," Anne said, sitting down again, "were made more heinous by the fact that they were only the backdrop, the red herrings, an elaborate subterfuge to disguise the tie between the four intended murder victims."

"You people are out of your frigging minds." Rinski laughed, shaking his head.

Ehrhart sputtered, "I had the best investigative team in the state working on that case, Miss Demming."

Anne stopped him. "That's because you didn't want them to find connections, and they conducted their investigation with that goal in mind."

The county executive leapt up. "That's a ridiculous lie!"

Engel looked over at him and smiled. Beck wondered what memory had slipped into lucidity. Whatever it was, it vanished as quickly as it had surfaced, and the inmate's impassive countenance returned.

"Good show, Ehrhart," Beck said. "Even roused old Tod here for a second. But if what you say is true, then how could a couple of relative amateurs like Miss Demming and myself, using publicly available documents, come up with the connection between the four?"

Ehrhart sat down, recovering some of his poise. "Maybe the data wasn't available at the time."

"Actually, the information is dated decades before the trial," Beck shot back. "It was there waiting, right under your eyes."

"Regardless," Bishop Langert interrupted eagerly, "what was the connection?"

Anne looked at him. "Four victims—Melin, Bartus, and the Reid couple—were originally from the same area of Austria." She tossed a yellow Michelin map to Beck. He and Baumschen unfolded it and taped it to the wall.

"The pertinent towns are marked in red." She pointed as she spoke. Matt could tell that she was reliving her journey. He started to move closer to be ready to take over but decided to trust her strength. If she needed help, she'd signal for it.

"Garnet Reid," Anne continued, "whose maiden name was Kahn, was from Langenstein. Her husband was from Schwertberg, where his real name was Rittenwald. Josef Melin, or Melindorf as his family is known, was born and raised in Feyregg. And Constance Bartenburg, alias Connie Bartus, was from the largest village here, the old Roman town of Enns."

"Thank you for the Austrian travelogue," Williams broke in. "But if I may be so bold as to ask, so what?"

"So it also turns out that these four were young Jews during Hitler's rampage. They arranged to be secretly baptized to conceal their heritage and then were commandeered to work as guards in the concentration camp nearby at Mauthausen." She circled the town on the map. "Right here. These angels," she said, holding up the one she had purchased in Feyregg, "Der Todengeln, Deathangels, were carved by inmates of that camp as a sign of resistance and hope. They are the same design as the ones found at the scene of each Deathangel murder ten years ago."

Beck wished he could have blood-pressure cuffs with pulse alarms on each man to determine whether their internal reaction was truly as cool as their external one. No one batted an eye at the name of the camp or the angels except for Ehrhart, who seemed affronted.

"If this is true," he said, "why wasn't it brought out at the trial? What does it have to do with the murders?"

Anne nodded to Matt.

"Excellent questions," Beck said. So far they were right on track and no one had tried to bolt. "Because that leads directly to the next issue. Given the victims' shared history, who is their killer?"

Rinski harrumphed. "The killer, you misguided son of a bitch, is sitting at that table right behind you." He jabbed a finger at Engel. "It's that psychopathic murderer who confessed to the frigging crimes, for God's sake!"

"Please, Commissioner." Langert frowned. "Father Beck is saying what I myself have avowed for years, and I'd like to hear someone's reasoning other than my own for a change." He gestured toward Beck. "Continue please."

"What the hell are you looking at?" Rinski yelled at Engel, who was staring at him. The prisoner dropped his eyes back to the table as Allen moved protectively to his side.

Beck pressed ahead, pleased that the crescendo had risen. "Commissioner Rinski is correct that Tod Engel admitted to the killings. However, the man sitting there is not Tod Engel."

Only D'Angelo appeared surprised. "What in the world are you talking about?" he said.

"According to his birth certificate, he is, in fact, Edward Clopton."

Engel stopped staring at the table and closed his eyes. Matt wondered if this was the calm before the unforeseen tornado. D'Angelo looked at Beck, who had instructed the sergeant to carry a canister of Mace as a precaution. Suddenly, Engel threw his head back and sneezed, startling everyone. The huge man wiped his nose on his sleeve and continued to stare at the table. The group regained their composure, though shifting uncomfortably in their seats.

"Listen to me, Beck," the County Executive said, angrily. "If you're going to retry this case for me, I'm leaving."

"We're not retrying it, Ehrhart, we're retelling it in its unexpurgated form, which is quite different from the way you prosecuted it."

"Such accusations had better have solid proof."

Beck held his gaze. It was the moment he had waited for. "We will do much more than that," he said with a calmness that enveloped an ominous threat like a velvet glove encasing a steel hand. He surveyed the group as he spoke. "We will show that each of you knew Tod Engel as Edward Clopton before the Deathangel murders were committed, that each of you used him for one purpose or another, that each of you had the motive, opportunity, and method to commit these crimes yourselves, and, finally, that each of you had good reason to wish this case would go away before your futures did."

It was as though he had thrown a funeral pall over the four. None of them moved, and neither did Beck, until Williams shattered the silence.

"You people are as certifiable as that nutcase there is. When you're finished spinning out your delusions, I have some nice isolation cells in the basement for each of you, padded so you won't hurt yourselves."

"Great. Let's begin with you," Beck said, turning to Allen.

Though he'd had no chance for a briefing, the chaplain picked up his cue and opened a folder on the table. I have here the written account of a Riker's Island prison guard named Richard Williams, the record of your—what shall I call it—your special relationship with one particular inmate there."

Williams sat with his arms folded and his lips tightly shut. The other three did not look at him, and Matt wondered if they knew. They must know. He suddenly worried about the one possibility he and Anne and Baumschen had not considered—that all of them were allied in this. If that were true, they might as well quit now as they would never break through those four horsemen.

Allen flipped through pages in the folder. "According to disciplinary records from Rikers, Warden, you were asked to resign your employment due to incidents of sexual impropriety with a mentally retarded inmate by the name of Edward Clopton."

Engel stretched his arms and legs, then abruptly stood and walked to the back of the room to lean against a wall. He seemed to be waking up. His eyes were brighter, more alert. What if, at some level, all the conversation around him was sinking in, dissolving the plugs of dulled recollections and letting them float to the surface? Perhaps what these men most feared was happening. Engel would reveal what had happened to him.

Williams face turned purple as his bulging eyes seared into Allen's. "That's a filthy lie!" he exploded. "I would not do such a thing!"

"Filthy? Yes. Lie? No," Matt said.

Allen merely continued flipping through the records he had faxed to Beck. "That episode was followed by a series of indiscretions involving prostitutes you beat up and physically mutilated when they couldn't make you perform."

"Stop it!" Williams shouted. "Stop it now! This is unfair, Beck! I was never convicted of those charges. They were trumped up by people who wanted to clear off their police blotter."

Allen responded, "It's true you were never convicted. But that's because nobody gave a damn about these women. The cops were probably just as happy to have them and you out of their hair and drop the whole deal. To your credit, there have been no further known occurrences."

Williams panted, gripping the arms of his chair.

"Except for the medication schedule for Engel," Allen added, holding up blue pages from the inmate's medical chart. Beck guessed he had gotten them from Petokis. "You steadily increased his medication dosage, causing him to deteriorate, and then you sent your goon to the infirmary this morning to feed him an overdose and kill him."

Ehrhart spoke up. Beck worried about why he was taking the heat off Williams. "In the first place, you've broken several laws by obtaining those records, which were presumably sealed employment files and court documents, none of which are admissable against him. In the second place, your argument is all speculative." Beck did not like the man's grin. "You have nothing of substance against him."

Or against you, Matt thought, or so you would like to believe.

"What we do have," Anne said as she got up to stand in front of the warden, "are several good reasons for you to be the real Deathangel."

"Yeah," Rinski smirked, "and your momma is the tooth fairy."

"If you would keep quiet, Commissioner," Bishop Langert said, "we might let her continue."

Beck handed Anne the folder from Allen, who moved back beside Engel, resting a hand on the man's shoulder.

"We know from the police record what violence you're capable of doing," Anne said, producing the rap sheet. "We know that you had opportunity because at the time you were between jobs. And we know that you had a reason to frame Engel—for reporting your sexual assaults on him and ruining your early career at Rikers, and I'm not talking about the little day job you had as a guard."

Beck thought Williams was about to erupt again. He hoped it would be with a confession rather than a defense.

Anne waved a sheaf of papers at the warden. "I'm talking about the lucrative illegal trade operation you ran with inmates and their families, kiting in—and out—whatever they wanted for the price you wanted."

"There's no way you can prove that," Williams said, seething.

"Then, to add insult to injury, you rebuilt your career at Weston on the battered body of Tod Engel, once you convinced the new county commissioner to finagle you a job here so you could watch him—and be close to him, I would imagine."

Williams's hands became clawlike against his chair. Beck guessed he was close to breaking. He wondered how Anne was managing to stay upright through this. He figured her adrenalin had picked up where the medication left off.

"Every time there was the least error in Engel's treatment," Anne said, "or he was written up for a security violation, or he was mishandled in any way, you managed to leak the report to the county commissioner, who presumably paid you, off the books, to act as a special monitor for this special inmate. The resulting firings almost always meant that you climbed another notch in the institution."

Ehrhart was turning as red as Williams. Maybe both would lose it at the same time. So far, so good.

"That is pure speculation on your part, Miss Demming," the County Commissioner snapped.

Baumschen spoke up. "But what is not speculation, Herr Ehrhart, is that Herr Williams—and each of you—has international connections, networks that could account for the recent terrorist activity in the Deathangel investigation."

Matt was surprised that none of them jumped to deny the accusation. Williams even laughed. He wondered if the warden would find Baumschen's next revelation funny.

"Yours, Warden, is a certain European spa in Feyregg," Baumschen said, "a stone's throw from Mauthausen."

Again no reactions from the other three, or from Engel, at the mention of the camp.

The inspector continued, "Your credit card and airline records show that you have traveled there at least once a year for the last twelve years. Would you care to comment on that?"

Williams flushed again. "I visit on vacation. There's no law against that."

"It's a special resort, right?" Anne said, looking at Baumschen. "Where no one asks questions and you can be totally anonymous, indulging in any whim you choose?"

"That is correct, Fraulein," Baumschen replied. "There are many such places in Europe. They are very costly, but the price is worth the pleasure, I suppose."

"Even if that were true, so what?" Williams muttered.

"The owner of the spa, according to our records at Interpol, is known to be quite sympathetic with certain fascist groups."

"How would I know that?" Williams said, with difficulty.

Rinski laughed. "Do they give a goose step with a Nazi blow job?"

Baumschen ignored him. "You might be aware of it, Herr Williams, because over forty percent of your contracts for products used in the prison are with companies connected with the owner of that spa."

"That's impossible," Ehrhart retorted. "To accomplish that, he'd have to circumvent state buying committees."

"If the stakes were high enough, you'd do the same," Anne said. "For instance, if there were certain photographs of you with employees from the spa, pictures that you would not like ever to appear in public or on the front page of the *Times* or *Post,* or an Internet Web site. You might even be persuaded to kill eight people, four of whom your friends have particular reason to hate. And the proximity of the spa to the town of Mauthausen would certainly provide access to knowledge of the angels."

Williams stood and faced her. "I don't have to take this crap off of you or anyone else."

She stayed nose to nose with him, and Beck took an uncertain step forward. "As a matter of fact, you do, Warden," she said. "And compared to what you have done to Tod Engel and others, this little dialogue is relatively painless, wouldn't you say?" She pointed to the chair. "Sit down. You're not in control here."

Williams glanced at Beck and Allen and returned to his seat like a chastened mutt. "This isn't over yet."

"It soon will be," Anne said, moving back toward the table.

Engel's gaping mouth let out a moan. He raised his arms, stretched, and yawned. D'Angelo touched the can of Mace, and the rest stared at the unshackled inmate. It was like having an uncaged, sleepy tiger curled up in a chair, giving no indication, no clear signal until it was too late, of whether he would drop off to sleep or pounce and kill. It was just what Beck had hoped would happen.

"Good point, Toddy, old kid," Rinski said, heading to the coffeepot for a refill. "I'm as bored with this shit as you are."

Matt filled his own cup and tapped it against Rinski's. "Then let's do you next, Commissioner."

"Do your worst, Beck. Throw your best shot in front of your chick, here. We'll see who's standing when you're finished."

"And because you are joined at the hip with Martin Ehrhart, we'll look at how the two of you worked so well together on this case." Matt stepped past them both and accepted two folders and a knowing glance from Anne. "First of all, we have determined from court records that your good friend, the county executive, back when he was a menial D.A. gofer cutting his teeth on night court in Manhattan, was well acquainted with Tod Engel as Edward Clopton."

"Court records?" the bishop asked seriously.

"Yes," Beck said. "Ehrhart is listed as the one who prosecuted Edward Clopton on charges of public intoxication on numerous occasions."

"It couldn't have been many," Ehrhart protested. "How can I be expected to remember some bum off the street I barely looked at in the long line of public defender cases? Hell, ninety percent of them I plea-bargained out. I never laid eyes on the person for more than the five seconds it took the judge to bang the gavel."

Anne pointed to the folder in Beck's hand. "Does the number thirty-two ring any bells for you?"

Ehrhart smiled. "Only thirty-two times in the three years I served in that court? Compared to the number of cases I prosecuted back then?"

"Thirty-two times in three months, Ehrhart," Beck said, stone-faced. "And these occurred at the end of that three-year period, just before you took the job with the Westchester County district attorney's office. You knew him."

Rinski shifted nervously in his chair. "Still doesn't prove shit," he said.

"Speaking of slimy substances," Matt said, "you also knew Edward Clopton before he changed his name."

"Did I?" The police commissioner did not smile. "Do the same court records say that too?"

"As the officer who arrested him the majority of those times, yes they do." Beck held up a sheaf of computer printouts. "And they're corroborated by the police blotter for the dates."

"Funny how quickly you forget a face," Rinski mumbled. Engel looked up at him for a second and then turned away.

Beck interrupted, "His prints turned up his old Clopton file, but you didn't think it was necessary to use that name in the trial, did you? 'Tod Engel' was a more sensational way to connect Engel to the killings, wasn't it?"

"Who cares what the hell his name is," Rinski lashed out. "He confessed to committing the crimes, Beck. His old rap sheet was irrelevant. He did the murders, damn it!"

"Did he?" Anne took Matt's place as he moved to stand by an intensely quiet Friedrich Baumschen. "Or did you?"

Rinski shook his head, but Matt could tell the man was far less confident than before. Surely he had to gather where they were headed.

"Why don't you tell me, lady?" Rinski looked her up and down. "And when you're finished, can we go to dinner? You talk a great story. I'll bet your loverboy Beck likes to hear them at bedtime."

Matt ignored the impulse to throttle the man. Anne could take care of herself. "Here's a bedtime tale I'm sure you'll remember," she said, brandishing a pamphlet and a photo she had snapped in the Mauthausen museum. "It's about Eduard Czahallerynsky. Your father."

Rinski sat silently with his chin cupped in one hand.

"I know that name," exclaimed the bishop. "Czahallerynsky was a Communist Party leader in Poland before the war. He cooperated with the Nazis completely in exchange for the promise of prosperity for his country during the occupation."

Beck observed Rinski's subdued response. He wondered if the man was holding in his anger. Would he lash out like the currently stoic Tod Engel?

Langert continued, "But then he disappeared during the war. I remember my parents sitting by our radio and commenting about it at the time. A lot of Polish leaders were sent to concentration camps when the Nazis reneged on their promise."

"He was one of them, Bishop," Anne said. She held up a second picture. This one showed an emaciated man clinging to a fence. "He became the liaison between the prisoners and the guards at Mauthausen. But when he learned of the Nazi atrocities in Poland he started helping the prisoners. He vanished after the camp was liberated."

All eyes turned to Rinski, who sucked in a deep breath. "Shit, this doesn't make any difference now anyway." He glanced at Baumschen, then at Beck. "As you probably already found out, my mother and I emigrated here when I was a child. I barely remember my father. After the war, he spent years working to send us money from Argentina and Chile, where he helped track former Nazis for the Nuremburg trials. Eventually, he joined us in the states." Rinski was solemn. "He died ten years ago."

"Ten years?" the warden said. "Then he could have been the one who committed the murders. He must have hated anyone connected with Mauthausen. If he had run into these people, he would have had every motive for killing them. What if he did the murders and you set up Engel to take the fall?"

That's good, Beck thought. Blame all this on a dead man so you can walk out of here free. "Is that possible?" he said to Rinski.

"Yes. And no," the commissioner replied. "He had not only the intelligence but the hatred and the will." Rinski crossed one leg over the other. "But he couldn't have done them. My father suffered from Alzheimer's. The last few years of his life, he lost all of his reason and memory. He lived somewhere in a small, safe corner of his brain until the disease invaded that too. You can check the medical records—and the tombstone."

Beck thought the man sounded defeated, not a bad strategy for avoiding the obvious next question. Another good try, but not good enough. "Then you could be Deathangel, killing to avenge your father's treatment in the camp or bringing in his network of antifascist operatives to kill them." Rinski looked up with a scowl, but Beck wasn't finished yet. "Like the blonde in the Chevy, and the person who rigged the Zyklon B to try to kill Langert—the same gas that was used in the showers at Mauthausen."

"You stupid shit!" Rinski shot out of the chair to grab Matt, but Baumschen rushed between them, his small body somehow forcing the bulky commissioner back to his seat.

"Not so stupid that I can't count," Beck said. "Including the number of angels submitted in evidence at the trial."

"All of which vanished from the property room that you broke into," Rinski said.

"Is that true, Sergeant?" Beck asked D'Angelo, who had sat across from Engel all this time.

"I believe you'll find the logs show that Father Beck was signed in with permission to that property room."

"At twelve o'clock at night?" Rinski said, incredulous.

"We get people coming in there at all hours," D'Angelo replied. "The father's covered."

Beck winked at the sergeant. Any debts between them were paid. "So I entered the property room and looked in the basket containing evidence from the trial." He switched his gaze to the county executive. "Perhaps Mr. Ehrhart's math skills are better than yours, Rinski."

"What are you talking about?" Ehrhart said, clearly annoyed.

"How many angels were there?"

Ehrhart stared back. "Six. There were six angels."

"Correct," Beck said. "The man tells the truth at last."

"There had to be six," Ehrhart fired out. "There were six incidents of murder."

"But," Back replied, softening his voice, "there should have been seven and you know it."

Bishop Langert spoke. "I may be a little dense, Matthew, but I don't understand. He's correct. There were six incidents. Are you saying there were more?"

"No." Beck answered him by holding up the *CityMag* issue again. "There should have been seven angels, because Rinski is seen here on the cover holding an angel he supposedly found in Engel's apartment at the time of the arrest." He slapped the magazine down on the table. "Six incidents plus one collar adds up to seven."

Richard Williams exclaimed, "A throw down!"

"Indeed it was, Warden," Beck replied.

"Throw down?" Langert asked.

Anne answered. "When a cop wants to connect a certain person with a particular homicide, he throws down, say, that person's gun next to the body, then pretends to discover it during the investigation of the premises." She glanced at Rinski. "That's what was done here, wasn't it? You lifted one of the angels from the property room and threw it down in Engel's apartment. You assumed no one would notice the difference or bother to count them all. And, at the time, you were right. But each angel is unique, Commissioner, and if we compare my photograph from that night with the police photos of the individual angels, we will see that this one had already been found near one of Deathangel's murder victims."

"But why?" Langert asked, his face puzzled. "Why would he do that?"

"Damn you, Ehrhart, I'm not doing this!" Rinski yelled. "Tell them!" Ehrhart sat unmoving.

"Then I will!" Rinski turned to Beck. "Sure, we had a deal." He looked at Ehrhart. "But it was a two-way street."

"Rinski," the county executive growled, "sit down and shut up."

Rinski paced back and forth in front of the group. Beck recognized that he was keeping his options open. There was no way he would take the fall for Ehrhart. If the case was collapsing, it wouldn't be James Rinski's body left under the rubble. Beck felt a spark of hope.

"Ehrhart's not as stupid as he looks. He can count, too, and he figured out I'd thrown down the angel. But he didn't want to prosecute me for it because it could have blown his case." He raised his hands as his voice grew louder. "It didn't make any difference. We all knew Engel was the killer. I took along an angel from the property room just for effect, for the press." He grinned at Anne. "It was the dramatic clincher for her camera. Ehrhart wanted to hold it over my head for the future. Which is exactly what he did for the two months preceding the trial. Had me doing all sorts of crazy-ass things for him. Like I was his trained puppy or some damned thing." Rinski glared at Ehrhart. "Shit, he even had me cut a piece of Engel's hair and stick it to the envelope left at the last murder scene."

"Rinski, you idiot," Ehrhart warned. "Don't do this."

"But then I got lucky." Rinski smiled. "I found something. Something

I could use against him in return."

"Rinski, shut up!" the County Executive roared.

"What was that?" Williams asked, frowning.

"A fingerprint turned up on the bedside table at the death scene of Connie Bartus. It belonged to the brother-in-law of Martin Ehrhart. The guy was inadvertently porking her the night she was murdered and woke up to find her dead."

So Ehrhart had lied about Rinski's involvement with the Bartus case. Beck wondered what else Ehrhart lied about.

"The perfect balance," Allen said. "Both of you had something on the other that, if revealed, would result in political disaster."

"Both, therefore, had everything to gain by keeping the Deathangel case under wraps forever." Matt motioned for Rinski to sit down. "And this relationship, forged by the pressure of mutual disdain, was supposed to blossom even further when Ehrhart became senator and Rinski became whatever Ehrhart wanted him to be on his staff. Who knows where they might go from there? The White House, perhaps?"

"Just for the record, Beck," Rinski said. "Go to hell."

"You first, Commissioner, considering you eminently qualify for the job of Deathangel, either alone for your father's sake, or with your tag-team partner Ehrhart." Matt handed a folder to Baumschen.

"At least you have made no secret of your foreign involvement, Herr Ehrhart," the inspector said. "You have even married a German woman. That, at least, was a good choice."

"Aber Deutschland nicht Oesterrich ist, Herr Baumschen."

"Correct. Germany is not Austria, but you have very close economic ties in both countries, ties to companies that your constituents might question."

"Such as?"

"Such as the ones selling technological equipment to build nerve-gas production plants in countries that are, shall we say, less than friendly to this one."

"Those are economic ties through my wife's family there, Herr Baumschen, not political ones," Ehrhart said.

"Try that answer on the campaign trail, Herr Ehrhart, and see how many votes it wins you when people learn you are mostly financed by Eurodollars—with expected future paybacks when you vote in the U.S. Senate."

Ehrhart tried to regroup, no doubt calculating how he might have his spin doctors counter this threat to his senatorial race.

"My own government frowns on such relationships as well." Baumschen looked at Anne. "Which would be one reason certain terrorist groups might wish to stop a reporter from investigating your connections to Austria." He exchanged glances with Beck. "Unless, of course, they were trying to solve a much larger problem for other reasons."

"Which would be?" Ehrhart said.

Matt clenched his fists at his side. "Which would be the discovery that you disposed of four Austrian Jews who surreptitiously escaped the Holocaust. Or who unfortunately escaped the Holocaust, to state the view of those in your wife's family. It would have been a small price for you to pay for their continuing financial support for your political aspirations."

Ehrhart moved to the front of his chair. The man looked like he was close to panic, but he said nothing. With Rinski spilling his guts and Williams's reputation in shreds, the man was rapidly losing allies.

Baumschen continued to drill. "We believe you used Herr Rinski in a scheme to frame Edward Clopton as Deathangel, including having Rinski or one of his agents take Engel to get his name changed and forging someone else's signature on the cash receipt."

Beck observed the bishop's startled look. He shook his head at Langert, signaling him to keep silent about assisting Clopton. Beck preferred to let the bishop believe he was still secretly his ally and to see where the false accusation might lead them.

Ehrhart turned on Rinski. "So you are Deathangel?"

"You bastard!" Rinski yelled and came out of his chair. Baumschen again pushed him back. "I never worked for him before Engel's arrest. If there was a setup, it was done by his own people, maybe Williams here. The blonde was on his payroll, too."

Someone pounded on the door. Baumschen went to answer it. He pulled back the heavy iron bolt and spoke to a man wearing livery.

"That's my driver," Langert said. "I believe he has my three o'clock medication. I must have left it in the car. I'm afraid I'm still recovering from the gassing incident." The bishop motioned Eslin in, and the inspector secured the door behind him. The driver handed Langert a small brown bottle, and the prelate took two capsules, washing them down with coffee. He passed the cup to the driver, who dutifully retrieved more hot coffee as a chaser.

Engel removed a cigarette from a disheveled pack and put it in his mouth. He stood, towering over the table and D'Angelo, moving his head in a circle, cracking his neck bones. All eyes in the room were on him, waiting. He burped loudly and, without making eye contact, sat back down, the unlit cigarette dangling from his lips.

"If only," lamented a distraught Williams, "you had left things alone." Then, to Matt's amazement, the man buried his face in his hands and wept.

Langert went straight to his side in a move Beck suspected was more than mere pastoral concern. They had finally gotten one of the four to weaken, maybe even nudged him to the cusp of a confession, and the bishop had stepped in to comfort, which might mean contain. What if Williams and Langert were working together and their common connection was Eslin?

"I think this harassment has gone far enough, Father Beck. If you have a point to make, do it. But stop the denigration of everyone here. Do you really think maligning these people serves the cause of justice? I admit I have always believed Tod to be innocent, but I cannot support championing his case at the expense of innuendo and aspersions cast upon the character of others."

Matt took a deep breath. So far no one had made an admission of guilt to criminal offenses that would hold water, and they could easily recant anything they had said. The rest of Beck's and Anne's arguments were speculation. If the four men decided to walk now, Baumschen had no way to detain them. Deathangel might escape once more. And Engel would probably not live to see the next sunrise.

"As a matter of fact, Bishop," Matt said, "it has not gone quite far enough. It has not nearly reached the proportion of suffering perpetrated on the murder victims and their families, including Kate Beck and myself, Tod Engel, and others who are no longer with us. Which brings us back to our brother in Christ, Joseph McCaslin, and to you."

Langert returned to his seat with Eslin at his side. "But I have no direct ties to Austria, or Germany for that matter. Except, perhaps, when you go back to my great grandfather."

"I did that," Matt said, "in the church archives." He recited the file from memory. "Your grandfather was born in the little town of Hinterzarten im Schwartzwald, the Black Forest in Germany. Even though the area was bombed, his church records remained perfectly intact. His U.S. data shows his emigration to a small town in Ohio, where your father and later you were born. You were an only child, and your school records, up through and including seminary are impeccably documented." He stared at the man who had been his mentor. "Perhaps too impeccably."

"What are you saying?" Langert replied, perhaps a little too glibly.

Matt hesitated just a moment. He never in his life thought he'd be speaking this way to John Langert. "I'm saying I think they're a lie."

Langert smiled in assurance. "I beg to differ with you. It seems to me the lies are deeply embedded in these other chairs."

Anne stepped forward. "Let me describe a slightly different scenario, Bishop Langert." She read from the folder. "An impressionable adolescent, born Karl Helliger in Germany, he is a deeply devout novice in a Roman Catholic seminary when the Brown Shirts come to prominence in his country. Church supporters of Hitler convince him to join them on this holy crusade. He mixes what he has learned of theology with the insane logic of National Socialism and becomes a religious fanatic for the Nazi cause."

Langert stared blankly at her. He sipped his coffee. Beck didn't like the look of it. The man appeared overconfident, which was either a sign of uncaring guilt or absolute innocence.

Anne folded her arms over her chest. "This Helliger rises through the ranks of the S.S. due to his family connections and to excellence in matters of deception, death, and torture, and the novel ways he extracts information from his victims. Ultimately, at the tender age of twenty-one, by special order of Der Fuhrer himself, as a reward to the young man's prominent and very wealthy Nazi parents during the final chaotic days of the Reich, he is placed in charge of the Konzentrationslager where he has been previously assigned. The concentration camp at Mauthausen."

Engel glanced up at the German word, grimaced, and blinked at D'Angelo as Anne continued.

"The night before the liberation of the camp on May 5, 1945, archives show that Kommandant Karl Helliger committed suicide. He left orders to be cremated before Mauthausen was occupied by the Allies. Eyewitnesses report that his body was burning, along with all photos and personal possessions, as the Americans came through the gates."

She held up a photograph. "Here, in the museum at the camp, is the urn containing his ashes."

"Or so the explanation beside the urn reads." Beck retrieved the folder and tried not to let his hands tremble. It was their most daring hypothesis, and their least provable one. "There are indications, rumors substantiated by evidence at the camp and by travel records for the period preserved by various agencies, that the clever young kommandant may have had someone else shot and burned in his place, while he escaped with a number of his staff to the Swiss border."

Matt could not make the next accusation. Everything within him rebelled against it. The negation of the years with Allen and Langert would be too much of a betrayal. He tossed the folder on the table and signaled to Baumschen.

"Let us suppose," the inspector said, "that eventually, with the help of other expatriots and Nazi sympathizers, the kommandant made his way to the United States, where they had all of his appropriate credentials properly falsified."

"And his name changed to John Karl Langert." Anne fired off the words like a shot in the night.

Langert was unmoved, though he sighed and shook his head in incredulity. "There is a quantum leap of credibility in that assumption, Miss Demming. Besides which, I believe the records show the last part of this rather wonderfully contrived fable to be patently untrue."

"Well, I'll be damned," Rinski barked, glaring at the bishop.

Matt prayed they were wrong. He desperately wanted any of the other three to break and confess so that Langert would be cleared, his story erased as mere fantasy. Yet, more than any of the others, this theory seemed to fit the events of the past. And, of all of them, Engel had been closest to the bishop. Reluctantly, Beck took up the verbal truncheon.

"Then let's look at your own canonical record," he said, unveiling a green-lined printout. "It shows that you completed seminary training and, following the usual ecclesiastical career pattern, were assigned as vicar to a series of struggling missions, which you led so well that they quickly developed into parishes. Over the years your abilities came to the attention of the diocese, and you finally managed to become rector of the small but promising Church of St. James the Fisherman in Hastings-on-Hudson." Beck tossed the papers aside. His eyes locked on the friend he was beginning to believe might have murdered his wife in cold blood. "Where eventually you admit you met Edward Clopton, took him in, and hid him from your congregation."

"Not long after that," Anne broke in, "when your position in the church had become more prominent, you could have accidentally run into Josef Melin in New Rochelle, selling papers on a corner."

D'Angelo passed her the trial records he had copied, from the court files. "Melin's bank account for several years before his death shows considerable cash payments accrued to him," she said. "You surely remember that the investigators testified at the trial that Melin must have been involved in illegal activity of some kind. But since it seemed to have no bearing on the case, it was dismissed."

"In actuality, it had incredible relevance to the murders." Beck turned from Langert to address Williams and Ehrhart. "In fact, I believe Melin was blackmailing the one of you who would become Deathangel."

"Which," the bishop said calmly, "could have been any of us here, as it appears that we all have potential but as yet unproven motives for such a heinous scheme."

"True," Anne said. "But just suppose it was the case that Melin recognized Helliger. He might have hinted that there were others who could identify the man, but perhaps he wouldn't reveal their names. It would not take much effort to follow Melin or have a confederate search his apartment to locate Connie Bartus and the old Reid couple. Or, conversely, someone could have paid Melin to give up the others, only to be executed himself. The only significance of the other deaths," she glanced at Matt, "was to distract investigators from the connection between these four. It was brilliant—and yet another atrocity."

"That is quite an insane theory, Miss Demming," Langert said, standing up, his clerical dignity surrounding him like a cloak.

"No," Anne faced him without flinching. "It is quite methodical, as are all of your actions."

"This is absurd!" Langert said, moving toward the table. Allen placed a hand on Engel's shoulder. "You have no proof of any of these disgusting and defaming accusations."

"I like the word defaming," Ehrhart said, "because that's exactly what they're doing." He also rose and straightened his suit coat. "I, for one, am tired of this unsubstantiated innuendo."

"Big words, Marty," Rinski muttered. "And big words usually mean you're trying to baffle them with bullshit. Sit down and let them finish," he said, mockingly, "unless you got some pressing need to leave, like you gotta take a piss—or you're Deathangel."

"It's true," Williams said, his weak voice gaining in strength. "You have nothing but guesses."

Beck pointed to the sack in front of Sergeant D'Angelo. "That's not a guess."

"I found it in the property room right where you said it would be, Father Beck," D'Angelo said, pulling a green telephone from the bag.

"You hid the damned thing! I knew you had it," Rinski said. "Looks like you can add theft of trial property to your charges when we leave here today."

Matt ignored him. "Did you call the numbers programmed into the phone, Sergeant?"

"Yes. The first three buttons dialed numbers that were food delivery businesses. You know, pizza, Chinese. The rest of the buttons were blank, but I tried them anyway."

"Could you identify any other numbers?"

"Yes, Father. One of them, as was brought up at the trial, was the phone number of the Reid couple. The other button did nothing, but the last button, even though it was unmarked, automatically dialed what was at the time the unlisted phone number of Bishop Langert."

Beck stared at the bishop. "And whose phone is, or rather was this, Sergeant?"

D'Angelo turned the set over to reveal its tag. "It was found in the apartment of Tod Engel."

Engel looked at the object and seemed about to reach for it, as if it had rung and was for him, but then he sat back in the chair, appearing puzzled.

"And you think it odd or somehow incriminating," Langert said with a laugh, "that the man I assisted for so long would have my personal number on his phone? My God, Matthew, I programmed it for him so he could reach me if he needed help."

You programmed it for him, Beck thought, his gut churning. Did that mean Engel couldn't set up the phone by himself? Had Langert then programmed in the Reids' number as well?

Ehrhart said, "We knew about it during the investigation, having called the number ourselves, but because of the bishop's support of Engel, we presumed even then that it was irrelevant to the case. That's why it was never mentioned at the trial."

Beck showed his dismay by hanging his head and staring at the floor. He had never expected the phone to be a determining factor, but he felt they had to raise the issue if for no other reason than to hear how it was explained. Given their joint defense, he worried again about the possibility of collusion.

"I believe it's time to call this travesty to a close," Ehrhart declared, again standing. "Wouldn't you say, gentlemen?"

Beck lifted his head and surveyed the group. "You forgot about the phrases," he said softly. "The words Tod Engel repeated constantly during the trial and still does today."

"The nonsensical ramblings of this poor man?" Langert chided, but Beck saw the chauffeur stiffen.

"The same phrases that were heard and then recorded in the diary of Joe McCaslin two nights before his murder."

Rinski looked surprised. "He wrote them down?"

Beck ran his fingers over the scab on his neck as he glared at the commissioner, wondering if it was his hand that wielded the knife that night. "Whichever one of you took the disk from me in the rectory kitchen didn't know McCaslin well at all. Not only was he a compassionate priest, he was also meticulous about keeping records. Written records, in addition to those newfangled computer files he hated." Anne handed him the diary. "I could read the entry to you, if you wish. But perhaps instead we can prevail on the man we are told is Deathangel to assist us."

Allen gently grasped Engel's arm. "Do you remember the words, Tod? Can you say them?"

"Can a rock talk?" Rinski mumbled. "Jesus."

Engel squinted at Langert. They were so close now, Beck thought, wishing the prisoner could put words to memories. Perhaps there was no conspiracy between the four, but smaller alliances—Langert and Williams, Ehrhart and Rinski, Williams and Ehrhart. The gathering had created deep cracks in their haughty defensiveness. Now it was up to the phrases to pry those cracks open. Beck prayed that whatever process of memory still operated, whatever capacity for competence still remained in that mass of synapses, would manage to come to the fore and cause Engel to repeat the condemning words he had said for ten years.

"Grabbin' wieners." Engel giggled. "Toad—toad sticker—Matthews." He frowned. His brow furrowed. "Con—concentrate—concentrate longer." He looked down and repeated, as if it was a logical conclusion, the same phrase he had said consistently since his arrest. "I am Deathangel."

"Like Langert said," Williams intoned, shaking his head, "the meaningless chant of a retarded man. He's no different from any of the other garble-spewing loonies locked up here."

"But the words are not meaningless," Baumschen said. "Not at all. Unless the German language is meaningless."

"You're gonna have to spell it out for us," Rinski jeered. "We obviously aren't taking the bait to confess for you."

Again, Matt wondered if the truth involved the four men being somehow together in this, or maybe they were just now seeing how their common interests were served by protecting each other until they could disperse from this place. He moved next to Anne, who would reveal the phrases as she had first seen them. "The words are phonetic but incorrect understandings of the German," Anne said. "And they all relate to Mauthausen." She spread several photographs on the table and showed them one at a time. "The first one—Grabbin' wieners—refers to the infamous Wiener Graben, the Vienna Grave where thousands of prisoners were buried in massive pits." She continued. "The second—toad sticker Matthews—is a mispronunciation of Todsteige Mauthausen—the Mauthausen Steps of Death, leading up from the stone quarry. Prisoners, weak from hunger and disease, were forced to work the quarry and carry huge granite blocks in back harnesses up the long hill of stone steps. Thousands died in the process." She did not stop. "The third—concentrate longer—is a misunderstanding of Konzentrationslager, which means concentration camp." She showed the photograph with "Arbeit macht frei" over the gate. "Mauthausen."

Beck pointed at the photos. "These words are ones Engel evidently overheard from one of you, perhaps as you spoke them on the phone or privately viewed old photographs, thinking he was too stupid to listen or understand them. But persons of his IQ often have excellent mimicking skills and can repeat what they've heard just once. Engel couldn't have gotten these words anywhere but from one of you. And that person could not have gotten them from anywhere but Mauthausen."

"More bullshit," Rinski said. "I don't speak German."

"That's not what your secretary says," Anne bluffed.

"That bitch!" Rinski bellowed, "What the hell did Charlotte tell you?" He pointed to Ehrhart. "He's the one with the Nazi inlaws, and Williams goes to a spa for perverts there. And Langert," the police commissioner's expression changed from anger to weary sadness just as Matt came to the same dispiriting conclusion, "or Helliger if that's his real name, may have actually been in the camp and persecuted my father."

Langert's driver drifted away from the group, one hand in his pocket. Beck's dad would warn him that both were bad signs. He could signal Baumschen to bring in his Interpol agents, but that might tip their hand too soon. They still needed a confessional confirmation.

The bishop's tone was upbraiding. He shook his head regretfully. "Are you so inconsolably angry about Kate that you have to destroy everyone you can, including those who have been your friends, in this pathetic attempt to attribute purpose to her murder? I pity you for your loss, Matthew, but I pity you even more for this shameful display. It can only lead to your downfall, and to yours, Father Allen, as you seek to shatter the lives of so many others who, had you left us alone, could have done so much."

He sighed. "I believe I must agree with the county executive now, Father Beck, in his demand that no further discussion take place without our attorneys present. I'm sure you know it will be important to have all this documentation at the disposal of the court, assuming you mean to bring charges of some kind against one or all of us. Until then, I want you to know how personally hurt I am by this desperate pageant of utter slander."

Matt's mind spun with discordant images. Joe McCaslin taking a final shallow breath in ICU. The blonde woman crushed beneath the police cruiser. Langert's gasping driver enveloped in a cloud of blue death. Anne pale and drawn, motionless in the hospital bed. Kate as she lay on the stretcher, the trickle of blood at the side of her mouth. Pain brought tears to his eyes and, like Anne, he too heard the screaming voices of the Mauthausen dead rising in a crescendo.

Like heart paddles in the ER, the voice of Art Allen shocked him back to the present. "They're rioting out there!"

Ehrhart's glance at the unperturbed Williams told Matt the commotion outside the door was more than coincidental. In seconds, a decade of feelings flooded his heart. Sadness, loss, despair, hope—all were drawn into the room and drowned out by the noise. The attempt to precipitate a confession had failed. Rinski, Ehrhart, Langert, and Williams had steadfastly held their ground. Engel would be the final victim. In what seemed like stop-frame strobe motion, Baumschen rushed to unbolt the door and let the Interpol agents in.

Hearing Anne shout, Beck whipped around to see Eslin pull something from his pocket and fire at the Interpol agent.

Baumschen spun to the floor in a whirl of red.

Chapter 17

"Everybody stay put!" Eslin yelled over the shouting outside. Beck watched Langert retrieve an identical plastic gun from his inner pocket.

"I had to do this, sir," Eslin said. "It was all falling apart. I couldn't let them have you."

Williams stared at the gun. "But everyone was checked!"

"The new German lightweights," Langert said. "And their plastic bullets will kill you just as dead as the lead kind." He turned to the policeman at the table, who had risen as if to strike, the Mace canister in his hand.

"Sergeant, ignore your stupid heroic thoughts and tend to Herr Baumschen." D'Angelo reluctantly dropped the can and moved to the fallen Inspector's side.

The bishop shook his head, a disappointed expression on his face. "I am sorry about this indiscretion on Earl's part, Matthew. He's very protective of me, of our cause, but I do believe we could have bought enough confusion with legalities to leave here quite peacefully." He motioned for Eslin to check the bolt on the door. "But not now."

"The man needs a doctor!" D'Angelo protested, stanching Baumschen's shoulder wound with his own shirt.

"You cannot escape," Beck warned. "There are guards everywhere responding to the shots."

"Exactly, Matthew. And while they're trying to put their prison back together, they will hardly notice a few of us guests trying to leave without getting harmed ourselves."

Langert pulled Anne over to stand in front of him, nodding toward Baumschen. "Now, if you would, please detach the sergeant's handcuffs from his belt and slide them across the floor to Earl."

Beck moved as slowly as he could, hoping to buy time to think or be rescued somehow. Langert was right. The guards and the Interpol officers would believe the shots came from the inmates, echoing through the hallways. And they would probably escort the bastard to his car on the pretense of protecting him, especially if he had a woman with him. If Matt could just get within striking distance, he'd have a chance. But Langert yanked Anne's hair taut and held the gun to her throat, shouting, "Do it now!"

Beck got the cuffs from D'Angelo and threw them to Eslin, who caught them and, in one fast move, slapped them tightly on Anne's wrists.

She winced and Matt stepped forward.

"Stop there, Father Beck," Langert ordered. "You know I'll kill her if you advance further."

He halted as Langert shuffled toward the door, Anne in tow. "You will not stop us," the bishop said. "There are too many of us who have devoted our lives to this effort." He smiled derisively. "We outsmart you at every turn, prepare ourselves physically and mentally, and use your ridiculous sense of trust and morality against you."

"Deutschland uber alles all over again, huh, Bishop?" Rinski remarked, inching forward. "You pompous asshole. Even if you do make it out of here, my men will be all over your ass like stink on a skunk."

"You and Mr. Ehrhart may stand back against that wall now, if you please, along with Father Allen." Langert smirked, "Do you really think I would enter here without a plan to escape?"

Beck started to speak, but Ehrhart cut him off. "I think you planned everything from the day you left Mauthausen."

"You overwhelm me with too much praise, Mr. Ehrhart, though you are correct that I always knew I would return to the church. It is the best and easiest vehicle to play upon the sentimentality and vulnerability of people and their pocketbooks. Once my network of connections had placed me at St. James, we strategized together how to rise to the top, to control greater sums of institutional finances and exert influence at higher levels of power."

Beck faced him only a few feet away. "So presiding bishop was not the last but the first step. What was your strategy? Funnel church monies to right-wing groups here and abroad, correct? You could move your people into key political positions, using religious resources while fronting a liberal, progressive platform."

Langert nodded. "You always were astute, Matthew, when you cared to be. It's a different kind of war now, fought not with guns and soldiers as before, but with subterfuge, with legislation and economic ties, as Mr. Ehrhart has so accurately suggested. Such a coalition, with the right terrorist connections, can wield power on an international basis that will eventually effect the flow of history.

"Don't you mean 'would have effected,' you insane bastard?" Rinski said.

Matt's mind reeled with options, trying to evaluate, how to stop Langert. "Ironic, don't you think, Bishop," he said, staring at Anne, "that all of this will end right where it started—in a prison?"

Allen spoke up. "The difference, of course, is that here the inmates are insane."

The bishop laughed. "Typical optimistic Americans. It is and always has been your downfall."

"And yours was your own superstitious Roman Catholic indoctrination," Beck said. "Was the fear of God's judgment so strong that you had to seek absolution from McCaslin before launching your great campaign, your next Endlosung—final solution?"

Langert smiled sadly. "You would do well to remember it is unwise to turn our backs completely on the divine. It was a necessary indulgence on my part. I needed absolution regarding the tortuous work and scientific experimentation I directed at Mauthausen before I could, with a clear mind, ascend to presiding bishop. It is a necessity that I've had time to regret."

"But why Joe McCaslin?" Beck, almost at a whisper, his eyes glued to Anne's.

"Small parish. Small man. He was expendable and unlikely to ask questions beforehand. I planned to confess and then kill him, but there was an untimely interruption. I foolishly left his fate to my associates. Who expected him to have the strength to take his assassins with him to the grave?"

"You didn't know my story in *CityMag* would talk about the phrases," Anne said through clenched teeth. "And it wouldn't have mattered anyway since McCaslin was supposed to be dead. It was just a bad coincidence, one you tried to correct by eliminating McCaslin and then searching my condo in case he had managed to contact me through Matt before his death."

"One man's coincidence is another man's plan, Miss Demming. I do regret that I could not kill McCaslin that night and avoid all the unpleasantness that has brought us to this point. But who knows? These events may speed up our timetable in other areas. All things work to good for those who love the Lord."

"Don't you mean the Reich?" Rinski said. "And what makes you think we'll let you live to accomplish any plans?"

"Strong talk from such an impotent man," Langert said, tightening his grip on Anne. "I have planned for this possibility, just as I have prepared for the unexpected examination of my church files." He raised his gun hand to punch a button on his watch. "I have just sent a signal to a relay in my car. That signal in turn caused the detonation of an incendiary device at the bishop's mansion. All records of my activities are being immolated as we speak."

"You won't make it ten feet past the gate, Langert," Ehrhart shouted, sweating.

"We will walk out of here under the personal order of Warden Williams, safely escorting Miss Demming to our car," Langert said, nodding to Eslin. His henchman grabbed Williams with a smile.

Beck understood what that meant for the rest of them. "So you'll have to kill those you don't take with you, right, Herr Helliger?"

"That depends on how cooperative you are, doesn't it?" The bishop turned to Williams. "And now, Warden," he commanded, "pick up that phone and order your guards to arrange safe escort to the car and the gate. Tell them you're concerned for our safety and are getting Miss Demming, my driver, and myself out first. The rest will follow in groups of three."

Williams said defiantly, "No."

The man had nothing to lose now, Beck thought, and Langert should know that. He was pushing Williams too hard in the rush to get out.

"Do it!" Langert fired once and Williams collapsed to the floor, screaming in pain. "The leg wound will heal, Warden. The next one to your brain will not. Get on the damned phone!"

Beck watched as the warden pulled himself into a chair and picked up the receiver. "This is Williams," he bellowed. "Listen to me."

There was a slight pause. Beck worried the man might faint.

Suddenly Williams yelled into the receiver. "Code Black! Conference room!"

Eslin rammed his gun into the warden's mouth, breaking teeth and smacking his head against the chair. "Bad move, old man."

"Don't shoot him, Earl!" Langert exclaimed, dragging Anne over toward the two men.

Beck looked to Allen, who explained, "Code for a hostage situation. They can't just stroll out of here now."

"The man finally grew balls," Rinski muttered.

"Unfortunate timing, however," Langert said, with a calm that told Beck he had planned even for this eventuality. "So now, Warden, you will order them to bring the limo to the nearest entrance and provide us safe passage to it."

Beck wondered how far Williams would go. He had mixed feelings when the man with the gun in his mouth slowly moved his head back and forth.

"Very well," Langert said, his voice lowering. "Since you clearly do not care whether you live or die, this time it is not your own life at stake." He motioned for Eslin to remove his gun and jammed his own tighter against Anne's throat. "Tell them or I will kill Miss Demming." He looked at Matt. "Just as I killed Kate Beck."

Matt's eyes widened. It was one thing to know it, another to hear it from the killer's lips. With all his heart he wanted to rush the murderer, but Anne's pleading eyes nailed him rigidly in place.

As if venting words hoarded for a decade, Langert spit out, "You did not deserve the little Jewess, Father Beck."

It was as if Langert was shedding a phony carapace, and real evil now surfaced unashamed and unstoppable.

"She only became a Christian to snare you into a marriage bed. She would have ultimately been your ruin, kept you from attaining the prominence I could have used you for, stifled your talents and the dreams I had for them." Langert stroked the muzzle of the gun along the side of Anne's chin. "And this one," he said in a disdainful tone, "is all talk and no show, far too loud and independent. She would have questioned everything I suggested, and I would have had her eradicated eventually. Unless you can leave your family behind—mother, father, sister, brother—you cannot know the kingdom of heaven. Consider that I am providing that for you, Matthew, when you think of cursing my existence. I am, in fact, simply doing you another favor."

"No!" Beck leapt forward and Eslin fired, but Rinski charged, throwing his weight against Matt and knocking him out of the way, onto the floor. As Rinski clutched his arms, Beck felt something being slipped into his hand.

Langert spoke to them both. "Enough games, gentlemen. You will stand over there with Father Allen as our friend the warden makes the proper arrangements now."

Beck slowly rose and stuffed both hands in his pockets. Williams reluctantly lifted the phone again.

"This is Warden Williams. There are two casualties here. We need EMS. I am guaranteeing the hostage-taker—John Langert—absolute safe passage to the bishop's limo, which you will leave running at the west exit. He is coming out now with a hostage. Do not take any action against him. Do you understand me? No action is to be taken against him!"

Beck noted Allen's tightened jaw and the slight movement of his head, but Langert saw it too.

"Thank you, Warden." The bishop motioned Eslin toward the county executive. "But just to make sure, I want you, Mr. Ehrhart, to put on my coat and hat and gloves from the chair there and move to the door."

Without looking at it, Matt tried to determine what the hell Rinski had pressed into his hand.

"Mr. Rinski will unbolt the door, and you will run out with him in front of you as though he is your hostage. If you make it, you're both free men. If the warden's people play cowboy, you both die and I cripple his other leg. It's clear now that I need to hold Miss Demming for later."

"Sounds good to me," Rinski said. "Let's do it and see what happens, Marty, old bud. Let's find out if the guards can follow the warden's orders or not. What do you say?"

Beck saw that Ehrhart could not move. Fear had frozen him beyond speech, and rightfully so. There was obviously no love lost between the two men. This could be Rinski's way of removing Ehrhart as a liability or retribution for years of condescension. Or maybe Rinski wanted the chance to escape, so that the he might survive to punish Langert for his father's sufferings at Mauthausen. Whatever the motive, Matt considered another action that might distract Langert and Eslin enough for the others to surprise and overpower them.

"I'll do it, Langert," Beck said, stepping away from the wall. "You're going to kill her anyway."

But Rinski bellowed, "No you won't, Beck. You ain't getting out of this a hero no matter how hard you try." He grabbed Ehrhart by the collar and forced the coat and hat on him. The county executive struggled, but he was no match for the commissioner's strength. When Ehrhart was draped in Langert's coat, Rinski marched him to the bolted door, standing in front of him as though the cop was a hostage.

"No!" Ehrhart choked out a whisper. "They'll kill me."

"Tough shit, Marty," Rinski snarled back at him. "Have some guts for once in your life."

Langert motioned to Matt and Allen with his gun. "You two get behind the door, out of sight of the opening. I'm not ready for you to die just yet."

Beck glanced at Williams, asking the obvious question with his eyes.

"My men follow orders explicitly," the warden said with a tone of certainty. "They would never disobey me."

Beck prayed as Eslin unbolted the door, waited one second, then opened it. With his arm around Ehrhart's waist, Rinski awkwardly dragged the county executive out behind him as though Ehrhart had a gun to his back.

There was a moment of leaden silence before the door slammed shut and the man in Langert's clothes shouted, "Don't shoot! I'm Martin Ehrhart! Don't—"

Beck closed his eyes. Ehrhart's screams were drowned out by the staccato blasts of automatic weapons fire that made Williams a liar. Clearly, the warden had somehow conveyed permission to take out the bishop. Matt wondered if he could distract Langert from fulfilling his promise.

"Stop this!" Beck yelled with all his fury behind it. "For God's sake."

"God has nothing to do with this, Matthew, or haven't you figured that out yet?" Langert said.

"No!" Williams cried. "They wouldn't shoot unless they were sure it was the hostage-taker. They made a mistake."

Langert fired a bullet into Williams's other leg. He frowned at the man's agonized screams. "A promise is a promise, Warden. Now contact them again or the next shot goes between your legs."

Sweat streaming down his face, Williams slowly took up the phone and spoke hoarsely to his guards. Matt heard the name Petokis and glanced at Allen, who shook his head. No secret codes this time. When Williams hung up, he told them the limo was in place and no one would fire on whoever left the conference room next.

Matt considered several tactics, then realized Anne was much closer to Langert than he was. At the same time, he identified what Rinski had given him.

"I hope they listened this time," Langert said. "After all—I am Deathangel."

Langert edged toward the door, Anne pressed in front of him as a shield. Desperate, Beck watched for any sign of carelessness from Eslin, whose pistol remained trained on the group against the wall. Movement from the corner of the room caught his eye. Engel stirred and languidly rose from the table. With surprising speed, he moved in the direction of the door, then stopped a few feet away from Langert and Anne.

Allen spoke to him. "Tod," he said calmly. "Tod, the man has a gun and will kill you if you don't get out of his way."

"How very pastoral of you, Chaplain," Langert mocked, pulling Anne's hair back so hard she cried out in pain. "Tell him I'll shoot the girl first, then him." He nodded to Eslin to unlock the door again.

"Tod. Wait. Think about what you're doing," Allen pleaded, inching closer to the inmate. "He will kill her."

Matt took advantage of the distraction to work himself closer to Eslin.

He tried to signal with his eyes to Anne, and to Allen, standing closest to her now. He only hoped she was aware enough, not so totally bound by the pain and medication that she could not put the action into motion. It was their only chance.

Engel stepped back a bit as Langert advanced, taunting him. "Too bad, Tod," the bishop said. "You should have taken the fall and shut up about it."

With a dreamlike smile, Engel moved aside and Langert turned to Beck. "Quickly, give Earl your collar." Matt obeyed, taking off his shirt but staring directly at Anne, trying to capture her attention for the one thing he would get to say. "Unlike us, they always stupidly pause before shooting a man in a clerical collar."

Eslin put on the black shirt and slipped the white tab in place. "Maybe they'll make an exception in his case," Beck said.

"I doubt it," Langert said, nodding to his driver to keep them covered. The bishop stuffed his gun in his belt and grabbed an oblong plastic object from his left pocket. "In any case, along with the chaos in the prison, this last diversion will keep them far too busy to worry about us, and my operatives will handle things once we're clear," he said. "You should be eternally indebted to me, Father Beck. This time you and your sweetheart will end up in the same place at the same time."

Beck ignored the comment, focusing on what he could now see was a grenade. He did not look at Anne, fearing the bishop would understand what he intended. "Then perhaps Anne and I had better grab that final tequila shot."

Langert looked puzzled, but he wasted no time responding. With his teeth, he extracted the round pin from the top and threw the explosive device into the center of the room.

"You have ten secon—" he said, when Anne slammed the back of her head into his face.

Engel leapt toward Langert as Allen grabbed Anne and pulled her to the floor. At the same moment, Matt emptied the contents of Rinski's experimental spray directly at Eslin, dropping him instantly.

Engel's huge frame engulfed Langert and twisted the gun arm around his back, snapping the bones at the wrist and shoulder. D'Angelo dragged the inspector toward the opposite end of the room, one arm supporting the immobile Williams.

Beck realized there was no time left, even to unlock the door. He fell to the floor to help Allen cover Anne from the coming blast.

Langert shrieked, and Beck heard a distinct snap as Engel cracked the

Bishop's ribs.

"Tod!" Matt yelled. "Get down, Tod!"

He watched the big man lift the gasping, flailing form of Langert, slam him down over the ticking grenade, and jump on top of him.

Beck ducked his head as the blazing, muffled blast propelled the two bodies into the air. Burnt flesh splattered across the room and onto his clothes. Flaming tissue fragments smoldered, sticking to the other people on the floor. The smell of cremated human remains wafted on the thick smoke, obscuring his view of anyone but Anne.

Sickened by the stench, trying not to vomit, Matt heard the door crash open and gazed through the haze to see the outlines of guards, police, and emergency medical techs rushing in. He shouted at them to attend to Williams and Baumschen as he and Allen struggled to help Anne out of the pungent, burning room. Looking back through the commotion and extinguishing smoke, he could see a rescue team pull the still moving form of Tod Engel off the fiery remains of Bishop John Langert.

He watched in horror as Engel, bleeding and charred, shoved his seared hand into a pocket, then tossed a small object onto Langert's smoldering body.

The carved wooden angel immediately burst into flames.

Chapter 18

The bright September sun shone down through huge, billowy clouds on the casket carried from St. Jude's Episcopal Church.

Matt stood with Anne and Baumschen and watched the new rector lead the procession to the hearse, where a balding funeral director slammed shut the rear door on the body of John Langert. Art Allen got in front with the driver and glanced back at them.

"Looks like he belongs here," Matt said to Anne. "With a new administration at the prison, it was a good time for him to move on—out into the world again. He can finally see daylight from here."

Baumschen anxiously checked his watch. "I'm afraid we must hurry if I am to make my plane. With these bandages around my shoulder, I do not move as quickly as I usually do."

"My car's around the corner," Anne said. "Since I'm feeling better, I'll drive." She took Matt by the arm.

Minutes later, they sped toward the Cross Island Parkway, and Beck tightened his seat belt. "Take it easy, Anne," he said. "Even I've had enough death for one week." He enjoyed her glare at him.

"We are lucky, actually, that Earl Eslin panicked when he did," Baumschen said. "Up until that point, Langert was right. We had little concrete evidence on any of them that would have survived the scrutiny of their lawyers."

Beck grinned as he heard Anne mumble, "Shakespeare was right."

"And you are a very fortunate woman, indeed, Fraulein Demming," the inspector added. "Langert was a dangerous, committed man who let nothing stand in his way. If you had not maneuvered a diversion and Tod Engel had not intervened, John Langert, by the rules, should have killed you."

"Yeah," Beck said with a smirk. "Anne has that effect on a lot of people. They know they should kill her, but they just can't bring themselves to."

Anne laughed. "And here I was about to thank you for that prompt with the tequila shot. I knew I had to try something fast, but that set it up perfectly and helped get Art ready to act in concert."

"Any time." He smiled as the Whitestone Bridge appeared in the distance. "Just not anytime soon."

Baumschen leaned over the passenger seat. "Please convey to Herr Petokis how much I appreciate his fast response to the debacle in that room." He eased back, grunting in pain. "It saved my life."

Anne glanced back at him. "So was Engel murderous, suicidal, or heroic?"

"All three," Beck answered, touching her shoulder. He would always be grateful to Engel. The man he blamed for so many years for murdering his first wife was the same man who had saved the life of the woman he was going to ask to be his second one. "He clearly wanted to get rid of Langert, though we'll never be able to fathom all the reasons. Mixed motives for a hero."

"As though all heroes' motives aren't mixed." Anne turned at the airport sign to the Long Island Expressway.

Matt said, "I think he reacted because the bishop had the audacity to admit that he was Deathangel—a title Engel claimed with proud notoriety for ten years, though he may not have known what it really meant."

"Apparently it meant everything," Anne said. "Ironic, isn't it? The identity that was created for him he embraced as his own. It brought him everything we all want—attention, notoriety, special treatment."

"Sodomy, beatings, drugging," Matt countered sadly.

"I agree it was the claim of the Deathangel title that set him off." Baumschen said. "Still, even for Helliger, an incendiary grenade is a horrible way to die."

"Like a Mauthausen oven," Anne said solemnly.

"And a hell of a way to survive," Beck commented, remembering Engel's scorched, peeling skin. Though Langert's body had taken the brunt of the impact, burning chemicals had spewed onto Engel's arms and legs. "Art told me he stopped by the prison infirmary this morning before the funeral to see Engel. He'll live, but it's going to take a lot of skin grafts and rehab."

"That's all he has now, isn't it?" Anne said. "Time?"

"And quite a story to tell, if he's able," Baumschen said.

"If the court order goes through today," Beck said, "Engel will be free to leave. He's not physically well enough to go anywhere on his own right now, so I made transfer arrangements to Grasslands, where he can recover in peace. Once he does, we'll find a placement. There are some good group homes up-county."

Matt wondered how happy the man would be in such a setting. Could he make the adjustment from the safety of a cell, the companionship of guards, and the respect of notoriety to being just another resident at a center for retarded adults?

Anne glanced at him. "Now if we could just locate a place for Rinski. Perhaps driving a cab in Beirut."

"What will happen to him?" Baumschen leaned forward again.

"A little chest wound won't slow him down," Beck answered. "My guess is he'll resign in exchange for the state not pressing charges of entrapment."

"For the wrongful incarceration of a mentally retarded person." Baumschen made a disapproving noise. "Incredible."

"It's the American way, mein Herr," Anne said curtly. "Even if a grand jury indicts him on conspiracy, falsification of records, and perjury, he'll claim coercion from the man he threw out the door to the firing squad— who is not here to refute the charge. Besides, Rinski still has political allies who will probably protect him because he's got the goods on them." She entered the expressway. "Save your pity for someone who's not so well connected—Richard Williams, for instance."

"Yeah," Beck said. "Poor guy doesn't have a leg to stand on." There were a lot of things he felt for the warden. Pity wasn't one of them.

"I'm serious, Matt. That man has no political protection. What will he do?"

"Art said Williams is taking a leave of absence during the investigation," Beck said. "He'll resign and lose his pension. He doesn't have any influential friends, but the state and county officials who should have been monitoring him would like all this to calm down before elections come up. They'll do what they can to drop it. Art said he's in bad shape, deeply shaken, and now he's on psychotropics himself." Matt twisted around to face the inspector. "Your friend Petokis was named acting warden of Weston this morning, by the way, for his efforts during the crisis."

"And D'Angelo got promoted all the way to captain," Anne said. "You know what's really funny?" She smiled at both of them. "Look what just happened."

Beck furrowed his brow, then smiled back at her, surprised he hadn't thought of it himself. "Damn!"

"I have obviously missed something," Baumschen said.

"History just repeated itself," Matt said. "The capture of Deathangel ten years ago propelled people into prominent positions through immediate promotions."

"The same thing occurred again," Anne explained.

"Except for us!" The inspector laughed.

"And we're much better off," Beck muttered, "Look what happened to those other guys."

They laughed together, but Matt was immensely grateful that one part of history had not repeated itself. Anne was still alive.

"However, there is yet a chance for me," Baumschen said. "I have been placed in charge of ferreting out Langert's European connections, which—from what we recovered from the house at Morningside Heights—are extensive. The bishop had no idea that his radio signal was trapped by those old, thick prison walls and was ineffective. We have already learned, by sifting through his incredibly meticulous records, that he kept in contact with many ex-Nazi units around the world." Baumschen suddenly became tight-lipped. "I will pursue the rest of the findings in Wien. Your CIA has already taken Langert's chauffeur there to join us for further interrogation. The minor wounds he received when the guards stormed into the room will heal long before he sees anything outside a prison cell again."

The three were silent as Anne pulled up to the Lufthansa departure gate. She turned to Baumschen. "You know, of course, that we have been followed the entire way?"

"Jaja, Fraulein. Those are what we in the business call, the good guys. They are my unofficial escort." Baumschen handed his bags to the skycap. From his briefcase, he removed a small leather-bound notebook and handed it through the window to Matt. "I thought you two might like this as a souvenir." Baumschen smiled. "We have copied its contents, and it is the information, not the document, that is important to us now. This is Langert's last journal, the only one in English. You, Fraulein, may find it useful for the story you are bound to write. And you, Herr Beck, may find the study of the man's descent into hell instructive in your own profession."

"Thank you, I think," Beck said. He wondered if it wasn't descent into as much as ascent from as he placed the journal in the glove box next to the LadyHawke.

Anne climbed out of the car. "As we say in Texas, Y'all come back, now, hear?" She hugged Baumschen close and whispered, "Thank you for everything."

Beck shook his hand. "Take care of yourself."

"Und Sie auch. Come to Wien. I will take you to Demel's and buy you Sachertorte. I promise to show you a better time than you had before, Fraulein."

"That won't be hard," Anne said. "Wiedersehen."

Beck waved to the man to whom he would always owe an unpaid debt.

Life was unfair in goodness as well as tragedy. Some things were never repaid.

"Wiedersehen." Baumschen disappeared into the terminal.

Back in the car, Matt looked at Anne. "Home, Jeeves," he said.

"Your place or mine?"

Beck reclined his seat all the way back. His drowsy eyelids floated shut. "Surprise me."

It was two minutes to midnight.

Richard Williams watched the digital clock in his office click to the proper time. He picked up the phone and punched in a number. "Ready," he said, and hung up.

One minute later he walked, with the help of crutches, to the infirmary where he knew Acting Warden Petokis waited. It felt like the longest walk of his life, following the most painful week of his life.

"He's been quiet all night long, Warden," Petokis said, opening the door.

"His room?"

"It has been kept unlocked, just as you requested, sir. He could see out into the hall and hear the noise from the other beds with no restrictions— other than his inability to get up, of course." Petokis nodded, and the guard opened the subunit leading to the hall of private rooms reserved for special inmates who needed closer security or for the occasional wounded guard who required comfort and privacy. For this short time, Engel was treated as the latter. "But he's stayed calm. He hasn't even hit the call light for pain meds or water. It's really odd."

"Did you explain it all to him?"

"Yes sir, I did. As well as can be expected, anyway. It's kind of hard not knowing if he's listening, or there with you, or understanding anything. But I've known Tod for a long time, and I think he got most of it."

Williams rested on his crutches. "What was his response?"

"Mumbled, mainly, without looking at me. He hasn't been hostile or even angry-sounding. A couple times he actually appeared to be whimpering."

"Could you make out any words?"

"Yes." Petokis hesitated.

"What were they?"

"Well, sir, he kept mumbling, 'I am Deathangel.' " The acting warden looked away. "I'm sorry, sir."

"Don't be, Petokis," Williams replied, a note of sadness creeping into his usually certain voice. "It's too bad."

"What's that, Warden?"

"That, after ten years, the one thing that meant something to Engel is being taken away from him."

"Sir?"

The warden paused, knowing it was obvious he spoke for himself as well. "His identity." Williams straightened up on the crutches and swung ahead. For the moment he felt back in control. Things were mostly settled. His path was clear. There was one thing left to do as his last official act as warden of Weston State Prison for the Criminally Insane.

Release Tod Engel.

And he would do it personally.

The two men approached the door to the infirmary room. Williams saw it first.

A small amount of red had spilled into the corridor.

The warden hurried as fast as he could to the open door. Petokis got there first, cursed, and spoke into his radio.

"Code Blue. Infirmary." His voice remained calm. They both knew the code team was futile. "Repeat. Code Blue. Infirmary."

Williams entered the room and beheld what Engel had done. In a final show of will, the inmate had ripped the central line out of his neck, allowing his heart to slowly pump all the blood from his body. But not before he left one last message.

Running feet sounded against cement in the background. Petokis touched the warden's shoulder. He did not need to point it out.

On the white wall next to the sodden bed, in letters scrawled with Engel's own blood, were the words, "I AM DEATHANGEL."

Epilogue

A breeze of cold air found its way through the slightly open window. The house on the mountain was otherwise still.

One voice spoke in the darkness. "You awake?"

"Yeah," Matt said. "I've been pretending I could sleep." He heard a sniffle next to him. "What's the matter?"

"It's just so sad," Anne said. "All those people killed. Lives ruined, families with horrid memories." She wiped at her cheeks. "And for what?"

Beck was silent. There was no answer to that question that made any sense to him. Maybe nothing was rewarded or punished. Maybe the only important thing was that they left things better in the world than when they arrived.

"When I was at Mauthausen, I saw a photo of a Texan who was one of the first liberation troops in the camp. The man was crying uncontrollably, tears of incredible sadness that humans could do that to each other, and of relief that it was over." She turned her head, and Matt could see her outline on the other pillow. "But it didn't die at Mauthausen, did it? It was just subdued. It broke out again here, through Langert and the Deathangel murders. And it will break out again somewhere else."

"Of course it will," Beck said, putting his hand on her arm. "It's only a matter of time. We do our best to contain it—that part of ourselves that wills power—but it's always temporary. We can subdue it for the present." He could make out the fear in her face, and it mirrored his own. "It's like that phrase from Compline—the last service of the day. 'Be sober. Be watchful. For your enemy the devil prowls around like a roaring lion, seeking someone to devour.' " He propped his head up with a pillow. "But the enemy's not external, it's internal, inside each of us. Sometimes it breaks out in groups like the Klan, or the militias, or in nations, like World War II, or Vietnam or Kosovo."

"So we contain it, imprison it, only for it to escape over and over?"

He pulled her to him. "Welcome to earth, Anne. This isn't heaven yet. It's the best we can do about anything—loss, evil, death, life."

Quietly, she leaned her head against his chest and said, "It seems so futile."

"Not really," Beck replied, kissing her softly. "Look how Deathangel transformed everything. You and Robert. Me and Kate. The lives of

Rinski, Williams, Art, and even Tod Engel. In so many ways it's been painful but absolving for me, healing for us both. This may sound ridiculous, but without it, I wouldn't be asking you to marry me."

She propped herself up on one arm. After a long silence, she touched his face. "And without it," she replied, "I wouldn't be able to say yes."

Matt wrapped his arms around her and kissed her. He heard her gasp. He backed away and asked, "How's your chest?"

"Still seeping through the bandages, I'm afraid." She caught her breath and kissed him gently. "We may have to wait a couple more days to celebrate."

"Celebrate which?" Matt said, taking her hand. "That we caught the real Deathangel and lived to tell the tale—exclusive to *CityMag*? Or that Tod Engel is being released," he leaned up and checked the lighted clock on the dresser, "as we speak?"

"All of the above," Anne said. "Plus asking Art Allen to do the honors at St. Jude's for us."

"Did we do that?"

"Not yet, but we will tomorrow. So on second thought, this calls for sex and champagne," she said, moving over him, "champagne later."

Beck felt her wince. "Tell you what," he said. "Let's get the champagne now. Maybe it'll act as a pain killer." He threw back the covers.

Later they were snuggled in a quilt on the living room couch, glasses in hand.

"I love you," Matt said as he clicked his glass against hers.

"I count on it," Anne replied. "I love you, too."

The phone rang as they sipped the bubbly liquid.

"I'm not on call," Matt said. "Let it go."

"What if it's Twitch and something's wrong?" Anne replied, reaching for the cordless receiver. "Hello?"

Matt squinted his eyes at her.

"Just a minute," she said into the phone, holding the receiver so they both could hear. "It's Richard Williams."

"Yes? What is it?" Matt stared at Anne as the news of Tod Engel exploded through the line. They listened without asking questions. There were none to ask, Beck thought, not entirely surprised at what the man had done.

"Thank you for telling us," Matt said when the warden finished. He clicked off the phone and reached for Langert's journal on the coffee table.

"What are you doing?" Anne asked.

"Making the final entry," Beck replied. He turned to the last page and wrote, "Deathangel is dead."

Anne looked at the words. She took the pen and added, "Again."

Beck closed the journal and tossed it to the floor.

They stretched out to watch the stars in the blackness outside, and held each other until they slept.

Acknowledgements

There are nearly as many people to thank for assistance with this book as there are characters in it. Susan Rogers Cooper, Barbara Burnet Smith, and Susan Wade diligently suffered through weekly chapter installments and applied their own well-honed mystery-writing instincts to critique and affirm the manuscript. Lt. Col. Carl Meyer served as a technical consultant on terrorism, most of which he learned from being my older brother. Mitch Lestico, D. Pharm. at St.David's Medical Center, tracked down information about the deadly Zyklon B and it's coloration. Texan Dr. Appletree Rodden and his German wife, Annegret Rodden, of Hamburg corrected my college German after they quit laughing at the words I remembered. The Austin Writer's League and Dave Hamrick of Barnes & Noble were unwitting accomplices to the publication of the book. They cosponsored a children's poetry contest and asked me to help with the awards, and it was there that I met Tom Southern of Boaz Publishing and introduced him to my wonderful agent, Kathleen Niendorf (who swears she does not ever represent this kind of book). I am indebted to Tom for agreeing to publish the manuscript and to his wife Elizabeth Vahlsing, for the excellent cover with the Austrian angel, purchased near the concentration camp at Mauthausen. Most of all, I am grateful for the support of my wife, Debi, and daughter, Michal. Debi, queen of the red-inked sticky notes, read and reread, red, re-red, critiqued, and proofed the tome with a sense of humor that always exceeded mine. Michal patiently lived with my ups and downs and endless hours at the computer, never failing to ask how it was going and celebrating the conquering of each new hurdle from rewrite to rewrite. Finally, the book masterfully edited through several incarnations by the excruciatingly meticulous Kathy Saideman who, much to my annoyance and chagrin, was (usually) correct in her comments.